A DISTANT MELODY

WINGS *of* GLORY
BOOK ONE

A DISTANT MELODY

A Novel

SARAH SUNDIN

Revell

a division of Baker Publishing Group
Grand Rapids, Michigan

© 2010 by Sarah Sundin

Published by Revell
a division of Baker Publishing Group
P.O. Box 6287, Grand Rapids, MI 49516-6287
www.revellbooks.com

Printed in the United States of America

Library of Congress Cataloging-in-Publication Data
Sundin, Sarah.
    A distant melody : a novel / Sarah Sundin.
      p. cm. — (Wings of glory ; 1)
    ISBN 978-0-8007-3421-3 (pbk.)
    1. World War, 1939–1945—Aerial operations, American—Fiction. 2. B-17 bomber—Fiction. I. Title.
PS3619.U5626D57 2010
813'.6—dc22
                                                                     2009042259

10 11 12 13 14 15 16   7 6 5 4 3 2 1

To my long-suffering husband, Dave—
I couldn't write about love if I didn't have yours.

1

Los Angeles, California

Monday, June 22, 1942

One whole delicious week together. Allie Miller clung to her best friend's promise and to the train ticket that would deliver it.

Allie followed an inlaid marble pathway through Union Station and breathed in the glamour of travel and the adventure of her first trip north. Anticipation trilled a song in her heart, but the tune felt thin, a single line of melody with no harmony to make it resonate.

She glanced at her boyfriend, who walked beside her. "I'm sorry you can't come."

Baxter shrugged, gazed at a knot of soldiers they passed, and pulled the cigarette from his mouth. "The war didn't stop just because Betty Jamison decided to get married."

Allie shrank back from the discordant note. Her bridesmaid duty might seem trivial, but she honored it as much as J. Baxter Hicks did his duties as business manager.

They entered the waiting room, which blended Spanish Colonialism and modern streamlining. A wood-beamed ceiling peaked overhead, and iron chandeliers illuminated hundreds of men in Navy white and blue or Army khaki and olive drab. None of the men cast Allie a second glance. Yet when Mother rose partway from her seat and beckoned with a gloved hand, she attracted dozens of stares with her blonde beauty.

Father gave Allie his seat. "Your ticket? Is it someplace safe?"

"In my handbag." She smiled at his protectiveness and settled into the deep leather chair. "And yes, Mother, I asked the porter to be careful with my luggage."

"Good. Oh, the thought of anything happening to that dress." She clucked her tongue. "Such a shame, this silk shortage, but you did a lovely job with my old ball gown. Why, you almost look pretty in that dress."

Allie stiffened but said, "Thank you." Mother meant well, and Allie could hardly expect a compliment. Nevertheless, sadness swelled in her chest. No—self-pity was nothing but pride in disguise, and she refused to indulge.

"So, Stan, any word on that parts shipment?" Baxter and Father strolled away to lean against the wall. The men could pass for father and son with their brown hair and blue eyes, well-tailored suits, and love for Miller Ball Bearings.

Mother picked a piece of lint from the sleeve of Allie's tan linen suit. "You've only been home one month since graduation, and off you go, gallivanting across the state."

Allie clutched her purse containing the ticket, purchased with the labor of overcoming Mother's objections. "It's only one week, and then I'll be home to stay."

"Not for long." Mother directed her large green eyes—the only good trait Allie inherited—toward Baxter. "You've been dating almost five years. He'll propose soon."

Baxter stood between towering windows, a dark silhouette framed by shafts of light slanting down through the haze of cigarette smoke.

Sourness shriveled Allie's mouth, her throat, her stomach. Did all women feel queasy at the thought of proposals? "Time for the arranged marriage."

"Pardon?"

Allie snapped her attention back to her mother. "That's not what I meant to . . . I meant—"

"Good heavens. You don't think this is arranged, do you?" she asked in a hushed voice. "Yes, Baxter's the only man your father would ever pass his company down to, but your welfare is our highest consideration, and—"

"I know. I know." Tension squeezed Allie's voice up half an octave, and she tried to smile away her mother's worries. "I know Baxter's a gift."

Mother's expression hinted at the approval that eluded Allie. "Isn't he? He's a fine young man and he'll make you so happy."

Happy? Baxter Hicks would never fulfill her childhood dreams of love, but he could give her a family, Lord willing, which would be enough to satisfy. Besides, this marriage was best for her parents, for Baxter, and for Allie herself. A dream made a worthy sacrifice.

So why did her heart strain for the missing notes?

★

Lt. Walter Novak leaned back against the wall at Union Station, one foot propped on his duffel. The coolness of the wall seeped through the wool of his uniform jacket. Felt good.

Almost as good as the mattress the night before at the home of Frank Kilpatrick, his best friend in the 306th Bombardment Group. His last furlough—ten good nights' sleep, thirty good meals, then back to base and off to combat. Finally he would get to use his God-given talents as a pilot and do something worthwhile.

Walt peered inside his lunch bag. Eileen was awfully nice to make him a chicken salad sandwich. After all, she had her husband home for the first time in months, three whooping little boys, and a belly swollen with another Kilpatrick.

Walt pulled out the best part of the meal—an orange from the Kilpatricks' tree—large and glossy and chockful of sugar. He planted a kiss on the skin, as nubby-smooth as the leather of his flight jacket. "Hello, sweetheart." To get this prize, he'd used a ladder to bypass dozens of lesser oranges in easy reach. Frank called him pigheaded.

Walt grinned at the memory. "Not pigheaded. Persistent." After a year of Army food, he longed for fresh fruit. As boys, he and his two older brothers would sprawl on the grass and eat nectarines until Mom pestered them to save some for jam, and they'd sneak plums just before they were ripe and claim the birds must have nabbed them.

A voice on the loudspeaker mumbled something about the Daylight. Walt plopped the orange in the bag, slung his duffel over his shoulder, and worked his way through the lobby as big as a hangar and swarming with servicemen. At his platform, a billow of steam evaporated to reveal the San Joaquin Daylight's black paint with red and orange stripes. Nope, the train wasn't ready for boarding yet.

Walt reined in his excitement, checked in his duffel, and jammed his service cap down over the dumb curl that always flopped onto his forehead. Then he wandered back inside to a newsstand to study the magazines. If he bought *Time*, he'd still have enough money for tipping the porters and for a couple of Cokes on the trip.

A pretty blonde in a blue dress stood in line at the newsstand. Her gaze fixed on the silver wings on Walt's chest and the gold second lieutenant's bars on his shoulders, and a smile dimpled the corner of her mouth.

Walt's throat constricted. Every limb froze in place. He couldn't have spoken even if he'd had something to say, which he didn't. That was why he was stuck kissing oranges.

Frank Kilpatrick, who could make friends with a doorknob, didn't understand, but for Walt, women came in two varieties—those who were taken and those who weren't. And those who weren't taken scared him more than a stalled engine on takeoff.

The young woman's gaze drifted to Walt's face. One nostril flicked up, and she looked away. He knew what she'd seen— the chipmunk cheeks and the Novak nose like an upside-down kite. Yep, unattached women were different. They hunted, scrutinized, judged, and he never measured up.

★

Allie stepped outside. Steam swirled about, heavy with the smell of burnt oil, and the train chuffed out a beat that quickened her internal melody.

"All aboard!"

Allie turned to her parents. "Thank you for this trip. I can't tell you how much this means—"

"We know," Father said with a warm smile. "You'd better go if you want a seat. Now, you're sure the Jamisons will meet you in Tracy for that train transfer?"

"Yes, and I have Betty's number and the information on the transfer just in case."

Mother adjusted the jeweled pin on Allie's lapel. "Remember everything we told you—keep your baggage claim check safe, keep your belongings close, and watch out for servicemen. A uniform alone doesn't make a gentleman."

Father chuckled. "Mary, you'll give Baxter nightmares about soldiers stealing his girl."

"Never have to worry about that," Baxter said.

Allie's tune dropped into a minor key. If only his trust lay in her faithfulness rather than her unattractiveness.

Father engulfed her in a hug. "I'll sure miss you, sweetheart, but have a wonderful time."

In the arms of her lifelong defender, Allie felt her heart rise. Then she turned to Baxter. Surely, he'd be moved by the romance of the train station, the departure, and the couples in sweet embrace.

Baxter bounced a kiss off her cheek. "Go along now. Have fun."

Her heart slumped down into its usual location. Just once to have a man look at her as if she were lovely and special. Just once.

Allie joined the crowd filing onto the train. At the top of the steps, she turned to wave but couldn't see over the Marine behind her. She stepped into the car, coughed at the dense cigarette smoke, and made her way down the aisle, avoiding open seats next to soldiers. The train filled quickly.

"Excuse me, miss. Would you like to join us?" A dark-haired woman indicated the seat facing her, already occupied by two small children. The woman held a baby and sat beside an older boy. "If you don't mind, that is. You'd be a bit cramped, and—"

"That would be lovely. Thank you." Allie settled into the seat of muted red cloth edged with darker red leather.

"I'm tree." The little girl to her right held up four plump fingers.

"Oh, what a big girl you are."

"Humph." The boy next to her thumped his foot against the wall of the train. "She can't even read. I can."

"Barely," said the older boy across from Allie.

"That's enough, children," their mother said. "Don't bother this nice young lady."

"They're no bother at all." Allie noticed the woman's ill-fitting red suit and felt self-conscious of her own elegant outfit. "And . . . and I could help with the children if you'd like."

"I'd sure appreciate it." She poked a bottle into the baby's mouth. "So, where are you going?"

"I'm visiting my best friend in Antioch, up on the Sacramento River Delta. I can't wait to see her again. Betty was my roommate at Scripps College over in Claremont. She's getting married, and I'm in the wedding." Allie cringed at her babbling. Why did she always do that when she was nervous?

"How nice. That'll be fun for you." She nudged the boy to her right. "Donnie, pick up your sister's doll, would you? Lonnie, stop that thumping."

Allie smiled. This mother didn't seem to need any assistance.

Then her smile collapsed. A lady stood in the aisle of the packed train, and none of the servicemen offered her a seat. Perhaps they would if she were young and pretty, or a frail grandmother. But she was heavy, middle-aged, and colored.

"Ma'am?" A man stood and motioned to his seat, a man in olive drab with an officer's cap over black hair.

The lady gave him a big smile, sat down, and grasped his arm. "God bless you. I pray for all you boys in uniform, ask the Almighty to keep you safe. What's your name, son?"

"Walter, ma'am, and thank you. I'd rather have prayers than a seat any day." He tipped his cap and stepped forward, closer to Allie, with a smile on his full face.

A uniform might not make a gentleman, but kindness and good manners did. Allie savored this deep new note and the rich chord it produced.

2

A vise tightened around Walt's throat.

Did she smile at him? That young lady with brown curls? Yeah, she did, and the vise cranked shut.

Then she turned striking green eyes to a boy and girl on the seat beside her. Oh, she was a mom. Taken. Breathing resumed.

The train jerked, lagged, and crept forward—Walt's favorite part. Always, for one suspenseful moment, he thought it couldn't be done. Then power kicked in, momentum built, and the train surged down the tracks.

A woman in a red suit said something to Green-Eyed Mom, who replied with a smile that grew as steadily as the train's speed and erased her schoolmarm look. Yep, any joke her husband told would be well rewarded.

The boy next to Red-Suit Mom grinned at Walt with teeth too big for his face. "Are you a pilot, mister?"

"Donnie, mind your manners."

"I don't mind." Walt smiled at the boy. "Sure, I'm a pilot."

"Wow! Shot down any enemy planes?"

Walt chuckled. "Haven't had the chance. Got my wings in

April, and last week I finished four-engined bomber training in Albuquerque."

"Oh!" Donnie bounced up in his seat. "Four engines—B-17 or B-24?"

The kid knew his planes. "B-17 Flying Fortress."

"Oh yeah? Where are you headed?"

"Hmm. Promise you won't tell? Loose lips sink ships, you know." When the boy nodded, eyes wide, Walt leaned closer. "Wendover, Utah."

The boy's nose scrunched up, and the women laughed.

Walt joined them. "We're still training. How about you, buddy? Where are you off to?"

"Fresno. We're staying with my grandparents for the duration. Papa just got inducted," he said with the nonchalant pride of a boy with a new word. "Someday I'm gonna be a fighter pilot." He did a vrooming, ack-acking fighter imitation, echoed by the younger boy across from him. Donnie's mother shushed them both.

Walt squatted next to the seat, and the boys fired questions faster than a machine gun. If only women liked planes. These ladies seemed interested, but they had sons, so they had to be.

The train crossed the High Desert, dotted with tumbleweeds, Joshua trees, and the small towns of Palmdale and Lancaster. When they passed Mojave, not far from Muroc Army Air Base, Walt stood to kick out kinks in his legs, and he felt the change in his pocket. "You kids want a Coke?"

"Yeah! Can I—" Donnie glanced at his mom. "*May* I go with him, *please*?"

"Yes, dear, and take Lonnie."

The boy on the other seat hopped to the floor, and Walt led both boys down the aisle. They were brothers? Then Green-Eyed Mom only had the little girl.

★ 15 ★

Walt paid for the Cokes with his last free nickels. They wove back through the forest of uniforms to find Green-Eyed Mom alone—with Red-Suit Mom's baby in her arms.

"Your turn to share with Connie," Donnie said to his brother.

"Nuh-uh. 'Sides, she's not here."

The train lurched. Walt grabbed the seat back and looked at the young lady in confusion. Who was Connie? The little girl? But . . .

"Her mother took her to the ladies' room. She let me hold little Bonnie. Isn't she sweet?"

She wasn't a mother at all. No ring on her left hand. He had to speak before paralysis set in. "Wait. Donnie, Lonnie, Connie . . ."

"And Bonnie," she said, voice taut.

"We rhyme," Lonnie said.

Green Eyes ducked her chin. "So you do."

Walt let out a laugh. The young lady shot him a look—though too polite to laugh, she shared the joke. She wasn't bad. No scrutinizing or judging, like a normal human being.

Red-Suit Mom returned with Connie on her hip. Right after they sat down, a tunnel snuffed out the sun. The kids squealed.

Walt took a bubbly swig of cola and squatted down again. "You'd better get used to tunnels. Eighteen through the Tehachapi Mountains. And the best part—in a few minutes we'll be at the Tehachapi Loop. Track runs in a full circle. You'll love it."

The boys flattened their noses against the window. Soon the train broke out of another tunnel and entered the loop, spread around an oak-studded hill. Walt pointed out the features, glad he remembered his research for that civil engineering class.

After the descent into the Central Valley and the stop in Bakersfield, Walt unwrapped his sandwich. His mom would have a fit if she saw him eat in the passenger car, but with the number of dining cars reduced for the war, he had no choice. He took a bite and closed his eyes in satisfaction. Base food was always mushy or tough, but this chicken was cool, firm, and mixed with onion and celery and—apple?—yes, apple.

"Mama, I'm hungry," Lonnie said. "When's lunch?"

"At Grandma's. Another hour or so."

Walt's sandwich didn't taste so good with all those little eyes watching him.

"Can't we buy something?" Donnie said.

"No, and quiet. We'll eat in Fresno." Her face matched her suit, and Walt suspected her purse was as empty as his wallet.

All he had left was an orange. One perfect orange. He pulled out the fruit, the same size as the hole in his stomach but not nearly as big as the holes in the children's stomachs.

"An orange?" Walt drew his face into a grimace. "Would your kids like an orange?"

"Oh no, thank you."

"No, really. Stayed at my friend's house last night, and his wife packed my lunch. I can't stand oranges."

She accepted. Walt dug his thumbnail into the peel and released a mist of fragrant juice, all citrus and summer and sunshine. He passed out slices, and the children stopped whining. More than anything, Walt wanted to lick his fingers and get a hint of flavor, but he used his handkerchief instead.

When they reached Fresno, Walt returned little boy salutes and received thanks for Cokes, orange slices, and stories.

"Oh, miss," Red-Suit Mom called over her shoulder to

Green Eyes. "Make sure to give that seat to this nice young man."

"Oh. Oh yes. Of course."

Walt looked around in desperation, but enlisted men filled the aisle—no women, none of his elders, and not one man who outranked him. Two sailors took Red-Suit Mom's seat and settled in for a nap, so no one could even rescue him in conversation.

Walt had no choice. He sat. "Thanks." He managed not to swallow his tongue.

"You're welcome. I think you've stood long enough." A quiver in her smile stirred something bold in his chest.

"Yeah. Yeah, I have." The train pulled from the station with a burst of steam and passed a bunch of warehouses. What could he talk about? "So, enjoying the trip?"

"Oh yes. It's nice to have a change of scenery."

"Same here. I've been in the desert too long. Can't wait to see grass again, even if it's brown. I like winter best—real green." Like her eyes, which were brighter up close, so bright he struggled to keep his airway open.

"So I've heard. I've never been up north before."

"Really? Where are you from?"

"Riverside."

Walt nodded. "Flew some training flights into March Field. Riverside's a great town."

"Thank you. I think it's the most beautiful city in California."

Could he tease her? One way to find out. "But you've never been up north."

Long brown lashes lowered, but her smile rose. "True. I should reserve judgment, but even if I find a more beautiful city, Riverside will always be my favorite."

Riverside—the name poked up a March Field memory. As

an engineer, Walt always bugged the mechanics so he could learn the planes inside and out. One day he'd been banished to sit on a crate to watch. The crate hadn't come far . . .

"Ball bearings," he said with a grin. "Miller Ball Bearings, Riverside, California."

She drew up her mouth so tight it almost disappeared, and she looked down at her book.

He stared at her. What? What did he say?

She turned a page with long fingers.

Roger and out. He sighed and pulled the rolled-up magazine from his pocket. If he couldn't talk to the girl, at least he could read the news, and finally some good news. Earlier in the month the U.S. naval victory over the Japanese at Midway ended six solid months of defeat.

After they passed through Merced, a magazine ad caught Walt's eye—a wife in a frilly apron served cake to her furloughed husband. Maybe Mom would have a cake tonight. Or a pie. His stomach gurgled, and he shifted position to make it stop.

He flipped some pages and read about the German advance on Sevastopol. The train swayed and bumped Walt against Green Eyes' shoulder. He mumbled an apology. No woman had to worry about an advance from him. Couldn't even make small talk.

Modesto whizzed past. Not long before he'd see Mom and Dad and have a big dinner, maybe roast beef. No, beef was scarce. His stomach rumbled, loud and insistent.

"Pardon me." The young lady rose, and Walt stood to let her pass.

Swell. Scared her off with ball bearings and stomach gurgles. He grumbled and read President Roosevelt's announcement of a rubber scrap drive, since Japanese conquests had cut off 92 percent of the rubber supply.

The next article made Walt burn: the Germans—the Germans themselves—announced the Nazi massacre of the Czechoslovakian village of Lidice. Stories like that heightened his desire to go to combat, and soon.

"Excuse me." Green Eyes looked down at him.

Walt swallowed his surprise in time to remember his manners and let her take her seat.

"Which would you prefer?" She held an apple in one hand and an orange in the other.

His gaze bounced between red and orange and back up to green. "Huh?"

She shifted her square jaw to one side and frowned at the fruit. "I wanted a snack and thought you might like one too. You were so kind to give part of your lunch to the children. This isn't as lovely as the one you had earlier—it's rather pale—but there's also an apple, and I'd be happy with either."

Walt smiled at her rapid speech. "Thanks. An orange sounds good."

She handed him the fruit. "I thought so. You said you hated oranges, but your eyes said you loved them."

He shrugged. "If she knew I wanted it, she wouldn't have taken it."

"Perhaps. But I believe every dilemma has a truthful solution."

"Not always." Walt peeled the orange. No juice sprayed this time.

"Oh. I assumed you were . . . well, never mind." She fussed with the apple in her lap.

He stared at her. She assumed he was a man of integrity, and a man of integrity never told a little fib for a good cause? Baloney. "I keep my word. But—well, a white lie's okay if your motive's right. Keeps things running smoothly—like ball bearings in the machinery of society."

She jerked her head toward the window.

Walt grinned in victory. What was her problem with ball bearings? Did Daddy lose a fortune on ball bearings in the Stock Market Crash? Or was her family in some rival industry, and mentioning ball bearings to her was like mentioning Stanford to a Cal man like himself? Or had she lost her true love in a freak ball bearings accident?

He pried off an orange slice, popped it in his mouth, and made a face. Bitter. Almost as bitter as his victory. *What's wrong with me, Lord? She buys me an orange, and I make a mess of things.*

The young woman chewed on the apple and gazed ahead at the round hills that edged the San Francisco Bay and the Delta. Her hair curled up around the base of her hat.

Walt cleared his throat. "I guess silence is a truthful solution to a dilemma."

Her gaze flowed back to him, a refreshing green river, and a smile bent her lips. "Yes, it is. Truthful and effective."

"I should try it sometime."

"Perhaps you should. How's the orange?"

Walt bit back a lie and made a show of shrugging and looking away.

She laughed. "Not very good?"

"A little bitter. How's the apple?"

"Dry. But I'm spoiled. We have an orchard full of apple and citrus trees."

He knew he liked something about her, besides her attention to his flying stories. "My parents also have fruit trees. My friend Frank says I miss the fruit more than my family."

"Is that true?"

"Nah." He swallowed the last orange slice. "Just that it's manly to grumble about the chow, but you're a homesick mama's boy if you miss your family."

"I understand."

The train slowed. Walt's sigh echoed the long, low whistle. First time he'd had a conversation with an available woman, and now he'd never see her again. He balled up his bag full of orange peel and got to his feet. "Well, Tracy's my stop. Thanks for the orange."

Green Eyes sat up taller and peered out the window. "Tracy? That's my stop too."

"Really?" She looked too sophisticated for the cow towns in the area. He stepped aside and followed her slim figure down the aisle. Once they disembarked, she looked around the platform and stepped into a phone booth.

Walt inhaled fresh Central Valley air to clear his lungs of cigarette smoke and his mind of Green Eyes. Then he headed for the station to buy a ticket for Train 53. The Daylight passed right through his hometown but didn't stop. Too bad he couldn't jump off.

"Walter! Walter!"

He turned to see his parents, and he braced himself for his mother's hug. For a small woman, she sure packed a wallop. "Hi, Mom. What are you doing here?"

She laughed. "Fine way to greet us after a year. We thought it would be fun to surprise you."

"Thanks. Swell idea." He pulled away to shake his dad's hand.

"Let's see those wings," Dad said. "Very good. Like Ray and Jack. Of course, Jack made captain."

Of course. Always one step behind.

"Goodness." Mom gripped him by the shoulders. "Hard to believe you're my baby. You get taller and broader in the shoulders every time I see you."

Walt grumbled, glad his traveling companion was out of earshot. "Let me get my bag, and let's get home. What's for dinner?"

"Not so fast, young man." Mom reached for Walt's arm. "Betty's friend from college came on the same train, and the Jamisons asked us to meet her."

Green Eyes? Could it be? He turned to the phone booth.

She stood in the doorway with the receiver to her shoulder. "Excuse me, Lieutenant. Is your name Walter Novak?"

He nodded, his tongue wooden. She'd be at the wedding. He'd see her all week.

She spoke into the phone, hung up, and walked toward him. He had to speak, had to speak. He nudged his mouth into a smile. "Looking for your chaperone?"

"Um, yes. I, well, Betty . . ." Her hand fluttered toward the phone booth.

Walt's chest felt fuller, wider with some need to ease her nervousness, and that need melted every frozen muscle. "Let me guess. Betty changed plans and didn't tell you."

"Um, yes." A breeze blew a brown curl across her cheek, and she tucked it back in place. "As bright as Betty is . . ."

"Sometimes she's a scatterbrain."

They laughed together, and an odd, warm sensation under Walt's ribs made him want to laugh with her again.

"You must be Allie Miller." Dad shook her hand. "I'm John Novak, and this is my wife, Edith. You've already met Walter?"

"Yes." Her gaze darted up to him. "Well, we sat next to each other on the train."

"But we didn't know who each other was—were—I didn't know who she was, vice versa."

"Well, come along." Mom took Allie's elbow. "Pastor Novak will transfer your luggage for you. Goodness, Betty talks about you so much I feel I know you already."

Walt followed his father and retrieved his duffel. Allie Miller. Yeah, Betty talked about her, but Betty talked too much about too many people. Now he wished he'd paid attention. For instance, did Allie Miller have a boyfriend? How come the most crucial detail was the hardest to recall? Oh well, if she had a boyfriend, he'd find out soon enough.

Walt and his father joined the women on the platform, and Walt grinned at the young lady beside him. He'd looked forward to this furlough for months—his family, his friends, and all the fruit he could eat.

But now it could be the best week of his life.

3

Antioch, California
Tuesday, June 23, 1942

Allie had heard of whirlwind tours, but with Betty Jamison, a tour was a full-blown tornado. Her feet hurt, her brain hurt, and her elbow hurt from Betty whipping her around corners. "I don't know how I'll remember all these names."

Dorothy Carlisle, a brown-feathered sparrow of a girl, peeked around from Betty's other side. "I don't expect you to keep this cast straight. I can't keep track of Betty's college friends."

Betty's smile lifted her plump cheeks. "Honestly, you two are such homebodies. Why do I love you so much?"

Allie squeezed Betty's arm. "Because we slow you down long enough to think."

"Oh, I hate thinking. Takes away time from the fun stuff. And oh, we'll have fun this week. I have something planned every day." Betty swung around a corner, and Allie scampered to keep up. "That's the end of the tour. We're early for dinner, but Mrs. Novak won't mind."

Allie glanced down the street lined with trees and well-kept homes, but nothing like her own Magnolia Avenue with its citrus groves and mansions. They crossed the street to a modest-sized Victorian painted yellow and white. A maple tree eclipsed the sidewalk, and an orange tree greeted them by the steps—depleted of ripe fruit.

As in so many homes, a white banner with a red border hung in the window. The Novaks' banner sported three blue stars. "Three sons in the service?" Allie asked.

"All three, and not even a daughter to keep them company." Dorothy rang the doorbell. "Is your boyfriend in the service? Baxter's his name, right? He must be aristocratic with a name like that."

Allie's grip on her handbag stiffened. Dorothy asked so many personal questions. "Baxter's exempt. His job is defense related."

"Hmm," Betty said. "He matches his first name more than his last. He's so neat and proper—a Baxter, not a Hicks."

The door opened, and Mrs. Novak untied an apron from around her slender waist. "My, you ladies are early. Well, come on in."

Chagrin knotted Allie's stomach. To arrive early and catch your hostess unprepared was even ruder than tardiness. "I'm sorry we're early, Mrs. Novak."

She grasped Allie's hand. "No apology is necessary. When the boys were still at home, the young people were in and out at all hours. Please make yourselves at home."

After she left for the kitchen, the ladies removed their hats and smoothed their hair. In the parlor Allie brushed her fingers over the keys of an upright piano. Three portraits of men in uniform sat on doilies on the piano top.

"You recognize Walt," Betty said. "These are his brothers. Aren't they gorgeous?"

Neither had Pastor Novak's odd nose or Mrs. Novak's full cheeks. Walter, however, inherited both. Since Allie also suffered from an unfortunate mix of family traits, she felt an affinity with him.

"Admiring my boys, are you?"

Allie looked up and smiled at Pastor Novak. "You have fine sons, sir."

"We're proud of them." He picked up the first portrait. "This is Raymond, the oldest. He followed his old man into the ministry but joined up when he saw war coming. He trains pilots at Kelly Field in Texas."

Pastor Novak proceeded to the next photograph. "Jack's also in the ministry, but he joined the Air Corps right out of seminary. He's based in Australia now. Quite a war hero, was in the squadron of B-17s flying into Pearl Harbor during the attack."

"Oh my."

"Oh yes," Betty said. "He got written up in the *Ledger* and everything."

"Then there's Walter." Pastor Novak gestured to the last portrait. "Chose engineering rather than the call of God. He's done well for himself, considering."

Considering what? Allie already knew the answer—considering he wasn't Raymond or Jack and didn't meet his father's expectations—as she didn't meet her mother's.

Footsteps sounded on the hardwood floor, and she looked up from Walter's portrait to his face. Black curls abounded on top of his head, although the sides were trimmed short. Goodness, she was glad the Air Corps didn't shave the men's heads.

"Hi, Allie." His tone was so warm, she again regretted being so touchy on the train.

"Look at you. Look at those wings." Betty sprang forward and grasped the silver wings pinned to Walter's khaki shirt. "But where's the jacket? The hat?"

He drew back but smiled. "Uh-uh. I'm on furlough."

George Anello's laugh rang from the entryway. "Should have known. Betty saw the uniform and forgot all about me."

"Nonsense, darling. You know I adore you." Fair, voluptuous Betty ran over and kissed her dark, lanky fiancé.

After George shook Walter's hand, he approached Allie with his uneven gait. One leg was longer than the other, which made him 4-F, "unfit for military service." His handshake bounced Allie's arm like a jitterbug. "Hiya, Allie. How was the grand tour? What do you think of Antioch?"

She searched for the truthful solution to her dilemma. "No town could live up to Betty's billing."

George laughed. "Ain't that the truth?"

Walter crossed his arms, a hint of a smile on his lips. "What did you like best?"

He knew what she was doing. Nondescript buildings flew through her mind, in contrast to Riverside's showcase of neo-classical, Mission Revival, and Spanish Renaissance architecture.

"The hills . . . the trees are lovely." The insufficiency of her answer appalled her. "Oh, and Pastor Novak, your church is a charming slice of New England."

He glowed with pride. "Thank you. Mrs. Novak is from Rhode Island, and she couldn't imagine a church without clapboard and a steeple."

Allie listened to him relate the history of the church. She refused to give Walter a glare or a triumphant smile, although either would have been deserved.

Before long, Pastor Novak excused himself, and Allie found herself alone in a room full of people. When had Betty's friends arrived? Blending into the ivy-patterned wallpaper was impossible, but joining a group was no less daunting.

Betty and Dorothy conversed with Betty's sister, Helen Carlisle, pretty and blonde and still heavy after the birth of her son. If only Helen had the baby along, Allie might have had an excuse to break into their tight circle.

The men's group rumbled with laughter. One man wore a blue sailor's suit that flattered his blond good looks—he had to be Helen's husband, Jim. The fourth man, a stocky civilian with brown hair and a mustache, cast a glance at Dorothy. Oh, what was the name of Dorothy's admirer? Oh yes, Art—Art Wayne.

Allie's stomach twisted. She enjoyed solitude, but not in the presence of others. She trailed her fingers on the piano keys behind her and started when she depressed one by accident.

Walter looked her way, eyebrows arched. Warmth crept up Allie's cheeks. What was more embarrassing—her musical faux pas, her isolation, or his pity?

"Dinner's served."

Allie let out a breath she didn't know she'd held. In the dining room she took the seat shown her between Jim Carlisle and Art Wayne. How awkward—two strangers. To avoid attention, she studied the china—a bit thick but simple and elegant and presented on embroidered linens.

After grace, Walter laid his napkin in his lap. "Roast beef. Mom, you're the best."

"I haven't seen you for a year, and I plan to spoil you."

Pastor Novak chuckled and sliced the roast. "The way this boy's been eating, you'd think the Army starves its airmen."

"He doesn't look starved." Dorothy Carlisle pinched Walter's cheek. He brushed her off with a glance across the table to Allie.

She looked down to smooth her napkin and to reduce his

embarrassment. Dorothy's comment was neither kind nor true. He had a nice, trim build.

"So, Allie," Jim Carlisle said from her left. "Did Betty show you our crater?"

Everyone laughed, and Allie looked about. "Crater?"

Betty peered around from Jim's other side. "We didn't get that far, Allie darling. Besides, it's been filled in."

"The four of us boys—we were a team." George formed a fist before his chest. "Jim came up with the ideas, and Art got the supplies from his dad's hardware store."

Art passed Allie her plate. His mustache twitched. "Scraps, rejects—all of them."

"Sure, they were." George winked at Allie. "Then Walt came up with the designs—amazing designs."

"Amazing any of them worked." Walter tore off a chunk of roll.

"Walt had another role," Jim said. "He's the pastor's innocent baby boy—threw everybody off the trail, told them we were engaged in harmless activities."

Allie spread butter on her baked potato. "Betty, you never told me your friends were a bunch of thieves and liars." She sucked in her breath. What an awful thing to say. Her gaze flicked around the table, but everyone laughed.

"See," Betty said. "Didn't I always say she was the missing member of our group? She's so quiet, but then . . ."

Too many people faced her. Allie scooped up some green beans. "The crater?"

"Oh." Walter took a sip of water. "I didn't compensate for the thrust—"

"No one wants an engineering lecture," Jim said. "You see, I got a chemistry set from a shortsighted uncle, and Walt designed a fuel-powered go-cart. Good thing we used Dodo's doll as a test driver."

"Don't call me Dodo." Dorothy glared at her brother. "And I loved that doll."

"A little glue," Walter said, his words broken by laughter. "You could have put it back together. Except we never found the head."

"Yeah, we did." George leaned forward, eyes bright. "How could you forget? That summer, climbing the tree in my front yard, the birds—"

"Oh yeah." Walter's laughter poured out. "The nest. They'd woven the doll hair into the nest—the head sticking out the side—"

Allie joined in the laughter. What would it have been like to grow up with a group of friends like this? Her grip on her utensils lightened as she listened to childhood stories. By the time Mrs. Novak served strawberry pie, plans for the week flew around the table, and Allie tingled with anticipation.

If only it could last forever. After this week, an eternity of isolation yawned before her. Every day Baxter ate dinner with the Millers, and then they wintered in the drawing room and summered on the porch. No movies, no picnics, no guests. Marriage would change nothing. Allie's tingles faded, replaced by asphyxiating sadness.

She gave her curls a flounce and laughed at the latest joke, although she hadn't heard it. She refused to let self-pity destroy this day, this week.

After dessert, the ladies cleared the table, but Mrs. Novak declined their help washing dishes. By the time they reached the parlor, Walter already sat at the keyboard.

He sent Allie a grin. "You're the visitor. What would you like?"

She would have liked to play, but she forced a smile. "Your specialty, please."

He launched into "Chattanooga Choo Choo," and Betty

linked arms with Allie and hauled her into the circle. Allie yearned for the keys. Walter had excellent technique, but he stumbled in fast sections.

When he finished, he blew out a puff of air. "Boy, am I rusty. How about something slower?"

Allie tensed at the first chords of "Green Eyes." When the song debuted the previous summer, she hoped Baxter would croon it to her, or at least give her a meaningful look when it came on the radio. A vain hope.

After the song dragged to a conclusion, Jim slipped his arm around his wife's waist. "'Don't Sit under the Apple Tree with Anyone Else but Me.'"

Helen leaned her head on his shoulder. "Never, my love."

Walter shook his head. "Sorry. Song's new, and I don't have the sheet music. I've been too busy with bombers to practice piano."

Disappointed groans circled the room, and Allie couldn't hold her tongue. "The song is quite simple."

Betty jiggled Allie's arm. "That's right. Allie knows it."

Walter gave her a look over his shoulder. "You couldn't play anything newer than Beethoven."

"Ooh," Betty said. "You just watch."

Beethoven indeed. Allie switched places with him and smoothed the skirt of her dress, a sage green crepe with an appliqué of a lily, which ran up the side and blossomed on her right shoulder. Then she dove into the song with plenty of splash. No stumbles, no sour notes, no dullness marred her performance. Afterward, she indulged in a smile in Walter's direction.

He frowned. "Don't get too comfortable. My piano."

"Not anymore." Her cheeks warmed at her own boldness and the group's laughter.

Betty requested "Tangerine," and Allie obliged with Latin flair. She had desired and earned her position, but Walter's frown pricked at her heart. Perhaps the piano bench was also his haven.

He cleared his throat when the song concluded. "How well do you sight-read?"

"Very well. Why?"

He motioned her off the bench, opened it, and pulled out a stack of papers. "Yeah, here they are. My brother Ray—his fiancée plays, so he arranges duets. Can you handle it?"

Although he had issued a challenge, Allie saw a compromise. "I'll try."

"Good." He sat to her left and set up hand-printed sheet music for "Little Brown Jug." They struggled at first with the fast pace and syncopation, but soon they coordinated the rhythm.

"Shame you missed that chord," Walter said.

Allie frowned at the sheet music. "Which chord?"

"That one." He flattened her hand on the keys, with dissonant results.

"Walter Novak!" Betty said. "You leave Allie alone. She's an only child. She's not used to teasing."

Walter's cheeks puckered. "Sorry. Let's try again." He started at the top.

Oh dear. Allie didn't want him to feel guilty, but how could she ease his discomfort? Then she turned the page, and inspiration struck. "Shame you missed that page."

"Page?"

"Yes." She slid the sheet music to the far right and leaned forward to block his view.

He burst out in laughter. "See? You're wrong. She can handle teasing."

Allie smiled at him over her shoulder, warmed by the

unfamiliar sense of inclusion and thankful she had grasped the welcoming hand he offered.

"Oh, Walt," Helen said. "Why don't you start over so we can dance?"

"Yeah!" Jim grabbed one end of the coffee table, Art lifted the other, and George rolled up the rug.

"I'm glad I'm at the piano," Walter said. "Can't stand dancing."

Allie shuddered. "Me neither."

"Really? Hmm." He plunked out a measure, then tried a different fingering. "Say, you know Betty paired us for the wedding—the two leftovers. Do you want to . . . well, *not* dance?"

She laughed. "Never in my life have I been asked to dance, and now I've been asked to *not* dance."

He made a face. "I—I'm sorry. That didn't—"

"No, no. I couldn't be more pleased." Her greatest anxiety about the week concerned the wedding reception. "Shall we not dance?"

Walter grinned and extended his hand. "Deal."

Allie shook—he had a pleasant amount of strength in his grip, not overpowering like George or insubstantial like Baxter.

When they resumed, Walter picked up speed and liveliness. His vigor energized Allie, along with the laughter, the swish of skirts, and the shuffle of shoes on the hardwood floor.

"This is so much fun," she said when the song was over. "Do you have more duets?"

"Sure do. Ray's prolific when he's in love." He retrieved the stack from the floor. "Let's see what else he's got. I picked the hardest one first."

The crinkle around his eyes made Allie laugh. "You wanted to ruffle my feathers."

"Nah, I wanted to trip you up. If I wanted to ruffle you, I'd say 'ball bearings.'"

Allie's mouth tightened. Why did this have to come up?

"Oh, relax, Miss *Miller*. The puzzle wasn't hard to solve. Daddy's rich, but you're not proud of your wealth; you're embarrassed by it."

"Well, yes." How often had she explained to Betty in vain? Betty loved her, but she didn't understand.

"People think you're a snob." Walter thumbed through the sheet music on his lap. "Even more so because you're quiet. All your life you've heard, 'That's Allie Miller. You know, Miller Ball Bearings. She thinks she's better than the rest of us.'"

"Yes," she said, eyes fixed on the profile of a man she barely knew, yet who understood. He actually understood.

"I've got the same problem." His nose wrinkled. "Not because I'm rich, obviously. Because I'm a pastor's kid. People think I have some holy link to God, that I spy for him or pass judgment."

"And they misinterpret your shyness as self-righteousness."

"Yeah." He turned to her, eyebrows high. "The fellows in the 306th Bomb Group call me Preach, because I don't drink, smoke, swear, gamble, or chase women. I think they're afraid of me."

Allie laughed. How could anyone fear a man with such an amiable face?

"Hey, Novak," Jim said. "My shore leave's ticking away. Pick some music so I can dance with my wife."

Walter selected "Moonlight Serenade," which was familiar enough to allow conversation.

"Thank you for sharing your piano bench," Allie said.

A grumble emanated from Walter's throat. "I should thank you for sharing."

She tilted her head. How far could she take this teasing? "It wasn't polite of me to invade your refuge. What do you hide from? Dancing or social interaction?"

He laughed. "Both. Dancing, more so. Two left feet. You too?"

"Oh no, I dance well. I just have bad memories."

"Memories?"

She'd said too much. She winced and concentrated on her fingering. However, she had a feeling Walter would understand. "Cotillion. The boys—well, they only wanted to dance with the pretty girls. How they rolled their eyes when they were paired with me."

"Yikes." His shoulders drew up, but he didn't miss a note. "I got the same reaction, but the girls also rolled their eyes in pain. Smashed toes, you know. I skipped school dances."

"Oh, I wish I could have, but Mother insisted. She was the belle of every ball, so she didn't understand. At least Father took pity and arranged a date for me my senior year. But then Baxter spent the evening talking to Mr. Jessup, the principal, so I still didn't dance."

"Hmm. On the sidelines again." He flipped to the last page. "Well, at the reception on Saturday, you won't have to dance, but you won't have to be alone either." He gave her a tentative glance. The lamp on the piano top revealed hazel in his eyes.

"I'm glad." Allie gave him her warmest smile in appreciation for his offer.

In tandem they struck the final chord. The tones melded, complemented, and lingered.

4

Wednesday, June 24, 1942

What a stupid deal. Walt had finally met a girl he could talk to, and he'd made a deal not to dance with her. Stupid, stupid, stupid.

He plunked a strawberry in his pail, unaware if it was ripe, only aware of Allie in the next row of strawberry plants. Ordinarily, he didn't like trousers on women, but he liked them on Allie. She wore some pink thing tied around her head to keep her hair back, which didn't work. She brushed little curls back from her face, and strawberry juice streaked across her cheek. Sure looked cute.

Yeah, one stupid deal. Two left feet? Not even true. He did fine when that USO girl dragged him out to dance, and never once did he smash a girl's toes.

He had to get out of that deal.

The worst thing about dancing was asking the woman, but he could talk to Allie, even with those eyes. *"Your green eyes with their soft lights . . ."*

He couldn't get that song out of his head. Why did he play it the night before? Must have looked like a fool.

Today he hadn't had a chance to talk to Allie, but if he could get Dorothy to pass him, he'd have Allie to himself.

Walt stood, stretched his arms high, and clasped his hands behind his head to deepen the stretch. Allie raised a slow smile to him and those eyes—"*those cool and limpid green eyes.*" What on earth did *limpid* mean anyway?

He nodded to her bucket. "How's it going, city girl?"

Her laugh was soft and low, not tinkly like Betty's or giggly like Dorothy's. "Just fine, country boy."

He grinned and set his hands on his hips. "Small town boy. Wish I were a country boy. Grandpa's farm is the best place in the world."

"It's lovely out here." She shaded her eyes against the noontime sun.

He followed her line of sight southwest, where golden hills marched in caravan toward Mount Diablo. "I always thought the hills looked like a herd of camels. You know, the grass looks like camel hair, and the oak trees—like little nomad camel drivers in green robes."

Another slow smile. "For an engineer, you have quite an imagination."

"You have no idea how imaginative he can be. Oh, the tales he tells." Dorothy stood to pass Walt. "Oh, Allie, you have something on your face."

Walt glared at the back of Dorothy's dark little head. Leave it to Dorothy Carlisle to ruin things for him in two different ways.

"Oh dear." Allie looked at the red smear on her handkerchief. "I wonder how long that's been there."

"Didn't even notice," Walt said. The lines in her forehead relaxed. Did she care what she looked like in front of him? He tipped his garrison cap further down over his forehead to confine his curls.

He squatted across from Allie. "You're doing well. One thing though—you've got to keep the tops on. Keeps them fresh. Take this one. It won't last." He pulled the reddest, shiniest berry from her bucket and popped it in his mouth.

"None of them will last with you around." She scooted her bucket away, her laugh as sweet as the berry dissolving in Walt's mouth.

"Grandma won't mind. She loves me."

Allie picked a strawberry, this time with top intact. "How nice to have your grandparents nearby. Mine are back East."

"Wow. Only you and your parents out West?"

"Mm-hmm. Betty wanted me to come up here on vacations, but I couldn't bear to leave them alone. And I'm sure you've heard Betty grumble about visiting my home."

Walt sorted through millions of Betty's unheard words.

Allie laughed. "I know. I can't remember half of what she tells me either. Anyway, my family prefers quiet evenings at home. You should see Betty fidget. She needs activity like the rest of us need air."

"Yeah." He chucked an overripe berry into the clumps of plants. "Sometimes I go back to base to rest."

"For me, home is almost too restful."

"Yeah?" He studied her downcast face. "Do you help with the business?"

She shook her head and sent curls across her cheek again. This time she brushed them away with the back of her hand. "My parents think it's shameful for a woman to work, but with the labor shortage, perhaps it's shameful not to work."

"Especially for a business major." He smiled at her surprised look. "Sometimes I listen to Betty."

Allie lowered those long eyelashes and smiled. Pretty. He had a hunch she didn't know, which made her more attractive, as if he'd found an undiscovered treasure.

"So why'd you pick business?" he asked.

"Well, I—I will inherit the company some day." Her cheeks turned red again, without the help of strawberry juice. "Baxter—he's Father's business manager—he's qualified to run the company, but I still feel I should understand business practices."

"Makes sense." He poked around a plant, but it was picked clean. Strange that she called the fellow by his last name.

"You must think I'm spoiled and lazy."

"Huh?" Walt snapped his thoughts back. "Because you don't have a job? No, of course not. Besides, you can volunteer."

"I wish I could." She moved forward. "My mother can't spare me around the house. Our housekeeper—well, she's Japanese and she was sent to a relocation camp."

He scooted up to join her, and his bucket left a circle in the rich brown soil. "Yeah. My best friend from the University of California too. Shame."

"You really think so?" Her voice was low, and she looked to him with wide eyes. "I—I suppose it's unpatriotic to say so, but I think it's horrible. Mariko's a citizen, as American as any of us."

"Yeah. The only sabotage Eddie committed was keeping me out of the top spot in our engineering class."

"I thought I was the only one who felt this way. My parents say it's for Mariko's safety. The city fired her husband, no one would sell to her, and the milkman wouldn't even deliver to her."

Walt shook his head and kept his voice down too. "Can't even help with the war effort. Eddie wanted to join the Air Corps with me, but they wouldn't take him."

She glanced down the row. "It's sad when those who want to serve aren't allowed to."

"Yeah." He followed her gaze and her line of thought.

"Nothing wrong with George's mind. He'd be great at a desk job, free another man to fight."

Allie leaned closer. "I hesitate to ask, but what about Art? Is he 4-F also?"

"Nope. 1-A and raring to go. His dad needs him at the store, made him promise not to join up. Art can't wait for his draft notice."

"His father must be proud of such a respectful son."

Walt shrugged and looked up to the white farmhouse. Grandma stood on the porch and beckoned through the circle of oak trees that screened the house from the wind. Lunch must be ready. Walt waved in acknowledgement. "Yeah, Art's respectful—too respectful."

"Too respectful? How can that be?"

"Sure, we have to honor our parents, but we have to honor God first." He stood and held out his hand for Allie's bucket. "Hey, everyone. Lunchtime."

Instead of the cold cut of a bucket handle across his palm, warm pressure enveloped his hand. Allie—she thought he was helping her up.

His throat clamped shut. *Oh Lord, not now. Don't let me freeze now.*

Allie got to her feet and released his hand. "My parents aren't Christians."

"Huh?" He swallowed hard. Maybe the deal wasn't stupid if he couldn't talk when he touched her.

"They think they are, but they're not."

Not what? He reeled his mind back. "Not Christians?"

"They think church membership makes them Christians, but in eighteen years at St. Timothy's, nobody talked about God the way Betty did—not just her words, but the way she lived."

"And you wanted what she had." He liked knowing more about her, but what did it have to do with Art and his dad?

"Yes, her assurance of God's love, her joy in his presence. It's what I wanted, what I needed." Allie headed for the farmhouse.

Oh yeah, lunch. Walt held out his hand again. "Here, let me take your bucket."

"Thank you."

She fell silent, and the distance across the green and brown striped field seemed longer than when he was a boy and hungry for Grandma's pie. He should say something, but what?

"St. Timothy's." Allie's eyes fixed on some point way past the farmhouse. "It feels so claustrophobic and petty, not joyful and peaceful like my church in Claremont."

Walt made a face. "Sounds like you need a new church."

She turned to him. "That's my quandary. How can I disobey my parents?"

Now he saw the connection to Art's story. "The real question is: how can you disobey God? You have to pray and find out what he wants you to do."

"I want to be where I can serve the Lord and do some good, but a family should worship together. Besides, I can't imagine walking into a strange church all alone. Why, I wouldn't even know where to look for a new church."

"If you'd like, I'll pray for you."

"Would you? You don't know how much I'd appreciate that."

Walt's cap slipped back, and the curl flopped onto his forehead. With a bucket in each hand, he couldn't do anything about it, but he didn't care. Allie had smiled at him, confided in him, and wanted him to pray for her.

★

"Hey, Walt." George pointed to the old wooden barn and winked.

Walt shot his friend a warning glare.

Betty pulled on her fiancé's arm. "Georgie, once we're married, you'll have to tell me. That story's been around since high school."

"Sorry, darling, I promised." George nodded to Walt.

He nodded back and leaned his forearms on the rough split rail fence. He could trust his friends not to tell stories told in confidence, even foolish boasts.

From around the corner of the corral, Allie gave him a curious tilt of her head. Walt rolled his eyes, and she smiled. Good. She understood.

An old red and white cow ambled toward him. Walt offered some grass. "Hiya, Flossie."

Grandpa Novak swung the corral gate open. "She can't hear anymore, you know. Stone deaf."

Walt nuzzled Flossie's fuzzy nose. "She can read my lips. You're still the prettiest girl in town, Floss. See, she knows me. She'd better. I named her."

"Yeah. Original," Art said with a grin.

Another head tilt from Allie. This one he could answer. "Hiram Fortner owns a dairy nearby, has a statue of a cow by the gate. Everyone calls her Fortner's Flossie."

"Except she disappeared the day before Pearl Harbor was bombed," Grandpa said. "Some kids pulling a prank, no doubt."

"Yeah," Walt said. "If Jack hadn't been at Pearl, I would have suspected him."

Grandpa chuckled and unbolted the barn doors. "That boy could never stay out of trouble. By the way, got a letter from him the other day."

"Yeah? I haven't heard from him for a while." Walt left the group behind and followed his grandfather into the barn. He savored the smell of hay, old wood, and livestock.

"That boy thinks he and his B-17 can take on the Japanese single-handedly."

"Great bird. Now we need to get Ray in a Fort too."

Grandpa mumbled and scratched his nose—the Novak nose. The only time Walt liked his nose was when he was with Grandpa.

"What?" Walt asked. "Ray needs to get out of that easy training job."

Grandpa shook his head. "Nope. Ray's a quiet soul. He's not cut out for the rough-and-tumble of combat like you and Jack."

Walt's shoulders felt straighter and broader. Grandpa thought he could handle combat.

"Okay, boy, put those Army muscles to use. Let's get the tarp off old *Jenny*."

Walt sprang forward, eager to prep the biplane for flight. The men worked in silence, another reason Walt loved the farm. Grandpa never talked much. In Walt's opinion, his parents had named the three boys well. Ray after Grandpa Garlovsky, soulful and musical. Jack after Dad, outgoing and driven. And Walt after Jacob Walter Novak, although he was glad his parents had reversed the names. Jacob was so old-fashioned.

"*Jenny* hasn't flown since Ray's last leave. Helped with the crop dusting."

The rudder felt stiff, so Walt squirted oil on the hinge. "Don't you think Ray wants to go to combat?"

Grandpa snorted. "Ray doesn't want to go to combat any more than you or Jack want to be pastors."

"Huh? Jack's wanted to be a pastor all his life."

"No, your father's wanted him to be a pastor all his life. Sooner Jack realizes that, the better."

Walt wiped his hand on a rag. True, he could never picture Jack in the pulpit—Jack, who was always coming up with schemes and getting Walt to cover for him. Still, Jack was a grown man and could pick his own career. And he had Dad's approval while Walt didn't. Grandpa understood, though. "You know, I never thanked you for how you encouraged me, stood up for me."

Grandpa grunted—but an appreciative grunt. "Didn't think the Army trained a bunch of sentimental fools. Come on, boy, let's get *Jenny* in the air."

Before long, the plane sat in the pasture. Walt slipped on his leather flight jacket. "Who wants a ride?"

Art was first, as always. The men climbed into the biplane, and Walt started her up. The engine's roar sounded almost as sweet as the duets with Allie. He glanced down at her and saluted, hoping he looked dashing and competent.

"Come on, Novak, let's go," Art called over the engine. "At least I can pretend to fight the enemy."

Walt coaxed the plane down the field and into the sky. Yeah, this was the way to fly. Sure, bombers were powerful, but in old *Jenny* he skipped on the air currents with the wind in his face.

Once he was over the town, he tapped Art on the shoulder, shook the stick, and pointed to Art. "Take the controls," he shouted.

Art gave him a thumbs-up. Walt pulled out his camera and leaned over to get aerial shots of his hometown. He'd received the camera for a college graduation gift and used the first batch of film on planes. Now he'd been away a year and wanted more—his family, friends, and home.

He took back the controls and wheeled *Jenny* toward the farm so George could have a ride. A crosswind on the landing allowed Walt to show off his deft hand with the controls. Too bad Allie wouldn't know how tricky a crosswind landing could be.

Walt and Art hopped out onto the grass.

"Boy, am I jealous," Art said. "You get paid to do that."

Walt flipped off his goggles. "Would you believe they pay me extra? Hazardous duty, they call it. Don't tell them, but I'd fly for free. Ready, George?"

"You betcha."

"No." Betty tugged on George's arm. "Oh, darling, not today, not three days before the wedding. I can't bear to lose you now."

"I won't—"

"But darling, the Army calls it hazardous for a reason. Please, not today."

George sighed and took Betty in his arms. "All right. Just this once."

Oh brother. Walt wanted one more ride, but Grandpa was busy with chores, Dorothy had never gone up, and Allie was too proper for an adventure. Or was she?

Allie hadn't taken her eyes off the plane. Walt recognized that look. He'd seen it on the faces of his fellow cadets the first day of flight school. He stepped in front of her. "You're thinking about it, aren't you?"

Allie's eyes widened, green as those cadets. "I've never flown before."

"Want to?"

"Maybe." Her lips barely moved.

He grinned. Yep, she might be the one for him.

Betty let out a scream. "No, Allie. I need you in the wedding."

Despite Betty yanking her arm, Allie didn't break her gaze with Walt. "Would it be like Art's flight? No aerobatics?"

"No loops, no snap rolls, no dives, I promise."

Betty hugged Allie's arm. "Don't believe him. He did it to George."

"Just once," George said, "and I asked for it."

Walt shuddered. "Yeah, and I had to clean out the plane afterward. Never again. Only when I'm alone."

"All right," Allie said.

Walt stared at her. "You'll go? Wow. Come on, let's get you suited up before this whiner changes your mind."

Her eager smile told him the whiner wouldn't win. Good. The woman had some spirit. He took off his flight jacket and handed it to her.

"Don't you need it?"

"Nah. Gotta get used to the cold. B-17s fly at over twenty thousand feet. Minus twenty degrees up there, sometimes colder."

He helped her with the leather flight helmet, careful to concentrate on the buckle, not on the soft skin under her chin. Then he stepped back to inspect his work. His jacket hung over her hips, the goggles covered her gorgeous eyes, and curls stuck out under the helmet. Cutest copilot he'd ever had.

"Okay, Allie, up you go." He laced his fingers together to brace her foot. "Is that 'Allie up' or 'Allie oop'?"

She laughed and climbed into the front cockpit. "If I slip, it'll be 'Allie oops.'"

Boy, did he like her. He climbed into the rear cockpit, nudged the plane across the golden pasture, and released her into the air. Allie's hands clamped the rim of the cockpit, and her curls whipped around her neck. After he leveled off, he put his hand on her shoulder. "How're you doing?" he shouted.

Allie's smile shone as bright as Walt's hopes. "I love it."

Yeah, she might be the one. Not only was she an attractive, intelligent woman, but she played the piano and liked to fly. She actually liked to fly. Most amazing—he could talk to her even though she wasn't taken. No doubt about that. No one had ever asked her to dance, and he had a hunch no one had ever told her she was pretty. He wanted to be the first. Too bad he didn't have Ray's way with words or Jack's way with a grin and a wink.

He'd just have to wing it. Walt chuckled at his unintentional pun. He tapped Allie's shoulder and pointed down at Antioch. She craned her neck to look over the edge, then turned and shouted something he couldn't hear. He shrugged. Allie cupped her hands together.

"Yeah. Like toys," he said.

She nodded and looked down to the miniature town in its grid along the river. Sure would be nice to take her into the hills or up the river. Still plenty of fuel. As a farmer, Grandpa would get unlimited fuel once it was rationed, but Walt didn't want to abuse the privilege.

He headed over the riverbank and poked Allie's shoulder. "Want a swim?" He pulled the stick to the right and depressed the right rudder pedal. Up went the right aileron, down went the left, and *Jenny* went into a tight right-hand turn.

Allie screamed, but the laughter in her scream made Walt smile.

Now he could impress her with the crosswind landing. He circled the white farmhouse and the weathered gray barn to approach from the south. The wind from the west had picked up, but not enough to worry him.

Walt lowered the upwind left wing and applied right rudder pressure to keep *Jenny* from turning left. Surely Allie could feel the struggle of the little plane against the wind. Boy, was it swell.

With flaps down and the stick forward, he eased the plane down, all the time compensating for changes in wind currents.

Now for the fun part—the momentary, one-wheeled landing required with a crosswind. That'd give Allie a thrill. About ten feet from the ground, Walt pulled the nose up for the flare to lose airspeed and settle to the ground.

Then he saw Flossie.

"Walt!" Allie screamed. "A cow!"

"I see her." At one o'clock, wandering into his path, and deaf—stone deaf.

Too late to get airborne again. Too little speed, too short a field. The left wheel touched down. If he turned to avoid the cow, he'd go into a ground loop, maybe flip the plane. But if he hit the cow . . .

"Lord, I need your help here."

The right wheel touched down. Flossie's backside rushed up before him. Walt eased the left rudder down enough to angle the nose away from the cow, but not enough to send them into a spin. "Oh Lord, move that cow or stop this plane."

Allie screamed. The plane shuddered and bumped down the field.

He applied the brakes as hard as he could without nosing the plane over. The right wingtip clobbered Flossie's rear end. An angry moo. The plane bounced to a stop.

Walt clenched the control stick. His breath came hard and fast. Oh, swell. He wanted to impress Allie and he almost got her killed. Now she'd never fly again. She'd never speak to him again. All because he watched her and not the field. Stupid, amateur, almost fatal mistake.

Allie turned to him slowly, her face white.

"You okay?" He dreaded her answer.

She nodded. "How's the cow?"

The cow. Walt glanced to Flossie, who trotted away with loud, indignant moos. "She's awful mad."

Allie laughed. She actually laughed, and she kept on

laughing. Walt joined in, relieved that they were alive and intact, and amazed at Allie's good humor.

Betty ran up to the plane. "Allie! Allie! Are you all right?"

She nodded, still laughing. "Oh, Walt, the cow—the way she mooed."

Fresh waves of shared laughter lifted him higher than any aircraft. He swung out of the plane and held up his arms. "Come on, Allie. Stop laughing long enough to get out of that death trap."

"I don't think I can stop." She climbed out onto the lower wing.

He put his hands on her tiny waist and lowered her to the ground. Her laughter tumbled sweet in his face, and it was all he could do not to hug her close and never let go.

"Say, Walt," George said. "Give me your camera. I'll get a picture."

"Great idea." He took off his goggles, then Allie's.

"Oh, not me."

"Yeah, you. You're my copilot."

The smallest smile crossed her lips. "Promise never to show my parents? I don't want them to know their only daughter played Amelia Earhart."

"See, you did something your parents wouldn't approve of, and you survived."

"Barely." The sparkle in her eyes stirred up all sorts of strange and wonderful things in Walt's chest.

He rested his arm along the fuselage behind Allie. Maybe when the fellows at Wendover saw the picture, they'd think she was his girlfriend. Who knew? Maybe by then, she really would be his girlfriend.

5

Thursday, June 25, 1942

"Oh, good," Betty said. "The men are already here."

Allie crested a grassy dune, and the San Joaquin River stretched wide and sparkling and gray blue before her. In a small cove, a lone willow tree trailed lacy branches over the beach.

Betty and Dorothy spread a blanket on the sand, and Allie set the picnic basket on top. She squinted at two men in a rowboat not far from shore. George, long and skinny, waved to the ladies. Art, smaller but sturdier, shielded his eyes before he added his greeting. A silver ripple formed in the water behind the boat, and Walt popped up. He smoothed his hair from his forehead, waved, and swam toward shore.

Allie helped Betty and Dorothy with another blanket. Walt had been so kind the last few days. Betty was appropriately absorbed with her fiancé, Jim and Helen had sequestered themselves with the baby, and Dorothy, for all her protests of not caring one whit for Arthur Wayne, stayed by his adoring side. Walt's company shielded Allie from loneliness.

Betty and Dorothy stripped to their bathing suits, and Allie removed the blouse that covered her yellow gingham suit. Walt's ripple approached the shore. Allie paused. It didn't seem proper to remove her wraparound skirt in front of him.

He emerged, panting, from the water and raked his hair back. "Hi," he said with a smile in Allie's direction.

She fought to keep her gaze from the trickles of water meandering down through the hairs on his solid chest, and her stomach clenched in an unfamiliar way.

Betty settled on the blanket and crossed her ankles in front of her. "Did you bring your camera, Walt?"

"Yep." He walked to a heap of clothing farther down the beach.

Allie took advantage of the moment to take off her skirt, sit next to Betty, and compose herself. She'd never had that reaction with Baxter, but then she'd never seen Baxter in bathing trunks. Why, he never took off his jacket, much less his shirt.

Betty flung her arms around Dorothy's and Allie's shoulders. "I've always wanted to be in a cheesecake photo."

Allie shrugged off Betty's arm. "Oh no. Not me."

"Yes, you." Betty pulled her down again. "We're a trio. Move over, Rita Hayworth, here come Dorothy, Betty, and Allie."

"Come on, Allie." Walt crouched down and focused the camera. "A man needs wallpaper for his barracks."

The thought of her photograph in a barracks was so ludicrous, she laughed.

The camera snapped. Walt looked up and grinned. "That was swell."

In the shade of the willow tree, over fried chicken and fresh strawberries, Allie bounced between conversations about wedding plans and the Allied progress in the Pacific, amazed at her ease with these people, most of whom she had known only a few days.

After the one-hour safety window, George and Betty appropriated the rowboat, Art and Dorothy went for a stroll, Walt took a running dive into the cove, and Allie followed.

Delta water was saltier than Lake Arrowhead water, and after a few laps it stung Allie's eyes, and she returned to the beach. She dried off and sat down, legs stretched before her. At first, the sun chilled her as the residual moisture evaporated, but then it warmed her through.

Allie closed her eyes and tilted her face to the sun, which painted bright patterns behind her eyelids. *Oh Lord, thank you for this day, this week. I'm having even more fun than I did at Scripps. If only . . .*

She expelled a deep breath and the sadness of the incomplete thought. *Thank you for Betty's friendship, for Walt's kindness to a stranger—*

"Hi, Allie."

Once again, Walt had sprung to her presumed distress. Betty must have commanded him to keep an eye on poor, shy Allie, abandoned by her boyfriend. She turned to him and smiled.

The camera clicked.

"Walter Novak!"

He plopped to the blanket beside her, his face too innocent. "As I said, a soldier needs cheesecake photos. Reminds him why he's fighting, inspires him."

She wrinkled her nose. "My photo would never inspire anyone."

"I heard that," Betty called from the boat. "She can't stand compliments, Walt, especially about her looks."

Allie held her chin high. "I was raised to be modest."

"No." The water seemed to magnify Betty's glare. "You were raised to believe you were homely. Nonsense. I've always thought you were darling, and no matter how much you roll your eyes, I'll still say so."

She closed her eyes to prevent them from rolling. This was always painful, but with men around, it was excruciating.

"Walt," Betty said. "Don't you agree? Doesn't she have the most gorgeous green eyes?"

Oh no. How could Betty do this to her?

"Huh?" Walt shot her a quick glance. "Oh. Um, yeah."

"Betty," Allie groaned. Poor man had probably never noticed.

"I wish I had eyes like yours," Betty said. "Blue eyes are so common, and with my blonde hair, I look like a German fräulein. I'm afraid they'll kick me out of the country."

George grinned at her. "And you're marrying an Italian man."

Betty laughed. "If I say *sayonara*, I'll never see American soil again."

"Axis spy!" Walt lunged forward into the water and thrashed to the boat. With a giant downward heave, he tipped the boat and its passengers into the water.

Allie laughed and brushed away the sand Walt had kicked up, relieved at the shift in attention.

Betty glided into the cove. "Come on, George. You wanted a swim anyhow."

Walt tossed the oars into the boat and pushed the craft ashore. "Say, Allie, you haven't gone out yet. Want a ride?"

"Sure." She got to her feet.

His face lit up as bright as when she'd accepted the plane ride.

"On the other hand," she said, "the last time I rode with you, we ran into a cow."

"All right, smart aleck. Just for that, you're rowing." With taut muscles, he steadied the boat while she stepped in and sat on the clammy seat. Then Walt gave the boat a push and jumped in. Allie gripped the sides until he sat and the wobbling stopped.

He draped his arms along the stern. "Okay, Miss Miller, all yours."

She bit down on her lip so she wouldn't laugh. He thought she played only classical music, and now he thought she couldn't row. She studied the oars with feigned confusion, then cranked the boat into a turn and headed across the cove. "Where to, Lieutenant Novak?"

"Well, I'll be." A smile worked into his cheeks. "You never fail to amaze me."

"You've only known me—four days."

"Can't wait for tomorrow's surprise." He settled deeper into his seat. "Nothing for me to do but put up my parasol, trail my fingers in the water, and whistle a romantic tune." He looked up to the azure sky, puckered his lips, and whistled "Green Eyes."

She gasped and let the oars slap the water. "Walter Novak, you're teasing me."

One side of his mouth twitched up. "I happen to like the song. Green's my favorite color. Now, you're strong enough to leave the cove. Don't go downstream—the Fulton Shipyard's that way. Head upstream toward the Antioch Bridge. Tide's coming in, so rowing won't be bad. I'll take over on the way back."

Allie looked over her shoulder to plot her course. She drew the oars back, ignored their sulky resistance, and released them to soar in glittering arcs.

"Where'd you learn to row, Miss Miller? It's not your typical debutante activity."

"I'm not a debutante." She smiled at his teasing. "My family went up to Lake Arrowhead each summer. I swam, I rowed, I imagined in the woods."

"Make good friends there?"

"Friends? Oh dear, no. But I still loved it."

Walt plucked a stick of driftwood from the water. "And this week?"

"I'm having a wonderful time. You're blessed to have such a group. I wonder—I wonder what I'd be like if I'd grown up with a group like this."

"Hmm." He leaned forward, elbows on knees, and studied the driftwood in his hands. "Not many friends at home?"

Allie guided the boat near the shore to avoid the current. "My parents are homebodies. We've always been content to keep to ourselves, except . . ."

"Except what?"

She gazed into Walt's dark eyes and knew he'd understand. "Since I met Betty, I haven't been as content at home, and now I don't have another school year to anticipate."

"Wow." His black eyebrows drew together. "I don't like to leave my friends, but they'll be here for my next furlough. And Frank's a good friend."

"Frank." Allie grasped at the change in subject. "He's in your bomb group?"

"Yeah. Great guy. He's married, three kids, fourth on the way. We did our advanced training together at Brooks Field. I had a bad night on the town and was real glad to meet him afterward, find someone who shares my values."

How did a man who didn't drink, gamble, or chase women have a bad night on the town? "Do I dare ask what happened?"

Walt grimaced. "I've only told Frank. Embarrassing."

"More embarrassing than admitting you don't have friends at home?"

"Suppose not." He grumbled and twisted the wood in his hands. "Okay. Just don't tell the others, all right? Makes me look bad."

"All right." She watched his face redden. Maybe she shouldn't have asked.

"First week at Brooks, three of the fellows invited me to the USO. You know how I feel about dancing, but I was bored, so I went. Well, they met four gals. I was paralyzed—couldn't speak. But this one girl talked so much, she didn't notice. Just glad to be with a man in uniform, I think." He snapped off a twig and scrutinized the remaining smooth branch. "Walked the girls home. Couldn't wait to get away, but out of the blue, she kissed me."

"Oh dear. What did you do?"

Walt glanced up at her. "I'm no fool. I kissed her back."

Allie laughed and averted her gaze to the contrast between the toasted hills and the lush reeds along the riverbank. From the tingle in her cheeks, she knew her face was as red as his.

"But then . . . um, she wanted . . . well, I went home. Only man who did. They gave me a tough time. Frank says I should invent a girlfriend to get them off my case. Imagine what they'd say if they knew she's only the second woman I've kissed." His cheeks agitated, much as they had the day before when George mentioned the barn.

"Does the first have anything to do with your grandparents' barn?"

Walt's jaw dropped. "How'd you . . . oh, swell. You've laid bare all my secrets."

Better his than hers. She smiled and sank the oars in the water. "I'm right?"

"My cousin."

Allie gasped. "Your cousin?"

"Not as bad as it sounds. My second cousin." He groaned, long and deep. "Her idea. We were seventeen. She had a big date coming up and wanted to practice. I was the right height, so she hauled me off to the barn."

The hint of a smile on his face made Allie laugh. She rowed around a clump of rushes protruding from the shore. "And you bragged to your friends because they think you're hopeless with women."

"I am hopeless," he said with a grin. "But I was the first to kiss a girl. Betty was still holding George off, Jim wouldn't give Helen the time of day, and Art and Dorothy—they just giggled at each other."

"They still just giggle at each other."

Walt snorted. "Aren't they something? Art's too shy to ask her out, and Dorothy—she flirts, she gives him the cold shoulder, she dates other men to make him jealous. I can't stand her games."

That explained the tension between Walt and Dorothy.

"Okay." He pointed the driftwood at Allie. "I told two embarrassing make-out stories. Your turn."

She gave him a smug smile and plunged the oars deep. "I don't have an embarrassing make-out story, because I've never made out." Her neck grew as warm as the sun on her bare shoulders. Oh dear, what would he think of Baxter?

"You've never been kissed?"

Allie drew herself up tall. "Have too. Ten times." The heat rushed up her face. Why, why, why did she admit that—only ten kisses in four and a half years?

Walt's lips compressed together, then crept into half a smile. "How can you count? Unless it's a peck. Otherwise—well, how can you count?"

Not only could she count, she could calculate—his birthday, her birthday, and graduation. "Just pecks," she said. She shut her eyes and wished she had shut her mouth.

"Wow. So no real kisses?"

"Not like in the movies." Not like people in love. She shook her head, as if she could shake off the sadness and humiliation of her secret, revealed for the first time. "Now we're more than even. I've thoroughly shamed myself."

He frowned. "Why would you say that? Reflects well on your character."

She paused midstroke. Is that how he saw the matter? That Allie was a lady of character, and Baxter a gentleman of noble restraint, able to resist the woman he loved? Fine. Walt's version was better than the truth.

"Are you sore?" He gestured to the oars. "Want me to take over?"

"Oh no." Although her shoulders were starting to ache, Allie leaned back and propelled the boat upstream. "I'd rather go on. It's lovely here."

"Yeah. This is a great place."

She gazed at the soft amber hills and the cattails edging the broad river, anything to distract herself from her relationship with Baxter. "How close can you get to shore?"

"Couple feet. Go ahead."

She steered closer and searched the reeds for a bird or a nest. Tiny white butterflies flitted about as if aiding her quest.

"When we were boys, George and I used to come here, pretend we were pirates on the bayou, explorers on the Nile, Huck Finn, you name it." Walt plucked a cattail and tapped Allie on the head with it.

She laughed. "What are you doing?"

He chucked her under the chin. "Trying to remember a Bible verse so I can impress you with my holiness."

"I'd be more impressed if you didn't beat me up."

"Psalm one." Walt grinned and rapped a rhythm on Allie's knees. "'He shall be like a tree planted by the rivers of water, that bringeth forth his fruit in his season; his leaf also shall not wither; and whatsoever he doeth shall prosper.'"

He was awfully cute. Why did he think he was hopeless with women? Why, if she didn't have a boyfriend . . .

Clunk!

Allie tipped back on her seat and slipped off with a little scream. She looked up to see Walt down on hands and knees. "Did I get too close to shore?"

"Nah. Sounded solid, metallic." He got up and offered his hand and a smile. "For the record, this time it was your fault."

If she didn't have a boyfriend . . .

She took his hand, and his warmth rippled right through her. The triangular hollow at the base of his neck deepened as he helped her back to her seat, and his lips had a nice, soft bend. What would it be like to—

"I wonder what we hit."

"What?" Allie stared at Walt, who squatted before her. "Oh, I don't know." She scrambled over the seat into the bow. The boat pitched, and Allie clutched the edge.

"Careful there."

"Sorry." The shore curved in and formed a pocket protected from the current, and the surface smoothed quickly. Through the murky water, she discerned black and white patches and large bovine eyes. "Walt, it's a cow."

He laughed and fished the oars from the water. "Now who's teasing?"

She beckoned, unable to break her gaze with the distorted image. "No, I'm serious. Come see. It's a cow—a giant metal cow."

They switched positions. Walt peered into the water and looked back to Allie, his eyes as wide as the cow's. "It's Flossie."

"Flossie?"

"Fortner's Flossie. I told you about her yesterday. The kids

who stole her must have panicked and dumped her here."
He sat down, backed the boat free, and rammed it into the
reeds.

She held on tight as he climbed out. "What are you
doing?"

He sloshed through the water. "Got to get her out."

"You're kidding. She's big."

He grinned over his shoulder at her. "About the size of
a calf. If Mr. Fortner doesn't want her back, think how
much scrap metal's in her. That's a lot of machine guns or
helmets."

Allie lowered herself over the side, and mud oozed between
her toes.

Walt stared at her. "You're going to help?"

"My patriotic duty." She untied a rope knotted to the bow.
"Would this help?"

"Yeah. Good idea. She's stuck in the mud."

Allie waded out waist deep and passed Walt the rope.

He tied it around the cow's neck. "Okay, I'll dive down,
loosen her. You pull."

"All right." When he dove, she tugged hard, but the cow
didn't budge.

Walt surfaced and flicked mud from his hands. "Should
have picked someone with more meat on their bones. You're
just a twig of a thing."

Enough affection shone in his smile to assure her he meant
it kindly. She wrapped the rope around her hand. "See what
this twig can do."

Down he went, and Allie pulled with all her might. This
time Flossie budged, and the next time the cow rolled to
her side. Allie slipped, and water rushed over her head. She
struggled to get her footing in the slick mud without losing
the rope.

A firm hand on her elbow helped her up. She wiped away the water streaming over her face. "Thank you."

"You're welcome." He smiled and pointed to the rope in her hand. "This twig may bend, but she doesn't break. Come on, let's get old Floss out of here."

"Then what?" She rearranged the rope around a less raw spot on her hand.

Walt wrapped his arms around the cow's midsection. "We're not far from the bridge. Gotta be a road nearby. Kids who dumped her had to get here somehow."

They dragged and laughed and slipped and bumped wet arms, sides, and legs—all of which gave Allie an unnerving, heady feeling.

Cattails brushed her back. "My, she's heavy."

"Won't be so heavy." He plunged back further into the reeds. "Once the water's out of her."

She felt solid ground underfoot, and soon the reeds gave way to dry grasses. Flossie slid out, and water gushed from her riveted seams. Allie fell to her backside, Walt collapsed flat on his back beside her, and they panted in the sunshine.

"You're muddy, Miss Miller." Walt poked her filthy calf with a brown toe.

She smiled down at him. In addition to the mud on his arms and legs, he had streaks of rust on his chest. "So are you, Lieutenant Novak."

He wiped his hands on his bathing trunks and laced his hands behind his head. "You and I have racked up the adventures, haven't we?"

She inspected her hands—the crisp manicure and the red rope burns. "I can't believe we ran into another cow."

Walt's laughter rang deep and melodious, and Allie joined in pitch-perfect accompaniment.

6

Friday, June 26, 1942

For the fifth time, Walt passed the door to the Belshaw building. "Next time I'll go in. Yeah, next time. You're a bomber pilot. What's so hard about opening a door?"

Across Second Street, Mrs. Llewellyn waved to him. The old gossip would tell the whole town she saw him pacing. Worse, she'd come over to extract all the details of the Flossie rescue operation so she could say she heard it straight from Walter Novak. All the details—how he and Allie recovered Flossie, found the road, and flagged down a pickup truck to find Mr. Fortner himself at the wheel. Of course, Mrs. Llewellyn really wanted to hear why Walt and this out-of-towner were traipsing around the countryside in nothing but their swimsuits.

Walt waved at Mrs. Llewellyn, ducked inside the Belshaw building, and climbed the stairs to the reception hall. White streamers hung from the center of the ceiling like a giant octopus. Mrs. Jamison and Mrs. Anello spread a cloth on a table across the room, Betty and Dorothy fiddled with some flower thing on another, and Allie stood on a ladder to Walt's right with a streamer.

"Walt, darling," Betty called out. "What are you doing here?"

"Hi." He tried to pull his hand out of the pocket of his khaki trousers, but got stuck. He released the item in his clutch and waved. "I'm bored. Dad's writing his sermon, Mom's cleaning, Art's working, Jim and Helen are out, and George's busy—the wedding's tomorrow."

"We know." Laughter bounced all around.

He winced. Stupid, foolish—

"We can find something for you to do," Betty said. "Allie, you need some help?"

"Sure. It'd be much faster if someone tore tape for me."

Time alone with Allie—just what he'd hoped for. He ambled over. "I should be the one up the ladder."

She lifted one eyebrow. "Do you tie bows?"

"Bows?"

"I didn't think so." She leaned down and handed him a roll of tape. "Just tear the tape, flyboy."

"Glad I can put my military training to use." He grinned and tore a piece for her. A boring job but not without benefits—like the shapely pair of calves at eye level. Why did women fuss about the stocking shortage? Bare legs were great.

"Nice view," he said. He snapped his gaze out the window and grimaced. Swell, he got caught ogling her legs.

"Hmm?" She bent down and looked outside to the tree-tops along the street below. "Oh. Oh yes." She didn't sound convinced.

Walt motioned to the window. "I like trees. Green." Like her eyes when she smiled at him. Was it always so stuffy in here? He tossed his garrison cap onto a table and rolled up his sleeves. Why was he tongue-tied? The day before was incredible. He couldn't believe they'd talked about kissing.

Wow, they talked about kissing, and she sure looked open to the prospect.

Allie looped the end of the streamer until it looked like some kind of flower. "I can't believe this week's halfway over." She held out her hand for tape, sighed, and twisted up her mouth.

"You okay, Allie?"

"Yes, I'm fine." Her smile wobbled. "I'm trying not to think about going home. Oh, you must think I'm horrible. I love my parents, I really do, and my home, and Riverside, and—"

"I know. No friends, no fun, no work, not even a good church."

She stared at him for a moment, then returned to her bow. "I wish things were different."

"Make them different."

She cast him a glance over her shoulder.

"I know you're shy, but you can do it. Visit a new church, check out the Red Cross." What was it about this woman that brought out his bold side?

She fluffed the bow. "It's not that simple. I mean, you—you understand me. I can't believe how well you understand me, but you don't know my parents."

"No, but you should have heard my dad when I told him I wasn't called to be a pastor. Yeah, it was tough, but I prayed and did God's will, and God gave me strength. You want to serve God. He'll honor that. Pray about it, and remember, I'll pray for you too."

"Thank you." Her bow done, she sat on a rung. "You need prayers far more than I do. I'm going home. You're going off to war." The puckers in her forehead told him she was concerned about him—and embarrassed to call attention to her own problems.

Walt hooked his thumbs through the roll of tape, as if it were a bomber's control wheel. "A while back, my brother Jack wrote that he'd rather face a whole squadron of Zeros than confront our father."

Allie's smile smoothed away those forehead puckers.

He eased the roll of tape back, ready for takeoff. "How about an even exchange of prayers?"

"Sounds wonderful," she said with a soft, long gaze.

Yeah, this plane was taking off. Everything was here—friendship, understanding, attraction, and the good stuff—their common faith. She'd pray for him. While he was off bombing the enemy and getting shot at, this lovely young lady would pray for him.

"We . . . we should get back to work." She glanced to the other women and stepped off the ladder. "Would you please bring over the next streamer while I set up over there?"

He balked at the thought of flitting about with a streamer. Might as well tie a pink bow on his head. "Uh-uh. I'll carry the ladder. You get the streamer." He put his hand to her lower back to guide her toward the octopus.

Walt carried the ladder to the next corner, pulled the object from his pocket, and set it on the top rung. He glanced at Allie. She sure looked better with the streamer than he would have.

She climbed the ladder and hesitated when she saw Walt's gift. "What's this?"

"Remember that driftwood I found yesterday?"

"You made this?" She sat on a middle rung and tucked the streamer under her leg. "Oh, Walter, what a sweet little cow."

"Carving's a hobby of mine. Usually do planes."

"When did you have time?" She traced her finger down

the cow's back, where Walt's fingers had been only moments before.

"Last night. After we all saw *Yankee Doodle Dandy*. Couldn't sleep." How could he with all those memories—rowing, flopping around in the mud, sitting real close in the movie, playing more piano duets, getting cozier with each song?

"You say I surprise you." She stroked the cow's nose. "Now you've surprised me. This is so well done."

"Well done? I wouldn't say that to a cow."

Allie laughed and covered small wooden ears. "Sorry, Flossie." Then she held it out to him.

"No, it's for you."

"For me?" A smile lit up her face. Why on earth did she think she was homely?

"Yeah. So you'll remember this week."

"Why, thank you, Walt. Would you like to come home with me, Flossie?" She kissed the cow on top of its head and tucked it in her skirt pocket.

How about a kiss for the man who made her? He raked the hair off his forehead.

She reached over and plucked the curl down again. "I don't know why you always push your hair back. It's cute like that. Quite the dashing pilot."

Cute? Dashing? Boy, if the others weren't around, he'd haul her down and give her that first real kiss right then.

Allie blushed, as if she'd read his thoughts.

"Taking a break?" Betty walked over and scowled at Allie. "Stop your chatter and get to work."

Allie burst out in a grin. "You've waited four years to say that."

"Absolutely." Betty patted Allie's hand. "I never thought I'd say it to you and Walt. To think I worried about you, since

I couldn't be with you much this week. I never thought the shyest people I know would get along so well. Why, you two have been inseparable."

Walt tore off a strip of tape. If he had his way, they'd be inseparable for life.

7

"Are you scared, Betty?" Dorothy asked.

Betty wound a blonde lock around a curler. "I'm marrying the sweetest man in the world, and we both love God, so how could I be scared? And I have my best friends to keep me company tonight in case I forget."

On the edge of Betty's bed, Allie placed a red stripe of polish down her last fingernail. Why did Betty think it was so important to marry someone who shared her beliefs? Couldn't a Christian wife's influence bring her husband to faith in the Lord? Baxter's salvation would be worth the sacrifice of her silly romantic dreams.

Dorothy sat next to Allie, her hair already set. "Are you excited about marrying Baxter?"

She screwed the cap on the bottle of polish and let out a noncommittal mumble.

Betty clucked her tongue. "You won't get anything out of her, Dorothy. She never talks about Baxter."

Dorothy's gaze bored into the side of Allie's face. "You know, I've barely heard you mention him."

"I'm a private person." Allie waved her left hand to dry the polish. She frowned. Come to think of it, she hadn't mentioned him much to Walt either.

"You have a baffling relationship." Betty glanced at Allie in the mirror of her dressing table and rolled another lock. "You kept Baxter's picture on your desk in our dorm room but you never pined over it. You didn't go crazy over the mail. When he visited, you weren't ruffled before he came, or giddy when he was there, or mopey when he left. Goodness, you know what I'm like. I always wanted to be as calm as you were."

Allie managed to return Betty's reflected smile. She always wanted to be in love as Betty was.

"I don't agree. I think feeling giddy is half the fun," Dorothy said.

Allie seized the opportunity. "Are you giddy with Art?"

"Art?" She sniffed. "Arthur Wayne is nothing but potential. Oh, he moons over me, all right, but he won't act."

"Could you do something?" Allie was stunned to hear herself ask such a thing.

Betty and Dorothy laughed together. "You should see," Betty said. "When she flirts with him, Art scurries for cover like a cockroach fleeing the light."

"Then he pouts when I date other men." Dorothy crossed her legs and rearranged her bathrobe. "But honestly, how long am I supposed to wait for him? I don't care what Walter Novak says. Ooh, I'm still seething over what he said last summer."

Betty whipped around. "Allie, you wouldn't believe what he said—Walter Novak, of all people."

Allie's hand paused midwave. She didn't care for Betty's tone of voice.

"Wait till you hear this." Dorothy crossed her arms. "Walt had the nerve to tell me I dated Reg Tucker just to make Art jealous, that I was playing games, being deceptive. Deceptive? Pot calling the kettle black."

Allie's gaze darted between her friends. Although she had to admit these ladies knew Walt better than she did, she longed to defend him.

"Come on, Allie." Betty rose from the dressing table and sat on the bed next to Dorothy. "I know Walt's your new pal, but I told you he stretches the truth sometimes. Oh, his heart's in the right place. He doesn't do it to hurt people."

Allie stood and retrieved the cold cream from her cosmetics case, her stomach in an unpleasant flutter.

"He sure hurt people last summer," Dorothy said. "He told me Art was dating Jeannie Llewellyn, which wasn't true. He thought he'd make me jealous, but he just made me mad. Art and Walt and I didn't speak to each other for weeks."

"Oh dear." Allie sat at the dressing table and unscrewed the jar of cold cream with her right hand, which was already dry. Now she truly understood the tension between Walt and Dorothy.

"In Walt's defense," Betty said, "he wanted to help. Sometimes he tells tales when he thinks it helps, sometimes to get his friends out of trouble, other times to save face. He's a pastor's son with two perfect brothers. He can't stand to be seen in a bad light."

Allie frowned and dipped her fingers in the sleek white cream. "I don't know. He's told me unflattering stories."

Betty's eyes glinted in the soft electric light. "Did he mention the barn?"

Allie saw her own eyes grow round in the mirror.

Betty squealed. "He did? Oh, tell us."

"Please?" Dorothy said. "You have to."

Allie paused, torn between loyalty to her old friend and her new. "I can't. I know how I'd feel if Walt repeated the story I told him."

"Oh?" Betty sat up taller. "What story? Something you haven't told me?"

"Well, yes."

"You can tell me. I'm your best friend."

Allie's heart wrenched at the hurt in Betty's voice, but if she divulged Baxter's ten pecks, Betty would pry out the horrid truth that they didn't love each other. She smoothed the cream in cool circles on her cheeks and gave Betty a weak smile. "I'm sorry. Telling the story once was painful, twice would be unbearable."

"Oh." Betty's nostrils drew up, her mouth drew up, and her chin drew up.

Allie sighed and massaged the last dollop of cream into her forehead, all too familiar with Betty's countenance. Betty wouldn't speak to her for days unless she revealed Walt's secret or her own.

Dorothy put her arm around Betty's shoulder. "Don't get in a snit."

She crossed her arms. "I'm not in a snit."

"Yes, you are," Allie said and laughed when Dorothy echoed her.

Betty's chin rose even higher. "What exactly is a snit anyway?"

"Just like that." Allie crossed the room, sat next to her friend, and poked her in the ribs. "Snit, snit, snit."

Betty's laugh sputtered out, and she poked Allie back.

Thump!

They jumped and turned to the window. "What was that?" Betty asked.

Clunk!

Betty scrambled to the window, peeked under the blackout curtain, and gasped. "It's George. And Art and Walt."

Strange musical notes filtered through the window: "'I

stand at your gate; and the song that I sing is of moonlight.'"

"'Moonlight Serenade,'" Allie said. "How romantic. Open the window."

"Oh no." Betty dashed for the bed and plopped between her friends. "I'm in my bathrobe, my curlers. I can't let George see me like this."

Of the three, only Allie didn't wear curlers and didn't have a romantic interest in the backyard. Then she hesitated at the thought of Walt seeing her in her bathrobe.

She stood up. Once and for all, she needed to banish these silly fantasies. She rolled up the blackout curtain and raised the sash, careful with her fresh manicure.

The song stopped. "Hello, Allie," three masculine voices called up to her.

"Good evening, gentlemen." She rested her elbows on the windowsill. In defiance of blackout regulations, someone flicked on the porch light and illuminated George with a ukulele, Art with a kazoo, and Walt cross-legged on the grass behind a toy piano.

"Where's Betty?" George asked.

"Hiding. She and Dorothy are in curlers." A pillow thumped her backside, and she laughed.

"Where are your curlers?"

Allie lifted a lock. "Natural curl. Sometime blessing, sometime curse."

"Always a blessing." Walt ran a tinny scale and grinned up at her. The single curl rested on his forehead, undisturbed.

Her face grew hot. Why had she touched him that morning? He had to think she was a horrible, unfaithful flirt. Why, she'd never flirted before in her life.

"You look lovely this evening, Miss Miller," Walt said with a wink.

She took a moment to recover from the wink and the compliment. Then she laughed. As always, he was teasing. She had never been lovely in her life, much less this evening. "And you look quite dashing, Lieutenant Novak. I think it's the grand piano."

"Must be." He played a few bars. "Should I bring it on our first date?"

A date? Allie's chest constricted. But of course, he was only teasing. He knew about Baxter, didn't he? "A date is somewhat of a . . . well, a moot question, isn't it?"

"Ah yes." He clapped a hand over his chest. "Ripped asunder by war's cruel hand."

Her laugh tumbled out. Yes, he was joking. "Betty says you're shy, but you're positively flirting."

"Hey!" George said. "I'm the one who's supposed to flirt. Where's my bride? I want my bride."

"Just sing, darling," Betty called out. "I'm listening."

Allie ducked back into the room. "Betty, you have to see. They're adorable. And this—this is a once-in-a-lifetime moment."

Betty chewed on her lips.

"I know," Dorothy said. "Let's cover our curlers."

Betty and Dorothy draped towels over their heads and clasped them under their chins, and the three ladies squeezed together on the windowsill. The ukulele twanged, the kazoo whined, the piano tinkled, and George and Walt sang deep and rough.

True, warm contentment snuggled in Allie's soul. The summer night breeze, the music, such dear friends, George and Betty's deep love—truly a once-in-a-lifetime moment. Although she longed for love like theirs, no bitterness tinged the sweetness.

Once again, Walt's understanding shone in his smile.

Whatever his faults, he was a kind man and a welcome friend. What would happen after she went home? Would he write? She hoped so. Friends were rare and precious, especially friends who understood.

A string on the ukulele popped, and George tossed it aside.

"'So don't let me wait; come to me tenderly in the June night. I stand at your gate, and I sing you a song in the moonlight. A love song, my darling, a moonlight serenade.'"

Betty sniffed and wiped her eyes. "I love you so much, George Anello."

"I love you too, and tomorrow you'll be my wife." He blew her a kiss and disappeared into the darkness.

Betty and Dorothy withdrew behind the curtain, and Allie reached up to lower the sash.

"Good night, Allie."

She looked down. Only Walt remained in the golden cone of light, the toy piano tucked under his arm. "Good night, Walt."

His warm smile struck a delectable note in her heart. Wouldn't it be wonderful if . . . ?

No! Allie shut the window and turned away. She twisted her hands together while her friends adjusted curlers. "Walt knows I have a boyfriend, doesn't he?"

"Of course," Betty said. "I told him all about you."

Allie frowned. After all, he didn't pay attention to Betty's stories.

"He knows," Dorothy said. "He talks to you, right?"

Betty laughed. "Poor Walter. He can only talk to a girl if she's taken."

8

Saturday, June 27, 1942

Walt stood in precise at-ease posture. If only his mind were at ease.

The paralysis was back.

As soon as Allie glided down the aisle of Riverview Community Church in that long green dress, every muscle froze. When she gave him her soft smile, he forced his mouth into some stiff position that probably didn't even look like a smile. Now only his neck muscles worked, but he couldn't control them. He should watch his father bless his friend's marriage, but Allie drew him like a pretty little magnet.

How was he supposed to dance with her if he couldn't move?

Allie's eyes turned to him. Walt whipped his head front, as if intent on Dad's words. Second time he'd been caught watching her.

Why now? Why was he freezing up now when he knew she was interested in him? No doubt after her flirting at the serenade, her dreamy look when he sang to her, and the look on her face when he said good night, as if she wanted him to scale the wall and kiss her right then. Last night he could have, but now?

Her waist looked even tinier in that dress, her hair curled so softly, and she had such a sweet expression. Boy, did he want to kiss her tonight.

Allie gave him a curious look. He snapped his head front so fast his neck hurt. Swell. She knew he was watching her. She knew something was wrong.

He frowned. He was too focused on the kiss. Just had to dance with her, talk with her. Conversation had been easy all week but now seemed as unlikely as Flossie flying.

If only she didn't look so nice—light as a glider.

Allie glanced at him. Caught again!

Before he could turn away, he thought he saw her tongue flick out, quick as a lizard. He blinked a few times. He wasn't seeing right.

She crossed her eyes.

One of the most ladylike creatures he had ever met was making faces at him in front of the wedding guests. A smile cracked the ice on his face. Allie knew he was nervous and wanted to make him comfortable. No one had ever understood him so well.

He dropped her a wink, packed full of affection. She smiled and faced front.

Walt flexed his hands and his toes. Yep, he could move. He could talk to her and laugh with her and dance with her. As for that kiss, well, he'd wait and see.

The knife pressed a valley in the snowy frosting and sank into the cake. Allie slid the cake server under the piece and transferred it to the plate in Helen Carlisle's hand.

"Almost done." Helen's gaze circled the room. "Dorothy has the beverage table under control, and the band is warming up. If the baby can wait ten more minutes for his bottle, everything will be set."

Allie smiled. For sisters, Betty and Helen couldn't be more different. Betty hated details, and Helen thrived on them. "I think half of Antioch is here. I'm amazed you obtained enough sugar for the cake."

"Well, when the grocer's son gets married . . ." Helen laughed and gathered two empty plates. "But of course, it was honest. We all chipped in our rations."

"Speaking of rations." Jim Carlisle approached the table with a squalling blue bundle. "Jay-Jay wants his milk ration. Your mom's busy, and mine—can't find her."

Helen glanced at the cake. "I'm almost done."

"I can finish," Allie said.

"But—"

Jim thrust the baby into Helen's arms.

She sighed and popped the bottle into her son's open mouth. After a few wails, Jay-Jay settled down with a whimper. Helen smiled at Allie. "Babies are adorable, but they sure ruin schedules."

Allie waved away the little family. Serving cake alone was manageable but awkward. The next few slices weren't centered on the plates, and one slice toppled in a crumbly heap. She pushed it aside to be her piece later.

"Hi, Allie."

The masculine voice behind her was right on cue—if anything, a trifle late. She had been alone almost five minutes. She smiled at Walt over her shoulder and turned back to the cake. "Come to help?"

"Nah. I came to brief you on our mission for tonight."

"Our mission?"

"You see those vessels—the USS *Carlisle* and the USS *Wayne*?" He leaned over her left shoulder and pointed to Dorothy at the beverage table and Art across the room. "Admiral Anello informed me of our solemn duty to engage the vessels on an intercept course."

While she was glad he had overcome his odd shyness during the ceremony, his proximity and boldness rattled her. She pulled herself together and set a cake slice on a plate. "Funny to hear a naval analogy from the mouth of an airman."

"Worked better with ships than planes." The puffs of his chuckle made Allie's hair and stomach flutter.

"Wait a minute." She set down the knife and faced him. He was so close and so handsome in full dress uniform, she took a step back out of necessity. "Haven't you meddled enough with Art and Dorothy?"

Walt's cheeks sagged. "She told you?"

"I know your intentions were honorable, even if your methods weren't."

He studied her for a moment, as if to ascertain the sincerity of her forgiveness. "I learned my lesson. This is George's plan."

She clasped her hands behind her back. "What's the plan, Captain Novak? Time's a-wasting. The vessels are drifting apart."

"Captain Novak—I like that." He grinned, then sobered. "But you won't like the admiral's plan. I told him about our deal not to dance, and he pulled rank on me. Seems if we sit out, Art and Dorothy will also sit out to keep us company."

"But if we dance . . ." A shiver ran up her spine, but was it apprehension or anticipation? "If we dance, they'll dance, and Betty thinks this evening of dancing will accomplish what countless other evenings of dancing have failed to accomplish."

Walt's smile bent his eyes into adorable half-moons. "For a newcomer, you've sure got everyone pegged. So, Sailor, can the admiral count on you?"

Something new and coy glimmered inside. "Actually, this sailor has a problem. I can't fraternize with an officer."

He stared at her, one eyebrow cocked. "Uh-oh. Fraternization is vital to the mission. How about a field promotion—Lieutenant Miller?"

She gave him a salute, energized by the glimmer. "Reporting for duty."

He grinned, grabbed her hand, and pulled her toward the dance floor.

"Walter, wait." She glanced over her shoulder at the cake and tried to ignore the warmth of his hand around hers.

"Oh yeah." He whirled back, a frown on his face. "I promised myself I'd do this right. No one's ever asked you to dance, and here I go, hauling you off. Won't do. Would you—um, do me the honor of dancing with me?"

For one brief moment, Allie wished Baxter away, wished Walt into her life forever and ever. What a disloyal thought, and besides, Walt was only being polite.

"Well?" he asked.

"Yes, but I have to . . . the cake." She tugged her hand free and returned to the table, afraid she was too shaky to handle a knife.

"Allie." A hand manicured with bright red polish reached across the table and grasped her arm. "I've been trying to get your attention for ages."

She looked up to see Louise Morgan from Scripps, her brown eyes enormous behind her glasses. "Oh, Louise, I hoped you'd come."

"How could I miss it? San Francisco's not so far." She glanced to Walt, once again by Allie's side.

She struggled to remember the proper order of introduction. "Louise, I'd like you to meet Walter Novak, George's friend. Walt, this is Louise Morgan, my dear friend from Scripps College."

After they exchanged handshakes, Walt turned to Allie, lower lip protruding. "I'm not your dear friend?"

"Of course, you are." She fought down an urge to push that darling lip back in place and faced Louise. "Where's Larry?"

Louise pointed to an Army officer at the beverage table. "Getting what passes for coffee. Doesn't he look great in uniform?"

"Oh yes."

"If you'll excuse me." Walt placed his hand in the small of Allie's back. "While you finish, I'll brief Art on the mission."

She nodded, smiled, and hoped her cheeks weren't as flushed as they felt.

After he left, Louise picked up an empty cake plate. "So, where's Baxter?"

"Baxter? Oh, he had a deadline at work and couldn't come."

Louise held out a plate for the slice Allie lifted. "I thought you'd broken up."

She dropped the cake onto the tablecloth. "No. No. Why would you think that?"

Louise glanced across the room to where Walt conferred with Art. "Walt seems attentive. Does Baxter know he has a rival?"

"Rival? Walt? Nonsense. He wouldn't try to steal another man's girlfriend." Allie hurriedly scraped the mess onto a plate. "I—I think Betty asked him to watch over me this week."

Louise brushed crumbs into her open hand. "Watch over you? Well, he's definitely watching you. He couldn't take his eyes off you during the wedding."

Oh no. Someone else noticed. She rubbed at a spot of frosting on the tablecloth with a napkin, aware she was making the stain worse.

★ 81 ★

"That pilot has a little crush on you."

"Nonsense." Her hand went in circles, but her mind fixed on an impossible truth. A crush would explain his attentiveness and also his awkwardness during the ceremony—he'd be embarrassed to have a crush on a woman who was spoken for.

"I think it's sweet he has a crush on you."

"Don't be silly. No one's ever had a crush on me."

"No one? What about Baxter?"

"Baxter?" Allie divided the last bit of cake. "That's different. We've been together so long." Yet four and a half years with Baxter Hicks had never generated a fraction of the emotions she'd experienced in one week with Walter Novak.

Walter Novak, who crossed the room, his gaze and smile locked on Allie. Walter Novak, who took her hand, led her away from Louise and the cake and Allie's own good reason, and drew her into his strong arms.

Walter Novak, who looked at her as if she were lovely and special.

All her life Allie had longed for the look in his hazel eyes, but she never guessed how splendid it was to truly feel lovely and special. His attraction sank deep in her soul, exhilarating and dangerous and enriching.

"Our primary objective is accomplished."

Allie blinked. "Hmm?"

Walt nodded to Art and Dorothy on the dance floor not far away. "As for the secondary objective, that's not in our hands."

She managed a smile but couldn't form any words. Maybe she could speak if she didn't look in his eyes. She studied his uniform instead—the olive drab wool, the gold lieutenant's bars on his shoulder straps, the U.S. pins on the collars, the

Army Air Force insignia on the lapels, and the silver wings over his left breast pocket.

The knot on his khaki tie bobbed. "So far no broken toes. But the night is young. You may get your Purple Heart yet."

She steeled herself to raise her eyes to him. "I doubt that. Despite what you say, you're a good dancer." No one would ever call him a great dancer, since he used only basic steps, but he led with gentle authority.

"And look, I didn't roll my eyes. In fact, I asked you."

"I know. Thank you." How could she ever forget?

The band began to play "A String of Pearls." Walt stumbled into the new rhythm, much lazier than Glenn Miller's orchestra played it. At least the minimal talent of the band ensured the tempo wouldn't outpace Walt's dancing ability.

"Allie," he said slowly. "Say, that's a nickname, isn't it?"

Oh, not this. She glanced to where George and Betty danced in wedded bliss.

He laughed. "Ball bearings all over again. Come on, tell me the truth or tell me a lie, but you have to talk. You're trapped." He squeezed her waist, as if she needed a reminder.

She sighed. "You'll never guess."

"But you'll make me, won't you? Let's see. Alice? Alma? Alberta?"

"No, I mean you couldn't possibly guess, because it's unusual, and I might as well tell you since Betty knows, but I never use it, and even my mother never uses it, and she chose it."

"You talk fast when you're nervous, you know that?"

"Fast." She looked at the shoulder she'd admired all week, now alive under her hand. "I suppose I can't help it. My name's Allegra."

"Allegra? Hmm. Your mom's musical too?"

"Yes, and I'm afraid she was a bit silly when she was younger."

"No more than my mom. My real name is Adagio."

Allie lifted an eyebrow. "I've been warned about your tales."

"Come on, play along. See, when we get married, we'll have a symphony of children." The mischief in his eyes neutralized the effect of his mention of marriage.

"A symphony?"

"Yep. First child, a girl, takes after her mother. We'll call her Allegretta."

As always, she enjoyed his sense of humor. "Then a son named Andante."

"You got it. Next comes Pianissimo."

"Quiet with this musical brood?" She shook her head. "Fortissimo is more appropriate."

"Yeah. Four kids. Pretty loud." He squinted at the streamer-draped ceiling. "Next comes the climax, our daughter Crescenda."

"Crescenda?" Allie laughed, even as she admired the dark stubble under Walt's jaw. "I thought Allegra was ridiculous."

"Nah." He lowered his chin and smiled at her. "Is the next kid Finis?"

"Goodness, I hope so. Six children is an exhausting thought for an only child."

"How many kids do you want?"

"More than one. One's too lonely." She gazed into his eyes and realized she and Baxter had never discussed children. "I always thought four would be perfect."

"Four it is." Walt's smile glowed with promise.

Promise? Impossible. He'd never come between her and Baxter—unless he didn't know about Baxter. Oh dear, what if he didn't know? She hadn't talked much about Baxter, and Walt hadn't asked about him either. Guilt and dread gripped her stomach. She needed to mention her boyfriend, but how?

Allie swallowed hard. "I'm surprised I've never had this conversation before."

"Kind of obvious with a name like Allegra."

He'd misunderstood. Allie pondered how to direct the conversation.

"With a last name like Miller, you should be glad to have an unusual first name. What if your name were Mary?"

"That's what Mother thought. Her name's Mary. She also thought Allegra was an enchanting name, suitable for the beauty her daughter should have been. Her great disappointment is having a plain daughter." She clamped her lips together. Once again, her familiarity with Walt led her to divulge too much.

Something fierce flashed in his eyes. "I can't believe people say you're plain. It's not true."

"Oh dear, I shouldn't have said that. I hope you don't think I'm searching for a compliment."

"You?" The ferocity dissolved into amusement. "Uh-uh. I've seen how you react to compliments. Besides, I'm no good with compliments, no good with words at all. But you're not plain. Your face . . . well, your face is memorable. If I walked into a room fifty years from now, I'd recognize you."

"Even with gray hair and wrinkles?"

"Sure. Your eyes won't change. And, well, anyone who says you're plain should be hung by their thumbs. A woman can't be plain if she has beautiful eyes."

He thought she had beautiful eyes. Allie almost forgot the dance step.

Walt's eyes narrowed as he examined hers. "Not just the color, which is . . . well, amazing. Something else. Ray's good with words; he could figure it out. Your eyes are bright, quick." He broke into a grin. "They're allegro. Yeah, that's it. But your smile is adagio, slow and quiet. Together—well, it's a swell combination."

She dragged her gaze down to her red fingernails on Walt's thick shoulder. "I thought you weren't good with compliments."

"I'm not. I'm also tongue-tied with women unless they're taken." His arm slipped further around her waist and drew her closer. "You, dear Allie, are the exception to the rule."

Red and olive drab mixed before her eyes in a strange blend. The exception? He thought she wasn't taken. That meant—

"What about me? Would you recognize me in fifty years?"

"What? Oh, I—oh, I don't know." Allie's line of thought both fascinated and frightened her, and she used every grain of will to concentrate on his question and look in his face. Would she recognize him? How could she not? "Yes. Your eyes."

"What do you see in my eyes?" He struck what he must have thought was a distinguished pose, chin high and turned to the side.

His expression was so comical, she laughed and pressed her hand to his cheek. "You have to look at me, silly."

Touching him was a mistake. His eyes shone even brighter. "Okay, I'm looking at you. What do you see?" His voice was as rugged as the stubble under Allie's fingers.

She managed to lower her hand to his shoulder. She couldn't voice what she saw in his eyes—the potential for all she longed for but could never have, not with Walt, not with anyone ever, because of loyalty and expectations and propriety.

He cleared his throat. "See a fellow with nothing but planes on his mind?"

"No, of course not." Fondness for him welled up inside. "I see intelligence and courage. I see a kind, understanding heart. I see . . . always I see your good humor."

He made a face. "Ah, you always talk up the men in your life."

"No. You know I don't feel comfortable with many people." Here was an opportunity to mention Baxter, but it would be a lie. On the rare occasions she was alone with him, the silence was deathly.

Walt leaned closer, until their cheeks almost brushed. "I'm glad I'm the exception."

Allie breathed in his heady fragrance of soap, wool, and aftershave. She couldn't tell him about Baxter now. What if he made a scene and tarnished Betty's wedding? What if he pouted and everyone talked? Silence was the only truthful solution to this dilemma.

And deep inside, she couldn't bear to destroy the moment, precious and yearned for and never to be repeated. Even though romance with Walt was impossible, all her life she'd have this moment in her memory of feeling beautiful, appreciated, and vibrant.

A moment to cherish.

9

Sunday, June 28, 1942

Walt scooped steamy scrambled eggs onto his fork. Never had his appetite been so robust.

He could still smell Allie's flowery perfume, feel that soft fabric, see her dreamy expression. And he'd still be tasting her kiss if that Dorothy Carlisle hadn't interfered.

"Why would you walk her home, Walt? I'm right across the street." He stabbed a chunk of egg. Yeah, Dorothy was still paying him back for last summer's mess.

No matter. He still had today. After church, George and Betty were leaving on their wedding trip. The rest of the gang didn't have plans, but someone would come up with something, and Walt would get Allie alone for that kiss.

Mom placed another pancake on his plate. "No more for you, young man. Your grandmother will be heartbroken if you don't save room for her chicken."

"Grandmother?"

Mom scraped the griddle. "Don't you remember? We're spending the day at the farm."

"Today? Why does it have to be today?"

"Don't use that tone with your mother." Dad set the *Antioch Ledger* on the table. "You've spent the whole week with your friends, and you leave Tuesday. One small day with your family isn't asking too much."

Even though his father was right, Walt grumbled. He knew it was childish, but this one small day was vital to his future.

Mom rinsed the pan in the sink. "Perhaps you could invite one of your friends. Maybe that nice Allie Miller."

What a great idea. Sunday dinner with his family—showed he was serious about her, showed he was a gentleman. But the farm was also chockful of romantic nooks and crannies. "Yeah. She might like that."

"Invite her after church." Mom cast Dad a glance over her shoulder.

Pride stirred in Walt's chest. Mom recognized what was happening with Allie. That validated it. Strange—George hadn't said anything. Usually the fellows were quick to tease each other. Must be too caught up in their own romances to notice Walt's.

Oh well. They'd notice soon enough.

★

"No, Walt. You've hogged her all week." Dorothy hooked her arm through Allie's. "Today's her last full day here, and my family has a big dinner planned."

Walt stared at Dorothy and restrained his anger and disappointment. He'd be at the farm for dinner and supper and long after—without Allie.

"Goodness," Allie said with a nervous laugh. "I never thought I'd see the day when two people would fight over my company."

He sighed. "No fighting. I know you have to go to the Carlisles."

She nodded, her smile sad but grateful. "Thank you for the lovely invitation. I'd say another day but . . ."

"I know. No more days." He had to cheer her up when he didn't feel cheerful himself. "But I'm taking you to the train depot tomorrow."

"Since when?" Dorothy asked.

He gave her a smug smile. "Makes sense. Dad's clergy. He'll get unlimited gas when rationing starts next month. You won't. Save it up."

✯

Monday, June 29, 1942

Walt walked up the path to the Jamison house and tugged his uniform jacket straight. Allie smiled at him from the porch. She wore a suit about the same shade of red as Dad's leather chair.

"Hi, there. Ready to go?"

She motioned to the door with a gloved hand. "Almost."

The door swung open. Dorothy and Mrs. Jamison came out, and Mrs. Jamison handed a basket to Allie. "Here's your lunch and some of the strawberry jam we made."

"How sweet." Allie hugged her hostess. "Thank you for your hospitality."

"Are you sure you'll be all right for that transfer at Tracy?"

"Yes, I'm sure. Thank you."

"All right, let's go." Walt loaded the suitcase and hatbox in the trunk, and then he opened the door and waited for Allie to be seated. Dorothy harrumphed and opened the back door.

He stared at her. "You're going too?"

"Of course. What kind of friend do you think I am?"

He clenched his hand on the door rim and suppressed a groan. She had a right to go, but it wrecked his plans. He had things to say to Allie, things he couldn't say in front of Dorothy.

Allie peeked up at him. "Did you forget something, or are you watching out for cows?"

He smiled. "Yeah, with you in the car, I'll have to keep my eyes open. Say, want me to put that basket in the trunk?"

"Would you, please?"

When he wedged the basket beside the luggage, an idea formed in his head. Yeah, it was sneaky, but this was his last opportunity to be alone with her. He might not get another furlough before he shipped out, and it could be years until he came home.

Walt sat behind the wheel and smiled at Allie. "Back home again, huh?"

"Yes." Her eyes darkened.

That was stupid—reminding her about home, where she had nothing to look forward to. He pulled away from the curb. "Well, you made lots of friends this week you can write to. Say, I need your address."

"Oh. Oh yes."

Walt dictated his address, and Allie wrote down hers. He wanted to read it right away and memorize it, but he tucked it in his left breast pocket.

At the depot he opened the trunk, removed the lunch bundle from the basket, and set it aside. He opened the car doors for the ladies and handed Allie the basket. "I thought Mrs. Jamison packed a lunch. Just jam in here."

Dorothy poked around inside. "Oh dear."

"It's all right," Allie said. "I can buy something at one of the stops."

"And lose your seat? That won't do." Walt pulled his wallet from his pocket. "Listen, Dorothy, run to the coffee shop and get her a sandwich while I take care of her luggage."

"Sure." She took Walt's dollar and dashed across the street.

He chuckled as he hoisted the suitcase from the trunk. That worked well. Perhaps the train would be full of servicemen, and Allie would have to wait another day. After all, military personnel took precedence over civilians. However, he couldn't count on it. He had to make the most of the few minutes he'd bought.

After Walt checked in Allie's bags, he joined her on the platform. She held the basket in both hands, the gloves taut over her knuckles.

"Promise you'll write?" he asked.

She gave him a shaky smile. "If you—if you write first."

Boy, did she look nervous. "Always the lady, aren't you? Except when you stick your tongue out at officers."

Allie laughed and looked down at her basket. "I can't believe I did that."

"Neither can I, but I'm glad you did. And I'm glad you'll write, 'cause mail call's the best part of the day—or the worst if you don't get anything. The fellows overseas live for mail call."

"A reminder of sanity in the world?"

"Mm-hmm." He swallowed hard. He was about to face the insanity, and it would be a lot better with a green-eyed girl writing to him and praying for him.

She raised those gorgeous eyes to him. "Promise me you'll be careful."

She wasn't nervous. She was worried, with good reason. Sure, the Army Air Force was the most sought-after service, but it was the most dangerous, and everyone knew it. Walt smiled. "As long as Hitler and Tojo don't put cows in the air, I'll be fine."

She laughed and loosened the grip on her basket. "I'd better keep quiet, or they'll develop a secret bovine weapon."

He laughed along. Now was the time for the words he'd rehearsed. "I'm glad I met you."

"I—I'm glad I met you too." But she wouldn't look up at him.

Now or never. Walt took a deep breath and cupped her chin in his hand. "You're a lovely woman, Allegra Miller, and you're very special. Don't let anybody ever tell you otherwise."

Allie's eyes got so big, Walt was sure he'd fall in. He leaned over and kissed her on the cheek. He had a lot to pack into that kiss—his affection and hope for a future and promises for more and better kisses someday.

He tore himself from her sweet softness and straightened up, his hand still under her chin. Her eyes opened so slowly he knew he could kiss her if he dared. But not in public. Not her first real kiss.

Walt stuffed both hands in his trouser pockets. He tried to smile, but his mouth didn't want to let go of the shape of that kiss. What was he supposed to say next? He was supposed to ask her to be his girlfriend, but how did he word it?

A loud whistle interrupted his thoughts. He turned to see the train pull in. Why now? He needed a few more minutes.

"Oh, good, I'm not too late. Ham and cheese okay?" Dorothy ran up and thrust a bag in Allie's hand. "Here's your change, Walt."

He groaned. God's timing might be best, but Walt didn't have to like it.

Allie and Dorothy hugged, with lots of "thank you's" and "I'll miss you's" and "I'll write you's." Women sure were sentimental, but at least Walt had an excuse for a hug. He wrapped his arms around Allie, and little brown curls tickled his nose.

She kissed him on the cheek, so quick he almost missed it. "Thank you."

"What for?" He'd only given her the wooden cow.

Her eyes looked damp. "For—for everything."

Walt understood. The week meant as much to her as it did to him. "You're welcome. Thank you for the same."

More good-byes and promises to write, and Allie disappeared onto the train. A strange emptiness formed in Walt's chest and grew bigger when the train chugged away. But he had her address in his pocket, her kiss on his cheek, and a future with her. He laughed for the joy of it all.

Dorothy looked up at him. "What's so funny?"

"All these years, all those jokes about me and women, but I might beat you to the altar."

"With whom?" She followed his gaze down the tracks. "You don't mean Allie?"

He rolled his eyes up. "Yes, I mean Allie. Have you been blind all week?"

Dorothy's upper lip curled. "I don't think her boyfriend would approve."

"Boyfriend? We're talking about Allie, remember?"

"Yes, Allie. She has a boyfriend. Don't you know that?"

Dorothy had always been spiteful, but this was ridiculous. Walt's fists clenched in his pockets. "You know what? I made a mistake last summer, but I admitted it and I apologized. As a Christian, you should at least try to forgive me. I lied to get you and Art together, but you—you're lying to keep Allie and me apart. That's plain malicious."

Her dark eyes flashed. "You think I'm lying?"

"I know you're lying."

"I'm not. Allie has a boyfriend. His name is Baxter Hicks, he works for her father, and they've been together for years."

Walt made a face and strode into the station. "Can't you make up a better name than that?"

"I'm not making it up. Ask Betty. She knows Baxter, so does George."

Dorothy's little heels clicked behind him out onto the sidewalk, and they'd have a long way to click, because he wasn't about to give her a ride home. Now she'd mixed up Betty and George in her lie.

George.

Walt stopped in front of the newsstand, where the *Ledger*'s headline read "British Retire in Egypt." George didn't tease him. Did he know something Walt didn't?

"Didn't Allie tell you about Baxter?" The anger washed from Dorothy's voice. "She doesn't talk about him a lot—you know how private she is. But you two talked so much, we assumed you knew."

Walt faced Dorothy, and his mind whirled over the memories of the week. Allie couldn't have a boyfriend. No one had really kissed her—ten measly pecks. No one had ever asked her to dance. And that one school dance . . .

Baxter.

"Baxter? But—but that was in high school." Arranged by her father. Baxter—her father's business manager.

Truth stabbed him in the chest. Allie had a boyfriend. Walt was a fool.

"They've been together a long time. I'm sorry. I thought you knew. We all did." The anger returned to Dorothy's voice. "I can't believe she didn't tell you."

Fury churned in his gut, but he wasn't about to let Dorothy know. Bad enough Allie thrashed his hopes, now his friends would pity him.

Without a word, Walt opened the car door for Dorothy. He felt a burning pain over his heart. Allie's address. He pulled the paper from his pocket, crumpled it, and dropped it in the gutter with his dreams.

10

Riverside, California
July 7, 1942

Sheer curtains hung at the tall drawing room windows, limp from heat so still that Allie's breath provided the only movement of air.

Allie sat at the grand piano to play after-dinner music for her parents and Baxter on the porch outside—every night the same. She knew coming home would be difficult, but she wasn't prepared for the depth of the void.

She pulled out Beethoven's "Moonlight Sonata." Perhaps the suggestion of moonlight would cool her and dry the perspiration that ran in nasty rivulets down the inside of her arms.

Mother's laugh floated through the window. How could she enjoy such an evening? Between the heat and the tedium, Allie thought she'd go mad. Quiet evenings were lovely, but only when they completed days of purpose and were punctuated by occasional social activities.

Allie had no friends, no fun, no work, and not even a good church, as Walt had worded it—blunt but true.

Even the promised letters hadn't arrived to relieve the

monotony. Perhaps it was too soon to hear from the newlyweds, but Dorothy should have written by now, and Walt . . .

However, she dreaded his letter. She couldn't bear any more of his tender words, and once he wrote, she'd have to tell him about Baxter. Already she mourned the loss of his friendship.

Never had "Moonlight Sonata" sounded so dreary, heavy, like the guilt on her heart and the boredom on her mind. If only things were different.

Make things different, Walt had told her.

But how? Allie lifted her hair off her sticky neck. Her parents would never approve if she went to work or changed churches, but without work or church, how could she make friends?

She flung back her head and sighed. Change was necessary, any change, and she had to start tonight. She folded the sheet music and went out to the porch, where three pairs of eyes looked up at her.

"I thought you were going to play," Father said.

"It's too hot." She gripped her hands in front of her. "I'd like to go for a walk. Who'd like to come with me?"

Three pairs of eyes grew wider. "A walk?" Mother said.

"Yes, a walk." She might as well have invited them to join the circus.

"Oh." Mother looked down to her embroidery hoop. "I need to finish these napkins."

Father smiled at Allie. "I'll stay with your mother. Baxter can go with you."

Baxter sat up taller. "I'd rather—"

"Please? Maybe you could show me your property. I've seen it from the street but not close up."

Baxter released a puff of cigarette smoke that drifted down in the heavy air. "I suppose so. Won't take long, will it?"

"No," she said with a sigh.

They strolled down the long, citrus-lined drive in silence. Allie tried not to think of Walt, their easy conversations, his attraction, and how she felt vibrant with him. Comparing the two men wasn't fair.

Even in the arid heat, Baxter wore his necktie knotted and his suit jacket buttoned. His build was slight, his brown hair impeccable under his hat, and he never gazed in her direction if he could help it. With Baxter, she felt dull.

Was that his fault? If she engaged him in conversation, paid him attention, maybe even flirted with him, his interest might grow and hers might also. Such behavior seemed natural with Walt, but with Baxter she'd have to plan. What could she talk about? With Walt, the most wonderful, most intimate talk began with a discussion of her name. She took a deep breath. "J. Baxter Hicks."

He looked at her, thin eyebrows raised. "Yes?"

"The J stands for Joseph, right?"

"Right." He rounded one of the brick pillars at the end of the drive and turned southwest down Magnolia Avenue, toward the setting sun.

She plucked a late camellia from a branch that beckoned through the Millers' wrought iron fence. As a girl, she'd loved to peel the endless pink petals. "I've always wondered why you don't go by Joe. Joe is such a nice, solid name."

"Joe Hicks?" His mouth drew up in disgust. "Joe Hicks is what I was called the first sixteen years of my life. Joe Hicks is the poor, uneducated dirt farmer I was bred to be. Joe Hicks is the reason I left Oklahoma. Joe Hicks has no dignity."

Allie frowned and cast aside the outer browned petals. "But J. Baxter Hicks?"

"I created J. Baxter Hicks, a man of dignity." He strode

down the avenue, eyes narrow. "J. Baxter Hicks takes a job at the cinema and studies how the movie stars dress and talk and move—how gentlemen act. J. Baxter Hicks puts himself through college, lands a top-notch job, and makes himself indispensable. J. Baxter Hicks earns the boss's friendship and the boss's daughter and builds one of the finest houses in town. J. Baxter Hicks makes a name for himself."

Even though the temperature exceeded ninety degrees, Allie crossed her arms against a chill. She was a mere cog in his wheel of fortune. Because she was a Miller, he would marry her, whatever her looks, her character, her personality, her feelings—or his. She dropped the camellia.

"Here it is." He turned onto a dirt path through an orange grove. "I'll build a long drive as your parents have. It'll be elegant once paved."

"Quite." She welcomed the tangy scent of citrus, glad she'd have the trees and fruit she loved—and Walt loved. She chased off the thought.

At the end of the path, wooden beams rose in a clearing. "The frame's up?"

"Started." Baxter picked his way around construction debris, set his hand on a beam, and scrutinized the length of it. "War production has priority over construction. Hard to get labor and supplies, but it should be done in time."

In time? Another chill raced up her arms. She stepped through the frame and glanced around. The house would be large and grand. How long would it take to complete? How long until it became her home?

A year, maybe less. The beams crowded about her like prison bars.

"Impressive, isn't it?"

"Oh yes." Allie stepped out and found she could breathe again. Then she remembered her resolution to show interest and gave Baxter a smile. After all, Walt liked her smile—and her eyes. A swell combination, he said.

Baxter looked up where the beams pierced the darkening sky. "I'll make your father proud."

"And your parents?"

He sniffed and wiped his shoe top on the back of his trouser leg.

"You never talk about your parents."

One side of his mouth curled. "Why would I? They have no part in who I am. They tried to hold me back. Why do you think I ran away?"

Allie couldn't even imagine leaving her parents, her home, or Riverside. "Don't you miss your family? The farm?"

"The farm?" He dusted off his other shoe top. "Nothing to miss. Filthy, stinking, hardscrabble life. Watched my father waste his life on that dirt patch. Every year he'd say, 'The Lord will provide,' and every year—nothing. And I left in '26, long before the Dust Bowl. Who knows what that place is like now."

"You don't write?"

"Why would I?"

"Oh my." Despite her current boredom, Allie couldn't bear to be separated from Father's guidance and encouragement, or Mother's company while cooking and sewing. "You haven't communicated with your parents for all these years? Don't you ever—"

"Why the interrogation? I know hot weather causes strange behavior, but can't you talk about something else?"

"I'm sorry." She pressed her lips together. Instead of finding common ground, she had plowed up an argument. "You . . . you prefer to talk about the present?"

"The present, the future, anything but the past."

Allie was surrounded by her future—the man she'd marry,

the property she'd roam, the house she'd decorate and fill with children, Lord willing. Instead of denying her future, she needed to embrace it. She needed to create the intimacy she longed for, the intimacy she'd tasted so briefly, so enticingly with Walt.

She moved closer to Baxter to make use of her eyes. His eyebrows lifted and drew together. She considered placing her hand on his cheek, but the gesture seemed too personal. Instead she laid her hand on his shoulder, so thin compared to Walt's.

Of course, he was thin. Unlike Walt, he'd grown up in poverty. She smiled with new understanding and sympathy. "The future is promising, isn't it? When J. Baxter Hicks marries the boss's daughter, he'll be in line to inherit the business. J. Baxter Hicks's children will never know the hunger and deprivation he knew."

He frowned. "Children."

Something in his expression frightened her, as if he'd never considered children. Dampness rose in her chest, rose in her throat, and if it rose any higher, she'd cry.

One corner of his mouth edged up. "Yes. They'll never want for anything."

The waters receded, and she smiled. She'd have children to love, and maybe Baxter would grow to love her, and she would grow to love him.

Allie reached up and kissed him on the lips. Eleven—maybe she'd lose count and forget all about Walter Novak.

Baxter pulled away, forehead furrowed. "We should get back. It's getting dark."

She lowered her hand from his shoulder. "Yes. Yes, it is. Dark indeed."

Allie sank into the white wicker chair. How could a short walk be so exhausting?

"Oh, Allie." Father rummaged through a pile of papers. "A letter for you got mixed up in my mail."

She reached for the envelope. Was it from Walt? How could she bear his affection right after Baxter's rejection? She smiled when she saw Dorothy Carlisle's rounded handwriting. Just what she needed.

> Allie,
>
> I am only writing out of necessity. Betty refuses to speak to you ever again, and I don't blame her.
>
> Walt and I have had our differences, but he is a good man and doesn't deserve the treatment you gave him. You should have seen the hurt on his face when I told him about Baxter.
>
> Betty and I are appalled, and Betty says you've betrayed her friendship. After all these years, she feels she hardly knows you. How could you conceal your relationship with Baxter? How could you flirt with Walt? How could you lead him to believe he had a future with you? Perhaps Betty and I should have noticed what you were doing and warned him, but neither of us thought you capable of such despicable behavior.

"Allie, are you all right?" Mother asked. "Is it bad news?"

She looked up. A weight crushed her stomach, her chest,

her throat. She was going to be sick in front of Mother and Father and Baxter, who all stared at her.

She stood, letter in hand, stomach roiling. "I—I'm going to bed." She didn't respond to their protests and questions, but ran, mouth clamped shut, up the stairs, down the corridor, into the bathroom, onto her knees.

Hurt on his face . . . appalled . . . betrayed her friendship . . . conceal . . . flirt . . . future with you . . . despicable behavior. Each phrase convulsed her with nausea.

At last she knelt, gasping, spluttering, staring at the mess she'd made. She cleaned herself and crumpled against the bathroom wall. With a trembling hand she pushed her hair off her forehead. Not only had she hurt Walt and lost his friendship, but she'd also lost Betty, her new friends, and her moment to cherish.

She had nothing, and she had no one but herself to blame.

11

Wendover Army Air Field, Utah

July 8, 1942

"Want some salt?" Frank Kilpatrick pried off a chunk of salt-crusted earth and stuck it under Walt's nose. "Too bad it's not sugar. Might sweeten that mood."

Walt swatted away Frank's arm and continued down the row of barracks toward headquarters. "We lost seven men in a crash last night. How can you joke?"

"Come on, buddy. We're going into combat. We'll take losses. Not to be callous, but we didn't even know the men. Besides, you've been sour since we got back. Today's no better or worse."

"Yeah? Well, not all furloughs are heaven on earth."

"So she had a boyfriend. Not your fault. All of us have gotten duped by a girl at some point. You know the type. While the cat's away . . ."

Was that what Allie was up to? Looking for a little fling on the side? Another heart to tack on her bulletin board? Didn't mesh with the woman he'd gotten to know, but lots of things didn't mesh. He picked up a rock and hurled it over the roof of one of the barracks. "Yeah, the mice do play."

"Look at it this way—you never have to see her again."

"Yep." Why did his heart sink lower? Allie sure had played him for a fool, and if Dorothy Carlisle didn't keep her mouth shut, everyone would know what a fool he was.

"Too bad sugar's scarce," Frank said.

"All right, all right. I'll get over it. Chin up, look on the bright side, always a silver lining. I know, I know."

"That's the spirit." Frank plucked off Walt's garrison cap and messed up his hair.

He forced a chuckle and jabbed his elbow hard into Frank's ribs. "Don't embarrass me, Dad. Just give me the car keys. Nah, forget the car. I want a plane."

"Don't we all? Can't believe we don't have our B-17s yet."

"Any day now. At least we get our crew assignments today."

They joined the mass of men in khaki in front of HQ. Frank received his crew list, but Walt's had already been taken. The squadron commander pointed to a blond man, who gestured to four other men with sureness and authority. The situation made Walt uneasy. After all, he was the aircraft commander.

He drew himself up to his full six feet. Still, the other man had several inches on him.

Blondie looked down at him with a movie star smile on his tanned face. "Hi. Are you on my crew?"

"I'm Walter Novak." He held out his hand for the crew list.

Blondie shook his hand. "Oh yeah. The other pilot."

Other pilot? Walt reached for the paper. "First pilot. And you are?"

"Lt. Graham Huntington."

Graham? As stuffy as Baxter. Walt scanned the list. "You're my copilot."

"Uh, yeah. I go by Cracker."

"Cracker?" Then Walt grinned—graham cracker. The guy couldn't be so bad if he had a sense of humor. "Because of your name."

"No, because I'm a crackerjack pilot." He gave Walt a flick of his square chin.

His stomach turned. Pride was a common—and dangerous—trait in a pilot.

"And he's a firecracker with the dames," an officer said in a Southern drawl.

Cracker smiled and lowered his chin. "So they say."

"Cracker and I did advanced together at Kelly Field." The Southerner smiled—a white line across a brown face under slick brown hair. "I'm Lt. Louis Fontaine, navigator, from outside Nawlins."

Nawlins? Walt blinked a few times as he shook the man's hand. Oh yeah—New Orleans. "Pleased to meet you."

"Novak," Louis said. "We had a flight instructor at Kelly by that name."

"My brother Ray."

Cracker frowned. "Slave driver."

"Yeah, he washed me out of pilot training," Louis said, "but a mighty nice fellow."

"Yep." Walt turned to the bombardier, Lt. Abe Ruben from Chicago. If his bombing was as sharp as the angles on his thin face, the Axis didn't stand a chance.

Now all four officers were introduced. Walt looked to his enlisted men—still three missing. Two men jogged up and snapped salutes. "Sorry we're late, sirs."

Cracker chuckled. "I told the others we like things informal in the Army Air Force. Crew's supposed to be family. No *sirs*, no *lieutenants*, and please no salutes."

While Cracker was correct, it was Walt's job to tell them.

The men smiled at Cracker with admiration, and Walt had to seize what little authority he had left. He shook hands with the enlisted men, all sergeants: Bill Perkins, the radio operator; and three gunners, Harry Tuttle, Mario Tagliaferro, and Al Worley. They looked awful young—eighteen, nineteen tops. Walt felt like an old man at twenty-four.

Al, a squirrelly, straw-haired kid, looked around. "Aw, nuts. I'm the shortest. You're gonna throw me down in the ball turret, aren't you?"

Cracker studied a rock by his toe.

Yeah, now he avoided the leadership role. Walt smiled at Al. "Sorry, but the ball's too cramped for a tall man." He inspected the others. "Mario, you're in the tail turret. Harry, you'll man the waist guns. Should have two waist gunners, but they think one will do." He read down the crew list. Still one man short—Technical Sergeant Juan Pedro Sanchez. When he looked up, a young man ran up.

Walt shook his hand. "You must be Juan."

"J.P., if you don't mind, sir."

Funny—no lecture from Cracker about informality this time. Walt smiled, pleased at the intelligence in J.P.'s big brown eyes. "Call me Walt."

"Ha!" Al cried. "He's shorter'n me. Stick him in the belly."

"Sorry," Walt said. "J.P.'s got the top turret. He's my flight engineer."

"He is?" The flare of Al's nostrils told Walt he didn't think anyone of Mexican ancestry was smart enough to be flight engineer.

"Sure is. Heard he's the best." He'd heard nothing, but Al didn't know that.

"Anyone know where we're going?" Louis Fontaine asked.

Abe Ruben laughed. "You're the navigator. You tell us."

Cracker set hands on hips and flicked that chin again. "North Africa."

Walt stared at his copilot. "It's all rumor."

"Heard it from high up. The Allies are building an invasion force. All the new bomb groups are going there."

"Possible," Walt said. "Along with Alaska, Australia, England, China."

"Mark my words." Cracker winked at the crew. "Get used to the desert, boys. We're going to the Sahara."

"Palm trees and belly dancers," Louis said. "My kind of place."

"Well, men." Cracker clapped his hands like a quarterback in a huddle. "We've got ourselves a fine crew. Finest crew in the squadron, finest squadron in the 306th Bomb Group, finest group in the whole Army Air Force."

The men cheered and punched fists in the air, and Walt stared, dumbstruck. The man was making speeches to *his* crew.

"Let's go, boys." Cracker beckoned with a sweep of his arm. "State Line Hotel. Drinks are on me. If we're going strong at midnight, we'll slide from the Utah to the Nevada side of the bar."

The men left Walt behind. He knew what would happen—the crew would get to know each other, get drunk, and get attached to that weasel.

Cracker stopped and turned to Walt. "Aren't you coming?"

"No, thanks. Don't drink."

"That's right. Heard about you. They call you Preach, don't they?"

He nodded, and Cracker turned away, but not before Walt caught a smirk on his face. Walt kicked a clump of earth. It shattered in the air.

12

Riverside

July 9, 1942

Allie buried her wet face in her arms on top of the desk. Why had she tried to write Betty? Even if she could find an explanation, Betty wouldn't read it. Betty's greatest fault was her temper, and this time her anger was warranted.

Allie had destroyed the best friendship she'd ever had, all for a fleeting romantic moment. *How foolish I am, Lord. Please forgive me for how I hurt Walt. I didn't know I could hurt a man in such a way, but that's no excuse. Please forgive me for how I betrayed Baxter. Even though we don't love each other, we're committed. And please forgive me for how I hurt Betty. Oh Lord, I miss her so much.*

A soft knock led Allie to draw her handkerchief and dry her face.

"Allie, are you all right?"

"Yes, Mother, I'm fine," she said with a traitorous tremble in her voice.

Mother opened the door, her face puckered with concern. "You don't sound fine, you don't look fine, and you haven't since that letter arrived the other day."

"I *am* fine." She crossed the room to her dressing table, where she neatened her hair. Confessing her transgression and its consequences was out of the question.

"Since you're fine, come help polish the silver."

Allie looked up, alarmed at the thought of too much time to think over silver and rags. "I—I can't. I'm going for a walk."

"A walk? But the silver—"

"I'll help later." She grabbed a purse and hat. "I need a walk."

"All right. If that's what you need." Mother frowned. "I'm worried about you."

Allie forced a smile. "A good, long walk, and I'll be back to normal."

As she headed up Magnolia toward downtown, she wasn't so sure. A walk also presented too much thinking time, and it was too early for the distraction of shopping or the escape of a movie. She passed a newsstand, ablaze with red, white, and blue. Every magazine cover displayed the American flag for the "United We Stand" campaign to boost morale and war bond purchases.

Everyone was doing something for the war effort, from military service to war production to volunteer work. Even the children were busy with scrap metal, rubber, and paper drives. And she—Allie Miller—was supposed to polish the silver.

She huffed. *I want to do something, Lord. I want to help. I want to serve. I don't even have friendships to add purpose to my life. Please show me how I can serve.*

She turned down a side street. She didn't know why. The neighborhood was unfamiliar, the houses small and getting smaller. Still, she pressed on until she reached an intersection with drab little houses on three corners and a church on the fourth.

Groveside Bible Church. Allie wrinkled her nose at the ugly, stuccoed building. Dingy tan paint peeled around dull, rectangular windows. Not one of Riverside's finer architectural examples. However, a cross rose from the steeple, the doors stood open in an inviting manner, and Allie crossed the threshold.

After her eyes adjusted, she inspected the sanctuary—floor in need of polish, faded brown pew cushions, worn Bibles and hymnals in the pew racks, a simple cross, podium, and piano in front. Nothing like St. Timothy's glorious stained glass, magnificent pipe organ, and gleaming wood.

Nothing like St. Timothy's.

A rustle and grunt to Allie's left startled her. She walked forward until she found a woman on hands and knees between the pews. The woman raised a head of gray curls caught back in a low bun. "Why, hello there. Didn't hear you come in."

"I was . . . I was just . . ." Allie gestured to the door.

"Oh yes. Thursday. Thursday. Ladies' Circle. Nine-thirty already?"

"Well, um." She glanced at her wristwatch. "Actually, it's not quite nine."

"Good. Good. Still have time. But you're half an hour early, love. Didn't you listen to the announcement on Sunday?"

"Well, I—"

"Never you mind. God has perfect timing. He sent you early to help. Do you have good strong nails, love? This is one ornery knot. Got to get these cushions aired."

"I'll try." She didn't suppose anyone could say no to this woman. Allie knelt. The knot tying the cushion to the pew was horrendous, shellacked by age and wear.

The lady squirmed to free her ample backside, and when she stood, her bosom flopped over the waist of a violently purple skirt. "I can't place your face, love."

"Well, I—"

"No. Don't tell me. Don't tell me." She bent closer and fixed little blue eyes on Allie. "What beautiful green eyes. You must be Mabel's granddaughter."

"Um, no." She ducked her head to concentrate on the knot instead of the man who commented on her eyes. Finally, she worked her thumbnail in.

"Strong jaw. Ruby's daughter?"

The knot gave way. "There."

"Good girl. Good girl. Such an answer to prayer. Grab that pile of cushions on the pew over yonder, and I'll get this bunch." She marched down the aisle.

Allie gathered the pile and smiled heavenward. *Well, Lord, I did tell you I wanted to serve.*

Outside, the lady struggled to tie a cushion to a clothesline strung between eucalyptus trees over a spotty lawn.

"Why don't you let me do that?" Allie took the cushion and tied it onto the line.

"You know, in my day girls stayed home, got married, moved down the street. Nowadays, you young people go away, get jobs—no, you call them *careers*—and come home so changed we scarce can recognize you. So what's your name, love? I give up." She picked up a broomstick and gave the cushion a whack.

Allie coughed at the musty cloud and stepped to the side. "Allie Miller." Surely, Miller was common enough not to be associated with Miller Ball Bearings.

"Miller. Miller. Still can't place you. Allie, you say? Hmm." No dust particle dared defy her, and Allie wouldn't have been surprised if the stains had leapt off at her command.

"Now you know my name," Allie said, "but I don't know yours."

A gray head poked from behind the cushion. "Don't know

my name? How can you not know my name? Everyone at Groveside knows me."

"I don't attend Groveside."

"You don't? Why are you here?"

Allie picked up the next beating victim and tied it in place. "I went for a walk. I'm sort of looking for a new church."

"You're a visitor? And I have you beat ratty old pew cushions? Now that's hospitality."

"I don't mind. Today I asked God to show me a place to serve."

The lady laughed long and hard. "The Lord always answers a prayer like that." She resumed her assault on dust. "Why are you looking for a new church?"

"I'm not really. I'm only thinking about it. My church is so empty."

"Everyone off to war?" The lady leaned on the pole, chest heaving.

"My turn." Allie tied on another cushion and took the broomstick. "Not empty of people; empty of Jesus. I don't feel the Lord's presence, I don't hear him in the teaching, and I don't see him in the people's lives."

"Hmm. Hmm." The lady rocked back and forth on her heels. "Harder, love."

She struck the cushion harder, her dust cloud a mere puff compared to the older woman's. "On Tuesday I went to Ladies' Circle with my mother. The women were more concerned about following Robert's Rules of Order than following Jesus. The only item of business was a fund-raiser for new Sunday school chairs."

"Chairs are necessary."

"Yes, but bickering isn't." She threw her all into the next blow. "A bitter division erupted between the rummage sale faction and the afternoon tea faction. They've lost sight of their purpose. They don't want new chairs so children can hear about Jesus, only to maintain proper appearance."

"All churches are full of sinning hypocrites, love, and don't you ever forget it."

Allie caught her breath while she strung up another cushion. "Yes, but in a good church, the people turn to God to overcome sin and hypocrisy. They love the Lord and want to serve him."

"Why don't you come to Ladies' Circle this morning? But I'll warn you. Our Sunday school needs new chairs." The lady picked up the rod.

Allie smiled. "New pew cushions too."

"Nope. I'll beat these into another year of service. Will you come today?"

"Will you tell me your name?"

She heaved a sigh and put one hand on her hip. "Dear Father in heaven, how I've failed your seeking child. Please forgive me, Allie. My name is Cressie Watts."

"Pleasure to meet you, Mrs. Watts."

"Not Mrs. Watts. Cressie. You're an adult and my sister in Christ."

She hesitated. The lady was in her sixties. Allie had never called one of her elders by her given name. "All right. Cressie?" she asked, unsure she'd heard correctly.

"Yes. Cressie. Hard to believe, but it's easier than my full name."

"What's that?"

She gave the cushion a smack Babe Ruth would have been proud of. "Crescenda."

Allie's jaw dropped. "Crescenda?"

"Yep. Pa was a choir director. I was the last of eight children, the climax, the crescendo."

Just like her conversation with Walt. Allie sank to the

pile of cushions and stared at the woman with the mighty arm and the musical name. A laugh bubbled up—the first in days—then more, a great stream, somehow mixed with her grief and guilt.

Cressie set hands on hips, and a smile fought a scowl. "All right, missy. Just because I press you into housekeeping doesn't mean you can laugh at my name."

"I'm sorry." She wiped her tears. "You must think I'm horribly rude. It's just—just that my name—Allie—it's short for Allegra."

"Allegra?" The smile beat the scowl. "I'm plumb flabbergasted."

"My friend Walt—" Allie gasped at the crush of pain in her chest. She drew a deep breath. "He—he joked that his name was Adagio, and we'd have children named Andante, Pianissimo, Fortissimo—and Crescenda." She almost smiled at the bittersweet memory, at the fragment of her lost melody.

"I must be your long-lost sister."

Tears welled in Allie's eyes again. "I could really use a sister right now."

"Well, sis. We've got work to do. On your feet. On your feet. We only have—you're wearing a watch? My, that's a fancy watch. What's the time?"

"Nine-twenty," Allie said in a shaky voice. She stood and added another cushion to the line. If only she could tell Walt about Cressie. How he'd laugh—that wonderful, resonant laugh. His grin would push up his cheeks, his hazel eyes would sparkle, his lips would tingle on her cheek.

She picked up the rod and pummeled the cushion. Baxter. Why couldn't she think of Baxter that way? Maybe if he actually kissed her, or held her hand, or showed an inkling of interest—

"Whoa, Miss Allegra. You'll beat the stuffing out of that one."

She dropped the broomstick, winded and embarrassed. "Sorry. Next?"

Before long, a row of brown cushions dragged the clothes-line low. Women arrived and entered the classroom wing. Cressie tucked wiry curls back into her bun. "Come along, love. Time for Circle."

Allie smoothed her skirt and adjusted her hat. She was in no state to meet people. Why, she'd left home in such a hurry, she'd taken a purse that didn't match her shoes. However, the ladies in the fellowship hall seemed oblivious to her oversight.

"Caught in Cressie's whirlwind, were you?" A tiny woman with white hair in a topknot clasped Allie's hand in gnarled fingers.

Cressie pressed a cup of tea into Allie's free hand. "I thought she was your granddaughter, Mabel."

"What a compliment." Mabel peered closer. "It was the eyes, wasn't it?"

"The Webers are all green-eyed monsters."

"Hush, Cressie. You'll drive away this sweet young lady. You see, Allie, most of our girls serve as nurses or work in the factories."

Allie glanced around. With one exception, she was the only woman under fifty.

Mabel lifted Allie's hand. "My, what long fingers. Do you play the piano by any chance?"

"Well, yes, I do."

"Oh, she is a godsend, Cressie." Mabel patted Allie's hand. "I'm the church pianist, but my rheumatism's so bad, I can't keep up with the more sprightly hymns."

Church pianist? She wanted to serve, but her parents would never approve.

"The choir practices Thursday evenings. I play at the service and for Sunday school beforehand."

"Oh my. I'm only visiting."

"Pray about it, dear."

The women pulled chairs into a circle. Opal Morris, the pastor's wife, prayed, and everyone opened bags and produced balls of yarn and knitting needles. Allie's idle hands perturbed her.

Cressie passed down a ball of yellow yarn and a pair of needles. "We're making blankets for our boys in the hospital at March Field."

Allie smiled, pleased to help in some small way.

Instead of conducting business, Opal read a Bible passage, and the ladies discussed it. Allie didn't dare speak, but she watched and listened and liked what she saw—love for the Lord, the Word, and each other. Allie studied the yellow rows gathering on the needle. Even if she didn't come on Sundays, she could attend Ladies' Circle.

When the business portion of the meeting started, no motions were tabled, no amendments were passed, and no minutes were taken. The Sunday school needed a dozen chairs. The men's board, although shrunken by the war, had rounded up lumber scraps, and Cressie's husband, a carpenter, would construct the chairs. The ladies needed to provide money for varnish and hardware.

"If you'd be interested . . ." Allie's cheeks warmed as all the ladies turned to her. "My—my father refinished my bedroom furniture last summer, and we have two or three cans of varnish left."

"What a blessing," Cressie said. "Why don't you bring it Sunday?"

"Sunday?" She glanced down at her yarn. "I—I have to ask my parents."

"How old are you?"

"Twenty-two."

Cressie's wide mouth bent, her message clear without words. As an adult, Allie could make up her own mind.

If only it were that simple.

13

Wendover Field

July 14, 1942

"What a great plane." Frank collapsed on his cot across from where Walt lay.

"Isn't she? How was your landing?" Walt tossed a baseball up and caught it right over his bare chest.

"As you said. Bounced all over the place. Don't know why the B-17 doesn't have the tricycle landing gear we trained on in Albuquerque. It'll take time to learn."

"Got to keep the approach straight."

"Yeah." Frank sat up and unbuttoned his khaki shirt. "Mail came?"

"Yep. Sorry, nothing for you today."

"Get anything interesting?"

Walt groaned, long and low. "Letter from George. Had a great wedding trip, loves married life, getting his materials ready to teach history at Antioch High." He tossed the baseball up.

Frank intercepted it. "Why the groan?"

Walt sat up and ran his hand through his hair, damp from

the desert heat. "His girlfriend—I mean, his wife—added a note about Allie."

"Yeah?"

Walt glanced around the smoky barracks, glad no men were in earshot. "Dorothy blabbed. Betty's mad at Allie, says she'll never speak to her again."

Frank threw the ball across to Walt. "Good. She had it coming."

"I don't know."

"You're not making sense, buddy."

Walt turned the ball in his hands. "You know, Allie never said she didn't have a boyfriend. She just didn't mention him. Betty insists she told me. Maybe, well, maybe Allie thought I knew."

"But she flirted with you."

"I thought she did. Don't have much experience with this stuff. What if I misinterpreted her actions? And now—well, she's lost her only good friend."

"Don't tell me you've forgiven her?"

Walt ran his thumb over the stitches on the ball. "No, but I should. After all, Joseph forgave his brothers who sold him into slavery, Jesus forgave the men who nailed him to the cross, and he forgave my sins too. I suppose I can forgive a girl for being friendly."

"Hmm." Frank tugged off his shoes. "Are you going to write her?"

"Not on your life."

Frank stretched out on the cot, silent. Walt got out his B-17 manual, eager to get his mind back on planes. He flipped through. All the men had to learn from the manual, since no one had experience in the Flying Fortress. The 306th still had only a handful of Forts, so the crews took turns, and the planes flew round the clock.

"You should write her."

"Huh?" Walt looked up from the takeoff checklist.

"Allie. You should write her. You really liked her."

Walt sighed. He didn't want to talk about Allie anymore.

"Did you like her as a person, or just as a potential girlfriend?"

Why did Frank have to talk everything to death? "Both, I guess. She's a great girl. We really . . . we understood each other."

Frank wiggled his toes. "You said she needs friends. Write her."

"Uh-uh. She knows I'm crazy about her."

"Why? What'd you say?"

Walt dog-eared the page with the takeoff checklist. "Um, I said she was lovely. Beautiful eyes. Glad I could talk to her."

Frank was quiet so long, Walt glanced over. Frank gave him a blank stare. "You're a regular Romeo, aren't you?"

He groaned and clapped his manual shut. He was a regular fool.

"Come on, I bet she doesn't know how you feel. Write her. Besides, if anything happens with what's-his-name, you'll be next in line."

That thought had occurred to Walt too. He shook his head. "That's not right. Anyhow, I threw away her address."

"Get it from your friends."

"Are you kidding? They know how I feel. I'd look like an even bigger fool, begging for crumbs of friendship. Short of going through the Riverside phone book, there's no way to get her address."

"March Field." Frank sat up, face bright. "Say, I know a fellow there. He can look it up for you."

Walt stood and slipped on his khaki shirt. "Last name's Miller."

Frank winced. "Too bad."

"Yeah. Too bad." He slung his lightweight A-2 flight jacket over his shoulder and walked outside. The sun blazed, but it had almost set over the jagged mountains in the distance. After he got his flight gear from the equipment shed, he headed to the runway. Not that they needed paved runways—a man could land a plane anywhere on the salt flats.

"Hiya, Preach."

He squinted into the sun and saw Harry, Mario, and Al walk toward him—away from the planes. "Hi. Where are you going?"

Harry unbuckled his parachute harness and shrugged it off. "Night navigational flight. Cracker says we don't have to go."

Walt's chest simmered. "Cracker's wrong. We fly as a crew."

"Why should we have to?" Al blew out a cloud of cigarette smoke. "Not a gunnery training flight."

"We all have to get used to the plane, the altitude, oxygen. Better now than in combat. Besides, don't you want your flight pay?"

Al cussed. "I'd rather have a night off."

Walt didn't want to order them, but he would if he had to. "We fly as a crew." He strode to the assigned plane, followed by his gunners, who spouted vocabulary that burned Walt's ears more than the desert sun.

"Wish Cracker was the first pilot," Mario muttered.

"Cracker says the CO must have had his reasons for putting Preach in charge," Harry said. "Can't imagine what they were."

Walt climbed through the rear fuselage door into the waist

compartment of the B-17, too furious with his copilot to admire the craft. He went through the radio room and bomb bay and into the cockpit.

Cracker lounged in the copilot's seat. "Say, Preach, what do you think?" He thrust a girlie magazine in Walt's face.

He snatched it and dropped it to the floor. "I think you should read the manual instead of that trash."

"Whoa, Preach. Get out of your pulpit." Cracker smirked and retrieved the magazine. "Hey, why are those guys here? I sent them back to quarters."

"You sent them. I didn't. We fly as a crew." He took his seat and tried to find the preflight checklist in his manual, but his fingers didn't cooperate.

Cracker turned in his seat and called down the length of the plane, "Sorry, fellas. I tried to get you out of it."

"We know," Harry called back. "Thanks, anyway."

Walt could barely see the print. Cracker had made him out to be a self-righteous slave driver, and to keep some shred of authority, that's exactly what Walt had to be.

14

Riverside

July 20, 1942

Dearest darling Allie,

    Can you ever forgive me? I received a letter today from Louise Morgan. She told me you didn't know Walt was smitten, and you were certain he knew about Baxter. Then I remembered how you asked me after the serenade whether Walt knew you had a boyfriend. Now I see your innocence in the matter.

    Can you ever forgive me for my rash words? I overlooked four years of precious friendship and all that I know of your character. How could I jump to such disgraceful conclusions? Please, please forgive me.

Betty begged Allie's forgiveness for two more paragraphs, then filled several pages on the joys of married life and the latest Antioch happenings.

Allie folded the letter. A dead weight lifted from her chest, and light filled its place. She still felt ashamed of how she treated Walt, sad over the loss of his friendship, and uncomfortable that Betty gave her more pardon than warranted, but her friendship with Betty was restored.

"Good news?" Mother smiled over the top of *Sunset* magazine.

"Oh yes." She picked up her mending and settled back in the wicker chair on the porch. She shared bits of Betty's news, and then the men returned to their evening conversation. The War Production Board had formed the Smaller War Plants Division to give companies like Miller Ball Bearings a chance for military contracts. All was well.

Until "He Wears a Pair of Silver Wings" played on the radio through the open sitting room window. Allie strained to concentrate on the description of the new bureaucracy, but then Father stopped talking, leaned forward, and gazed down the long drive.

"Who would come to visit in a taxi?" he asked.

Allie looked over the porch railing. A taxi stopped where the driveway circled in front of the house, and two men stepped out. Both wore khaki shirts and trousers. One man was tall and lean with red hair under his cap, but the other man . . .

Dinah Shore's voice floated through the window, soft and mellow: "'He's the one who taught this happy heart of mine to fly. He wears a pair of silver wings.'"

Why was Walter here? How did he—oh yes, she gave him her address. But why? After how she treated him? Oh no! He'd come to expose her behavior—just what she deserved, but oh no. Her heart raced, and she wished it would gallop away and take her along.

"Hi, Allie." Walt waved up at her with a bright smile.

A smile? Allie could only follow his lead and weather the storm when it broke. "Hi." She stood, and her mending slipped to the floor. Her hand trembled when she stooped to retrieve it. "To—to what do we owe the pleasure?"

He climbed the porch steps. "Flew into March today. Traded in our old B-18s for brand-new B-17Es. We fly back to Wendover in the morning. I figured while I was in town, I'd drop by."

"Oh. Oh, how nice." She sensed three people on their feet behind her. Now came the dreaded moment.

"Hi, I'm Lt. Walter Novak." He extended his hand to Father. "I grew up with George and Betty Anello. I met Allie at the wedding. And this is my friend, Lt. Frank Kilpatrick."

"How do you do? I'm Stanley Miller. My wife, Mary."

Allie shook Frank's hand, dazed by the pleasantries and handshakes, as if this situation were normal.

"You must be Baxter." Walt offered his hand. "Good to finally meet you. You wouldn't believe how much Allie talks about you."

Those words kicked her in the breastbone, so hard she couldn't breathe. Would he expose her now? No, he chatted amiably with Baxter. With those words, he'd flattered Baxter and portrayed Walt and Allie's friendship as innocent. For some reason, he protected her instead of exposing her. Allie's breath returned, ragged but reviving.

Walt and Frank took the seats Father showed them on the porch. Allie's legs almost gave way as she sat. The scene was surreal. In the cool of the early evening, Father, Mother, Baxter, Walt, and Frank discussed B-17s, ball bearings, and the progress in the Pacific.

"Listen, Baxter," Walt said after some time. "I need to ask you something. You see, I asked Allie to write me. But our friend Betty—boy, did she give me a rough time. She says I can't write another man's girlfriend."

He still wanted to correspond? He was asking Baxter's permission? Allie stared at him—a gentleman, a friend.

Baxter shrugged. "Why would I mind? I've never had a reason to be jealous."

Allie twisted her mending in her lap. If only he knew.

"Well, I wouldn't like it if the woman I loved started writing some scruffy pilot all of a sudden."

She forced herself to breathe. He actually thought Baxter loved her?

Baxter tapped out a few cigarettes and offered one to Frank, who accepted, and Walt, who declined. "If she wants to show her patriotism by writing servicemen, it's fine with me. Better than if she joined the WAACs."

Allie stiffened. What if she did join the WAACs? Wasn't that her decision to make?

Frank lit the cigarette and shielded the flame with his cupped hand. Then he took the glowing cigarette from his mouth. "Say, Walt, don't you think you'd better ask the lady whether she wants to write a scruffy pilot?"

He chuckled. "Sorry, but you promised to write. I figured you keep your promises."

Allie nodded, her head heavy with the meaning of his statement.

Mother straightened the stack of magazines on the wicker table. "You gentlemen must be thirsty after that long flight."

"Yes." Allie sprang to her feet, embarrassed to have slighted her hostess duties and relieved at the chance of temporary escape. "Iced tea, lemonade, or water?"

"Lemonade? Come on, Walt." Frank got up and set hands on hips. "Would you look at our proper hostess, flustered because her guests want to help." He grabbed Allie's elbow and steered her across the porch. "I'm one of eight children, and I'm already up to four myself. Boys, girls, everyone helps in a big family. Did I mention my wife had a baby girl a few weeks ago? Finally, a girl after three boys. I get to meet her tonight. Kathleen Mary Rose. My wife and kids caught a train from L.A., and I'm meeting them at the station at eight o'clock."

"Congratulations. I'm so happy for you." She smiled at Frank and fumbled for the doorknob. Goodness, he talked a lot.

"Talks as much as Betty, doesn't he?" Walt said behind her.

She laughed, nodded, and swung open the front door.

"You know what they say about the Irish—full o' the blarney," Frank said in an affected brogue. "Isn't this a grand house? I've never been in one this big."

Jaws dropped at the sight of the marble entryway, the sweeping staircase, and the crystal chandelier. Allie winced.

Frank let out a low whistle and peered into the sitting room to the right and the dining room beyond. "Wow. How many rooms has this place got?"

She edged toward the kitchen. "Plenty."

"She doesn't like to call attention to her wealth." Walt gave her a smile and pointed with his thumb to the drawing room on the left. "Is that where you play?"

"Yes." Her stomach knotted when she saw the room through new eyes—the opulent woodwork, the plasterwork on the ceiling, the antiques, the Persian rug, the oil paintings, and the grand piano like a jewel in the center of the room.

"Wow," Walt said. "I've always wanted to play a grand piano."

"Please do. After all, I played your piano."

"Hardly a fair exchange, but I won't turn you down." He headed to the piano. "What are you working on? I was right. Beethoven."

Allie laughed. His teasing was as unexpected and welcome as Betty's letter. Dorothy and Betty must have been mistaken about his feelings. "No, you said I couldn't play anything newer than Beethoven, and I believe I proved you wrong."

"Boy, did you. Frank, this lady plays a mean piano."

"Looks like a nice piano to me. Say, Walt, you want to play a grand piano, well, this is my dream." Frank hoisted himself up and stretched on his side along the piano top.

Allie gasped, then laughed. Never had anyone dared to sit on the Miller piano.

"Play me a song, flyboy," Frank said in a falsetto. He leaned over and flicked off Walt's cap.

Walt chuckled and slapped his cap on. "Sorry. Your dream doesn't appeal to me."

Frank sat upright, eyes flashing. "No, we need a woman. Behold, I see a woman." He hopped to the floor, and before Allie could protest, Frank grabbed her around the waist and set her atop the piano.

She looked down into his brilliant blue eyes and laughed. "My mother would kill me if she saw me up here."

"First she'd have to get past two of Uncle Sam's finest." Walt played a few measures, and a smile flickered on his lips.

"You're right, Novak." Frank leaned closer to Allie. "She does have the most gorgeous green eyes."

Her gaze flew to Walt. The flicker left his lips, traveled up his cheek, and settled in his eyelid. Allie's stomach crumpled into a wad of remorse. Dorothy, Betty, and Louise had not been mistaken about Walt's feelings, and neither had Allie. However, his presence and behavior suggested he had forgiven her and his crush had disintegrated into regret for silly words spoken in haste.

"You're right, Frank," she said, her eyes fixed on Walt. "You're full o' the blarney."

Walt looked up to her without smiling, yet his gaze filled her with a warm glow. She didn't deserve his forgiveness or friendship, but for some reason, he'd given them to her. What a blessing.

Like Cressie. Allie broke into a smile. "Oh, Walt, you won't believe what happened. I'm so glad I can tell you." She relayed her introduction to Groveside Bible Church and Cressie Watts.

He laughed long and hard, as she had imagined. "Crescenda? You're kidding."

"You know I'm not."

Walt's eyes shone, that delightful hazel mixture of warm brown and lively green. "How was Sunday?"

"Oh, I didn't dare go." She glanced up with a sudden shock. What if her parents came in and saw her on the piano, or heard what she'd said about Groveside? She'd been gone longer than necessary to fetch lemonade. She eased herself down and straightened the skirt of her dress. "I mustn't forget the lemonade I promised."

"Groveside?" Walt asked.

Allie headed for the kitchen. "I did go back to Ladies' Circle last week and I plan to return. I told Mother I went for a walk, which was true."

"And Sunday?"

She quickened her pace and ignored the two sets of heavy footsteps that followed her through the entry and down the hall into the kitchen, where she removed two glasses from the cupboard.

"Allie, silence is not a truthful solution to this dilemma. Groveside. Sunday."

She sighed and pulled out the ice cube tray.

Frank inspected a crystal bowl of lemons on the counter. "Give up. He learned his interrogation techniques from the master—me."

Walt leaned against the counter, arms crossed. "You just need a good story. Say an old friend invited you and would be heartbroken if you didn't come."

Allie dislodged the ice from the metal tray and gritted her teeth against the nasty squeak. "I'm not going to lie."

"You're staying at dreary old St. Lucifer's?"

She laughed and dropped ice cubes into the glasses. "St. Timothy's. Lucifer is no saint—the prince of darkness, I believe."

"Yeah. Well, it sounds like the church of darkness. God doesn't want you there. He led you to Groveside and friends and a chance to serve—what you want and need."

"Yes, but, oh dear."

"So your parents will fuss. No offense, but Christians have put up with much worse persecution. Remember, God will give you strength. Don't forget I've been praying for you."

"You have?" Goose bumps ran up her arms, and not from the chilly glasses in her hands.

"Told you I would." Walt's smile was so gentle, Allie could hardly bear it. In Antioch he had seemed like a dream, but now he stood in her kitchen, a real man who hurt and forgave and prayed.

"I'm praying for you too." Her voice hovered just above a whisper.

"May I? I'm dying of thirst." Frank reached for a glass, and Allie gave the men their drinks, careful not to touch Walt's fingers.

Walt sipped and murmured his gratitude. "Say, our labor

wasn't in vain. Hiram Fortner donated rusty old Flossie to the scrap metal drive. Big hoopla in town about it."

"I know." She headed for the doorway to lead them back to the porch. "Betty told me."

"She—she did? How? Did she write?"

Walt sounded so surprised, Allie turned back. "Yes, I received a letter today." Why would he be surprised, unless Betty told him of her decision not to write—and the reason why? Oh, how awful.

"I haven't heard from them," he said. "You know how newlyweds get. Thought they'd neglected everyone. Guess it's just me."

She smiled with relief. "I'm sure they haven't forgotten you. Would you like to come to the porch?"

"Just a minute. Could you do me a favor, and not tell Betty we're writing? I told you she gave me a rough time about writing you. Well, it was a real rough time. Even with Baxter's permission, she'll still think it's improper."

Behind Walt, the light came through the kitchen windows at a slant, dappled through the surrounding orchard, and Allie couldn't read his face. How had Betty given him a rough time if she hadn't written? Was he lying? If so, which was the lie—that Betty had written, or that she hadn't?

She squinted through the glare. "I'm not comfortable with that."

Frank stepped to Walt's side. "So Betty has some strange notions. Humor her. You don't have to lie—just don't mention it. You and Walt know this is innocent." He flung his arm around Walt's shoulder. "Come on, the poor man needs letters."

"I do. My friends neglect me."

Allie smiled, unable to resist his pout. "All right, but if Betty asks, I'll tell the truth."

15

Westover Army Air Field; Springfield, Massachusetts
August 18, 1942

Walt dug his knife into the wood, and a golden curl wound to the grass. In a few days he'd have a wooden model of a Flying Fortress. He sat cross-legged near the hardstand, the small concrete parking pad for his brand-new B-17, one of the first F models off the assembly line.

Sure was plenty of wood to carve around here. Lots of trees, taller than the California live oaks he was used to, and packed close—pines, maples, oaks, and who knew what else. As eager as he was to head overseas, he almost wished they could wait to see the New England fall colors.

Did Britain have fall colors too? Seemed likely. When the 306th was assigned to the U.S. Eighth Air Force, Walt's victory was doubly sweet—they'd be stationed in friendly, civilized, historic England—and Cracker was wrong. Today's newspaper trumpeted the Eighth's first mission, in which twelve B-17s bombed rail yards in Rouen, France. Soon the 306th would add to the conflagration.

Walt eased his knife over his model's vertical stabilizer, the B-17's distinctive rounded tail fin. What a great bird. Sleek lines, not boxy like the B-24 Liberator. The F model had many improvements over the E model: more armor, wider propeller blades, Wright R-1820 Cyclone engines, and a frameless Plexiglas nose to increase visibility for the bombardier and navigator.

"Hiya, Novak. Mail call." Frank Kilpatrick loped toward Walt. The man did nothing slowly except get out of his cot in the morning. "Took the liberty of grabbing your mail. Figured you'd be out here ogling the girls." He nodded to the planes.

Walt laughed and held up his hand for the mail.

"Let's see what we've got here." Frank lifted an envelope for inspection. "Mom and Dad. Thick, but not thick enough for cookies. Say, what's this? Could it be? Yes, a letter from the lovely, charming, and elusive Miss Allegra Miller."

Walt's heart jolted. "Just give it to me."

"Not so fast. I can see through the envelope: 'My dearest darling, your manliness made me realize what a fop Brewster is.'"

"Baxter. And he's not a fop."

"Didn't you feel his handshake? Foppiest fop I've ever met. Surprised he has a *girl*friend, if you know what I mean."

Walt rolled his eyes. He agreed, but he wouldn't let Frank know. "Letters?"

"Yeah, yeah, yeah." He popped them into Walt's hand and sat down.

As soon as Frank was occupied with his own mail, Walt opened Allie's letter, his first from her. As expected, the lady had waited for him to write. He sent out letters once a week— seemed like a good rate for platonic correspondence—and he hoped she would write as often.

He unfolded cream paper covered with delicate handwriting. In the first few paragraphs, Allie asked polite questions, described the weather, and mentioned a house Baxter was building. Subtle, yet obvious—Walt knew where he stood. He read on:

Walt, I did it! Before your letter could arrive and nag me about Groveside, I decided to go. I can't begin to tell you how nervous I was or how perplexed and upset my parents were, but I stood my ground.

The service was wonderful. Daisy Galloway from Circle invited me to sit with her family. Daisy's a sweet girl, fresh out of high school, who works the swing shift at a local factory. Pastor Morris's sermon was biblical and inspirational, and I felt the Lord's presence in that dingy building.

After the service, Mabel Weber, the church pianist, introduced me to the pastor, who offered me the church pianist job. Walt, I took it! I refused the pay, but Pastor Morris insisted. He said it's a paid position, and if I declined payment, it would set a bad precedent. Since I can't tell my parents I have a paying job, I decided to tithe, buy war bonds, and open my own little savings account.

Do pray for me to stay strong. Father supports me, although he doesn't approve. Mother, however, remains opposed, and I'm afraid we've had some unpleasant scenes.

Please know you are in my prayers.

Whenever I hear a plane overhead or see a man in olive drab, I say a prayer for you.

Walt smiled. With March Field nearby, he'd get plenty of prayers.

"Nice, long letter." Frank peeked over his shoulder. "I told you—sparks. I saw sparks between you two. Stick in there."

"Don't talk like that. Besides, you saw her house. Too rich for me." He stuffed the letter in the envelope and opened the letter from his parents. Not much new, except his brother Jack's squadron had been declared war-weary and would be transferred stateside.

Figured. Just as Walt was leaving. He hadn't seen Jack since before Pearl Harbor. At least he'd seen Ray this spring while training in Texas.

The envelope wasn't thick with words but with pictures—Walt's furlough pictures. His parents in front of the house, his grandparents by the old almond tree, George and Betty and their new bungalow, Jim and Helen and baby Jay-Jay, the aerial shots of Antioch. Walt paused over the next picture—the biplane, Allie in his A-2 flight jacket, the same one he wore right then, and Walt with a foolish grin. Yeah, foolish, all right. Then Dorothy, Betty, and Allie hamming it up on the blanket by the river, Allie's mouth open in laughter. Then Allie alone, pretty legs stretched out, and a drowsy, sunwarmed smile aimed right at him. Cheesecake, and mighty fine cheesecake, but not his.

"Who's the dame?" Louis Fontaine plucked the photo from Walt's hand.

He looked up in alarm.

Louis and Abe Ruben stood before him and studied Allie's picture. Abe whistled. "She's not bad. Too good for you."

Walt groaned. "That's the absolute truth."

"You never said you had a dame," Louis said with admiration in his voice.

A lie formed in Walt's throat, but he opened his mouth to tell the truth.

"Because Allie's a lady," Frank said. "Not a dame. Not the kind of woman a man brags about." He gave Walt a grin that said, 'Take this ball and run with it.'

How many times had Frank urged him to invent a girlfriend to get the men off his case? Already Louis and Abe looked at him with a whole lot more respect.

"Yeah. Allie's a lady." Walt stood, took back her picture, and smiled. "What kind of gentleman lets fellows ogle his girlfriend?"

16

Riverside

September 4, 1942

"Hundred degrees outside, and we have blankets on our laps."

Allie smiled at Daisy Galloway beside her on the bus to March Army Air Base. Allie's thighs stuck together under a chin-high stack of the Ladies' Circle's handiwork.

"If I go up in flames, at least it's in service to my country." Across the aisle, Cressie Watts lifted her pile a bit and flapped her knees together.

Not ladylike at all, but Allie's arms and legs blazed with damp prickles, and she almost wished she weren't a lady.

When they reached the base, Cressie stood and led the two women down the aisle.

"Isn't this exciting?" Daisy's cherry lips spread in a wide smile. "We're a part of the war effort."

"Not until we actually deliver the blankets." Allie gave her a smile and a nudge with her colorful pile. She had never been that chipper even at eighteen.

The ladies stepped off the fume-filled bus, and Allie let out a sigh when the hot Santa Ana wind dried her bare legs. A

rumble behind her grew in intensity. She looked back to see a large airplane approach for a landing—four engines, a tail fin curved like a bell, a clear nose, a glass bubble underneath, and another bubble behind the cockpit. Yes, a B-17. She smiled, proud she could identify one type of plane, and proud she knew a man who could fly the powerful machine—a man who wrote delightful letters.

"Come along, Miss Allegra," Cressie said. "Come along."

Allie's gaze followed the B-17 in an arc, and the wind generated by the plane whipped her curls behind her.

Daisy's brown hair strained against the red bow tied around her head. "Allegra?"

"Um, yes. Silly, isn't it?"

Daisy glanced at the B-17 and back to Allie with a slow grin. "Allegra Miller."

"Yes, but I go by Allie." She shook her curls off her face, unable to smooth them with her arms full. Why was Daisy so intrigued by her name?

"Why didn't I put it together before? My dad helped your pilot find you."

Allie gave her a quizzical look.

"Did you get a visit from a couple of pilots a while back?"

She stopped and stared at Daisy. "Well, yes. My friend Walt, and one of his friends, but how did you—"

"Oh, this is the most romantic story." Daisy scampered to catch up with Cressie. "Let me guess, he got out of my dad's taxi all casual-like and never told you it took two hours to find you. Isn't that just like a man?"

"Two hours?" Allie struggled with the wind and with Daisy's statement.

"He didn't know your address. Lost it, he said. Also just like a man." She climbed the steps, and Allie forced herself to do likewise. "He gets in Dad's cab and gives him a page he tore from the phone book—all the Millers in Riverside, and that's no small number. Now people shouldn't rip up phone books, but I forgive him. After all, he said he had to find you before he shipped out. *Had* to."

He searched for her? Allie tried to speak, but her mouth formed no words.

"He knew you were rich, so that narrowed the search. But goodness, aren't there a lot of swanky neighborhoods in Riverside?"

Allie's cheeks tingled at the mention of her wealth.

An orderly stepped outside and held the door open for the ladies.

"Dad started at the top of the alphabet and lost count how many houses they went to. Two hours till they found you. No need to tell you my dad sure liked that fare, although he gave them a discount, seeing as how sweet the whole thing was. Daddy's nothing but a big old tenderhearted teddy bear, and your—Walt?—seems he's cut from the same cloth."

The tingles flowed down Allie's cheeks to her chest and arms. Two hours? Stanley Miller—they would be near the end of the list. "Yes, Walt's a sweet man." Then she shook her head, shook off the tingles. "But he's—he's not mine. He's a friend."

Daisy gave Cressie a look. "A friend."

"Take her at her word, love. Take her at her word." Cressie led the way across the lobby, peppered with small groups of men talking and smoking.

Allie pondered an explanation, but then she gasped. A man sat in a wheelchair, one leg amputated above the knee, the other below the knee. The man standing next to him had his pajama sleeve pinned up over the stump of his arm.

As if he'd heard her gasp, the man in the wheelchair looked

right at Allie. He couldn't have heard due to the noise in the lobby, but that did little to soothe her guilt and regret. She should expect such sights in a military hospital.

To atone, she offered a smile to him and his companion. "Good afternoon."

"Good afternoon, miss." The man in the wheelchair gave her a grin that compensated for his missing legs.

The other man leaned his stocky frame against the wall and took a drag on his cigarette. "I hope it's *miss* and not *ma'am*." Then he winked at Allie.

She almost dropped her blankets. Was he making sport of her? Or flirting? Or just being friendly? Something genuine in their smiles made her decide on the latter. She smiled back and hurried after Cressie and Daisy. Such a small gesture, a smile and a greeting, had brightened the day for those two men—and for her.

The ladies turned down a corridor, pungent with disinfectant, and entered an office. A poster on the wall showed a tiny girl with a pale blue scarf over her blonde curls, clutching a doll and sucking one finger. Flames and debris behind her accentuated the message of the slogan: "War Relief—Give!"

Behind a steel desk heaped with papers, a stout woman with a dark complexion and a gray Red Cross uniform rose to her feet. "Cressie—my star volunteer. Look at those wonderful blankets. Oh, so many. These will do the boys a world of good." She swept stacks of manuals from chairs to the precarious tower on her desk.

They set the rainbow of blankets on the wooden chairs. Cressie introduced Allie and Daisy to Regina Romero, who directed the Red Cross Hospital and Recreation Corps at March—the Gray Ladies.

Cressie frowned at the desk. "Swamped with work as always, love?"

"As always." A stack of books slipped from its perch and threatened a paper avalanche, but Regina righted it in time. "Never enough help. All the young women want paying jobs nowadays."

Guilt sank in Allie's chest. Her pianist job took but a few hours a week and made no contribution to the war effort, other than enabling her to purchase more war bonds.

Regina picked up a clipboard and discussed the papers with Cressie. A poster by the door drew Allie's attention. A Red Cross lady offered a snack up to a soldier leaning from a train window. What a difference the Gray Ladies made.

Lord, I want to make a difference too. This is something I could do, something I should do.

★

"You did what?"

"I volunteered with the Red Cross, Mother." Allie pulled silverware from a drawer in the sideboard. Nervousness bored acid holes in her stomach. "I know forty hours a week is a lot, and you'll miss my help at home, but it won't be any different than when I was at Scripps or—" She swallowed. "Or after I'm married."

Mother marched to the archway between the dining room and the sitting room. "Stanley, did you hear what your daughter did? Speak to her."

Father settled back in his red leather armchair and ground his cigarette into the ashtray. "Sorry, dear, but this will be a good experience for her. We'll look harder for paid help."

"Thank you, Father." She set the silver around his plate, the knife protecting the spoon from the fork.

"Baxter?" Mother said. "You speak to her."

Allie grimaced. The poor man was caught in the middle.

"Volunteer work is a very high-class activity," she said. "Many ladies from Riverside's best families volunteer."

"Is that right?" Baxter said. "Well, Mrs. Miller, maybe this is what Allie needs. She's been so strange and restless this summer."

Strange and restless? The doorbell rang, and Father rose to answer. Allie strode to the kitchen for the mashed potatoes. If joining a God-fearing church and volunteering to help wounded servicemen was strange and restless behavior, then she hoped to be even stranger and more restless.

"Allie, a package for you," Father said.

"For me?" She frowned, set the potatoes on the table, and went to the sitting room where Father held a box about two feet square and eight inches high.

She sat in the wing chair, the box heavy in her lap. Her name was written in all capitals with the first letters taller than the others—Walt's handwriting, a style he'd learned in engineering school.

What on earth had he sent? All too conscious of everyone watching, she worked off the string and opened the lid. A letter lay on top of wadded newspaper. She scanned it for news to relay. After the wedding fiasco, she was diligent to mention something good about Baxter in every letter to Walt, and just as diligent to read Walt's letters to her family.

"It's from Walt. He says his group is going overseas soon. He knows where but can't say. Since he's in Massachusetts, he must be going east. He says they received new planes. Hmm? Again? I thought they received new planes last month. Oh, and as the pilot, he has the right to choose the name—*Flossie's Fort*," she said and laughed.

"*Flossie's Fort*?" Baxter asked.

Allie told of the loss and recovery of Fortner's Flossie, but the story seemed deflated compared to her memory, and her memory recalled details she didn't dare relate, details which brought telling warmth to her cheeks.

She glanced down at the letter:

> Baxter's property sounds swell, and so does the house. Remember when my dad told you how he built Riverview Community Church just as my mom wanted, because he loves her so much? You never have to doubt the love of a man who builds something for you.

Mouth dry, Allie paused over the tidbit she should read aloud. However, he was mistaken. Baxter built out of pride, not love. She continued:

> Now to explain the model. I sent these to my family and friends to remind them to pray for me. Besides, you already have a model of Fortner's Flossie, so I thought you should have Flossie's Fort. J.P. Sanchez, my flight engineer, did the artwork on the real plane and the model. He's good, isn't he?

Allie dug through the newspapers. "It's a model of his plane. He carves." She gasped in wonder at how well he carved. The model stretched almost a foot and a half from wingtip to wingtip. The details were exquisite—why, even the wheels and propellers spun. It sported green and olive drab camouflage paint on top, gray paint underneath, and a white star on a blue circle on each side. On the nose, a bust of Flossie the cow, in a leather flight helmet and jacket, raised a hoof in salute.

She looked up, expecting disapproval of such a personal and time-consuming gift, but everyone was enthralled. She'd write Walt that evening to report their delight and tell him about the Red Cross.

Allie took the model to her room and set it on her desk next to the wooden cow. She folded Walt's letter and added it to the others in a desk drawer.

He told Mr. Galloway he'd lost Allie's address? More likely he'd torn it up after what she'd done. He'd be embarrassed to ask Betty for her address—that's why he didn't want Betty to know they were writing. And yet he searched for her. What a precious sacrifice of time and pride, all for the sake of their friendship.

Allie ran her hand over the wooden plane and rested on the cockpit.

You never have to doubt the love of a man who builds something for you? She had to be careful not to read too much into that statement.

17

Gander, Newfoundland

September 6, 1942

"Sixty miles per hour . . . Seventy," Cracker Huntington called out.

Walt nodded and eased the throttles forward.

"Eighty . . . Ninety."

They were committed now, had to take off. Walt frowned. *Flossie* felt sluggish for the calculated weight: nine crewmembers, a mechanic flying as a passenger, luggage, and the eight hundred gallon auxiliary tank in the bomb bay needed to fuel the 2,100-mile flight across the Atlantic.

"One hundred . . . Hundred ten."

Above stalling speed, enough for takeoff as calculated, but Walt wanted more. J.P. Sanchez hunched between the pilots' seats, trusted as always to watch the instrument panel while Walt watched the runway.

"One fifteen . . . One twenty." A question mark hung in the air. They were supposed to take off at one fifteen.

Walt shook his head. The plane rumbled down the runway, and the trees rushed toward him in the twilight. Just a little more speed.

"One twenty-five," Cracker said, a tense edge in his voice.

Walt guided the control wheel back. Up went the nose, and the rest of the plane followed, but the resistance made him hold his breath until he cleared the trees. "Wheels up."

"Check," Cracker said, still with the edge. "Too close to the end of the runway."

"Feels mushy." Walt peered around his left shoulder and watched the landing gear fold into the nacelle of engine two. "Up left."

"Up right. Don't forget we've got eight hundred extra gallons of fuel back there."

"Tail wheel up," Harry called on the interphone from the back of the plane.

"Yeah. Still doesn't feel right." Walt followed the other planes in his squadron, little lights in the darkening sky. Thirty-five planes from the 306th were leaving Gander for the eleven-hour trip to Prestwick, Scotland—nine planes each from three squadrons, and eight from the fourth.

Walt leveled off at an altitude low enough not to require oxygen. To maintain hands-free flying, he adjusted the elevator trim wheel on the center console. He frowned again. It didn't just feel wrong, it *was* wrong—*Flossie* was heavy in the tail. Didn't make sense. The bomb bay, with most of the extra weight, was located at the plane's center of gravity.

"Take the controls," he said. "I'm checking out the back."

"Why? They'd tell us if something was wrong back there."

Walt caught a flash of alarm in his copilot's eyes. Yeah, something was wrong. "Take the controls," he said. He unplugged his headset, swung his legs to the side, and maneuvered over the open passageway that led down to the nose compartment.

"Good takeoff, Novak," J.P. said, "but you're right. Mushy."

He smiled and patted his flight engineer's shoulder when he passed. J.P. was the only crewmember who didn't call him Preach.

Walt squeezed around the top turret apparatus in the back of the cockpit and squirmed through the door to the bomb bay. The B-17's interior was cramped enough in regular clothes but was awfully tight in his sheepskin-lined B-3 flight jacket and with a seat-pack parachute slapping the back of his knees.

He clutched the metal supports as he walked the narrow aluminum catwalk in the bomb bay. The engines' power vibrated through his gloves and sheepskin-lined boots. The auxiliary tank looked fine.

When he entered the radio room, four men sat up straighter on the floor.

"Hiya, Preach." Bill Perkins took off his headphones at his seat at the radio desk. "What's up?"

"Flying heavy in the tail. I'm checking her out."

Al Worley scrambled to his feet and blocked the door to the waist compartment, which was closed to keep the men warm. "I don't think you should go back there."

"All the more reason to go." Walt shoved the little man to the side with the back of his arm.

"Really, Preach. Luggage all over the place," Harry Tuttle said.

Walt opened the door and moved to step through. He couldn't. He could only stare.

Luggage lay heaped on top of the housing for the ball turret, and stacks of wooden crates filled the tubular waist compartment. He read the labels on the crates—bourbon, gin, rum.

What on earth?

The crates weren't there when he did the preflight inspection. Guaranteed. When? How?

The parachute.

He'd set his parachute on the pilot's seat before preflight. This—this was why it disappeared. This was why he had to trudge all the way back to the equipment shed and fill out all the stupid forms to get a replacement. This was why the men insisted Walt enter through the nose hatch instead of the waist.

"What's going on here?"

Silence. He faced his men. "I repeat—what's going on here?"

Bill fidgeted with the radio cord. "Well, we stocked up so we can sell to the Brits. Cracker said not to tell you. He knew you'd get riled up, because you hate booze."

Walt's fists clenched as tight as his gloves allowed. "It's not the booze, it's the weight."

He picked up a duffel and tossed it into the radio room so he could get through the door. Just how much weight was there? He counted forty-eight crates. If each crate weighed forty, fifty pounds, he had about a ton of cargo.

He waded through the bags to the left waist window and threw a duffel to Mario Tagliaferro, who stood in the doorway, mouth wide open. "I need some help," Walt said.

"What are you doing?" Mario asked.

"Ditching the weight." Walt lifted the top crate by the window and slammed it down in the space he had cleared on the floor. Now he had room to work.

Al pushed past Mario. "Hey, that's our profit."

"Profit? Fat lot of good that'll do if you're at the bottom

of the ocean." He dropped another crate, with a satisfying crunch of breaking glass.

"Stop it!" Al leaned over the crates Walt had moved, his face red and twisted. "We put a lot of money in this."

"Too bad. Stupid investment. Would've frozen anyway." He slid the Plexiglas window open. The Arctic wind gusted in and knocked his breath away. He braced himself against the slipstream and heaved a crate through the window.

Al grabbed his elbow. "You can't do that."

Walt whipped around, fury hot in his veins. "I can and I will. If you don't want to join your cargo, you'd better get to work."

One of Al's eyebrows twitched, as if he knew Walt just might follow through on his threat. He grumbled and backed off. "Just 'cause you don't drink doesn't mean we can't have our fun."

Walt plugged in his headset by the window. "Fontaine, recalculate the fuel consumption data with an extra two thousand pounds of weight." He pointed to Al, Harry, Mario, and their startled passenger. "And you—get to work."

"Yes, sir," Al said, no mask over his hostility.

Over the next few minutes, Walt and the men dumped the crates into the Arctic Ocean five thousand feet below. Despite the cold, sweat dampened the sides of Walt's undershirt. The exertion and some muttered prayers took the edge off his rage.

When the booze was gone, Walt returned to the cockpit. He took his seat without a word to his copilot. Sure enough, the elevators had been re-trimmed. Must have gained altitude.

He plugged his headset in and pressed the mike button on the control wheel. "Pilot to navigator. Fontaine, do you have those calculations?"

"Um, yes."

"And . . ."

"And—we probably wouldn't have made it."

"What if we'd had engine trouble?" He glared at Cracker, who wouldn't meet his eye.

"Um, no. Definitely not."

"Okay, crew, get to praying. Pray your stupid stunt didn't cost us too much fuel on takeoff. That water is icy down there." His fury cooled with the satisfaction of being proved right. "If you'd been honest with me before we left, you could have gotten your money back. I might even have let you keep a few cases."

One more point to drive home hard. "Dishonesty always has a price."

18

Bedford, England

September 9, 1942

"Like a fairy tale," Frank said.

"Yeah." Walt stuffed his hands in the pockets of his flight jacket and glanced over the embankment to the Great Ouse River. Thanks to Cracker's scheme, they'd landed on fumes the other day, but thanks to God's mercy, they landed. Now Walt was actually in England, in Bedford, where John Bunyan wrote *Pilgrim's Progress* while in prison, and swans actually swam in the river.

The place didn't remind him so much of a fairy tale—more like the colorful pictures in the black and white checkered Mother Goose book Mom used to read to him. "I half expect Little Miss Muffet or Wee Willie Winkie to run by."

"I'd rather see Lady Godiva."

"Hey! You're a married man."

Frank cocked his head to the side. "Speaking of naked ladies, gotta get something for my Eileen."

Walt laughed and turned right onto who-knew-what street. During the invasion scare in 1940, the British had torn down the street signs to confuse German paratroopers. Now the

American invaders were confused. Bedford's streets lay like wheel spokes, not in a grid like Antioch's. Walt and Frank passed the Swan Hotel on the right and the tall white spire of St. Paul's cathedral on the left. A fourteenth-century cathedral—he couldn't believe it.

Frank turned left. "This street looks good. Lots of shops."

"Not much in them." Walt peered through the store windows at the empty shelves. Across the street, a line of women and old men stood outside a store called "Marks & Spencer." Must be a grocery. The people showed the results of strict rationing, all thin and pale. Some airmen from the 306th swaggered around the line and flirted with the prettiest girl with gum-smacking Yankee vigor.

"Let's check in here." Frank nodded to a jewelry store and ground his cigarette butt into the flagstone sidewalk. "Can't wait to see what the Brits do when an Irishman waves money in their faces."

Walt stopped to let his eyes adjust to the dark store. A man with wispy gray hair and a worn tweed jacket stood behind the display case. "How may I assist you?"

Frank leaned one forearm on the case and pulled out his wallet. "Looking for a grand necklace for me wife," he said in his fake Irish brogue.

Walt stifled a smile and looked down through the glass at a collection of gold crosses. One grabbed his attention. Long-stemmed flowers formed the four arms of the cross. "Excuse me. What are these flowers called? On this cross?"

The jeweler glanced over and sniffed. "Those would be called lilies, sir."

"Oh yeah. Like Easter." Leave it to the English to make a man feel like an uneducated dolt. Lilies—he knew that. Why did he think of Allie? Oh yeah. One day she'd worn a dress with a big lily up the side. Sure was pretty on her. That cross would look pretty on her too.

"Getting something for your girlfriend?"

Walt looked up. "Hi, J.P. Didn't see you come in."

"Ah, Sergeant Sanchez," Frank said. "Faith and begorra, it's good to be seeing you this fine afternoon."

J.P.'s eyebrows drew together at Frank's accent, and Walt fought a chuckle.

Frank's eyes lit up, and he turned back to the Englishman. "Must be doing your heart good to be seeing so many fine American lads. Don't you be worrying. We'll be getting you out of this war as we got you out of the last one." He was breaking every rule in the handbook the American servicemen received about dealing with the British, and he sure was enjoying it.

"He's joking," Walt said. "We know you can handle yourselves. We're only over here to get in a few licks of our own."

The jeweler straightened his thin shoulders. "Would you gentlemen care to see anything?"

Frank fingered one necklace. "Sure and me wife would like this sapphire."

"Nothing for me," Walt said.

"What about your girlfriend?"

Walt glanced over at J.P. This story of his required as much maintenance as an aircraft engine.

"Saints be blessed, Walter. 'Tis your Allie's birthday soon, 'tisn't it?"

"'Tisn't it?" He raised an eyebrow at Frank, who shrugged.

Walt had no idea when Allie's birthday was and no business buying her jewelry, but he couldn't keep his eyes off that cross. He didn't remember Allie wearing a cross. Surely he could make some excuse for a gift like this. "Yeah. Yeah, I'll take this cross."

The jeweler boxed it up, and Walt's misgivings melted away. She'd like it. Pretty, distinctive, and a sign of her faith. Besides, it felt nice to buy her something.

J.P. picked out a bracelet for his girl in San Antonio. "Another plane came in from Prestwick after you two left—with some news."

"Yeah?" Walt stroked the velvet box in his pocket. He'd never bought jewelry before.

"That missing crew from the 367th Squadron made it— but barely. Ran out of fuel off Ireland, ditched the plane in shallow water, and walked to shore. The next tide washed their Fort out to sea."

"Wow. So we're down to thirty-three planes." Walt held the door open, and the men walked out into weak sunshine. One plane from the 423rd Squadron had disappeared in a bright flash not long after takeoff. "At least the men made it this time."

"Yeah." J.P. nodded across the street to a half-timbered pub, full of airmen on liberty. "I think the booze did them in."

"They weren't drinking, were they?"

"Nope. Had a full load in the back of the plane. Sound familiar?"

Walt tripped over a flagstone. "You're kidding."

"Uh-uh. Al Worley—he turned even whiter than usual when he heard. And Harry and Mario—they're singing your praises."

"Glory be, 'tis wonderful news."

Walt laughed. "Knock it off, Frank. We're out of the store."

"Sorry. Can't help myself. But say, that is good news. Tell the CO. Cracker will crumble in your hands."

"Nah. I forgot to tell you. Talked to Colonel Overacker this morning. Seems Cracker's from some hoity-toity family. Can't get rid of him. And Overacker doesn't want to switch crews. He knows Cracker's weak. That's why I got him."

"That's a fine compliment," Frank said.

Walt snorted. "I'd rather have a fine copilot."

19

Riverside

October 8, 1942

"I couldn't pick if I were her either," Daisy Galloway whispered, then stuffed more popcorn in her mouth. "Bing Crosby or Fred Astaire? Bing Crosby or Fred Astaire? They're both dreamy."

Allie shushed her—again. Daisy guffawed during the cartoons, crunched popcorn during the newsreel, and chattered during the movie. Allie had seen *Holiday Inn* before, but not this week's newsreel, which showed U.S. aircrews landing in England after a mission over Nazi-occupied Europe. She had strained her eyes looking for Walt. Although he couldn't say where he was stationed due to censorship, his references to Mother Goose and *Pilgrim's Progress* indicated he was in Great Britain.

"Oh, Fred. Definitely Fred," Daisy said when his tap-dancing feet set off firecrackers.

"Oh, Bing. Definitely Bing," she said when he crooned "White Christmas."

Allie sighed, but she did enjoy her outings with Daisy after Ladies' Circle every Thursday, her day off from the

Red Cross. What a joy to tell Walt she now had friends, fun, work, and a good church, all of which brought purpose and contentment, despite Mother's comments that Allie had abandoned her.

The house lights flipped on, and the ladies filed out of the Fox Theater, a Mission Revival building with a bell tower over the box office.

Daisy sang "I've Got a Gal in Kalamazoo" as they strolled across Seventh Street in the sunshine.

Allie frowned at a crowd ahead of them. A shipment of something scarce must have arrived at the grocery. Beef? Coffee? Even bobby pins would be nice.

"Sugar," Allie overheard.

"Sugar." She gripped Daisy's elbow. "They have sugar. Do you have your ration book?"

"Yeah. Do you?"

"Yes." Allie opened her pocketbook. She always took the family's ration books when she went out. The apple trees were in peak production, and now they could make applesauce. For once, she'd make Mother happy.

✦

Allie counted Mason jars. The Miller family had rations for six pounds of sugar for October. Allie had poured two pounds into the empty sugar crock, and the remaining four pounds would yield over twenty quarts of applesauce. With Daisy's help, she could finish before choir practice.

Daisy wiped her forehead and stirred the kettle of boiling apples. "Why does canning season have to be the hottest time of the year?"

"I think it's part of Eve's curse." Allie ladled cooked apples from the second batch into the food mill.

"That and men." Daisy set her hand on her hip. "Could

you believe the nerve of that soldier at the theater? Asking me out—a stranger, and I don't even know if he's a Christian."

"Mm." Allie cranked the food mill, her stomach as jumbled as the apples.

"I'd never marry a man who didn't share my faith, so why would I date one?"

"Mm." Allie didn't dare speak up, not until she found that Bible verse about how a believing wife could help her husband come to Christ. But what if Betty and Daisy were right, and she was wrong? She couldn't be wrong. She had to find that verse.

After Allie fed the batch through the mill, she shook out her sore arm. Then she stirred in sugar and cinnamon, poured the applesauce into quart jars, sealed them, and eased them into a kettle of boiling water on the iron top of the white enamel stove.

"Do I smell applesauce?" Mother pulled an apron out of a drawer.

"You sure do, Mrs. Miller. But dontcha worry. We'll be outta your hair by dinnertime." Daisy cracked her gum.

Allie winced at Mother's tight smile. Mother had never said a word about her new friend, but she clearly disapproved of her unpolished ways.

Allie wrapped towels around her hands and hefted the kettle of boiled apples to the sink. "Sugar came in today. I'm thankful I had the ration books with me."

"Oh, good. Baxter can have lemonade again." Mother peeked in the sugar crock, then looked up. "Is this all?"

"Well, yes. We need to put up the apples. Two pounds should meet our needs this month." She drew back from the steam of the drain liquid—and Mother's rebuke.

"It'll meet our minimum needs, but you should have saved

some for lemonade. Poor Baxter hasn't had a glass for almost a month."

Now steam rose in her head, unfamiliar yet uncontainable. "Poor Baxter can put a twist of lemon in his water. These apples need to be put up. We haven't been able to make cake or pie for months, I know I won't have a birthday cake, and you're worried about Baxter's lemonade?"

"Allie!"

She flung limp apples from the colander into the food mill. "If Baxter wants lemonade, he can buy his own sugar."

"Allegra Marie Miller!"

"No. He's over here every single night, eating all our meat, drinking down our entire sugar ration, but does he ever help? No." How dismaying, how satisfying to speak out.

"Allie . . ." Daisy poked her and motioned to the door.

Baxter stood there, a brown bag in his arm. "The grocer had sugar. I bought a couple pounds—for you."

The satisfaction of her anger drained away and left her dismay unbalanced.

"Apologize to Baxter this instant." Mother's voice climbed and shook, unaccustomed to such heights. "You ought to be ashamed."

She was, but she couldn't voice her shame at raising her voice, at speaking ill of Baxter—to Mother, to Daisy, to Baxter himself.

"No apology is necessary." Baxter set the bag on the counter. "I've taken your hospitality for granted for too long."

"But Baxter, we don't begrudge you at all." Mother patted his shoulder and glowered at Allie. "Why, you're practically family."

Allie gripped a Mason jar as if she could extract the sugar from the applesauce. She was wealthy, and he came from poverty. He probably never had lemonade in Oklahoma. "I—I'm sorry. I was rude, and—and what I said was uncalled for."

"Nonsense. You were right." He smiled, walked up to Allie, and took her hand. "Sugar is scarce, and I consume more than my fair share."

"But I—"

"Hush." He laid a kiss on her forehead. "I don't want to hear another word about it. Water with a twist of lemon sounds delightful."

Allie stared at him, as stunned by his tender kiss and merciful gaze as she was by her own behavior. "Thank you," she whispered.

20

Thurleigh Air Field; Bedfordshire, England

October 9, 1942

"Four o'clock in the morning," Frank mumbled.

"At least it's not a false alarm today. Finally, our first mission." Walt guided his razor over his chin. He needed a close shave so the oxygen mask would fit right.

"Four o'clock." Frank pounded his shaving brush into the soap in his mug. His cheer wouldn't come out until the sun did.

"Hurry up, y'all," Louis Fontaine called from across the ablution hut, where the men washed up. "I hear we get real eggs before combat, not that powdered slop."

Walt caught a strange light in Louis's eyes—too bright. The men reacted to fear in different ways. Abe Ruben's hands shook as he dried his face. Frank had some saint's medal stuffed in his shirt pocket. Cracker dragged from a hangover, even though the bar in the Officers' Club closed at 2000 hours the night before. Walt felt—well, normal. Eager but calm. Was he peaceful because of his faith, or was he stupid?

If he was stupid, he wasn't alone. Frank perked up over heaps of real eggs for breakfast, and excitement charged the air in the briefing room. The jokes stopped when the group commanding officer, Col. Charles Overacker, took the stage at 0500 hours. Walt leaned forward in his chair. Where would the 306th first rain bombs on Hitler's Third Reich?

Colonel Overacker drew back a blue curtain that covered the map at the front of the room. A red string stretched from Thurleigh across the Channel. One hundred eight bombers would hit the Compagnie de Fives steel and locomotive works at Lille in France. The 306th would join the veteran 92nd, 97th, and 301st Bomb Groups in B-17s, and the 93rd would fly the first mission in Europe with B-24 Liberators. It was the biggest mission the Eighth Air Force had ever sent up.

After the briefing, the men went to the locker room to get their flight gear and rations. Then Walt stood in line to turn in his personal effects to the intelligence officer. If they were shot down, the enemy could gather information from letters, diaries, even pictures. Walt only had his wallet and his Bible, in case he had five minutes to read—which he didn't.

He pulled Allie's photograph from his Bible for one more look. He'd sent his service portrait a while back, and she'd responded with her graduation picture. Seemed more respectful to have her portrait in his Bible than that cheesecake snapshot.

He closed his eyes. *Thank you, Lord, for strengthening Allie, for giving her a church, work, and friends.*

Louis nudged him from behind. "Give her a kiss and move it."

Walt laughed and kissed Allie's picture. He tucked it in the Bible and gave his stuff to the intelligence officer. Now he only carried two written items—his dog tags and a Scripture verse on a slip of paper in the pocket of his heavy flight jacket.

"We've got Jerry in our sights now," Louis said when he climbed into the truck that took the crews to the planes.

"Abe's Norden bombsight." Abe had already left to carry the top secret bombsight to the plane and install it under armed guard.

Walt hoisted himself into the truck, his parachute slung over his shoulder. "We'll put those bombs in the pickle barrel today." That was the claim of the Norden. The bombardier dialed in altitude, airspeed, wind speed, and direction for precision bombing. Let the RAF carpet bomb under cover of darkness. With the Norden, the U.S. could inflict strategic damage with minimal civilian casualties.

The truck pulled up to *Flossie*'s hardstand in the dim morning light. The bombs had been loaded in the middle of the night, but the ground crew still scurried about, making sure "their" plane was in top shape.

Al Worley hopped out of the truck first. "Still can't believe we have to fly in a plane named after a cow." But he grinned at Walt.

He smiled back. "My girlfriend gave me a tough time about *Flossie*. She said it's wrong to dress a cow in leather." The crew's laughter smoothed out the wrinkle of guilt when he called Allie his girlfriend. Besides, Frank was right—no one questioned Walt's manhood anymore or bugged him about going out to pick up girls. And Allie's frequent and lengthy letters made this story easy to tell.

While the gunners installed their machine guns in the mounts with help from the armorers, Walt and Sergeant Reilly, the ground crew chief, filled out Form 1A and walked through the preflight inspection. At quarter to seven, Walt gathered the men by the nose hatch. After he ran through the mission once more, he burrowed under his Mae West life preserver and parachute harness and into the pocket of his flight jacket. He had misgivings about reading Scripture to the men, but God gave him no choice.

"First mission, men. We've got a great crew and a mighty good plane, but we can't put our trust in machines or ourselves—only in God. The eighteenth Psalm reads, 'I will love thee, O Lord, my strength. The Lord is my rock, and my fortress, and my deliverer; my God, my strength, in whom I will trust; my buckler, and the horn of my salvation, and my high tower. I will call upon the Lord, who is worthy to be praised: so shall I be saved from mine enemies.'"

Cracker's mouth contorted, but before he could make a wisecrack, Bill Perkins sang out, "A mighty fortress is our God, a bulwark never failing."

Wow. The man could sing. Walt wanted to join in, but Bill had a soloist's voice.

After Bill finished, Louis clapped Walt on the back. "Say, Preach, you've got yourself a choir director."

Walt laughed and checked his watch. Seven o'clock. "Okay, to your stations."

With the ancient hymn playing in his head, Walt settled in the cockpit, strapped on his throat mike, and put on his headset.

A green flare sprang from the control tower, and his heart lurched. This was it.

He started each of the four engines, which sputtered to roaring life. The final checks of engine performance looked good, and he stuck his hand out the window to signal the ground crew to remove the wheel chocks. He taxied from the hardstand to the perimeter track around Thurleigh's three intersecting runways. Twenty-four bombers rolled in a rumbling line. Their propwash flattened the grass and buffeted *Flossie*, forcing Walt to keep firm pressure on the rudder pedals under his feet. His eagerness flared into full excitement at the power of the sight.

Overacker's plane sped down the main runway at 0732, and

the other planes followed. *Flossie* was heavy from ten 500-pound general purpose bombs in the bomb bay, but takeoff was smooth. Cracker's hangover made him useless. Good thing J.P. was dependable.

The 306th orbited the field, and the Forts slipped into formation. First they formed three-plane elements in a V, then lined up three elements abreast. Frank's plane, *My Eileen*, flew to Walt's left, his nose lined up with Walt's tail.

He checked the altimeter—ten thousand feet. "Okay, men, put out those cigarettes. Time to go on oxygen." He turned to Cracker. "I need you now. Oxygen checks every fifteen minutes."

He nodded. He looked like a bug with his bloodshot eyes and the black rubber mask hanging off his face. Walt strapped on his own mask, heavy and clammy.

Once over the Channel, the gunners entered their turrets and tested their guns. The .50-caliber machine guns in the top turret, ball turret, waist, and tail, and the two .30s in the nose chattered in short bursts.

The promised escort of RAF Spitfires never came, but neither did the Luftwaffe. Walt climbed to the bombing altitude of 22,000 feet, and soon he saw a wavy white line far below. The blue gray Atlantic gave way to France's brown and green patchwork. Little black clouds appeared before them. Flak.

Hard to believe he was over France, and on the ground were the real, live, Hitler-saluting, goose-stepping Nazis he saw in newsreels. The flak proved it. Behind each black puff stood a Jerry with an antiaircraft gun trained on a B-17.

"Tail?" Cracker said to make sure no one had oxygen problems. A man could pass out in a few minutes without oxygen and could die in less than twenty minutes.

"Check," Mario said.

"Waist?"

"Check," Harry said.

"Ball?"

"Check," Al said from the ball turret, which hung like an udder below *Flossie's* fuselage. "But it's right cold. Could you send some heat down here?"

A black burst at one o'clock low rocked the plane, and Walt steadied her. Shrapnel pinged the underside of the fuselage. The Germans really did want to kill them. Well, of course they did. But this was the real thing. This was war.

Al cussed. "That's not the kind of heat I meant."

Walt laughed, muffled in his mask. Felt good, took the edge off. "Okay, men. Fun's over. Intercom discipline, please. Keep your eyes peeled for fighters."

The flak lessened past the coast, still no sign of the Luft-waffe, and the group appeared intact. Overacker dropped from the lead, number two engine down, its propeller blades feathered—turned parallel to the wind to lessen drag.

"We're at the IP," Louis said from the navigator's desk in the nose.

The Initial Point, start of the bomb run. "Okay, Abe, aim for that pickle barrel."

Abe and Walt worked together on the bomb run. The Norden bombsight was connected to the Pilot's Directional Indicator on Walt's instrument panel. As Abe lined up the target, the PDI showed Walt how to maneuver the plane. He was glad the Eighth Air Force didn't use the Automatic Flight Control Equipment, which allowed the bombardier to fly the aircraft through the autopilot. Walt wanted to control his own plane.

Flak picked up again when they neared Lille. Walt sensed his grip on the wheel was too tight. He relaxed his hold to keep his feel of the plane.

"Okay," Abe said. "I've got it. Take that, Hitler. Bombs—"

An explosion overrode the thunder of engines. The left wing lifted, and Walt fought to right *Flossie*. "Any damage?" The gauges for engines one and two looked fine.

"Clear." J.P. stood on a platform in the back of the cockpit, his head in the Plexiglas top turret.

"Clear," Harry said from the waist.

"Looks okay. Some dings," Al said from the ball turret. Only he could see under the wing.

Too close. Walt felt sweat on his upper lip, or was it condensation from the oxygen mask? He peeled off the target with his squadron and increased airspeed.

"We missed," Mario said from the tail. "Our bombs fell too far north."

Walt sighed. The flak burst must have thrown off the aim at bomb release.

"Uh-oh." J.P. spun his turret around. "Fighters. Three of them. Two o'clock high."

"I see 'em," Harry said.

"A little closer, and I can get them," Abe said, his bombsight exchanged for the right nose gun.

Walt watched with dread and fascination. The famous Luftwaffe swooped down in Focke-Wulf 190s, among the finest fighter planes in the world. Long, yellow noses identified them as Goering's best "Abbeville Kids," named after their home airfield in France.

White flashes zipped toward Walt. Three of *Flossie*'s machine guns opened up. The cockpit filled with the cough of J.P.'s gun and the clatter of bullet casings on the metal floor. The Fw 190s rolled to their left, following their prop torque. Walt nudged the wheel slightly left to evade.

Cracker yanked his wheel. *Flossie* careened to the left. J.P. cried out. Walt heard a crack and a thud behind him.

They were going to collide with *My Eileen*. Walt tugged

his wheel right to counteract Cracker. "What are you doing?"

"Evasive maneuvers."

"Not like that! Not in formation." He glanced over his left shoulder. No sign of Frank. "Mario, where's *My Eileen*?"

"She's out of formation," Mario said. "Turned to avoid us—just missed—caught our propwash, fell back."

Out of formation. Most dangerous place to be. Sitting duck for the Luftwaffe. "Come on, Frank. Get back in formation."

"She's coming back," Mario said.

"Hey, what do you think you're doing up there, Preach?" Harry said. "Had those Krauts in my sights till you knocked me down."

"Our copilot's idea of evasion." He looked behind him. J.P. sat on the turret platform, forehead in his hands. Blood oozed between his gloved fingers. "J.P.! You hit?"

"No. Cracked my head when I fell. I'm okay."

"One bogie at five o'clock low," Mario said.

Walt fixed a glare on Cracker. "Keep your hands off that wheel."

"You'll get us all killed, you—"

The words he used burned Walt's ears. "Hands off. That's an order."

Sharp pops under the fuselage. "I got him," Mario cried. "I got him. Smoke off his engine."

"Ah! I'm hit! I'm hit! Blood! Blood all over."

Al in the ball turret. Walt craned his neck, though he couldn't possibly see anything. "Harry, get him out of there."

The fighters left to pick on another squadron. Walt worked the wheel between his fingers as if he were milking a cow. "Come on, Harry. Get him out."

"I got him." Harry swore, and Al screamed. "A lot of blood.

Can't find the wound. Where were you hit, Worley? Come on, show me."

"I've got the first aid kit. I'll go back, give him some morphine," Bill said from the radio room. "Oh no. The syringe—it's frozen."

Lord God in heaven, help him. We're still an hour from base.

"Um, Preach? We found the wound," Harry said, laughter in the background.

Laughter?

"Al wasn't hit. A hydraulic line in the ball turret was. The red liquid isn't blood—it's hydraulic fluid."

Laughter had never felt so good, never in his life, not even with Allie. He couldn't wait to tell her this story.

When they landed at Thurleigh, Walt and Sergeant Reilly inspected the plane and finished Form 1A. Other than the broken hydraulic line and a few dings, *Flossie* looked great. Only Cracker dimmed Walt's mood.

A sick feeling churned his stomach as he watched the co-pilot swagger around, slapping backs and ruffling hair. During debriefing, he'd have to report Cracker's poor judgment and insubordination. At this rate Cracker would never exchange his gold second lieutenant's bars for silver first lieutenant's bars as Walt had. But he couldn't leave Cracker's discipline to the squadron commander. No. To prove his leadership to the brass, to the crew, and to Cracker, he'd have to confront the man, and now.

The crew stood on *Flossie*'s right, shrugging off flight gear and recounting the mission in loud voices to the ground crew. Walt caught Cracker's eye and motioned him over in front of the left wing.

Walt ran his hand down the smooth edge of a propeller on engine one. "I've put this off too long. It's time we had a talk."

"In private, huh?" Cracker peeled off his flight helmet and smoothed his blond hair. "I don't appreciate this. When you chewed me out, you did it in front of the men, but when it's time for you to eat crow, you want to do it in private."

Walt gripped the propeller tip so hard he was amazed it didn't snap off. The man's pride knew no end. "I'm not eating any crow."

"You're not? Well, then, you're wasting my time. I've got logs to fill out." He looked over Walt's head and moved to step around him.

Walt raised an arm to block him. "This is the problem—your arrogance and your incompetence. I can't decide which is more dangerous."

"Incompetence?" Cracker jutted his chin out. "I saved your tail today."

"Saved?" Walt moved closer. It'd feel good to put a fist in that smirking face, but that wasn't how officers solved problems. "You think you saved my life? That's the arrogance I'm talking about. You almost got us killed—twice now. That's plain incompetence. You don't know the ship, you don't know her limits, and you don't know the regulations."

"Regulations?" Cracker's chin stuck out more, right in Walt's face. "Regulations are for cowards who can't think on their feet."

For the first time in years, Walt itched for a fight, but he wouldn't give Cracker the satisfaction. "Regulations are common sense. You don't make evasive maneuvers—"

"You're just afraid to admit my actions—not yours—saved the day." He jabbed Walt in the chest. "You're afraid to admit I'm the better leader."

"Arrogant, incompetent, and deluded." Walt thrust a finger in Cracker's face. "Like it or not, I'm in charge. I'm responsible for the success of our mission, for the safety of the plane, and for the lives of these men. I will not let you interfere. Now, this is an order. You do your job, you stay out of my way, and don't you ever show up with a hangover again or—I don't care who your family is—I'll—"

Footsteps thumped beside him.

"You want to kill me, Novak? Do it man to man." Frank stormed up and shoved him.

He stumbled to the side. "Whoa, buddy, not what you think." He gestured to Cracker, who snickered and sauntered toward a truck.

"I swear. That jerk." Frank ran over and spun Cracker around. "What on earth do you think you're doing? Nine men on my plane. I've got a wife and four kids at home. No room in this squadron for idiots like you."

"Hey, back off!" Cracker pushed him away.

Frank threw a wild punch, and Walt grabbed Frank's arms from behind. As much as he'd love to see Cracker beaten to a pulp, he didn't want Frank to get in trouble. "Come on, he's not worth it."

"I'd like to break that pretty-boy nose." Frank strained against Walt, his face redder than his hair. "You'd better apologize."

"Apologize? You're crazy."

Walt grunted and tightened his grip on Frank's flailing arms. Already a crowd was gathering, rooting for a fight. "Apologize, Cracker. You owe him."

"You're both crazy. We didn't get shot up, did we? Thanks to me." Cracker shouldered his way out of the crowd.

If Walt hadn't been occupied with Frank, he would have given in and thrown a punch of his own. "Arrogant fool."

"You said it," Louis said, his face set hard.

Abe nodded. "Yeah. You make a mistake, you own up to it."

Finally, everyone saw Cracker for who he was, but it didn't feel as good as expected to see him overthrown—not when his blunder could have cost eighteen lives.

Frank's arms went limp in Walt's hands. "My dad turned to drink after the last war. Now I know why."

21

Riverside

November 7, 1942

Allie stepped off the bus and hugged herself against the chill. An older couple at the bus stop gave her an appreciative smile. Allie smiled back, proud of her Red Cross uniform—a gray dress with white collar and cuffs, and a white cap with a gray veil in the back. It represented Clara Barton tending the wounded on Civil War battlefields, decades of wartime aid and disaster relief, and Allie's own small sacrifice.

She hurried down a street in an undesirable part of town. Twilight had fallen, and no light issued from street lamps or windows. If it did, a Civil Defense warden would pounce on the perpetrator. The CD had been stricter than ever since Japanese planes dropped incendiary bombs in the Oregon forest twice in September.

Allie squinted at house numbers and frowned at her own pride. Could she even call her work a sacrifice? She read to the men, helped them write letters, served coffee, and played the piano in the recreation room. She never broke a sweat or dirtied her hands, much less placed herself in mortal danger like Walt, Jim Carlisle, or Louise Morgan's husband, Larry.

The closest she'd come to danger was in her dreams. Twice she'd dreamed of Walt flying under fire. She'd written him about the first dream and regretted it as soon as the envelope tipped down into the mailbox. How improper to tell a man she dreamed about him.

Allie stopped. Cressie's house had to be the tiniest bungalow she had seen, probably a living room and kitchen, one bedroom and a bath. Even in the dusk, she could see the house was yellow—not subtle, but sulfurous.

What would the ladies from St. Timothy's think to see Mary Miller's daughter enter such a house? She laughed and knocked on the door. They'd never see her, because they'd never set a well-shod foot in such a neighborhood.

"Allie? Is that you? Come in, love."

She gasped. Women packed Cressie's miniature living room—Cressie, Daisy, Opal Morris, Mabel Weber—why, the entire Ladies' Circle.

"Surprise! Happy birthday!"

Happy birthday? Tears welled in her eyes. She clapped her hand to her chest and felt the cross from Walt. Two surprises for her birthday. Walt's gift arrived a week before, but for the life of her, Allie couldn't remember mentioning her birthday to him.

Cressie crushed Allie in a hug, and then pulled back and clucked her tongue at her. "You'd have thought someone died by the look of those tears."

She sniffed them back. "Oh my. Thank you, everyone. Thank you, Cressie."

Cressie turned for the kitchen and flipped her hand over her shoulder. "Daisy's idea, love. Daisy's idea. We all put in a bit of butter and sugar for the cake."

Allie turned to Daisy, whose brown pompadour defied gravity. "Oh, I don't need a cake."

"Sure you do. You made me sad ranting to your mom about not getting one."

Allie's stomach knotted at the memory of the scene she'd made—in front of Daisy, no less.

"Ooh, is that new?" Daisy took the cross in her hands. "Sure is pretty."

"Isn't it? My friend Walt sent it from England."

"What'd Baxter get you?"

"Earrings." She smiled, relieved at what she *hadn't* found in the jeweler's box.

Daisy's forehead puckered, and her gaze bounced between Allie's bare earlobes.

"He bought the wrong kind. I don't have pierced ears."

"Didn't even notice." Daisy rolled her eyes. "Just like a man."

Allie didn't want to be critical, but somehow Walt noticed she didn't own a cross, while Baxter failed to notice her ears weren't pierced.

Cressie returned with a white cake and had Allie sit in the seat of honor, where the upholstery sported giant red and orange roosters strutting on a turquoise background. A spring poked her thigh. She crossed her ankles to relieve the pressure and set her elbow on a doily on the armrest. A purple doily. Where had Cressie purchased such thread, and why?

Yet the confidence that allowed Cressie to use purple doilies appealed to Allie. Cressie never fretted about appearances and propriety and what people thought—only what the Lord thought.

At least Cressie had better taste in her baking. The cake was almost as sweet as the friendships that produced it.

Cressie refilled the ladies' teacups. "I apologize for not having coffee. I love you, Allie, but not enough to give up my coffee."

Allie laughed. Since coffee was scarce, rationing was scheduled to start November 29 and would provide less than a cup a day. Everyone grumbled, but Allie didn't mind tea.

Tea. Did Walt drink British tea and eat genuine British fish and chips? Had he been to London to see Big Ben and the Tower and Buckingham Palace?

Much too soon, the ladies rose to leave. Allie lingered to thank her hostess again. While she waited for the others to depart, she studied a photograph on the wall. A handsome young man in a dark suit gazed down at a young lady in a white shirtwaist and long, slim skirt. Allie drew in her breath. Cressie hadn't been plain; she'd been ugly—coarse features, a broad mouth and crooked nose, and thick black eyebrows. Age had been kind to her. Extra pounds softened her features, and gray hair reduced the effect of the eyebrows. Yet her husband adored her—in the photograph and now, some forty years later.

"I love that picture," Cressie said. "Doesn't Bert look smitten?"

"That's what I noticed. Was this taken when you were engaged?"

Cressie snorted. "Couldn't have been. We married out of necessity—oh, not like young people do nowadays. You see, Bert was orphaned at eighteen. He had five little sisters to care for, a house to mind, and a business to run. He needed a wife, and fast, and I was the only marriageable girl in our Kansas town."

An ember of hope lit in Allie's chest. "Your love grew after you married?"

"Yep. I went to a revival meeting and met Jesus Christ. Imagine that, the daughter of the choir director had never let the truth sink through her thick skull. Well, Bert fell head over heels with the new Cressie."

Allie stroked the polished wood frame. "Was he—was he a believer?"

"Nope. Stubborn young fool. But after a very long year, God got ahold of Bert and wouldn't let go. That's when I fell for him."

Allie recited the verse she'd promised herself to find and memorize, "As the Bible says in 1 Peter 3: 'Likewise, ye wives, be in subjection to your own husbands; that, if any obey not the word, they also may without the word be won by the conversation of the wives; While they behold your chaste conversation coupled with fear.'"

Cressie was silent. Allie tucked her pocketbook under her arm and reached for the doorknob.

"That's a strange verse to memorize," Cressie said.

"I like it. Isn't it—" Allie turned back to Cressie and rolled the doorknob in her hand. "Isn't it encouraging? Hopeful?"

Cressie's little blue eyes narrowed, almost lost in her cheeks. "Your young man—I thought he was a brother in Christ. He isn't?"

Allie winced. Why had she let that slip?

"That verse—read it again. Peter's talking to married women, to wives who come to Christ after marriage, like I did, not to unmarried women."

Allie tilted her head. What was the difference?

Cressie looked up to the ceiling and drummed her fingers on her thigh. "Where's that other passage? Corinthians? Yes, 1 Corinthians 6—pretty near certain."

"I'll read it." She put on her grateful guest smile and hugged Cressie. "Thanks again. It was a lovely party."

"You deserve it, love. You deserve it." Cressie almost smothered Allie in her soft shoulder. "You're a special girl."

She pulled back and smiled. "You're special to me too. You're one of my favorite people in the world."

"One of?" Cressie leveled a glare at her. "Who's my competition?"

Allie laughed. "Betty, of course." The person who introduced her to Christ, to friendship, and to fun. "And Walter." The person who understood her, forgave her, and encouraged her.

Cressie released a rueful sigh. "Should've known. The way you talk about those two."

22

Thurleigh

November 13, 1942

Wait till the folks back home heard he got to see King George VI.

Walt pedaled a bicycle down the road heading west from the living sites, past a flurry of bikes and men. Not only was the king visiting, but also the top Eighth Air Force brass—Generals Carl Spaatz, Ira Eaker, and Newton Longfellow.

Walt passed through the technical site, the complex of workshops and administrative buildings, dominated by four massive hangars in camouflage paint. He swerved around a pothole in front of HQ. The weather that had grounded the 306th for a month had turned the base into a muddy pit. He had to change into dress uniform before the visit, but the less laundry he had to do, the better.

"Hiya, Preach."

"Hi there." He let go of the handlebar and waved to Frank's copilot.

"You're going the wrong way," Petrovich called. "Gotta shine those shoes."

"Later. I want to check out *Flossie* first."

"Yeah? While you're over there, check out *Pearl*."

He gave a salute, but he had no intention of doing so. The nose art on *String of Pearls* showed the rearview of a blonde lying on her side, smiling over her shoulder, wearing nothing but high heels and her namesake jewelry. It annoyed him. He liked that song. He'd danced with Allie to that song.

When he reached the control tower, he turned left onto the perimeter track. Thirty-six hardstands for bombers stuck off the perimeter track like leaves on a vine.

"Preach?" Bob Robertson, *Pearl*'s pilot, ran toward him. "I need a word with you."

From his tone, Walt knew it wasn't a friendly word. He swung off the bike. "What's up?"

"You behind this? How could you do this to *Pearl*?"

"*Pearl?*"

"Don't play innocent. Look!" Bob grabbed Walt's arm in his meaty grip.

He shook him off and let the bike clatter to the ground. "Let go. I'm coming."

A dozen men surrounded the Fort, pointing and arguing. For once, Walt could look at the nose art, because the woman was clothed. She now wore a flight jacket, which covered her backside and slouched off one shoulder to show off her pearls.

He blinked. Wow. That looked good.

"You did this, Preach. I know it," Bob said.

"Nah, I'm no artist."

"He's lying," someone said. "I've seen him carve."

"Yeah, technical stuff—planes. I'm an engineer, not an artist." But he knew someone who was, someone with experience painting flight jackets.

"You know," one man said. "I think she looks better, more alluring."

Catcalls.

"You're kidding."

"Are you blind?"

"No, Joe's right. Makes you curious, makes you want to see her goods."

"But we could already see her goods."

Bob squinted at his plane. "You know, Joe may have a point."

Since he was off the hook, Walt left the men to their debate. He mounted his bike and made his way to *Flossie's* hardstand, one of several tucked around Whitwickgreen Farm. He'd never seen civilians and livestock and crops at a U.S. airfield, but the British needed farmland as much as they needed air bases.

Flossie looked great. The ground crew had done a good repair job. After the month of bad weather, Walt flew three missions in a row. On November 7, the 306th flew to Brest and bombed the U-boat facility with no casualties or damage—a "milk run." Then they returned to Lille and lost one B-17. But the next day some idiot at Bomber Command ordered them to bomb St. Nazaire's U-boat pens at the low altitude of 7,500 feet. The flak couldn't miss, and three planes fell.

Most of the men got rip-roaring drunk that night.

Flossie's Fort took minimal damage. Her crew insisted the cow and the Scripture reading gave them good luck. Walt hated to see them rely on superstitions and rituals, but at least the crew was working as a unit. Cracker was still useless in the cockpit, but his star had dimmed with the men, and he knew well enough to lie low.

Walt coasted the bike up to his plane. J.P. Sanchez stood on a scaffold and painted over the metalworkers' patches on his artwork. Pete Wisniewski, the right waist gunner, waved at Walt. The first mission proved one waist gunner wasn't enough, and new gunners were recruited from around the base. Pete, a big, yellow-haired kid, had come to Thurleigh as a medic.

Walt planted his feet and leaned on the handlebars. "There's a ruckus with *Pearl*'s crew."

"Is that right?" J.P. dabbed black paint on a verse printed below the cow: "The Lord is my rock, and my fortress, and my deliverer; my God, my strength, in whom I will trust."

"Seems someone painted a flight jacket on the lady," Walt said.

"Defacement of government property? *Sí, sí, señor.* Blame the wetback."

Walt chuckled. "I'd say it's improvement of government property."

"You know, the king's coming. Can't have him look at naked ladies."

Pete nodded. "At twenty thousand feet I get icicles on my eyebrows."

Walt laughed. "So we wear leather and sheepskin, but Pearl . . ."

J.P. shrugged and dipped his brush in the paint. "She looked cold."

★

"Look. Eleanor Roosevelt promised warmer socks and faster mail when she visited London last month, and she came through." Frank waved a letter in Walt's face. "Only two weeks old."

Walt sorted his pile of mail. "Now for those socks."

"I'll settle for mail. Warms my heart, don't care about my toes."

Walt sat on his cot in the Nissen hut, the half-cylinder of

corrugated steel that thirty-two officers called home. He had letters from Mom and Dad, one from Ray in Texas, a really old one from Jim Carlisle in the Pacific, and two from Allie. Also a package from Allie, big and heavy. What did she do? Chop up the B-17 model and mail it back?

Frank knotted his tie. "You don't have time."

"Just the package. Won't take long." Walt cut the string with his pocketknife and lifted the lid. Sheet music and a note:

> Yesterday I bought more music to play for the patients at the hospital, and I remembered you mentioned a piano in the Officers' Club and a shortage of sheet music. I hope you can use this. "Tangerine" reminded me of how you gave away your orange on the train. What could be more appropriate for you than a song about a girl named after fruit?
>
> I also hope you'll enjoy the applesauce. Baxter says it's a good batch.

Applesauce! Walt flung aside wads of newspaper and found a glass jar—no, two jars, quart jars.

"Applesauce?" Frank said. "First the peach jam, and now this. That girl's mad about you."

If only it were true. He smiled though. Frank's comment was intended for the other men. He was a great accomplice, as was Allie—although unwittingly.

"Preach got applesauce from his girl," Abe Ruben said. "Who's got spoons?"

He clutched the jars to his chest. "Get away, all of you. Mine, all mine."

Frank set his cap on. "We know. Don't get between this man and his fruit."

"Come on, you know I'll share." He held up a jar. Flecks of pulp and cinnamon clung to the glass. He swallowed. Sure looked good. Baxter said it was good.

Baxter knew what a wonderful woman he had, didn't he? Of course, he knew.

So why . . . ?

Walt huffed and took off his leather jacket to change into dress uniform. He'd wasted too much time stewing over Allie and Baxter. If she loved him, why hadn't she talked about him that week? If he loved her, why had Allie seemed so receptive to Walt, so unfamiliar with attention and compliments and all that? Why didn't he go to church with her? And what about those pecks? How could he not want to kiss her? Didn't make sense.

"What's this?" Frank picked up the sheet music. "'Tangerine'?"

"A joke. Allie thinks I should have a girl named after fruit."

Frank laughed. "Sounds about right."

Walt buttoned up his jacket, the same one he'd worn at the wedding reception, the same sleeves that had circled Allie's waist. He'd rather have a girl named after music.

23

Thurleigh

November 23, 1942

"I got him," Mario Tagliaferro said. "Two hundred yards. Broke apart."

"Yeah, Tagger got him. Saw his chute." Al Worley drained his slug of whiskey.

Mario rolled his shot glass between his hands. "Fw 190s everywhere."

"Everywhere." Cracker's hands shook as he lit another cigarette. "*Pearl* didn't stand a chance. They pounced on her, picked her out."

"I counted six chutes," Pete Wisniewski said.

"Seven," Al said.

"Slow down, everyone. One at a time." The intelligence officer gestured with his pencil at *Flossie*'s crew seated around a table in the briefing room. He pointed at Walt. "You said the Luftwaffe attacked head-on?"

"Yep. Never seen that before. Crazy, isn't it?" Crazy wasn't a strong enough word. Walt still couldn't shake the shock, the terror of fighters rushing straight at him. The closing speed had to be close to six hundred miles per hour. Walt sketched a B-17 nose in his logbook and racked his brain for a solution.

Louis tipped up his shot glass, but it was dry. "They know. They know we're weak up front. The .30s in the nose—the range is too short, can't reach 'em."

Abe rocked back and forth in his chair, hands deep in his jacket pockets. "The nose guns—they angle too far to the side. Can't train them to twelve o'clock."

Walt sketched a .50 in the nose, straight out front. But how could it be braced? The Norden bombsight was right underneath.

"That's how they got *Pearl*." Cracker took a drag on his cigarette. "Head-on. Shot up the nose, killed the pilots."

"How do you know?" the intelligence officer asked.

"The blood on the cockpit windows." Cracker banged his fist on the table. "Do you think I'm blind?"

"Calm down," Walt said. "You know they have to make sure. Next of kin."

"They're dead. We're all dead. The Jerries have it out for us. The 306th has lost seven planes. Seven! We're all dead men."

The intelligence officer poured Cracker another shot, which he gulped down.

Walt shook his head and drew braces straddling the bombsight. Whiskey wouldn't help. Yeah, tonight Cracker would get a good drunk on, but when he sobered, the pain and anxiety would come right back.

The Germans did seem to have it out for the 306th. They had the highest losses in the Eighth Air Force. Granted, they were now the grizzled veterans. The other bomb groups transferred to the Twelfth Air Force in North Africa after the U.S. invaded on November 8. The 91st, 303rd, and 305th Bomb Groups had arrived with B-17s, and the 44th with B-24s, but no one got picked on like the boys from Thurleigh. They could only muster eight planes today, and four aborted with mechanical problems. The fewer planes, the more vulnerable they were to Goering's men.

"Tell me about the flak," the intelligence officer said.

"Flak?" Al drummed his shot glass on the table. "Saint Nazaire's flak city."

The door to the briefing room opened. Walt sighed in relief. Frank made it back to base. *My Eileen* had straggled at the French coast, one engine feathered.

Frank's men sat around the empty table at Walt's right. Another intelligence officer would interrogate them as a crew. Walt counted six men. Who was missing? Petrovich, the co-pilot; Willard and Russo in the nose; Thompson, the flight engineer. Oh no. Were they killed? Wounded?

Frank's face was rigid, and his hands lay like wood in his lap. He stared at the table, at the shot glass in front of him.

Walt's chest tightened. Frank never drank. He'd seen how alcohol destroyed his father after the First World War—seduced him with forgetfulness, stripped him of dignity and ambition, and burdened his family with a drunkard husband and father.

Frank groped for the glass.

"Frank," Walt said.

He couldn't have heard over the noise in the room, but he looked up. The expression in his eyes socked Walt in the stomach—empty, haggard, despairing.

Walt shook his head slowly.

Frank's face collapsed in a grimace. He shoved the drink away with the back of his hand and splashed amber liquid onto the table.

Cracker was right. They were all dead men. With seven

planes down in less than two months of combat and no end to the war in sight, it didn't take a mathematician to calculate the odds of survival. Walt wasn't bothered much. He knew where he'd spend eternity. Sure, his family and friends would mourn, but unlike Frank he didn't have a wife and kids who loved him and depended on him.

For the first time, he was glad things hadn't worked out with Allie. What if they'd fallen in love, and then he'd been killed? No, this was better. He couldn't stand for her to be devastated.

Flossie's crew was dismissed for the mess hall. After dinner the enlisted men would go to the Red Cross Aeroclub. If Frank was okay, he and Walt would go to the Officers' Club to play chess, read magazines, and maybe play some tunes on the piano. At some point, one of the men would stand on two other men's shoulders and use a cigarette lighter to burn the mission into the ceiling: "11-23-42 St. Nazaire."

Mission number nine. If Walt survived one more, he'd get an Oak Leaf Cluster for the Air Medal he earned after the fifth mission.

Louis held the door open for Walt. "Coming with us or waiting for Kilpatrick?"

"Waiting." He leaned back against the building's brick wall.

"I'll save seats for y'all. I guess the other four . . ."

"Yeah. We'll find out."

Walt opened his Bible, retrieved from intelligence, and a chilly breeze lifted the pages. The psalms came alive to him as never before. Now he understood how enemies attacked, pursued, hurled spears and arrows and bullets and shells at you, wanted you dead.

What was it like to live like that all the time? For the Marines slogging through the jungle on Guadalcanal? For the soldiers racing tanks across the Sahara? For the sailors like Jim Carlisle never knowing when a sub or plane could send you into the drink? Walt's war was strange, civilized. Three square meals, cots and showers, a cozy Officers' Club—then adrenaline-charged missions with hours of action and danger.

The door opened, *My Eileen's* crew filed out, and Frank sent his men off to the mess.

"Hungry?" Walt asked.

Frank faced him, his eyes still empty. "Can't eat. I don't know. I don't know what I want. Go to bed and sleep for days? Walk and walk and never come back?"

Walt didn't know what to say. That's why he was the only Novak brother not in the ministry.

"Gotta walk. Yeah, walk." Frank strode down the road toward the living sites.

Walt's stomach gurgled. Oh well. He had a Hershey bar by his cot. It'd have to do tonight.

Frank walked in silence, hands in trouser pockets. They passed a cluster of Nissen huts, like giant tin cans half-buried in the ground, then a clump of trees under the clear sky, then the communal site with the mess halls. Walt's stomach rumbled. They always had great food after missions. Did he smell steak? Oh, swell.

Frank turned south down a path that ran behind the living sites to the village of Thurleigh. Never—never had he been silent so long.

"His head," Frank choked out. "Petrovich. The right—the whole right side of his head—gone. They shot it off. They killed Petrovich."

Walt's stomach turned, hunger forgotten. John Petrovich was a nice guy, always wisecracking about the food, quick with a practical joke, first to sing when Walt sat at the piano.

Now he was gone, and Frank saw it, saw his copilot die, saw the blood.

Dear God, no.

"Willard?" Walt swallowed to moisten his dry mouth. "Russo? Thompson?"

"Wounded. Willard's in bad shape. His leg—he'll probably lose his leg." Frank's breath came out in hard puffs. "What am I doing here? What on earth am I doing here?"

"I—I don't know." He clutched his Bible tighter. "Maybe you should look into a transfer."

Frank stopped under a tree that clung to its last withered leaves. "A transfer? You're kidding."

"I'm serious." Walt poked the hedge along the road with his toe. "This is a voluntary service, you know that. You can transfer to ops, intelligence, no questions asked. Remember?"

"Yeah? So why hasn't anyone done it? Not one man. I tell you why—they're not chicken, and neither am I."

"Of course not. But how many of us are married? Not many. Even fewer are fathers, much less fathers of four. No one would call you chicken."

"I would."

"Swell. You're a hero. How are you going to get through this, huh? Turn to drink like your dad?"

Frank thrust a finger in Walt's face. "I didn't do it, Novak, and you leave my dad out of this."

He knew he should keep his mouth shut. "What about Eileen?"

Frank's hand folded into a fist.

Walt was going to get a black eye, but he stood his ground. "What about Eileen? What about your kids?"

"What do you know?" Frank's fist trembled, a pink blur in front of Walt's eyes. "You had to make up a girlfriend."

A bloody nose would have been better than that, but he

refused to stand down. "Yeah, so I've got nothing to lose. Unlike you."

Frank scrunched his eyes shut and pressed his fist down on Walt's shoulder.

"Come on, buddy. Leave the air war to us single guys."

24

Riverside

December 12, 1942

"Hiya, Miss Miller. Over here. I get her first, boys." Lieutenant Patterson rolled onto his side in bed and pushed up onto his remaining elbow.

"Good morning. Would you like me to write a letter for you?" Allie sat in the chair next to his bed and stifled a yawn. Last night she'd awakened again, compelled to pray for Walt.

"Nope. Doc says I've got to write left-handed. I just want to lose myself in those pretty eyes."

When Allie first started at March Field, the men's flirting bewildered her. Now she knew they flirted with anyone in a skirt, regardless of age or beauty. She smiled and got to her feet. "If you only desire my company, come join us in the rec room after lunch, but meanwhile—"

"That's not all I desire." Lieutenant Patterson waggled his eyebrows at her.

Heat rushed up her neck. Why, oh why, must she blush? And when would she learn not to use words like *desire* around the men? She turned and crossed the aisle. "Good morning, Lieutenant Duncan. Where did we leave off yesterday?"

"Hello." Lieutenant Duncan looked up at Allie through the holes in his bandages. "Second Corinthians. I think we finished chapter 5."

She settled in a chair and exchanged her clipboard for a Bible. The fire in the cockpit of Lieutenant Duncan's fighter plane had scorched his hands and face but had kindled a deeper love for God's Word.

Allie flipped to 2 Corinthians. A few weeks before, she and Lieutenant Duncan read the chapter Cressie recommended. What was Cressie thinking? All that talk about harlots and fornication? Why, Baxter might not be a believer, but he could hardly be compared to a harlot, and they would be getting married, not . . .

She shuddered and started to read. Occasionally Lieutenant Duncan stopped her, asked her to repeat a verse, and said it to himself.

She turned a page and continued at the fourteenth verse: "'Be ye not unequally yoked together with unbelievers—'"

Second Corinthians, chapter 6. That's what Cressie meant. There it was in brutal black and white.

"Miss Miller?"

She forced herself to respond. "Yes?"

"I have this section memorized." He spoke slowly, his face stiffened by scars. "'Be ye not unequally yoked together with unbelievers: for what fellowship hath righteousness with unrighteousness? And what communion hath light with darkness? And what—'"

"Why?" She cleared her throat, unable to break away from the text. "May I ask why you memorized these verses?"

Lieutenant Duncan chuckled. "My mother made me. The first girl I brought home only attended church for holidays, weddings, and funerals. Mother thrust my nose in this passage and wouldn't let me date again until I memorized it and took it to heart."

"Did you?"

"Of course. I'd rather have a wife who loves the Lord than one who belongs on a magazine. I hope—I hope I can find—" His eyes squeezed shut.

Allie swerved from her predicament to his. She'd seen his portrait. Before his accident, he had been a handsome man. "I know—I know someone will see past the scars."

"Well, if it isn't Allie Miller, ball bearings heiress." A nurse stood behind Allie, her arms crossed over her white uniform. She looked familiar—a gorgeous brunette with a smirk. "Josie Black, Riverside High School. Josie Black *Cummings* now. But you wouldn't remember me. You always thought you were too good for the rest of us."

Allie's mouth fell open. Josie and her popular crowd had looked down at *her*, but this was hardly the place for an argument. "I—I assure you I never thought any such thing. Now, may I help you?"

"Yes, you may," Josie said with a tilt of her head. "Isn't this interesting? Your daddy bosses my father and my husband all day on the line, but I get to boss you."

Although Allie reported to Regina, not the nurses, in the interest of peace she stood and placed the Bible on the nightstand. "Pardon me, Lieutenant Duncan. We'll finish later. Now, how may I help, Lieutenant Cummings?"

Her smile didn't even approach her eyes. "We're short staffed today, and the bedpans need to be scrubbed."

Allie swallowed a mouthful of pride and disgust. "I'm here to help."

"Good." Josie flounced down the aisle. "Imagine Allie Miller scrubbing bedpans. You'll have to take off your fancy jewelry first." She stopped and glanced at Allie's hands. "Oh, no ring. Still not married?"

"Not for long. My boyfriend and I will be married soon."

"Oh? Someone from high school?"

"No. Baxter Hicks, the business manager at Miller Ball Bearings. Perhaps you've heard mention of him."

Josie's eyes widened. "Um, yes."

Allie had the upper hand, but guilt from resorting to snobbery eradicated her enjoyment. "I'm here to help. Where are those bedpans?"

Alarm flashed across Josie's face, but she matched Allie's smile and led her to a workroom where a stack of enameled bedpans sat by a stainless steel sink. "Here you go. Soap, disinfectant, scrub brush."

Allie unbuttoned her cuffs and rolled up her sleeves. She refused to pucker her nose at the smell and give Josie the satisfaction. At least the bedpans had been emptied.

Josie leaned against the wall. "So Mr. Hicks has a girl-friend."

Allie put a bedpan in the sink and turned on the water. If they were short staffed, why was Josie still there? "Yes. We've been seeing each other for five years."

"Five years? Oh my. Well, I'm glad to hear it. What a relief."

"A relief?"

"Well, yes. I'm sure you've heard the rumors. Don't you hate hearing such nasty things about people? I'm so glad it isn't true." Josie's eyes stretched too wide.

Allie rinsed the bedpan and let it fill with water, as a chill twined about her. Josie's bait hung within reach—the juicy bait of gossip—and Allie knew it was best to ignore it, but . . . "What—what rumors?"

"Oh, you've heard. The men at the plant don't even think it's rumor; they think it's fact. You know how Mr. Hicks walks, how he watches the men, how chummy he is with Mr.—well, your father, but I'm sure that's ambition rather than . . . well, you know."

"No. No, I don't know." Allie gave the soapbox a vigorous shake.

Josie leaned closer, no longer pretty at all. "Don't you know everyone says he's . . . well, homosexual?"

"What?" Allie snapped up to her full height.

Josie pressed her lips together, a laugh in her eyes. "You don't know what that means, do you?"

"I know what that means, and I assure you, Mr. Hicks is most definitely not—not what you say." Now was the time for snobbery. She lifted her chin high enough to actually look down her nose at Josie. "My father will be most upset to learn such vicious rumors fester in his factory."

Josie's face pulled into several expressions, none of them attractive. "I—I'll leave you to your work."

"That would be wise," Allie said in her most regal air.

After Josie left, Allie plunged the brush into the suds and tried to scrub away the thought, but the gossip stained her mind with doubt.

Was that why Baxter never looked at her with interest? Why he never really kissed her? Why he didn't love her?

No, it couldn't be. Besides, if he really were what Josie said, he wouldn't have a girlfriend, much less entertain the thought of marriage.

Flats and sharps collided, as if a child pounded on a piano in her head. What if Baxter was using her—not only for the inheritance and social position and favor with her parents, but also for respectability, to prove the gossips wrong?

No, it couldn't be. The men on the line simply didn't recognize refined mannerisms and mistook them as effeminate.

So why did her tears dimple the puff of suds in the sink?

Oh Lord, it can't be true. She scrubbed harder. The water swirled up and dampened her sleeves. She didn't care.

She dragged her mind away to the rest of the day. After she finished this task, she would go back to the ward before her afternoon in the recreation room. She'd have time to finish reading with Lieutenant Duncan.

"Be ye not unequally yoked together with unbelievers."

Allie groaned and dumped the water down the drain. *Lord, you know I have to marry Baxter. It's best for everyone, and with that rumor around, it's vital for Baxter's reputation. And remember, I'm doing this for you, to bring him to you.*

She scoured another pan, but harmony eluded her. Why this growing unease? Why this nagging about marrying an unbeliever? Why did she feel her sacrifice wasn't pleasing to the Lord?

"Goodness, Allie, you're drenched."

"I'm fine, Mother." She slouched off her raincoat and hung it on the coatrack in the marble hallway. "I forgot my umbrella."

"Yes, dear." She fingered Allie's dripping hair. "But what about your hood?"

Allie shook her head. She had no answer. She hadn't put up her hood, because the rain felt right, stinging her eyes, matting her hair, washing her mind.

"I hope you aren't coming down with something. That hospital runs you ragged." Mother pursed her lips and patted Allie's cheek. "Go change out of those damp things. Oh, you got some letters today."

"Letters?" She dashed to the hall table and gasped. Lots of letters—one from Betty Anello, one from Louise Morgan, and three from Walt. Three—what a treat. Even though he wrote regularly, his letters arrived in fits and starts.

"Those can wait until after you've changed."

No, they couldn't—not today.

After Allie wrapped her hair in a towel turban, she sat cross-legged on her quilted white satin bedspread and studied the envelopes. This had to be done right, in chronological order, so Walt's came first. She opened the first letter, dated November 13, and admired his precise handwriting.

> Dear Allie,
>
> Curtsey when you read this, because the hand that wrote it shook hands with the King of [censored]. Can you believe it? A small town pastor's kid talked to royalty. I guess the war's not all bad. He called _Flossie's Fort_ a "smashing aeroplane." I hope he doesn't mean she'll end up in pieces.
>
> Mail call is either feast or famine, and today it was feast. Two letters from you and applesauce! Allie, you're the best friend a man could have. All the fellows agreed it was the best applesauce ever, and Baxter is one lucky man. I prefer to say he's blessed. By the way, Frank said if you want to write him, he'd be fine with that. He likes cookies.
>
> We've got four bomb symbols painted on _Flossie's_ nose, one for each mission, and four swastikas. Mario Tagliaferro in the tail earned

three of them. The crew calls him Tagger. I feel
good about what we're doing here. Some of the
missions have been tough, but we've done lots of
damage.

I'm still digesting something in your last
letter—along with the applesauce. You said
you woke up and felt compelled to pray for me.
Allie, that was the day of our first mission. The
middle of the night in California corresponds
with the time [censored]. Do me a favor, and if
you're ever led to pray for me again, please do so.

Allie stared at the letter, warmed by Walt's cheer, struck
by his comment that Baxter was blessed, and stunned that
her dream corresponded with his mission.

What about the other dreams? She crossed the room to
her desk and drew a slip of paper from under the model of
Flossie. Nine dates—ten after she recorded today's. Now she
was glad she had mentioned them to Walt.

She read the next letter, dated the eighteenth, and another
from the twenty-third.

Dear Allie,

We flew a mission today. Did you wake
up again? Tonight I read your letter from
November 9. You said you woke up three nights
in a row—I flew missions all three days. If
we weren't both Christians, I'd mark this as a
coincidence, but there are no coincidences, only
God. I have no doubt the Holy Spirit prompted
you to pray. I'm honored. Lots of people pray for

me in general, but I'm amazed how you pray
for me when I'm in the thick of combat.

Could you include Frank in your prayers?
He's having a rough time. [Censored] He's
taken it hard, of course.

Allie could barely read the rest of the letter. Her dreams, her awakenings, her compulsion to pray—all came from God. Goose bumps ran up her arms like notes up a scale. "Thank you, Lord, for using me like this."

Next, she read Louise's letter, in which she described San Francisco's twenty-fifth air raid alert and her search for roommates. Dear, sweet Louise—so resourceful to take in girls to help pay the rent, so patriotic to relieve the city's housing shortage, and so lonely with her husband deployed to North Africa.

Last came Betty's letter. Betty wrote as she spoke, and her letters always topped six pages whether anything had happened in Antioch or not. Today's letter, however, filled less than a page. Allie frowned and read:

Dear Allie,

Please pray for us. How I wish you were
here. You have always been a comfort to me,
and I've never missed you more than I do now.
Yesterday my sister, Helen, received a telegram.
Jim's destroyer was torpedoed off Guadalcanal a
month ago. Oh, Allie, Jim was killed.

Jim Carlisle? Handsome, charming Jim Carlisle, who teased his sister about her doll, who jitterbugged with his wife, who fussed over his baby son? How could he be dead?

Allie had hardly known him, but her tears left pockmarks on Betty's letter. "Oh, Father in heaven, poor Helen. She's only twenty, Lord, and now she's a widow—a widow with a baby boy. Oh, and baby Jay-Jay won't know his daddy."

Allie couldn't fathom the loss. Her mind careened as she thought of each person now in mourning. Dorothy lost her brother, Betty lost her brother-in-law, Walt and George and Art lost their childhood friend. And Walt—he couldn't know yet. Poor Walt, he was going through enough already. And Mr. and Mrs. Carlisle . . .

Allie sobbed at the thought of the Carlisles' white house with its high hedges of oleander.

A gold star would replace the blue in the Carlisles' banner.

25

Over Paris

December 20, 1942

Walt stole a glance from the instruments, his group's sloppy formation, and the charging Focke-Wulf 190s. Even from twenty thousand feet, he recognized the Eiffel Tower. If he survived, he had something good for his next letters. If not? Well, at least he'd seen Paris before he died.

One hundred eighty miles inland, the Eighth's deepest penetration yet into enemy territory. The air depot at Romilly-sur-Seine was a great target, and the Luftwaffe attacked as if they knew the Americans were headed to their servicing center. Ever since the Spitfires had turned back from escort duties at Rouen, the squadrons of Fw 190s attacked in relays.

With the chatter on the interphone to call out fighters, the stutter of *Flossie*'s guns, and the zing of incoming bullets, a man could go mad, or he could do his job.

Walt did his job. Was he fatalistic? Who cared? He was calm.

Frank, on the other hand . . .

Walt sighed. Frank was a nervous wreck at the briefing and

barely got past the physician screening for combat fatigue. If only Doc had nabbed him. If only Frank would transfer.

Walt looked down through the blur of prop blades to the silver trail of the Seine River. The fighters slacked off—must be flak ahead—but they'd be back, refueled and ready to hassle the remainder of the hundred bombers on the return run.

Sure enough, flak appeared—how could he describe it in his letters?—like dirty black cotton balls. Nah. He'd leave the poetry to his brother Ray.

"We're at the IP," Louis called on the interphone from the nose.

Walt made a thirty-degree turn to start the bomb run and glanced at his watch—1229. They'd been under attack for a solid hour, since about 0330 California time. Was Allie praying again? Was that why he was calm? Something warm filled his chest. He never thought she'd write as much as she did—twice a week now and Walt matched her.

Lots of flak. None near *Flossie*. Walt drew a deep breath and felt light-headed. Yep, the bag on his oxygen mask was icing up. He squeezed it to break up the ice. With the temperature at forty below zero, his fingers were stiff, even with gloves and what passed for a heater in the cockpit. But the waist gunners, with those open windows, had no relief.

"Oxygen check, Cracker. It's been a—"

Black cloud, flaming red center—twelve o'clock low. *Flossie's* nose lifted, and shrapnel hit the windshield like gravel. Walt whipped his head away in reflex. He looked back and leveled the nose. Cracks in the Plexiglas let in frigid darts of air.

"Fontaine? Ruben?"

"We're fine," Abe said. "Got some new ventilation. Coming up on the target."

"They're—they're getting a bead on us." Cracker clenched the wheel.

Walt had to distract him. "Oxygen check?"

"Yeah. Yeah." Cracker nodded too many times and called through the stations—engineer, radio, ball, right waist, left waist, tail. "Tail?" he repeated.

No response from Mario. Walt and Cracker shot each other a look.

"Wisniewski, check on Tagger," Cracker said to the right waist gunner. Pete would have to crawl through the narrow tunnel to the tail turret and drag Mario out.

"On my way. Glad you have a medic on board?"

"Sure am." Walt winced at the draft, like icicles carving up his face.

Another round of flak lifted the right wing, then the left. Too close.

"Pete's got Tagger," Harry called on the interphone from the waist. "He's unconscious. Pete's got him on a portable oxygen bottle, says he'll come around."

"Good. Stay with him." The lead squadron dropped their bombs and peeled away. "Ruben, you got the target yet?"

"No. The bombsight—couple dials damaged in that flak burst. Can't—"

Boom!

Something kicked *Flossie* in the tail. A string of explosions rocked the plane, hurled her down and to the right. Walt's seatbelt cut into his thighs, blood rose to his head. Clunks pounded the left side of the Fort. Walt pulled back on the wheel. Had to stop her, she was going into a spin. "Gotta get the nose up."

"Harder," Cracker said.

The two men braced their feet and pulled the controls, muscles straining. Harder than it should be. Elevators must have been hit on the tail. Rudder too—she slipped to the inside of the turn. Walt eyed the flight indicator on the instrument panel until it was level again. Sweat made his oxygen mask even clammier.

"Navigator? Bombardier?" Cracker ran through the stations again. All okay.

Walt scanned his ship. Still had two wings and four engines, and the gauges looked okay, but the damaged elevators and rudder would make the return home a challenge. Considering the destruction in the tail section, Mario would be glad he'd blacked out. That iced-up oxygen mask saved his life.

Walt guided *Flossie* up into formation. He felt his pulse against his earphones. "What was that?" he asked.

"A—a Fort," Al said from the ball, his voice smaller than his turret. "A Fort. Took a flak burst—in the bomb bay."

Walt and Cracker looked at each other and shook their heads. That explained the series of explosions. The plane still had a full bomb load. There would be nothing left.

His face grew cold, even colder. A B-17. Close. To his left. Behind him.

Frank.

"Who is it?"

Silence.

"Who—is—it?" he asked, voice hard.

"Preach," Harry said. "It's—it's *My Eileen*."

Whacked him in the chest, knocked all the air out. "Chutes! How many chutes?"

"Preach, there—there aren't any."

Walt pounded the wheel, made *Flossie* bounce. "Count the chutes!"

"Preach . . ."

"Keep watching. That's an order."

"Walt!" Harry said.

He sat up straighter. Harry Tuttle never called him Walt.

"Walt, there's nothing—there's no way anyone could have survived."

His breath came fast and shallow. Couldn't be. Frank. Blown to—no! Not Frank. Not Frank!

"Novak." Cracker suddenly looked alert and controlled. "The bombs. Our squadron's bombing."

He blinked over and over. Holes in the windshield. The strap for his throat mike—the strap was too tight. Not Frank.

"Ruben? Can you get a fix?" Cracker asked.

"Nope. Just have to follow the others. Bombs away."

The plane rose with the loss of weight. From behind, J.P. put his hand on Walt's shoulder. "Walt, you okay?"

He filled his chest with air, took charge, and turned *Flossie* away with the squadron. "I'll get us home."

He wouldn't think. He'd do his job—hands firm on the wheel, mind fixed on the instruments, the formation, the adjustments he had to make due to the damage. He'd learned to fly before he could drive. It was automatic.

He bounced over the flak, didn't flinch when the fighters attacked, kept *Flossie* in formation, crossed the Channel, made a complicated but flawless landing, filled out forms, and logged damage. He answered questions during debriefing, listened to the description of *My Eileen*'s demise, stayed detached and professional.

But now what? Back to quarters, then what? He could feel his men watch him on the truck ride back to the living site. Louis held open the door at the end of the Nissen hut, looked with concern at Walt, then over Walt's shoulder to Abe and Cracker.

Walt took in the scene before him and stopped. Half a dozen men he didn't recognize stood around Frank's cot and the cots of the three ops officers who had just taken over as replacements on Frank's crew. The strangers tossed things to each other.

"What's going on here?" Walt asked.

One of the men shrugged, a husky man who wore a ground crew cap with the earflaps flipped up. "Just cleaning up. This fellow went down."

They weren't cleaning—they were looting. "Those aren't your things."

"Just helping."

Abe stepped beside Walt. "Just helping yourselves, you mean."

"Not as if they need this stuff anymore." He snorted and lifted a brass picture frame—Eileen, three little boys, and a tiny baby girl.

Something lurched deep inside Walt. He charged forward, yanked away the picture, and planted his fist in the man's face. "Get out!"

The thief screamed, grabbed his mouth.

"Get out!" Walt swung again, right into the man's meaty stomach. Felt good.

The man doubled over and spat drops of blood on the floor.

"Hey, back off! We're leaving, we're leaving," another fellow said.

Walt coiled for an upper cut, but someone grabbed his arm.

Abe. "Preach! It's okay. They're leaving. If they don't, we'll bring up charges."

The thief stumbled to the door. "He's crazy. Crazy."

"Kilpatrick was his best friend." Cracker called them every filthy name in his considerable vocabulary.

Walt panted, shrugged off Abe. His right hand smarted, and he inspected it—tooth marks. He was bleeding. His left hand—the picture frame—cold in his clutch. Eileen, so pretty, a wash of freckles over her cheeks. Frank Jr. looked like his mom. Sean and Michael were the spitting image of their dad. And Kathleen Mary Rose—too soon to tell—just a little blob.

Dear God in heaven, no!

"Here, I've got an empty box," Abe said. "Anyone else have boxes?"

"Yeah, a few," Cracker said.

Louis set his arm around Walt's shoulder. "Don't worry. We'll get his stuff packed up for his wife. The other men's stuff too."

Walt nodded, his neck stiff, his gaze on Eileen and the kids. What would happen to them?

Walt felt his mouth hanging open, his lips drying out.

"Sit down." Louis guided him to his cot. "Whoa, watch out for your mail."

He sat. Mail? Yeah, a letter, a package.

"You're getting Christmas presents already."

Christmas? Yeah, five days. Oh no, Frank's family. When would they get that telegram?

"You know what?" Louis had the whitest teeth Walt had ever seen. He pried the picture from Walt's hand and gave it to Abe. "A present is just what you need."

A present? Walt's gaze drifted to the box. How could he open a present now?

"Come on. If you don't, I will. It's from your girlfriend. She sends food." Louis set the box on Walt's lap.

His hands were heavy and thick, but he opened the box. He had to. If he sat still, he'd think. He unwrapped tissue paper and found a brown leather satchel—casual and masculine.

"Anything inside?" Louis asked.

Walt opened the flap. Sheet music—loads of it. New stuff—

"When the Lights Go on Again," "Serenade in Blue," "Praise the Lord and Pass the Ammunition," "White Christmas." And a note:

> Merry Christmas, Walt. I hope this will remedy the shortage of sheet music. With the damp and rainy weather, I thought the bag might be useful to carry papers, as well as music. Perhaps the bag will blend in with your flight jacket so Flossie won't be upset by yet more leather.

"Swell bag," Louis said.

"Swell girl."

"Might as well open the letter. News from home will do you good."

Dad wrote this one, on the typewriter as always, the same Smith-Corona he wrote his sermons on, lowercase *a* filled in, uppercase *T* set too high. Walt could almost hear the clatters and dings, smell the walnut desk in Dad's office, see Dad chew a pencil as he typed. He used a typewriter. Why the pencil?

Walt's throat swelled shut. Sure would be nice to be home, hear Dad's voice, taste Mom's cooking. Mom always knew what he needed, let him stew, then listened when it all gushed out. Who would listen today?

Dad's note rambled. Dad never rambled. Then Walt hit the last paragraph:

> There's no good way to relay bad news. I wish I could tell you in person, but obviously, these aren't ordinary circumstances. I'm afraid Jim Carlisle was killed in action off Guadalcanal.

*You can imagine the impact on his wife and
parents, as well as your group of friends. Now
the grief has crossed the ocean to you. I wish
I could be with you, son. Now more than ever,
you're in my prayers.*

Whacked in the chest—again. "No. No. Not Jim."

"Huh?" Abe glanced up from the box he was packing.

Walt looked up to the corrugated steel arching over his cot, to the snapshots tucked in the grooves. There it was—Jim with that dumb sailor cap over his crew cut, his arm around Helen's shoulder, her light hair blowing behind her, baby Jay-Jay cradled in her arms, Jim's hand holding one tiny, bootie-covered foot.

"Jim. Friend—from home. Guadalcanal. Ki-killed."

"Oh no," Abe said. Louis sighed. Cracker cussed.

Walt's head shook from side to side. He couldn't stop it.

"The Swan?" Louis said.

"No, too crowded," Cracker said. "I know a pub in town. Locals only."

"Come on." Louis took Walt's elbow and pulled him to standing. "It's time you became a man. We're getting you drunk."

"Uh-uh."

"Yes, we are." Abe slid a box under his cot. "We're paying. No arguing."

"Uh-uh."

"You heard the man. No arguing," Cracker said. "You need this tonight."

"What about tomorrow?"

Cracker stared at him with eyes as blue as the sky that had swallowed Frank, the sea that had swallowed Jim.

"What about tomorrow? Am I supposed to get drunk

tomorrow and the day after and the day after? Will that bring Frank back? Or Jim?"

"Of course not." Louis came in front of Walt and set his hands on Walt's shoulders. "But you're in shock. We've just gotta get you through tonight."

"Thanks. Thanks." Walt turned to his cot and dumped the music out of the bag from Allie. "But that's not how I want to get through tonight."

"Walt . . ."

"No." He grabbed his stationery, his Bible, letters, whatever he could reach, and stuffed them in the bag. "I gotta go."

"Where are you going?"

"Don't know." He tipped them a salute, slung the bag across his chest, and strode out the door. He got on the first bike he saw and rode south, away from the base, around the village. The pedals pumped, the chain squeaked, and memories invaded.

Jim and Art, tagging after Walt and George in grade school. Pests—until they realized Jim had great ideas and Art had access to hardware. Jim at twelve, chasing Helen Jamison on his bike until she fell and twisted her ankle. Jim at eighteen, chasing Helen Jamison until she fell for him. Frank, setting Allie on the grand piano, smoothing a prickly situation. Frank, tossing a carbon dioxide canister into the stove in the Nissen hut—the explosion, the coal dust everywhere. Frank, always laughing, talking, moving.

Dead! How could they be dead?

He rode harder. The road blurred. Moisture ran across his cheeks and into his ears.

No. He wasn't crying, was he? He hit the brakes and wiped his face. It had to be from the wind. He lifted the bike over a hedge, climbed over, and barged into the trees.

"No!" He whapped a branch aside. "No, Lord! Why Frank?

Why Jim? They're husbands, dads, for crying out loud. You should've taken me. Not them. Me! Why? I'm not good enough for you?"

It wasn't the wind. Honest to goodness crybaby tears. He kicked a tree, sank to the ground, and swiped away the tears.

It would all gush out now. He opened the satchel and pulled out stationery. Couldn't write Mom with what he had to say. She'd fret. Couldn't write the fellows. Had to be tough.

No, he'd write Allie. She understood him. She had that gift of praying for him when he needed it. Besides, he'd never see her again. If she thought he was crazy, so what?

He wrote so hard he ripped the paper a few times with his pen. He didn't stop to think about censorship. He didn't stop to catch the stupid teardrops. He didn't stop when he heard his own choked sobs. He didn't stop until evening blended ink and paper into gray.

Then Walt prayed. He raged and questioned and mourned. Eventually he found peace—not peace like some still pond, but peace like a river, jostling over rocks, hurtling over falls, whirling in eddies.

Authentic, rugged peace.

26

Riverside

December 25, 1942

The formality of Allie's deep green velvet gown required gemstone jewelry, and the emerald pendant was the best choice, but she still felt wrong taking off the cross from Walt. She stretched the necklace flat on the mirrored tray on her dresser. Mother wore a cross to church and stashed it in her jewelry box the rest of the week, but Allie had resolved never to keep her faith—or her cross—in a drawer.

The smell of Christmas met her at the top of the staircase—cool pine, roasting turkey, and tangy mincemeat pie. Plenty of vegetables would make up for the small turkey, but there would be no butter to spread on them. Butter was scarce, but she'd scraped together half a batch of cookies a week before to send to Walt and Frank. If only she had sent them in time to arrive before Christmas.

Mother swept down the stairs behind Allie, and her garnet velvet dress shimmered with her movements. "Shall we see what Santa brought?"

Allie laughed. "Mother, I'm twenty-three, not three."

"Don't remind me."

"What have we here?" Father stood at the base of the stairs, his tuxedo a mirror image of the white and black marble floor. "If it isn't Riverside's two greatest beauties."

Allie tripped and caught herself on the banister. Father never complimented her looks—her mind, her character, her achievements, but never her looks.

"Thank you, darling." Mother brushed a kiss onto Father's cheek, her voice cool. Including Allie had diminished the compliment to Mother.

What did Mother care? Every day Father told her how beautiful she was, but Allie had heard it only twice in her life, and only once had she felt beautiful. She touched her necklace and stifled disappointment when she found the emerald.

Baxter stood to kiss her cheek when she entered the drawing room. Couldn't he be bothered to say she looked nice, or let his eyes light up, or do something to show appreciation? Josie's vile accusation dug into her mind, and she shoved it out.

She knelt in front of the tree. The pine scent evoked equal shares of memories from Christmases and from summer vacations at Lake Arrowhead. Hand-painted glass ornaments twinkled in the glow of tiny electric lights and reminded her of the gorgeous porcelain doll she received when she was five, the exquisite dollhouse when she was eight, her first diamonds when she was sixteen. The Millers always had quiet celebrations, just the three of them until Baxter came along.

Baxter. Allie scanned the gifts and saw a small, cubical present. To Mary, from Stanley. She released her breath.

Allie passed gifts to Father and Baxter in their matching leather chairs flanking the fireplace, and to Mother on the settee she favored, then returned to her childhood position on the floor beside the tree.

Soon she had a pile of books and records before her. Baxter

admired the smart briefcase Allie had bought him. She'd spotted the satchel at the same store. It had the same tone, smell, and feel as Walt's flight jacket, and the right casual air for an aviator. Perhaps it was too nice a gift, but she couldn't resist the chance to spend money she had earned on a dear friend.

Only one present for Allie remained, the cardboard mailing box from Walt marked, "Don't open till Christmas." She worked the string over one corner, opened the top, and removed crumpled newspapers, the *Stars and Stripes*.

She found a wooden grand piano, not much larger than her hand, painted black, with graceful legs. A brass key protruded underneath, and when Allie turned it, Beethoven's "Für Elise" played. Next to the key, tiny white letters read, "Für Allie. W.J.N. '42."

The letters swam before her, and she blinked to clear her vision. It was the sweetest gift she'd ever received—beautiful, handcrafted, personal, and he even squeezed in some teasing.

"How lovely," Mother said.

"Isn't it?" Allie ran her finger down the painted keyboard, almost expecting Walt's hand to flatten hers. "Walt made it himself."

"He certainly sends nice presents," Father said, a sharp edge in his voice.

She looked up. Surely he didn't think Walt had a romantic interest in her. "He—he sends nice things to all his friends." Why did that sadden her? She couldn't expect to be the sole beneficiary of his generosity.

"Speaking of gifts." Baxter set his cigarette in an ashtray on a marble top table. "I hope you don't think I've neglected you."

The music box wound down and hung up on the final notes.

"Oh. No, of course not." That's right. She hadn't opened anything from him.

"I wanted to wait. Save the best for last."

The best? Oh no. The music stopped, the phrase hovering midair, its promise of completion unfulfilled.

Allie gripped the little piano in her lap, but she had to set it aside, had to take the box from Baxter. *Oh, please, Lord. Please let it be earrings again. Clip-on, pierced, I don't care.*

However, the pride in Baxter's smile left no doubt about the box's content. The only surprise was the opulence of the setting—almost gaudy.

"Only the best for my future wife."

Her breath came out choppy, her eyes blinded by the dance of light in the numerous diamonds, her ears deaf to her parents' exclamations of joy.

Yoked. Yoked together. Unequally yoked together.

"Oh, look, Stanley," Mother said, her voice choked. "She's speechless."

Allie met her mother's eyes, and for the first time she found the approval she longed for.

Baxter stooped in front of Allie, pulled the ring from the box, lifted her limp hand, and slipped the ring on. He didn't ask. She didn't accept. He kissed her on the lips. Number thirteen, but she rejected superstition.

It was done.

Allie's eyes clouded. A loveless marriage, but it was a worthy sacrifice, a necessary sacrifice. Now Stanley Miller could pass his company to a capable man and still keep it in the family, Mary Miller had found a suitable match for her homely daughter, and J. Baxter Hicks had earned the boss's favor, the boss's daughter, an inheritance, prestige, and respectability.

She clutched the music box on the floor by her right hip.
What would she tell Walt? Oh, why was she even thinking
of Walt?

Baxter was talking. ". . . almost done. The floors go in
soon, and the decorator will have the place ready in June. I
wanted a June wedding, but July will have to do."

July. Seven months.

"Well, come here, dear," Mother said. "I want to see."

She got to her knees, her feet, and stumbled, her foot caught
in her dress. Her parents laughed. Apparently they thought
she was overcome with happiness.

Allie made her way to the settee, where Mother took her
hand.

"Oh my. Isn't that—isn't that dazzling?" She stood and
clasped Allie's face between her hands. Her green eyes, so
much like Allie's, brimmed with tears. "Oh, I'm so proud of
you. And look at you, crying for joy."

A tear tickled as it dangled on Allie's jaw, then scurried
down her neck. She was going to cry harder—great, gulping
sobs no one would mistake for joy. "I need to go. I need to
show Cressie."

"I'm sure you can't wait to show your friends."

Allie nodded her face free and headed for the door.

"You don't mean now, do you?"

"Yes, now."

"But—but dinner."

Allie gripped the doorjamb between the drawing room and
the entry, looked over her shoulder, and prodded her mouth
into a smile. "I can't wait. I won't be long."

She knew she was a sight, alone on Christmas Day on the
streets of Riverside, no wrap, no hat, no purse, her formal
gown whipping around her ankles.

As soon as she knocked on Cressie's door, she realized she'd made a mistake. The sounds of many voices drifted from the saffron-colored house. She winced and turned away, hoping no one had heard her knock.

"Hello?"

Allie turned back, one foot on the top porch step.

A woman in her forties peered through the screen door. "May I help you?"

"I—I'm sorry." Allie twisted her hands together and longed for a purse. "I was—well, I thought I'd drop by and see Cress—Mrs. Watts, but I wasn't—well, it's Christmas, of course, and I don't mean to impose, so I'll come back later."

The woman opened the screen door and squinted. Evaporating tears tingled on Allie's face. "Ma, you have a visitor."

"Oh no. No, really, I'll come back later. Tomorrow, perhaps."

Cressie appeared in the doorway and grinned. "Allie! What a sur—" She squinted too. "Are you all right, love?"

Her concern made Allie lose whatever composure she'd maintained. Her chest heaved, a sob erupted, and she held up her diamond-encrusted hand.

"Allie, Allie." Cressie wiped her hands on her apron, stepped outside, and took her hand. "Oh my. Oh my, that's a fancy ring. I suppose I should congratulate you." She locked questioning eyes on Allie.

She gulped and nodded.

Cressie put her arm around Allie's shoulder and guided her to a porch swing. Despite the gray layer of dust, Allie sat.

"Well, I'm plumb flabbergasted," Cressie said.

"Flab—flabbergasted?" Allie's legs bent as Cressie set the swing in motion.

"Yep. I thought he'd wait till after the war so he could ask in person."

"What do you mean?" Allie wiped her face as best she could with her hand.

"You need a hanky." Cressie dug in her apron pocket and handed Allie a plain white handkerchief. "Flabbergasted. Your young man sounded like such a romantic fellow."

Baxter? Romantic? She dabbed her eyes and inhaled a deep, ratcheting breath.

"That's one fancy ring, but I see why you're upset. Not romantic to mail it."

Allie looked up from the handkerchief. "Mail it? He didn't mail it."

Cressie frowned. "How'd he get it from England?"

"England! Oh dear, no. No, that's Walt, my friend Walt. He's—he's not my boyfriend. Baxter is."

"Who's Baxter?"

Not again. Allie flattened the handkerchief over her face. "I know—I *know* I talk about him. I make sure I talk about him. Baxter Hicks. He works for my father."

"I'll be." Cressie didn't speak for a minute. "Hmm. Well, you did say Walt was only a friend, but then you kept talking about a boyfriend, so I thought things had changed. Hmm. So that's why you sometimes talk as if he's right here in town. Two different men, two different men. You've got yourself in a fine pickle, Miss Allegra."

"A pickle?" She pressed her eyeballs until golden lights appeared.

"Yep." The chains on the porch swing squeaked when Cressie halted its motion. "Hmm. You got me so discombobulated when you quoted 1 Peter, because I thought your young man was a brother in Christ. Let me get this straight. Walt's a believer and Baxter isn't?"

"Yes." Allie tensed herself for a lecture.

Cressie set the swing rocking again. "Baxter. Hmm. What

have you told me about Baxter? Hmm. Your parents are right fond of him, are they?"

"Uh-huh." Was that all she'd mentioned about him?

"Hmm. Walt's the pilot. Searched for you in Herb Galloway's cab. Writes those letters you talk about all the time. Didn't you call him one of your favorite people in the world?"

Allie nodded and groaned. Oh, how bad that sounded. Now Cressie thought she was in love with Walt.

"Yep," Cressie said. "A fine pickle."

27

Thurleigh

January 7, 1943

"Ready to be paddled?"

Earl Butterfield walked out of the CO's office and rubbed his backside. Nervous laughter rumbled in the hallway where Walt stood with half a dozen other first pilots and one co-pilot—Cracker.

"You're next, Preach." Butterfield leaned close enough for Walt to see brown hairs in his blond mustache. "Watch out. Armstrong's nothing like Overacker."

That's why Armstrong was there. On January 4, Ira Eaker, the commanding general of the Eighth Air Force, had visited Thurleigh to investigate the high losses and high level of aborts in the 306th. He found lax discipline and low morale, and replaced Overacker with Col. Frank Armstrong, who had led the Eighth's first mission back in August.

Walt made sure his service jacket was straight, walked into the CO's office, and snapped a salute. Armstrong sat behind his desk, his head bent over a file.

"At ease, Lieutenant Novak."

He clasped his hands behind his back and waited while

Colonel Armstrong read the file. If he wanted to make Walt nervous, it worked. Even though he had nothing in his file to be ashamed of, he felt as if he were back in the principal's office for putting gum in Lulu Parker's hair.

The colonel set the file down and raised a sharp-lined face. "On December 30, seventeen out of eighteen bombers from this group aborted the mission."

"Yes, sir." And the one that continued was shot down.

"You didn't fly that day, Lieutenant."

"No, sir. My plane took heavy damage over Romilly. She's still in the hangar."

"You've never aborted one mission."

"No, sir. Sergeant Reilly and the rest of my ground crew do a great job."

Armstrong fixed his gaze on Walt. Behind the steel, Walt saw something he liked—integrity and intelligence. "I saw your designs for a nose-mounted gun. As you know, an armorer and a welder from this group implemented something similar."

"Yes, sir. No connection to my design."

The CO flipped through some papers in the file. "Your record is exemplary, and your squadron commander speaks highly of your performance. The strike photos show good accuracy."

"Lieutenant Ruben is an excellent bombardier."

Again with that gaze. "And the rest of your crew?"

Walt paused. With one exception, they were great. "Lieutenant Fontaine has never let me down at the navigator's desk, nor has Sergeant Perkins in the radio room. Sergeant Sanchez is one of the most intelligent and dedicated men I've ever met—officer material. As for my gunners, their records speak for themselves."

Armstrong leaned back in his chair and waited—for Walt's

assessment of Cracker, no doubt. "I thought so. Now, I'm making changes around here. More work, more discipline, and I've put you in for a promotion to captain."

Walt reminded himself to blink. He wasn't getting paddled. He was getting promoted.

"You'll make a fine squadron commander—and soon."

Squadron commander? He wasn't just catching up with Ray and Jack, he was passing them. What would Dad say about that?

"One problem—Lieutenant Huntington's record is abysmal. How this man passed flight school is beyond me. In fact, I have a formal protest letter in his file from one of his flight instructors—interesting, a Lt. Raymond Novak. Any relation?"

"My oldest brother, sir."

"His concerns were well founded. I know you won't object if I transfer Huntington to a ground job."

"We fly as a crew." Walt frowned. Why would those words of his come back now when he had a chance to get rid of the man who'd been a jagged pebble in his shoe? "Sir, we fly as a crew."

"Pardon?"

"We fly as a crew, sir. That's what I tell the men when they try to get out of a practice mission. I can't go back on my word now."

Armstrong's forehead furrowed. "I can't make you a squadron commander with a copilot like that. He couldn't be relied on if something happened to you."

"I understand, sir."

"I admire your loyalty, but it's misplaced."

Walt dug his fingernails into his palms. He couldn't believe he had to say this. "I've never respected the man, but he was invaluable over Romilly."

"Romilly. A Fortress exploded near you that day."

Like sandpaper on an open wound, but Walt didn't let his face show anything. "Yes, sir. The Distinguished Flying Cross I received—it belongs just as much to Lieutenant Huntington. He had to—had to take over for a while. He fulfilled his duties."

Armstrong glanced at the file. "The chaplain noted the pilot of the other plane, Lieutenant Kilpatrick, was your best friend."

"Yes, sir. He left a wife and four children."

"And you? Your file says you're single. Do you have a girlfriend back home?"

Walt stopped breathing. Although he wanted to maintain consistency, lying to his CO would be just plain stupid. "No one who affects my performance, sir. I'm in love with a girl, but we aren't committed."

✸

That was the truth, wasn't it?

Walt tramped back to the living site under a lumpy gray sky. He'd never been in love before, but he'd never felt this way about a woman before, either. When he said it out loud, said he loved her, it felt right, not a lie at all.

Swell. Wasn't that swell? What a sorry excuse for a man. Sure, he might make captain, but he'd fallen in love with a woman who was spoken for.

Walt banged open the door of the Nissen hut, and a dozen men startled.

Earl Butterfield poked around inside the coal stove to coax out some heat. "Preach just met with Armstrong."

The other men murmured their understanding.

"How'd it go?" Louis Fontaine asked. "Get whipped like Butterfield?"

"No, it went okay." Walt unbuttoned his uniform jacket and hung it on the rack that ran the length of the hut over the cots. "I think he'll make some good changes."

Louis snorted. "Yeah, you would think so."

Something soft hit Walt's back. He looked down to see a balled-up sock.

The door opened, and a sergeant brought in a burst of cold air. "Mail call. Fontaine . . . Granger . . . Jansen . . . Novak."

Walt took the letter from his brother Jack and sat on the end of his cot, as close to the feeble stove as he could. Jack had transferred to the 94th Bomb Group in Texas, not far from Ray, and the two brothers were able to visit each other. Jealousy and homesickness slapped Walt. He hadn't seen Jack for over a year, and Ray for nine months. Jack's group was in the final stages of training and expected to go overseas soon. Jack hoped for England so he could meet up with Walt. Knowing Jack, he also wanted to meet up with some English girls.

Walt sighed and folded the letter. Jack wouldn't come. The Twelfth Air Force in North Africa siphoned off the new bomb groups—and all other resources as well. The Eighth Air Force still had only four B-17 groups, two B-24 groups, and not nearly enough replacement crews, aircraft, or spare parts.

"Novak." The sergeant held up a package.

Even from across the hut, he recognized Allie's handwriting, and his heart skipped like a bad landing. When he opened the box, he found ginger cookies. No wonder he'd fallen in love. If only she weren't so sweet, so kind, and such a good cook.

Her note was dated December 13:

It happened again yesterday. I'm no longer surprised when I read of a mission the following

day in the paper. Do you suppose my dreams
are an intelligence breach? You said you were
honored, but I'm much more honored that God
chose me for such service. If my prayers offer
any strength or peace, I'll gladly sacrifice some
sleep.

I'm also honored to include Frank in my
prayers. The censors blacked out the reason for
his distress, but the Lord knows his needs. At
least I can fulfill his request for cookies.

Walt dropped his head in his hand. Every day, just when
he thought he was over his grief, something came along and
punched him in the gut again. "Say, Preach, don't tell me you
got a Dear John letter." Louis inspected a brand-new bottle
of that hot Tabasco sauce he liked.

Guilt compounded his grief. Louis, Abe, and J.P. had all
become good friends, and they all believed his lie. "Allie sent
cookies—for Frank."

Louis winced. "Oh, boy."

"Here. Have one." Walt reached across the aisle and handed
him a cookie, took one himself, and bumped them together
like a toast. "To Frank."

"To Frank. A good man."

The hut was silent. Walt stood and passed out ginger-
snaps. Felt like communion. Maybe that was a sacrilege, but
it seemed fitting. He took communion to remember Christ's
sacrifice, and today he remembered Frank's.

The tightness in Walt's throat rose to his face and threatened his tear ducts, so he lifted his chin and his cookie high.
"To Frank Kilpatrick—a devoted husband and father, one
fine pilot, and my best friend."

"To Kilpatrick," the men said, their voices throaty and raw.

Louis raised his cookie. His jaw worked back and forth a few times. "To John Petrovich, master of the practical joke."

"To Petrovich."

"To Bob Robertson," Earl Butterfield said in a fierce, loud voice. "A good friend and a talented artist, whose work inspired us all."

"Hear, hear!"

"To Robertson."

So it went, around the room, as the men remembered their fallen friends. Some memories were solemn, some stirred up rusty laughter. How long had it been since they'd laughed together?

Walt ran his thumb along the edge of the cookie. Allie had no idea what her simple gift had done, how much she helped them remember, mourn, and heal.

★

Walt settled in the upholstered armchair in the Officers' Club and read the story in *Time* again. Eddie Rickenbacker, World War One flying ace and Walt's childhood hero, had been in a Flying Fortress that crash-landed in the Pacific in October. While adrift in a raft for twenty-four days, the crew held twice-daily prayer meetings. Once, after praying for food, a seagull landed on Rickenbacker's head. The men ate it raw.

Walt smiled. God made the front page.

"Hi, Preach."

Walt looked up. Cracker stood in front of him with two Coke bottles. He held one out to Walt.

"Thanks." He didn't know what surprised him most—

Cracker taking a seat next to him, Cracker buying him a Coke, or Cracker drinking a Coke. "Cutting back?"

"Yeah." He set elbows on knees and stared at the glass bottle. "You're right. Doesn't help."

"Hmm." Walt tossed the magazine onto the coffee table. Cracker's tan had faded, and his hair had dulled in the English overcast. Didn't look so much like a movie star.

Cracker scanned the club. "Quiet tonight."

The crews that had survived the mission on January 3 had put down at St. Eval in Cornwall with damage and were stranded there by the weather. The rest of the men were licking the wounds Armstrong had inflicted.

"Yep. Quiet." Walt sipped and let bubbles fizz in his mouth.

"You were right about a lot of things."

Walt almost spat out the soda.

"Armstrong lit into me today, called me arrogant, incompetent. Seems I've heard those words before." He pointed his bottle at Walt. "He says I owe you—a lot more than a Coke. He told me what you did. I don't know why you'd give up squadron command for me."

"Neither do I." Walt lifted his drink to Cracker.

He chuckled and clinked bottles together. "Listen, I may be arrogant, and I may be incompetent, but I'm not stupid. I know a second chance when I see one. I want to be the crackerjack pilot I claim to be, and I'm determined to get you that squadron commander position."

Walt stared into Cracker's eyes. The man was serious. Walt had done it. He'd earned the respect of every crewmember. "We have to work together. We've been competing since that first day at Wendover."

"The better man won." Cracker took a swig and made a face, as if disgusted to find Coke and not beer.

Walt couldn't gloat over his victory. His crew was demoralized, and there was no end to the war in sight. He crossed his ankle over his knee. "I think God put us on the same crew for a reason. You have skills with people that I lack."

"Maybe. But you've got the crew's respect. I lost it."

"So we work together as we did over Romilly. That alone will help morale. You could do some other stuff with the men, as you did stateside."

"Yeah." Cracker tapped his thumbnail on the glass bottle. "Like a baseball game against another crew, football maybe."

"With this weather, maybe water polo."

Cracker laughed, then nodded to the table. "We could at least share cookies."

Walt grinned and offered him the box. "Have one. From my—" His lie stuck in his craw. "From Allie."

"Thanks. You know, that's another thing you did right—found a good woman and stuck with her. That's what I should do."

Walt popped a gingersnap in his mouth, his lying mouth. Frank knew the truth. Frank winked at the story and made it feel like a joke. But with Frank gone, Walt's lies ate at him, and his readings in Proverbs didn't help. This morning he read, "Lying lips are abomination to the Lord: but they that deal truly are his delight."

How could a little white lie get so complicated?

28

Riverside

January 14, 1943

"Really, Allie, you mustn't cover your ring. People will think you're ashamed of your engagement." Mother tapped Allie's right hand, clasped over her left.

"Sorry, it's a habit." She offered her mother a smile as flimsy as her excuse. The habit was born of many stares at a ring too glamorous for hospital wards and Groveside Bible Church.

She reversed her hands and glanced out the bus window at the Parent Navel Orange Tree, brought to Riverside in 1873, the source of the local citrus industry, ensconced in a park on the corner of Magnolia and Arlington.

If only fresh oranges could survive the trip to Walt in England. But they wouldn't make a dent in his mountain of grief. Three days had passed since she'd received his letter, handwriting slanted hard, content blackened by the censor's pen, paper ripped and pocked by rain or—could it be tears?

Frank Kilpatrick was dead. Despite censorship, that much could be deduced. Allie couldn't decide if it was cruel or kind that Walt learned of Jim Carlisle's death on the same day. All she knew was her grief for a man she'd met once but memorably, for his widow and children, and for Walt.

Poor, dear Walt, crushed by guilt for surviving while Frank had perished, guilt for wishing such a fate on his own crew, even guilt for writing Allie such an emotional letter.

The bus crossed Fourteenth Street, Magnolia Avenue changed to Market Street, and Allie gazed at Riverside's beloved architecture. How could she comfort a man thousands of miles away? Her condolences seemed empty and impotent, as did her reassurances that she respected his transparency and was honored that he chose to unburden to her.

"Allie, Eighth Street." Mother's tone said she was repeating herself.

She rose and followed her mother off the bus and under the Spanish-style arcade along Eighth. Mother opened the door to Miss Montclair's dress shop.

"Dearest Mary, how are you?" Miss Montclair glided over, kissed Mother on the cheek, and took both Allie's hands. "Oh, what a charming bride you'll be. How have you been, dear? We've truly missed you at St. Timothy's."

What was the truthful solution to this dilemma? Allie stared at Miss Montclair, who, despite her aristocratic bearing, seemed to have risen from the local hills, craggy and sharp angled.

Mother draped her garment bag over an upholstered chair. "As I told you, Agatha, she's doing volunteer work at a church for the needy."

Church for the needy? Volunteer work? Mother's warning glance silenced the retorts on Allie's tongue.

"How gracious of you, dear Allie. We who are blessed with a church like St. Timothy's often forget those who aren't so fortunate."

She sandwiched her tongue between her teeth. Groveside's

congregation was far more blessed, but she had to respect her mother's need to maintain proper appearances.

"May I see what you brought?" Miss Montclair opened the garment bag and pulled out Mother's wedding dress. "How exquisite. I can design something more modern, even with the silk shortage. How generous of you to let us alter your gown. Here, Allie dear, try it on."

She stepped into the dressing room and removed her bottle green hat and suit.

"I'm thrilled about this wedding, Agatha. I've dreamed of it for five years. Why, Baxter's already like a son to us. Allie should have the most beautiful dress Riverside's ever seen, silk shortage or no silk shortage. I won't force her into yesteryear's fashions because of my own selfish nostalgia."

Allie stared at herself in the mirror. All her life she'd seen the portrait over the drawing room fireplace of her parents on their wedding day in 1918. Now she wore the dress. It would be refashioned, and she would have her picture taken with Baxter on July 3, and she'd see the portrait over their fireplace for the rest of her life.

Nausea swirled in her stomach. She sat down hard on the little stool and leaned her cheek against the cool wall until her stomach stilled. She'd spent her whole life trying to earn her mother's approval. Now that she had it, why did it fail to satisfy her?

Oh Lord, please help me. You heard my mother, how happy she is. Your Word tells me to honor my parents.

She could see Walt standing among the strawberry plants in the summer sun, his head turned toward his grandparents' farmhouse, his hand extended to help Allie to her feet. *"Sure, we have to honor our parents, but we have to honor God first."*

"Allie, are you ready in there?" Mother called.

She stood and took a deep, steadying breath. "Yes, I'm ready."

Mother and Miss Montclair descended on her with measuring tape and pins.

"That long collar must go."

"Yes, and I'll take in the bodice. Perhaps a sweetheart neckline."

"That would be pretty. What about the sleeves?"

"Shorten them, puff them. The skirt will be the hard part."

"Much too narrow."

"Yes, but I have plenty of lace in stock. I'll create some insets, and it will be the height of fashion."

Allie stepped on and off a platform, raised and lowered her arms, turned and stood still, all while avoiding the mirror.

"She's rather glum for a bride," Miss Montclair whispered.

Allie didn't meet Mother's eye.

"An acquaintance of hers was killed over France," Mother whispered back. "She took it quite hard."

"Well, we're done for today." Miss Montclair set her hand on Allie's shoulder. "Yes, these are difficult times, dear."

Allie had never noticed the kindness in Miss Montclair's stone gray eyes, and she ducked into the dressing room before tears welled up. Difficult times? Yes, for Walt and for Eileen Kilpatrick and for Helen Carlisle. But Allie was only indirectly affected.

Why, she had a wedding approaching. She should be celebrating. So why hadn't she told Betty? Why hadn't she told Walt? She had a date set at St. Timothy's, a reception room reserved at the Mission Inn, and her mother's wedding gown about to be cut to pieces. It was time to tell everyone.

★

"Poor Agatha," Mother said with a sigh as they strolled up Orange Street.

Allie glanced away to the old Post Office, now used by the Fourth Air Force, in charge of the defense of the southwestern United States. A captain in dress uniform trotted down the wide steps of the Italian Renaissance building and tipped his hat to the ladies. Perhaps his attention would distract Mother from a story Allie had heard too often.

"Good afternoon," mother and daughter said in unison. Allie said a quick prayer for Walt, as she did whenever she saw a man in olive drab.

Mother sighed again. "Poor Agatha's never been pretty. She was fresh out of school when we moved to Riverside after our wedding, and she wasn't pretty even then."

Allie crossed Orange Street and cringed at Mother's tone, which implied that unattractiveness was a character deficiency.

"I know you could have made over the dress, but I like to give poor Agatha the business whenever I can. It's sad to see what she's fallen to."

Allie waited on the corner to cross Seventh Street. Few cars traveled the city streets, since nonessential driving was forbidden, new cars hadn't been produced since January 1942, and tires were unavailable. Perhaps when they arrived at the Mission Inn for lunch, Mother would forget to finish the story.

"So sad. She was well situated after her parents died in the flu epidemic. If only she hadn't fallen for that swindler in 1925. Hmm, or was it '26? No, no, '25."

Allie murmured to steer her mother around the obstacle of a trivial detail.

"No, it was '27. I still can't believe a bright woman like Agatha Montclair let a rogue talk her into selling her father's company—her own father's company, mind you—and putting all her money in stocks."

Allie concentrated on Riverside's landmark across the street. The Mission Inn covered an entire block with tile-roofed Mission Revival buildings, which glorified California's Spanish days.

"I saw through the man right away," Mother said. "One of those cads who preys on homely women of means."

Homely women of means—like Allie. Finally, they could cross the street and stroll under the vine-covered arcade along Seventh.

"Then in '29, the Stock Market crashed, and there she was with no stocks, no money. With her looks, she couldn't find a husband, certainly not at her age. At least she found that seamstress position and eventually bought her own shop. Still, so sad."

Allie sighed in relief at the familiar end of the story. She glanced through one of the arches in the arcade, across Seventh Street, to City Hall with its square tower and palm trees.

"If only she'd listened to her family."

Allie turned back to her mother. That wasn't how the story went. "Her family?"

Mother tucked a blonde curl back under her navy blue hat. "I suppose I've never told you this part. It's rather shameful, and I didn't want to warp your view of Miss Montclair when you were younger."

Allie raised her eyebrows. "But now that I'm older . . ."

"Now you're old enough not to repeat stories." Mother greeted a lady from St. Timothy's Ladies' Circle, the afternoon tea faction. "If only Agatha had listened to her family and kept her engagement."

"Her engagement?"

"When I met her, she was engaged to a fine man, Herman Carrington."

"Carrington Citrus Company?"

"The same. It was a splendid match—his citrus groves and her citrus packing company. Her grandparents set it up after her parents' deaths, and Mr. Carrington agreed to the match, even though he's quite a handsome man."

Another plain woman in an arranged marriage. "What happened?"

"Agatha always had a willful streak. She insisted he didn't love her and he'd—" Mother leaned closer and hushed her voice. "Well, he would cheat on her. Isn't that a disgraceful accusation?"

Allie swallowed hard. "Yes. Yes, it is." As disgraceful as Josie's accusation.

Mother lifted her chin and gave her curls a shake. "I told her she was foolish. With her looks, she couldn't afford to be choosy. And she certainly should have had the sense to follow her family's advice."

Allie unglued her tongue from the roof of her mouth. "Certainly."

"I was always afraid . . ." Mother's eyelashes fluttered, and then she gave Allie a smile. "Well, I'm glad you have Baxter, and you have far more sense than Agatha."

Allie could hardly breathe as she passed through the Mission Inn's courtyard with its lush greenery and brilliant flowers. She saw the parallels as clearly as Mother did, saw the lessons to heed in Miss Montclair's story.

So why did she feel the Lord was pointing her in the opposite direction?

29

January 27, 1943

Walt stepped off the train onto American soil, under California sunshine, into a Delta breeze. Dad and Mom waved from
the platform, so did Ray and Jack, Grandpa and Grandma
Novak, George and Betty, Jim and Helen. Walt squinted in
the heat. Where was she?

Boy, the sun was hot. He looked down. No wonder he was
frying—he wore full, high-altitude flight gear, complete with
life preserver and parachute.

Walt scanned the crowd. Everyone he knew was there—the
whole Kilpatrick clan, Art, Dorothy, Eddie Nakamura from
Cal. But where was Allie?

There she was, way in the back. He shouldered his way
through the crowd, threw his arms around her, and swung
her around in circles. Wasn't that what coming home was
about—swinging the girl you loved around in circles?

"Oh, Walter darling." She took off his flying helmet and
ran her fingers deep into the curls on top of his head. "I don't
love Baxter. I love you."

Even though the sun roasted his cheeks, he smiled. This
was what coming home was really about—kissing the girl
you loved. He bent toward those pretty lips.

"Okay, you lunkheads, up and at 'em."

Walt opened one eye. He had one hand under his meager pillow, the other buried in his own hair. Of all the lousy times for reveille.

The Charge of Quarters walked down the aisle, shook shoulders, and thumped backsides. "Mission today, you good-for-nothings. Rise and shine." The sergeant relished this duty. When else could an enlisted man insult and abuse officers?

Walt groped for his wristwatch. Three o'clock? He pressed the cool glass to his cheek. Yeah, he was burning up again. All his covers were kicked off, even though his breath condensed in front of him. Before the Charge of Quarters could smack his bare feet, Walt swung them to the icy concrete floor and kicked aside a chunk of dried mud. Every muscle ached, down to his fingers and toes.

He popped a couple of aspirin into his mouth, grimaced at the bitter taste, and swallowed. The aspirin would knock out the fever before briefing, and if he could manage not to cough, he might get past the doc.

He couldn't go home until the war was over, and the war wouldn't be won nursing a cold in bed. Too bad his homecoming would be nothing like his dream. Frank and Jim were dead, Eddie Nakamura was locked up in a desert camp, and Allie wouldn't be there. Nope, she ran her fingers through Baxter's hair, if he ever let it get mussed up.

Walt coughed and groaned at the pain in his chest. That was new.

"Wow. That's one bad cold." Louis had wrinkles pressed into his cheek from the pillowcase.

"It's not that bad." He stood and closed his eyes against a rush of dizziness and guilt. Every day God made it harder to tell fibs. "No, it is bad, but I'll get through."

The aspirin worked, some hot tea with breakfast steamed

the rattles from his chest, and the briefing knocked out any misgivings. When Colonel Armstrong pulled back the blue cloth at the front of the room, the men went wild.

Germany. For the first time, the Eighth would hit the enemy's heartland, and the 306th had the honor of heading the force, with Colonel Armstrong in the lead plane. The men of the 306th would be the first Americans to bomb Nazi Germany. The red ribbon on the map ran round the continent, over the North Sea, to the shipyards at Vegesack, with the secondary target at the shipyards and docks at Wilhelmshaven.

No stupid chest cold would keep Walt from this historic mission. This was a story to tell his kids, or more likely, his nieces and nephews.

★

"Give us some milk, Floss." Cracker patted the cow on the nose of the plane.

The rest of the crew followed, laughing and adjusting flight gear. "Make it a milk run."

"We love ya, Floss."

"Give Papa some milk."

Walt smiled, although even his lips hurt. Morale had never been higher, thanks to Armstrong. Sure, the men groused about the strict discipline and training at first, but they flew better and they knew it.

"Okay, men." Cracker clapped his hands together. "Germany. Today we'll drop bombs right in der Führer's face. Ruben, you got those coordinates dialed in?"

Abe grinned. "I'm aiming for his mustache."

"We'll blow it right off." Cracker's face lit up with his old luster. "We've had milk runs lately, and today won't be any different, not with our captain at the helm."

Captain—sure sounded good, as good as those double silver bars felt on his shoulders, but not as good as it felt to have a unified crew. He had never seen a man work as hard as Cracker had the last few weeks. When they weren't flying a combat or practice mission, he studied the B-17 manual and racked up hours in the Link Trainer, which simulated instrument flying conditions. As Walt suspected, when the men saw their pilots work together, they rallied.

"What's the Scripture for today, Preach?" Bill Perkins looped his yellow "Mae West" life preserver over his head.

Walt dug in the shin pocket of his olive drab flying suit—escape kit, bottle of aspirin, scrap of paper with Psalm 91 written out. He'd read it before, but no one tired of the promises of the Lord's protection.

He watched the men climb into the Fort, coughed, and braced himself against the fuselage, his hand on the large blue squadron identification letters. *Lord, please give me strength. I can't deprive the men—or myself—of this mission.*

What a long mission—the longest the Eighth had flown yet, three hundred miles to the target. At least the Jerries were caught off guard. They sent up plenty of flak but didn't aim well, and compared to the fighters over France, these guys didn't know what they were doing.

When the 306th reached Vegesack, solid clouds prevented bombing, so they turned for the secondary target of Wilhelmshaven, where fifty-five B-17s dropped their bombs from 25,000 feet through a hole in the undercast.

On the return flight the aspirin wore off, and Walt began to shiver. He poked two aspirin under his oxygen mask and choked them down dry.

Didn't help. The shivers became shakes. The coughs ripped deeper into his lungs, and he had to take off his mask every once in a while to clear his mouth and nose of nasty brownish gunk.

Good thing he'd been flying all his life. Good thing Cracker could finally be trusted. Together they kept *Flossie* in the "combat box," which had been developed by the 305th Bomb Group and lately adopted by the whole Eighth Air Force. Each group flew in a tight, staggered formation to maximize defensive firepower.

The English coast looked good. Walt could almost feel the pillow under his head, the heavy blankets over his frozen body. *Flossie* landed unharmed, and all sixteen planes from the 306th returned with only minor damage. Another milk run.

Half a dozen reporters greeted *Flossie's Fort*. The crew cheered and hammed it up for the cameras, and Harry and Mario hoisted Walt up on their shoulders. He looked down, the ground blurred, and he squeezed his eyes shut against the dizziness.

"Hiya, Captain. How'd it go?"

Walt opened his eyes. A man in a brown suit circled him with a movie camera. What if he was in a newsreel and Allie saw him? Or his family? Had to look healthier than he felt. He grinned. "We showed Hitler, showed him not to mess with the USA."

The men hooted and hollered, and the camera wheeled to Cracker. Yeah, he'd look good on film.

J.P. shrugged off his parachute. "Wouldn't that be something if we made a newsreel?"

"Your girlfriend would like that, Preach." Mario jostled Walt as he and Harry headed for the truck. "See your ugly mug on the silver screen."

Walt laughed, which churned up another gurgling mess of coughs. At least the coughing prevented more lies. He just couldn't lie anymore. Hurt more than his chest. Allie called silence a truthful solution, but was it? Was it truthful when it perpetuated a lie?

The men lowered him to the ground, and he stumbled to the two-and-a-half ton truck. *What do you want me to do, Lord? Am I supposed to tell them I've been lying to them all along? Lose their respect, this unity? Can't do that.*

Abe extended a hand to help Walt into the truck. "Your cough's a lot worse."

He climbed in, embarrassed that he needed help, that his knees buckled as he sat, that he hacked into his handkerchief and the men stared.

"I'll talk to the driver," Abe said. "We'll swing by Sick Quarters first. My dad's a doctor, and I know what rust-colored sputum means."

Walt did too. He'd had pneumonia when he was eight. Only this felt worse.

30

Riverside

January 28, 1943

"Look how much scrap I got, Miss Miller." Ricky Weber dumped the contents of his red wagon onto Groveside's spotty lawn, where the Ladies' Circle sorted the neighborhood collection.

"Oh my." Allie knelt and rummaged through tin cans, tools, cookware, and what looked like a car fender.

"I guess I'll be going now." Ricky dropped the wagon handle, drew back his little shoulders, and walked away.

"Ricky, your wagon."

"No, Miss Miller. That's a whole lot of metal could be used for the war effort."

Her heart ached at the quiver in the boy's voice. The Webers couldn't afford another wagon, and toys with metal or rubber parts weren't being produced anyway. Ricky wouldn't have a wagon to help with the next scrap drive.

She sprang to her feet. "Ricky, wait. Come back."

He gave her a puzzled look and returned.

Allie picked up the wagon handle and held it out to the boy. "Your wagon is already part of the war effort."

"It is?"

"Of course. Look how much scrap you collected. This wagon is as important as a jeep or a B-17."

His smile exposed brand-new front teeth surrounded by gaps. "You think so?"

"I know so. Take your wagon, soldier, and bring more scrap." She gave him what she hoped was a decent salute.

"Yes, sir—ma'am." Ricky ran off, his wagon clattering behind him.

Allie smiled and knelt to sort the haul. A child should be able to keep his favorite toy. This war had caused enough loss.

Cressie came over and set down an orange crate. "Tin in this crate. Tin only."

"Wow. Look at all this." Daisy squatted next to Cressie.

"Thanks to Ricky and his trusty wagon." Allie tossed cans into the crate, as well as a tin cookie jar, which reminded her how she gave up cookies for Lent last year.

"What are you giving up for Lent?" Allie asked. "I usually give up sweets, but with rationing, it's hardly honest. The only thing I can think to give up is movies, but that seems too dear. I couldn't stand to miss the newsreels."

The only response was the fragrant rustle of eucalyptus leaves and the clunk of metal. Allie frowned and readjusted the silk scarf around her hair. She must have demonstrated the immaturity of her faith. "Maybe I should give up movies. Isn't that the point? To give up something dear?" But how could she? She'd never spotted Walt, but seeing the Flying Fortresses land with four circular propeller blurs, seeing the men bundled in their flight gear, jubilant and victorious— those images reassured her.

"What do you give up for Lent, Cressie?"

"I don't."

"Me neither." Daisy chewed her gum and blew a bubble.

Allie smiled and reached over to pop it. "Maybe you should give up gum."

Daisy poked in the shreds of gum. "Honestly, what's the point?"

For once, Allie was in the teaching role. "By giving up something we love, we show unity with Jesus in his sacrifice."

"By giving up gum? Seems silly. If God wanted me to give up something, wouldn't he want me to give it up for good, not just for forty days?"

Allie stared at Daisy, whose brown hair was tied up in a red polka-dotted scarf, leaving a round pompadour up front. "I've never thought of it that way before. But—but sacrifice is pleasing to the Lord. The Bible tells us to present our bodies a living sacrifice, holy, acceptable unto God."

"Miss Allegra," Cressie said. "Busy with your memory work again. Good for you. Good for you. And you're right. Doing God's will often means sacrifice."

Daisy clasped her hands and gazed heavenward. "Not the gum, Lord. Not the gum."

Allie smiled and added a tin pot to the crate.

"Silly, isn't it?" Daisy said. "Giving up luxuries. Makes you feel holy without making you holy."

Cressie got up and dragged over another crate. "Sometimes we do that, love. Sometimes we choose our sacrifices."

"Choose our sacrifices?" Allie stared at the diamond ring, so heavy on her hand.

"Sure. We think we're doing something to please God, but down deep we're only out to please ourselves."

"Ooh. King Saul and the Amalekites." Daisy nodded to Allie. "Just taught it in Sunday school."

"Refresh my memory," Cressie said.

Daisy dropped a frying pan in the crate. "You see, the

Lord told King Saul to slay the Amalekites, every last one of them, livestock too. But King Saul, he kept the best animals, said he wanted to offer them as a sacrifice to the Lord. But he disobeyed. Boy, was God mad—Samuel too. Samuel told the king, 'Hath the Lord as great delight in burnt-offerings and sacrifices, as in obeying the voice of the Lord? Behold, to obey is better than sacrifice.' That was the kids' memory verse this week. Isn't it a good one?" she asked with a snap of her gum.

"Yes." Allie rolled her fingers on the edge of the crate. The sunlight reflected off the diamonds and pierced her eyes as the words pierced her soul. "'To obey is better than sacrifice,'" she whispered.

✦

Was she like King Saul?

Allie walked down Eighth Street that afternoon, her pocketbook tucked under the sleeve of her chestnut wool suit. *Am I offering this sacrifice for you, Lord, to lead Baxter to you? Or is it for me, to gain my parents' approval?*

Oh Lord, you couldn't possibly want me to break my engagement. She smiled and nodded at a lady who worked at the grocery, while a shiver ran up her arms.

If she broke her engagement . . .

The shiver coursed through her whole body. Her parents would be disgraced to have raised an unfaithful, disrespectful daughter. Oh, the shame, the scandal, how everyone would talk. The gossips would dissect poor Baxter. That awful Josie would feel vindicated. And what about Father and Baxter? They were business associates, close friends, almost family. Would their relationship be marred or shattered?

And the hassle of a broken engagement. Baxter's house pressed closer to completion, built with Allie in mind, complete

with a music room and a sewing room. And the wedding—
the church was booked, the invitations were ordered, and
Mother's precious wedding dress lay in pieces.

The wedding dress . . .

She was supposed to be going to the dress shop. She stopped
and looked around in the winter sunlight. She stood at the
corner of Eighth and Lime. Miss Montclair's shop was back
between Orange and Lemon Streets. Miss Montclair . . .

Miss Montclair broke her engagement, and people still
talked more than twenty years later.

Allie sighed and turned back. Miss Montclair greeted her at
the front door. "Ah, there you are, dearest Allie. I saw you pass
right by. Brides do tend to be scatterbrained creatures. Well,
come along. I have everything set out for you." She showed
Allie a chair at a long table heaped with bolts of lace.

Miss Montclair wore a long-sleeved charcoal jersey dress,
which brought out her unusual gray eyes and the gray streaks
in her black hair, worn back in a snood. She spread sketches
of wedding gowns before Allie, each fashionable and distinctive, and Allie pointed to the middle one because it was
in the middle. Then Miss Montclair held up bolts of lace
to Mother's wedding gown on a dress form and described
the merits of each, and Allie selected the first because it was
first.

"My, you decided quickly." Miss Montclair rolled up a
bolt of delicate Chantilly lace. "Newly engaged ladies are
usually so giddy."

"I've never been much of one for giddiness." She studied
the chosen sketch—the short, puffed sleeves, the nipped waist,
the skirt with cascades of silk and lace. "Miss Montclair, are
you happy?"

"Excuse me?"

"I—I'm sorry." Allie bent to pick up her pocketbook and

to conceal the rush of heat in her face. "That was a personal question and none of my business whatsoever."

Miss Montclair chuckled, and Allie glanced up to her. Miss Montclair rested on the edge of the table, leaned back on her hands, and crossed her ankles—very Katharine Hepburn. "Your dear mother never understood me. So what is your question? Am I happy in my tragic poverty? Or am I happy as a pathetic old spinster?"

"As a spin—I mean . . ." Allie's cheeks flamed.

"I know what you mean. Yes, I am happy, despite what Riverside society says. As for my poverty, I never wanted to run a citrus packing plant. Perhaps I should regret putting my money in stocks, but if I hadn't, I never would have gained this."

She spread her arms wide, and her eyes gleamed like polished pewter. "I never would have discovered my talents for dressmaking and design, my business acumen, my gift for fulfilling dreams. And I certainly wouldn't be happy if I'd married the man my family selected."

Allie scrutinized her face. This was no brave front; her happiness was genuine.

"Why not, you ask?" Miss Montclair directed an amused look down the craggy tip of her nose. "Can you imagine anything more miserable than living with a man you don't love?"

Allie tried to swallow, but her tongue felt like a slab of concrete.

"Oh, not that silly, romantic love. Heavens, it's fun, but it won't sustain you. No, in this business you watch and learn. Good marriages are built on deep love based on respect and friendship."

Respect? Friendship? Although she respected Baxter, she'd never considered him a friend.

"Are you marrying your best friend?" Eagle eyes peered down from a stony aerie.

Her best friend? Who was her best friend? Definitely not Baxter. Betty had been her best friend for over four years, but now they only corresponded by letter.

Letters. Allie's mouth dried up like the local Santa Ana River in the summer. Whose letters did she long for most? Whom did she think of first when she had a story to tell? Who understood her best? Who chose her when he needed understanding? With whom did she share respect and friendship?

"Perhaps . . ." Miss Montclair fingered the sleeve of Mother's gown. "Perhaps I should wait before I make further alterations."

But Allie could only hear Mother's voice in that very store, brimming with joy and approval: *I'm thrilled about this wedding, Agatha. I've dreamed of it for five years.*

"No." Allie stood with a harsh scrape of chair legs over the wooden floor. "No. Get on with it."

31

2nd Evacuation Hospital; Diddington, Huntingdonshire
January 29, 1943

He should have stopped after the second letter.

Walt's cough reverberated off the walls of the Nissen hut that served as a medical ward.

"Would you like some more cough medicine, Captain Novak?"

He pried his head off the pillow. Lieutenant Doherty smiled down at him. The nurse's striking looks had led half the men in the ward to ask her out in the two days he had been there.

"No, thanks," he croaked. No medicine could make him feel better. He let his head flop to the pillow, and he stared at the three letters on the mattress beside him.

The first letter was great. George and Betty Anello were expecting a baby in June. At least this kid would never lose a dad to war as the Kilpatricks had.

The second letter was also great. He'd dreaded Allie's response to his crazy letter the day Frank died, but why had he doubted her? She understood. She always understood. She mourned with him, comforted him, and even encouraged him to unburden on her again.

Then he'd read the third letter. July—Allie was getting married in July. He was supposed to rejoice with her. That's what a friend would do. That's what she'd do for him. But no, the pain in his chest worsened, raw from coughing, heavy with phlegm, and now a stupid ache in his heart.

Lieutenant Doherty came beside Walt's bed, tucked a strand of dark red hair under her nurse's cap, and laid an icy compress on his forehead. "I hope you didn't get bad news from home."

Coolness seeped down to his eyelids. "Depends on your point of view."

"Point of view?" She placed a chilly hand behind his neck and eased him up to sitting.

Walt swallowed the aspirin she gave him. "The woman I love is marrying another man." Wow, the truth felt good, even if Lieutenant Doherty's face fell.

"I'm so sorry, and what an awful time for you to find out."

The compress slipped, and he pressed it to his forehead. "Nah, it's not like that. She's a good friend, but she's dated this fellow for years. She doesn't know I love her."

"Why don't you tell her?"

"Excuse me?"

"Why don't you tell her?" Lieutenant Doherty smiled and poured some medicine. "If she's upset, you can chalk it up to feverish delusions."

Walt chuckled, which brought on a coughing fit. "No. No more lies."

"Good, so you'll tell her the truth."

"What good would it do? I'd look like a fool." He choked down the nasty cough medicine.

"Nonsense. Even if she's upset, deep down she'll be touched. And what if—what if she loves you too, and she's waiting for you to say it first?"

He scowled at her. "Don't feed my feverish delusions."

She laughed. "Think about it, Captain. You have nothing to lose and everything to gain." She crossed the room to help another patient.

Walt slipped down in his cot and stared at the arch of corrugated steel over his head. What did he have to lose? Allie's friendship, her letters, and her prayers. What did he have to gain? Not her love. Lieutenant Doherty watched too many Hollywood movies.

He rolled his head to the side and picked up Allie's first letter. She admired his honesty after Frank's death. Maybe she'd admire his honesty about his love. Wouldn't it feel good to tell the truth?

He closed his eyes. *Lord, I don't want to lie anymore. It makes me sicker than these germs in my lungs. Please help me tell the truth.*

"Hiya, Preach. Trying to get out of flying?"

He looked up to see his crew file into the hut. "Hi, fellas."

"Boy, do we have good news for you." Abe sat on the empty cot to Walt's left. "McKee—one of the pilots shot down over Romilly—he evaded capture and made it back to England."

"Say, that is good news." Walt hitched himself higher and set aside the compress.

"Wait till you hear this." J.P. sat next to Abe. "He said a bomb fell on a mess hall that day. Two hundred fewer Nazis in this world."

"Wow."

"Kilpatrick's revenge," J.P. said.

"Yeah," Walt said quietly. Nothing could make up for

Frank's death, but at least he and his crew didn't die in vain.

"Say, Preach, do me a favor." Louis stood at the foot of the bed and ogled Lieutenant Doherty's shapely figure across the hut. "Cough on me, would you?"

Cracker whistled. "You're one lucky man."

Al Worley craned his scrawny neck to see over Louis's shoulder. "You don't need to cough on me. I feel a fever coming on."

"All right, men, leave her alone," Walt said.

"Did you say something about a fever?" Lieutenant Doherty crossed the room with concern all over her face. She pressed her hand to Al's forehead, making his hair stick up like straw. "We'll need to give you a nice, long sponge bath."

"Y-y-yes, ma'am."

"Sergeant Giovanni?" she called to a burly orderly. "You'll see to it, won't you?"

"Sure thing, Lieutenant." Giovanni cracked his knuckles and nodded at Al. "That the fella?"

"You know, I—I feel a lot—a lot better," Al said.

Walt joined his crewmates in laughter. Lieutenant Doherty turned and dropped Walt a wink over her shoulder—she appreciated his protection, but she could handle herself.

"Whoa, Preach, I saw that wink," Louis said. "Allie will be mighty jealous."

Walt glanced up to nine smiling faces. *Lord, don't make me do this. What harm is this story doing?*

His chest contracted in a spasm of coughs. This story was a lie, and it was doing plenty of harm, tearing him up like the pneumonia. The man his crew respected didn't exist. Only Walter Novak existed, a man living in disobedience to the God he claimed to love.

"Allie." He squeezed his eyes shut. Why was it so much easier to tell a lie than the truth? "Allie's getting married."

"What?" Abe said. "She sent you a Dear John letter?"

"No. No." Walt set his letters on the nightstand. "Allie's not my girlfriend. She never was. She's just a friend. She never loved me, never will. I'm afraid I've been lying to you."

"You lied to us?" Louis said. "Why on earth would you lie about that?"

"I was tired." Walt let his head fall back, and he winced when he struck the wall. "I've never had a girlfriend, never even had the guts to ask a girl out. I was tired of the wise-cracks, tired of everyone pestering me to go out on the town. If I had a girlfriend, everyone would leave me alone."

"Something's wrong with a man who can't ask out a girl." Cracker's eyes glinted in a way Walt hadn't seen for months.

Walt swallowed hard. He hated pride in others—and in himself. Pride led him to lie in the first place. "You're right."

Abe got to his feet. Anger sharpened the angles of his face. "No, something's wrong with a man who lies to his friends."

"You're right." His stomach knotted up. What harm had his lie done? He insulted his friends.

Bill Perkins stepped forward. "Come on. You guys are always bragging about conquests—all lies, and you know it. Why are you getting on Walt's case?"

Al grasped the footboard and leaned toward Bill. "'Cause he's always on our case. He preaches at us, won't let us have any fun, makes himself sound so holy with all that Bible talk, and all this time he's lying to us. He's nothing but a hypocrite."

Walt flinched. What harm had his lie done? The worst possible—he discredited God.

"Come on, men," Cracker said. "Let's get out of here."

Walt looked away when they left so he couldn't see the disgust in their eyes. Just because he deserved it didn't make it easier.

He scooted under the covers and rolled to his left side. J.P. still sat on the cot next to him. Something lightened in Walt's chest. He ventured half a smile. "Wow. That was bad."

J.P. traced the blue and gold piping on the garrison cap he held between his knees. "You know, in my last letter home, I told Mama there was no man I admired as much as Walter Novak. I told her I wanted to be just like you, go to college, become an engineer, be the kind of man everyone respects." He looked up, his dark eyes narrow and distant.

Walt sighed. He'd lost that respect.

"Reminds me of something you once told the crew," J.P. said. "Dishonesty always has a price."

32

Riverside

February 14, 1943

"God of Our Fathers" sounded grander on St. Timothy's pipe organ, with rousing trumpetlike blasts before each verse, but Allie pounded the chords on Groveside Bible Church's piano with grand enough results.

"'Lead us from night to never-ending day,'" the congregation sang out, voices full and throaty with emotion. When she finished, sniffles and sighs rewarded her far more than a standing ovation would have.

Could Baxter feel the difference between St. Timothy's stuffy service and Groveside's genuine worship? Allie glanced at her fiancé in the third pew in an immaculate navy pin-striped suit, his face set in polite appreciation.

Allie returned to her seat beside him, still in disbelief that she had persuaded him to come. She had pleaded with him, explaining how she'd prepared a special piece for the service and wanted her fiancé by her side. To her surprise, her pleas worked.

Since the Lord seemed to insist she had to marry a Christian, Baxter needed to become a Christian—and soon. *Please, Lord, let the sermon touch his heart.*

Baxter sat straight, his hat in his lap, his head inclined at a gentlemanly angle, and Allie grew tense as she looked through Baxter's eyes. For the first time in months, she saw the shabby interior and the unfashionable attire of the members. She heard the twang in her pastor's speech and the *amens* around her. She felt the grungy pew cushions and the sunlight unfiltered by stained glass.

Could Baxter hear the Word of God if his mind was prejudiced against the bearers of the message? If he didn't listen at Groveside, where would he hear? Certainly not at St. Timothy's.

From Allie? She hadn't been able to sway him in five years—five years in which he was supposedly courting her. Why would five more months make a difference?

What about after they were married? Allie sucked on her teeth and opened her eyes wide to dry the threatening tears.

"Love each other, love and serve the Lord together, and he'll bless your marriage," Walt had written in his last letter, which brimmed with congratulations and cheer even though sent from the hospital. What a dear friend he was.

She had to stop thinking about Walt. This wasn't about Walt. This was about Allie and Baxter and God. But Walt's statement stung her heart. She and Baxter didn't love each other, and Baxter didn't love or serve the Lord, so they could hardly do so together.

"Allie," Baxter whispered. He nudged her and cocked his head toward the piano.

Silence. Pastor Morris smiled down at Allie. She'd missed her cue for the closing hymn. "Young people in love," the pastor said.

Gentle laughter bruised Allie's ears as she walked to the

piano. She stumbled over several chords in the simple hymn. In love? If only they knew.

After the service, Baxter guided Allie down the aisle and allowed her to make only cursory introductions. Even though his disapproval hung thick in the air on the brisk walk home, an incongruent peace settled in Allie's heart. God wanted her at Groveside, the right and best place for her, and nothing Baxter could say would take away her joy.

"I counted seven employees of Miller Ball Bearings," he said when they crossed the Miller property line.

"Yes?" She tucked her hands in the pockets of her camel-colored coat. She knew what he meant, but she wanted him to voice his snobbery.

"It isn't seemly for management to worship with labor."

"Why not?" she said, unable to keep a note of enjoyment from her voice.

Baxter's mouth spread and twisted. "It isn't seemly. It's bad for authority. It implies you're equals."

"We are."

"Don't be ridiculous."

"I'm not." She gave a dry leaf a flip with the toe of her shoe. "Jesus Christ—King of kings and Lord of lords—he associated with the poor. Why shouldn't I? Besides, worship is about God, not social status."

"Don't be naïve. Everything's about social status."

Allie stopped and faced him. "Especially your choice of a wife."

"Well, yes. And for our sake, you need to remember your place in society." He flung an arm in the direction of Grove-side. "Those people. I've spent my entire life getting away from people like that. You—you have everything—wealth, breeding, social position, yet you throw it away and sully your family name."

Her neck stiffened. "I fail to see how I've sullied my family name."

"The gossip, Allie." His gaze ran the length of the Millers' wrought iron fence. "Everyone is talking. Your parents are humiliated, as am I. Your mother tells people you're doing charity work, but no one believes it. They know that filthy little church is taking advantage of you. You're only a bank account to them."

She laughed. "Why would that bother you? That's all I am to you."

Baxter's eyes rounded. "That—that's not true."

"You're right. I'm so much more to you. I'm an inheritance and social standing and respectability and a chance to please my father."

"This is nonsense." He turned and strode down Magnolia, his voice quiet, but not quiet enough to conceal a tremor. "You changed the subject. We're talking about that church. They run you ragged like a common laborer. You're above this kind of work. You should be behind the scenes like your mother, raising money for worthy causes."

"That's not what I want. I want to serve." Allie matched her stride to his.

He shot her a glare. "I've tolerated this because I knew it was temporary, but I've had enough."

"Temporary?"

"After we're married, you won't have time for the Red Cross and you will not attend that church."

"Yes, I will." But could she? Could they actually attend separate churches? What about their children? Would he let her take them to Groveside? She mustn't let them attend St. Timothy's.

Baxter turned to her with strength in his gaze Allie would have found attractive in different circumstances. "I forbid it.

In fact, I forbid it right now. You'll give appropriate notice to the Red Cross, and you'll never return to that church."

He expected her to give up her volunteer work and go back to St. Timothy's? To return to a drab, purposeless life? To disobey God? That was what he demanded—for her to defy God's will. She stared into his sharp blue eyes under his navy blue hat. Mr. and Mrs. J. Baxter Hicks would try to play a duet, but they would play in different keys, and they would always do so unless Allie succumbed to the temptation to slip into Baxter's key for the sake of harmony. Something precious would drain from her soul if she honored Baxter rather than God.

Baxter's face softened. He took her elbow and led her down the street. "Come on. It's for your own good."

This was what unequal yoking was. She could already feel the yoke on her shoulders, binding her to Baxter. He would pull in one direction, the Lord would pull in another, and Allie would be torn apart.

Suddenly scandal, gossip, inconvenience, even her parents' anger and disapproval seemed a small price. Her blood seemed to stop and congeal, as did the thoughts in her head. It was time to choose obedience.

Oh, dear Lord, if this is truly your will, please give me strength.

Baxter guided her around the brick pillar at the base of the driveway. Allie drew a deep breath, which caught several times on the way in. "Baxter, I can't do what you ask of me."

"Excuse me?" He faced her under the glossy leaves of an orange tree. When he saw her expression, his eyebrows twitched, and his grip on her elbow tightened. "Don't you—don't you always say you have to obey the Bible?"

"Yes." She felt taller, stronger, and braver than ever before.

"Well, the Bible—" The line of his lips undulated like an ocean wave. "The Bible says a wife must submit to her husband."

"Yes, it does." Allie pried Baxter's hand off her arm and worked the engagement ring off her finger. "That's why I can't become your wife."

"What?" His cheeks paled.

She held out the ring. "I won't submit to a man who asks me to disobey God."

"I—I'm not—"

"Yes, you are." With peace and resolve, she pressed the ring into his palm and folded his fingers around it. "I'm sorry. I know your house is almost finished, and there will be gossip and scandal and awkwardness, but this is for the best. Why, we don't even love each other."

"How can you—how can you say that?"

Allie sighed and gazed into his stricken face. J. Baxter Hicks had come so close to fulfilling his dreams, and now she had dashed them. "I'm so sorry. I do care for you, but I don't love you, and I know you don't love me."

"Love?" Baxter's eyes narrowed. "Need I remind you? You're rather plain to be choosy."

"*You're a lovely woman, Allegra Miller, and you're very special,*" Walt had said to her on the train platform, his eyes and kiss confirming his words. "*Don't let anyone ever tell you otherwise.*"

"How dare you? That's not true." The forcefulness of her voice surprised her. "Even if it were, that doesn't mean I'm unworthy of love. Cressie was never pretty, and her husband adores her. I want a marriage like that, based on love, friendship, and faith. If I can't, I'd rather not marry at all. Why, Miss Montclair is happy, and I can be too."

"This is absolute nonsense. Come on. We'll discuss this later."

Allie followed Baxter to the house, but no discussion was necessary. She looked down at her ring finger. Her hand and her soul shivered in the freedom and delight of nakedness.

★

Father folded the newspaper in his lap when Baxter and Allie entered the sitting room. "How was the service?"

"She won't be going back," Baxter said in a low voice.

"Yes, I will." She crossed the dining room with a swing in her arms and entered the kitchen. "Hello, Mother."

"Well, hello." She slid the chicken into the oven. "How was church?"

"I loved it. Baxter hated it." She draped her coat over a chair and suppressed a bubble of laughter. She'd made a decision that would upend the household, and she wanted to laugh for joy.

"Oh?" Mother said. "You sound remarkably cheerful about that."

"Strange, isn't it?" Allie washed her hands at the sink, and Mother came to her side to fill a pot with water. Allie looked deep in her mother's eyes. If only she'd understand. If only she'd still approve. "Please be happy for me."

Mother's forehead crinkled. "I'm very happy for you. You're marrying a fine man." She glanced down to Allie's left hand, to her right, back to her left. "Oh, Allie, your ring. Don't tell me you lost it. Oh dear, where could it be? Does Baxter know?"

She sighed. "Yes, he knows. It's best if we discussed this after dinner."

However, Mother took off her apron and dashed through the kitchen door.

Oh no. Not now. Not like this. Allie hastened to follow her into the sitting room.

"Baxter, I'm so sorry," Mother said. "We'll find that ring if we have to turn the house inside out."

"The ring?" Baxter's shock dissolved into a smile. He fished the ring from his breast pocket. "I have it right here. Don't worry, Allie, I kept it safe for you."

"Thank goodness." Mother took the ring and brought it to Allie. "You had me worried for nothing."

They smiled at her, Baxter with an extra measure of satisfaction.

Allie had been presented an escape route from parental wrath. She straightened her shoulders, as if throwing off the yoke again. "I gave it to Baxter for a reason, but I'd rather tell you after dinner."

"Nothing to worry about," Baxter said, his smile stiff but assured. "Just a little lovers' spat."

She rolled her eyes. A lovers' spat? They'd have to be in love to have a lovers' spat.

"Allie, be careful what you say in an argument. Never say anything you'll regret later." Mother took her hand to give her the ring.

She pulled free. "I'd rather talk about this later."

Mother's face began to lose its color, Father rose to his feet, and Baxter settled back in his chair with a smug smile. Allie glanced to an alpine landscape hanging on the wall. *Lord, I need a mountain of your strength now.*

Father stepped next to Mother, his face set. "Allie, put your ring on."

He wouldn't be her defender this time. Her heart sank, and she drew a breath to buoy it. "No, I won't. We didn't have an argument, and I'll never regret what I did. I've prayed about this and I know I've done the right thing."

Baxter lit a cigarette. "She'll get past this. All brides get cold feet."

Allie wrestled back her exasperation. If she lost her temper, they'd think she'd made a rash decision. "My feet have never been warmer. I've broken the engagement. I will not marry you."

"Allie . . ." Mother turned the garish ring in her fingers.

Poor Mother. "I'm so sorry. I know how awful this is for all of you. I know how this marriage fulfills your dreams—but I won't let that happen at my expense."

"Your expense?" Baxter blew out a plume of smoke. "The expense of silly schoolgirl fantasies? Go ahead. Explain your reasoning."

She searched her parents' eyes for mercy. "What's silly about wanting a marriage as happy as yours? I can't marry a man I don't love, I can't marry a man who doesn't love me, and I certainly can't marry a man who doesn't share my faith."

"Oh," Mother gasped. "How can you say such things?"

Father pointed to Baxter. His arm shook. "Allie, you'll apologize to Baxter this instant."

"I do apologize. I apologize for the hassle, the shame, the disappointment, but I refuse to apologize for my decision."

Mother's lips quivered, and Father's face reddened. Allie shook her head and turned to go upstairs. She wouldn't have dinner today, but in all likelihood, no one else would either.

"Don't worry, Baxter," Father said. "She's a sensible girl. She'll come around."

"I won't cancel anything," Mother said. "You'll be married July 3."

Allie sighed. The ordeal was far from over, but the Lord would help her. He'd already helped beyond measure, with all that strength and peace and joy. She glimpsed herself in the mirror in the entryway and halted. She didn't look *almost* pretty—she looked pretty, with a slight smile and a gleam in her eyes.

Allegro and adagio. A swell combination. Her smile lifted in a crescendo, and her heels tapped a pizzicato on the stairs.

In her room she pulled out stationery and penned a long letter to Walt, relaying the day's events, including the irony that his blessing on her engagement helped her break it. The letter overflowed with joy.

When she finished, she reviewed the pages and frowned at the intimacy of the letter. What if Walt felt responsible? What if he thought she harbored inappropriate feelings for him?

Allie puffed her cheeks full of air. She needed time and prayer to figure out how to tell him in a proper manner.

Proper? Was it proper that the first person she wanted to tell was Walter Novak?

33

Thurleigh

February 18, 1943

"Come to the hardstand at 1500."

Walt studied the note on his pillow in Cracker's handwriting. What? Was this like the "meet me on the playground after school" note he'd gotten from Howie Osgood in fifth grade? The note that led to his first black eye? At least Howie's shiner had been bigger than Walt's.

He sat on his cot and pulled out the letter to Allie he'd started before lunch. He was in no condition for a fight. He'd only been discharged from the hospital that morning and he still felt as if a B-17 had crash-landed on his chest.

Walt stretched out on his back and read Allie's letter again. Strange letter—sounded flat. She described her work and activities, but it was like a newspaper account without her usual color and humor. At the end of the letter, she rambled about obedience and sacrifice, and then she asked his opinion and ratcheted up the level of their communication again. She had a spiritual question, and she didn't ask her fiancé, pastor, or church friends. She asked him.

Apparently she needed his friendship as much as he needed hers. Good thing he'd decided not to tell her of his love.

He rolled to his side and pulled out the concordance Dad gave him for a high school graduation present, convinced Walt would be a pastor. The concordance came in handy today. Allie wanted godly instruction, and he was determined to give it to her.

After a while, he had several passages marked, and he picked up his pen.

That's one interesting verse you asked about. Couldn't you have asked about something simple like John 3:16? No, I take that back. What's simple about God loving us and sending his Son for us? I'll give this my best shot, but remember you asked Captain Novak, not Pastor Novak.

Wow, there's a lot in the Bible on this topic. We know God is pleased with sacrifice and asks us to make offerings to him, but sometimes sacrifices displease God and he rejects them. You've already found 1 Samuel 15:22—strong verse, isn't it? In Micah 6:6–8, the prophet tells us what the Lord prefers over sacrifice—justice, mercy, and walking humbly with God. Psalm 51:16–17 reads, "For thou desirest not sacrifice; else would I give it. . .The sacrifices of God are a broken spirit: a broken and a contrite heart, O God, thou wilt not despise." Hosea 6:6 is so good, Jesus quotes it twice in Matthew: "For I desired mercy, and not sacrifice; and the knowledge of God more than burnt-offerings."

See the theme, Allie? When we're not following God's will, our sacrifices aren't acceptable to him. What God wants most is for us to be broken before him, walk with him, know him, and obey him.

Am I preaching to you, or are you preaching to me? This sure addresses something I'm going through. I joined the Army Air Force more than willing to sacrifice my life for my country. I sacrificed my opportunity to be squadron commander to keep the crew together. Sacrifice makes me feel good and noble.

But the Lord wants my obedience. Remember the orange on the train? You didn't say a lot, but I could tell you were disappointed in me for saying I didn't like oranges. I've always been able to justify my little white lies. But lately God has given me a tough time about honesty and shown me how my lies come from pride. I hate pride. God detests pride. I realized I had to stop telling those ball bearing lies. Worse, I had to confess to my crew a lie I told them—a whopper, I'm afraid. I didn't feel good and noble. I felt like a louse. I let everyone down and lost the respect I worked so hard to earn. Times like this I really miss Frank. It's been lonely since

I fessed up. I did the right thing, but obedience can be tough.

Wherever God wants your obedience, Allie, I hope the consequences are light. Even if they aren't, you must follow God's will. As always, I'm praying for you.

Walt signed his name, sat up, and stretched. Still had time to stop by the PX and mail the letter before going to the hardstand to take the consequences of his obedience.

No, the consequences of his sin.

★

"Hey, what's he doing here?" Al scrambled to his feet and scowled at Walt.

Cracker stood in front of Al. "Sit on that scrawny backside, Worley. He's the reason you're here. Yeah, in more ways than one."

Walt clenched the lining of his trouser pockets. The whole crew sat on the hardstand by the hut the ground crew had assembled from broken-down crates to keep warm while they worked.

Cracker leaned against the wall of the hut. "Glad you came, Preach."

Walt studied the men's unwelcoming faces. J.P. wouldn't even look at him. "Thanks for the party invitation."

"Got anything to say to us?" Cracker had a slight smile on his face, but not a malicious smile. What was he up to?

"Um, well, yeah. Once again, I'm sorry I lied. I showed you a lack of trust and respect, and I disobeyed God repeatedly. I'm sorry. I won't lie to you again."

Al spat into the grass. "Can't trust a liar, my mama always says."

"Ever tell a lie, Worley?" Cracker asked.

"Uh—"

"Of course, you have. Ever lie to Preach?"

"Uh—"

"Remember when we tried to import liquor? All of us lied to him except Sanchez, because we didn't tell him, and Wisniewski, because he wasn't there."

"That—that's different."

"You're right, that's different. Our lie almost got us all killed. His lie made us think he had a girlfriend. So what?"

Walt's jaw went slack. Cracker was defending him?

"That's why I called this meeting." Cracker set one foot on a crate and leaned his forearms on his knee. "Preach apologized and promised to be straight with us. We shunned him for the three weeks he was in the hospital. That's more than enough punishment. We're a crew, and we need to work together."

"Go ahead," Al said. "I'm putting in for a transfer to another crew."

"Me too," Harry said.

Louis sighed and glanced over his shoulder to the gunners. "Don't be stupid. Y'all know Preach is one of the best pilots in this outfit." His voice was heavy though, and he didn't look at Walt.

"The best," Cracker said. "How many scrapes has he gotten us out of? He's not just a good pilot, but also a good man. His example got me out of the bars and into church services and settled down with Margaret."

"That's irony for you." Walt still couldn't believe he wasn't getting beaten up.

"Yeah, I noticed," Cracker said. "But you know what, men? Now I like Preach more. He's not so perfect; he's human."

"Too human." Walt lifted half a smile. His nemesis had become his ally. He never would have guessed it.

"Yeah." J.P. chucked a pebble into the bushes by the hut. "But I don't lie to my friends, much less keep on lying to them."

"He could have kept lying, you know. We never would have known." Abe looked up over his shoulder to Walt. "You told us the truth. That takes integrity. You didn't have to do that."

"Yeah, I did." Walt sat down cross-legged on the tarmac.

"Besides," Cracker said. "We drove him to it."

"Huh?" Walt said.

"We gave you a tough time for being a good man."

Walt coughed a stiff, dry cough. "Nope. A sorry excuse for a man."

"Won't argue with you there," Louis said, but a smile cracked his face.

"Neither will I." Cracker grasped the door of the shed. "Which is why I have a mission for the men of *Flossie's Fort*. Preach shouldn't have to make up a girlfriend. Men, our target for today—sorry, I couldn't find a blue cloth."

He flung open the door of the shed. Two pictures were tacked to the inside of the door, joined by a red string. The first picture was a stick figure—had to be Walt, judging by the double bars on the cap. The second showed stick figure Walt with his stick arms around a stick figure girl.

Walt laughed. "You've got to be kidding."

"We thought St. Nazaire was a tough target," Abe said.

The way the men laughed told him Cracker had succeeded. Now Walt owed *him* a Coke. A lot more than a Coke.

"I won't lie to you, men," Cracker said with a wink at Walt. "This is one rugged mission. Weather will be bad, flak will be heavy, and opposition will be intense. But this is our mission—find Walter Novak a real live woman."

✫

February 26, 1943

"She's here, Preach," Louis said.

"Who?" Walt stuffed his gloves into his pockets and crossed his arms underneath his flight jacket to warm his hands in the fleece lining.

"The Red Cross girl. She's sweet on you. I can tell by the way she watches you."

Walt rolled his eyes. No one had ever been sweet on him.

Cracker glanced over the heads of Butterfield's crew, ahead of them in line for coffee and doughnuts before debriefing. "Say, that's Emily Fairfax. She's Margaret's best friend." He turned to Walt, his blue eyes wide. "You're the one she likes? Well, I'll be. Operation Novak is cleared for takeoff."

"You must have had a kink in your oxygen hose today." Walt stamped his feet for warmth. It had been one of the coldest missions ever, so cold most of the B-24s had aborted. The Liberators didn't function at a temperature less than forty degrees below zero.

"Now it all makes sense. Margaret said Emily never bothers with the dances here on base, because the chap she fancies never attends," Cracker said in a decent British accent.

"Come on, I've never even met the girl." Walt glanced at her out of the corner of his eye—a brunette with small, close-set eyes.

"All the pieces are in place. She doesn't know your name, just likes your face. Can't imagine why."

"See, it can't be me." Walt scanned the room. The 306th seemed to have emerged intact today, although the crew saw several Forts fall in other groups.

"Coming up on the target." Abe stepped forward in line. "Looks clear, Preach."

"Yeah. As clear as Bremen today." The thick cloud cover over Bremen had forced the Eighth to drop their bombs on Wilhelmshaven instead.

"Who needs the Luftwaffe?" Louis said. "You're shooting yourself down."

Walt groaned and burrowed his hands deeper under his jacket. Still numb. Emily caught his eye over Butterfield's shoulder and lifted a shy smile, kind of like Allie's.

"She likes you." Cracker nudged him in the ribs. "Make your move."

"Come on . . ."

Butterfield stepped away from the counter, and Emily smiled at Walt. "It's good to see you chaps. You were absent so long, I started to fret."

Louis slung an arm over Walt's shoulder. "Preach here was in the hospital with pneumonia."

"Oh dear. I didn't know you were ill."

"I'm okay now." He took the doughnut she offered. She noticed he was gone? Why? Cracker couldn't be right.

"I'm so pleased to see you're well." Emily poured a cup of coffee.

Louis jiggled Walt's shoulder. "Better make it a double for Preach. He could use some beefing up after that illness."

Cracker leaned his elbows on the counter. "And some cheering up after those lonely days in the ward."

Emily's eyes were hazel, like Walt's. She slid him the cup of coffee and another doughnut. "Would an extra doughnut help, Captain Preach?"

The men howled with laughter, and Walt had to smile despite Emily's confused expression. "Preach is a nickname," he said.

"His name's Novak," Abe said.

"Walter Novak." He wrapped his hands around the coffee mug, and his fingers were so cold they registered the heat as ice. Wait, his fingers were frozen, but his tongue wasn't. She was available and interested, and he was talking to her.

"So, Captain Novak," Emily said with a sweep of brown lashes. "Why do they call you Preach?"

"My dad's a pastor, and I've never been ashamed of my faith." The pain in his fingers mellowed to warmth. Emily's smile seemed warmer too.

"And Walt's a straight arrow," Louis said. "Don't come any straighter."

"If your faith is so important, why have I never seen you at St. Paul's?"

She was flirting. She was actually flirting, but his throat didn't tighten and his tongue didn't swell. In fact, he smiled. "I go to church here on base."

"Maybe you should visit St. Paul's sometime and see how we British worship."

Perhaps the situation with Allie had served its purpose and shown him he didn't have to freeze up with a woman. He drew on everything good from his furlough and smiled at Emily. "Maybe if I knew I would see a familiar face."

She pulled the spigot on the coffee urn. "If you'd like, you could sit with my family, and if you'd like, you could have Sunday dinner with us—if you'd like." Her cheeks darkened to a deep pink.

The last bit of weight lifted from his chest. This was how he could get over Allie. The solution stood right in front of him, nervous and—yes!—sweet on him. On him—Capt. Walter J. Novak.

He grinned at her. "I'd like that."

34

Riverside

March 13, 1943

"Congratulations, sweetheart." Father smiled and slid Allie's Red Cross service ribbon back to her across the dining room table. "You've earned it."

"Thank you, but volunteering is its own reward." Nevertheless, she ran her finger along the red ribbon with its thin gold stripe.

"A thousand hours." Mother clucked her tongue. "If you spent even a fraction of that time on wedding—"

"Mother, please." Allie rose and gathered the serving dishes from the patriotic meatless dinner.

"Don't worry, Mary," Father said. "Allie's intelligent and loyal. She'll come around."

Baxter dabbed his mouth with his napkin. "How *are* the wedding plans coming?"

Allie escaped to the kitchen. She didn't know what was more exasperating—Father insisting she'd come to her senses, Mother fussing over a wedding that wouldn't occur, or Baxter acting as if nothing had changed. Allie had taken to spending evenings in her room or out with Daisy on her evening off.

She set the dishes on the counter, determined to wash up before Daisy arrived.

"No, no, Miss Miller." Juanita, the new housekeeper, grasped her shoulders and turned her toward the door. "This is my job. Enjoy the evening with your family."

If only she could. Allie groaned and returned to the dining room.

"I need to discuss something with you, Allie," Mother said after Juanita cleared the table. "Oh, such a problem. Mrs. Rivers called from the florist. Roses are unavailable. All the flower farms—well, the Japanese owned them, and now they've been converted to food production. You must go to the florist on Thursday and see if there are any acceptable alternatives."

"No wedding, no flowers." Allie stood, pushed in her chair, and smiled at her mother. "I'm going out with Daisy. Have a lovely evening." The doorbell summoned her from maternal protests.

"Your timing couldn't be better, Daisy." Allie shut the front door and slipped on her spring coat.

"Are they still treating you like—"

"I'd rather not talk about it. Only pleasant topics, please." Allie trotted down the front steps and smiled at her friend. "I love your new hat." While made of cheap materials, the curve of the brim flattered Daisy's round face.

"Thanks. Daddy says I look like Ingrid Bergman in *Casablanca*."

"Well, come along, Ingrid. Let's make a night of it." Allie hooked her arm through Daisy's and sauntered down the driveway.

"I'm so glad you broke up with Baxter. You're much more fun now."

Allie laughed. "The joy of obedience. But Baxter is not a pleasant topic. Change subjects, please."

"Okay. Get any letters today?"

"Yes, I got a nice letter from my friend Betty in Antioch."

"She's the one who's expecting, isn't she?"

"Yes, in June." She mentally reviewed the letter for news to relate. The death of Jim Carlisle had brought Dorothy and Art closer together—Jim's sister and his best friend. On the other hand, Helen Carlisle dealt with widowhood by immersing herself—drowning herself, Betty insisted—in committees and volunteer work. However, Daisy knew none of these people.

"What's she think of your broken engagement?"

"Who? Betty? Oh, I haven't told her."

"You haven't? Why not?"

"Hurry. I see the bus." Allie picked up the pace down the driveway.

"It's going the wrong way, and so are you. Don't tell me you're going to change your mind about Baxter."

"No, never." Allie looked both ways and headed across Magnolia. "It's just that I want people to hear the news firsthand. For example, what if I told Betty, and she wrote Walt, and her letter arrived before mine? I don't want that."

Daisy's eyes twinkled under the rim of her fedora. "What's Walt have to say?"

"There's our bus." Allie raised her arm to hail it.

"Ooh, she dodged the question."

Allie sent her an amused glare and dug in her purse for the fare. "Walt's fine. I received a letter today. He's out of the hospital."

"Thank goodness. I know his pneumonia worried you."

"Now I can just worry about combat." He had to be flying again. Her dreams had returned.

Daisy led the way up the steps of the bus. "What else does he have to say?"

Allie deposited her fare and considered how to describe his letter. She sat next to Daisy. "Remember when we discussed obedience and sacrifice at the scrap metal drive?"

"Yeah?" Daisy cracked her gum.

"I asked Walt's opinion, and he answered with a wonderful, clear, biblical analysis. I've already obeyed, but he reassured me."

"Didn't you say his dad was a pastor?"

"Yes, and I don't think Walt would be as bad a pastor as he claims. Of course, he's meant to be an engineer, a pilot, but he has such a strong and genuine faith."

Allie smiled. When he told her of his decision to tell the truth, she respected him more than ever. His candor touched her, his courage impressed her, and his new commitment to honesty filled her with even greater admiration. He was growing, changing, allowing God to reach him. The Lord had worked on them both with similar issues, and now they both had to endure the consequences of their decisions.

Warmth swirled in Allie's chest, deep and sweet and fulfilling. Somehow God bound them together in their struggles.

"But what does he have to say?" Daisy asked. "You know, about the engagement?"

Allie's gaze darted out the window. They were still several blocks from the theater, which eliminated the silent solution. "Well, I—I haven't told him."

"What? You're kidding. Why not?"

She rubbed her thumbs over the soft russet leather of her handbag. "I don't know. I try, but I can't find the right words. I crumple up every attempt and send my usual letters. Oh dear, and the longer I wait, the more awkward it gets. Now I have to explain why I waited a month to tell him."

"That's where all your fancy college words hang you up.

Tell him straight out." Daisy made a hacking motion. "I broke my engagement. I don't love Baxter. I love you."

Allie felt her jaw descend. "But I—I—"

"Yeah, I know it's brassy. That's the fun of it." Daisy looked at Allie, arched one eyebrow, and chomped her gum a bit. "Don't tell me you don't love him."

Allie could only stare, her thoughts mired as if in Daisy's chewing gum. "I—I—"

"Oh, come on. You're crazy about him. You should see your face when you talk about that man. Why, you light up brighter than that marquee used to before Pearl Har—oops! The theater."

Daisy stood, grabbed Allie's hand, and hauled her down the bus aisle—just as well, because Allie was incapable of independent movement. Why would Daisy think that? Why? Allie didn't love Walt, did she?

"Ooh, *For Me and My Gal*." Daisy studied the poster. "Judy Garland and some new fellow—Gene Kelly. Isn't he cute?"

Allie stared up at the bell tower over the box office of the Fox Theater. Was she in love with Walt?

They had a strong friendship grounded in respect, affection, and faith. And yes, she got a warm glow whenever she thought of him. The attraction lingered—and oh my, it had deepened to something more.

"Allie, are you okay?"

She lowered her gaze to Daisy and pried her tongue from the roof of her mouth. "I do. I do love him."

Daisy chuckled. "Of course. Everyone knows that."

Allie pressed her hand to her forehead to stop a wave of dizziness. "Please don't say that. Please don't tell me you think I broke up with Baxter because of Walt."

"Nonsense. Baxter didn't love you. But now he's out of the picture, and Walt's slipped right into your heart."

"He has, hasn't he?" Allie slid her dime to the lady in the box office. "Or was he always there?"

"That's a penny, miss."

Allie looked down to see Lincoln's likeness on steel—the new pennies to conserve copper for wartime use.

Daisy took Allie's purse, pulled out a coin, and gave it to the woman. "Forgive her. She's in love."

She pulled Allie into the theater, and Allie found herself laughing. "I am. I'm in love. Oh my goodness, Daisy, I'm in love."

"Oh, you got it bad."

"And that ain't good." Allie laughed at the title of the popular song. "Now what?"

"For a college girl, you're not that smart." Daisy led the way to seats in the center of the theater. "Now you tell him. At least you tell him you broke up with Baxter."

Allie settled into the plush seat. She couldn't tell him she loved him. That would be ridiculous. But she could tell him she broke her engagement, and tonight she'd write that letter.

The newsreel flashed black and white comfort—English fields, trim B-17s, and men in layers of sheepskin. Then Allie listened, really listened, and Daisy gripped her arm.

The Eighth Air Force announced a new policy, in which combat crews would finish their tours after twenty-five missions and then be transferred to stateside positions. No longer would they have to fly until this interminable war ended. No longer would they have to fly until they were horribly injured, captured, or killed. Now there was an end in sight. Now there was hope.

Twenty-five missions! Why, Allie already had eighteen probable missions marked on the slip of paper under *Flossie*. Walt could finish in a month or so. Then he'd come home.

She could see his smile, hear his laugh, smell the wool of his uniform, and feel the soft crush of his embrace.

Allie's eyes opened wide to the flickering image of a neat formation of Fortresses. Now she knew why she hadn't told him of her broken engagement. She had to see his face when he heard the news. She had to tell him in person.

35

Thurleigh

March 18, 1943

"Come on, fellas," Abe said. "I'm tired. I did the flying today."

Walt held open the door of the Officers' Club. "Just on the bomb run."

Abe yawned. "There I was—my bombsight linked to the autopilot for the first time. Still can't believe Preach gave up the controls, let the Automatic Flight Control Equipment kick in, let me fly for once."

"He didn't have a choice." Cracker nudged Abe through the door. "Sanchez and I held him back, and Wisniewski came up and gave him a sedative."

Louis stuck a finger in Cracker's face. "Preach gave up lying. Don't you start."

Walt chuckled and followed his officers into the club. Despite the length of the mission, heavy flak, and two hours straight of Luftwaffe attack, only Abe complained of fatigue. Walt felt energized. They'd been briefed to hit the submarine yards at Vegesack several times, but always had to turn for secondary targets due to cloud cover. Today, however, they had clear skies and near perfect bombing—seven U-boats mangled, unable to harass Allied convoys again. And for the third mission in a row, the 306th had no losses.

Walt glanced over at the piano. Good. No one was playing. He wanted to belt out some rousing tunes. He stood in line at the bar, but as soon as the Coke bottle hit his hand, the first chords of "In the Mood" hit his ears. Swell. Someone else wanted to belt out some rousing tunes.

He leaned back against the bar and sighed. The guy at the piano had his back to Walt. He was a major from the gold leaves on the shoulder straps of his shirt, and he was pretty good. While he played, he jiggled his leg and dipped his shoulder to the beat.

Jack did the same thing. Homesickness jabbed Walt in the stomach. He hadn't had a letter from either of his brothers for over a month.

"Who are those fellows by the piano?" Louis asked. "Never seen them before."

Walt shrugged. There were over two thousand men at Thurleigh, including almost three hundred officers.

"Must be a replacement crew," Cracker said.

"With a major?" Walt squinted at the group. Couple majors, couple captains.

Earl Butterfield leaned his elbows on the bar while his glass was refilled. "Didn't you hear? Four new bomb groups coming to England. We get two squadrons for training."

Walt's gaze flew back to the pianist with the jiggling knee and dipping shoulder. "Which group—94th?"

"Something in the nineties."

Couldn't be. He set his Coke on the bar and headed for the piano. With each step the man looked more like Jack—wavy black hair like Jack, broad shoulders like all the Novak men. No, wait—this guy had a mustache.

Then he turned to Walt with Jack's blue eyes and broad grin. "Figured the best way to draw Walter Novak out of the crowd was to play some music."

He just nodded and grinned. Seeing his brother was almost like being home—a face he'd seen all his life, a voice he'd heard all his life.

Jack stood and extended his hand.

Walt grasped it and pulled his brother into an embrace. "Jack Novak, what on earth are you doing over here? Haven't you heard there's a war on?"

"Sure have. Why do you think I'm here? Heard you fellows needed help." He thumped Walt's back and pulled away. "You do need help. You look ten years older. What happened to Mom's chipmunk cheeks?"

Walt frowned and felt his face. "Still there."

"Nah, you look different. Still ugly, but different."

Walt chuckled. "Speaking of ugly, why'd you grow the mustache?"

Jack stroked it and waggled his eyebrows. "The ladies love it. You should grow one."

Walt puffed up at the chance to brag. "Don't need one. Got a date on Saturday."

"You're kidding me."

"Nope. Red Cross girl from Bedford. She's coming out to the base for the dance."

"You? A girl? A dance? You're lying."

"Not lying. Never again. It's the truth—me, a girl, a dance."

"Wow." Jack's eyes widened—same gray blue as Mom's. "Can't believe my kid brother has a girlfriend."

Walt made a face. "She's not my girlfriend. I've been to church with her a couple times, dinner with her family. This is our first real date." And he barely felt like he'd given the invitation. Emily's hints about the dance were so broad, it would have been rude not to ask her.

"Say, let's find some chairs." Jack grabbed his flight jacket from the piano bench. "I've gotta hear this."

"Yeah." Walt frowned and scanned the room. Other than bragging about his date, he didn't want to talk about Emily, because he couldn't figure her out. She gave him those mooning looks Art Wayne gave Dorothy Carlisle, but Walt didn't know why. They didn't have much in common. Why did she like him? Because he was an American officer? Because her best friend was dating Cracker?

Made him uncomfortable. So did the stupid nagging feeling he was cheating on Allie. All that time pretending she was his girlfriend must have messed up his thinking.

Walt spotted his friends and a chance to distract Jack. "Want to meet my crew?"

"Yeah, and you've got to meet Charlie de Groot." Jack motioned to a man leaning on the piano. "Charlie was my bombardier with the 7th in the Pacific, and then we came to the 94th together."

Walt shook his hand. Charlie was a few inches shorter than Walt and Jack, and his round face, yellow hair, blue eyes, and pink cheeks made Walt think of Easter eggs. "Good to meet you. The way Jack talks, you're the best bombardier in the Army Air Force."

"I'm hurt." Abe Ruben's voice came from behind.

Walt turned to see his officers. Abe had a pout on his angular face. Walt flung an arm over Abe's shoulders. "But Jack's wrong. This man here's the best bombardier in the Army Air Force."

"Too late, Preach."

Jack chuckled. "Preach? I'll never get used to that. You realize he's the only Novak man who isn't a pastor?"

"Men," Walt said. "Meet my brother Jack."

Cracker shook Jack's hand, then Charlie's. "94th Bomb Group, I hear?"

"That's right," Jack said. "94th, 95th, 96th, and 351st are coming over. We're a lead contingent to set up training. Two of the squadrons from the 94th will go to Bassingbourn to train with the 91st, and two will come here. Since I'm squadron commander, they let me bring my men here so I can pester my kid brother."

Walt couldn't contain his grin. Some brotherly pestering sounded awful good—it even overrode the twinge of jealousy that Jack was a major and a squadron commander, and Walt wasn't.

Charlie stuck a cigarette in his mouth and gazed at the ceiling of the Officers' Club, where someone had added "3-18-43 Vegesack" to the smoky inscriptions. "How's it really going over here? The newsreels back home make it sound as if you had Hitler cowering in a bomb shelter, but the papers can't gloss over the losses."

"It's getting better," Walt said. "We're finally getting replacement crews and planes, and we're hitting some targets in Germany."

"And y'all are doubling the B-17 force over here." Louis took a swig of beer.

"If only we had fighter escort to keep the Germans away," Walt said. "The Spitfires the British loaned us are great little fighters, but they have to turn back at the French coast when things get rugged."

"The 4th Fighter Group just got P-47 Thunderbolts," Cracker said. "They've got better range, but still won't get us to Germany."

Charlie's cigarette waggled as he stared at the ceiling. "Twenty-eight missions? Anyone finished their tour yet?"

The men laughed. "Nowhere near," Walt said. "Not with aborts, damage, illness. We're pretty near the top at nineteen."

"Yeah," Cracker said. "We get Preach out of the hospital, and the brass sends us to the 'flak shack' at Stanbridge Earls for a week's R & R. Missed three missions."

Jack raised his eyebrows. "You went to some old English manor? You sure have it rough over here."

"Indubitably." Louis pinched up his face and lifted a pretend teacup, his pinky held high. "I do say, old chap, we sampled the finest tea and cr-r-r-rumpets, and saw Captain Novak play a smashing game of croquet."

Walt laughed, both from the memory and from his navigator's Louisiana-spiced British accent.

"We do mean *smashing*," Abe said. "He took out an old English manor window."

"Just a little one." Walt measured an inch between thumb and forefinger. "Don't tell Dad, or I'll tell him what really happened to his *Smith's Bible Dictionary*."

Jack clapped him on the back. "We need to catch up. It's been great meeting all of you."

Walt spied a table across the room. "There's a spot." He took the Coke bottle Louis had brought over for him, and the brothers staked out the table.

Jack tipped his chair back and crossed his ankles. "What's this about you not lying anymore? Who'll cover for me now?"

"Sorry. If you can't stay out of trouble, you're on your own."

Jack dropped him a wink. "Guess I'm on my own."

Walt chuckled and raised his bottle to his brother. Jack didn't need his help. His good looks and easy charm could get him out of any fix, get him anything he wanted, any woman he wanted.

If Walt had a fraction of Jack's gifts, Allie would be marrying him instead of Baxter the fop. Walt swallowed some soda to quench the spark of resentment. Ray and Jack had it all, but they were good men.

"Did you go home before you shipped out?" Walt asked.

"Ten-day furlough. Forgot how beautiful Antioch is this time of year—everything green, wildflowers coming up."

Walt nodded. "How are Dad and Mom?"

"Grayer. Funny how people age when you only see them once a year."

"Yeah, I noticed. The war's not helping."

Jack waved to Charlie over by the bar and made a drinking motion. "For the first time, they'll have two sons in combat. You were training when I was in the Pacific, and when I came back, you shipped out. They act brave, but I know Mom's anxious."

Walt frowned. Mom had a right to be anxious. Twenty-one crews from Thurleigh were gone now, either in German prison camps or killed. The odds said at least one Novak brother wouldn't come home.

"Grandpa and Grandma look good," Jack said. "Slowing down, of course. I got Grandpa to admit he maybe, perhaps might possibly think about considering hiring on more farm help after the war."

Walt smiled. "For Grandpa, that's as good as surrender."

Charlie came over with a cup of coffee and swept a long bow. "Anything else, my esteemed skipper?"

"No," Jack said with a laugh. "Thanks, buddy."

Charlie pulled Jack's cap over his face and left to join the other men from the 94th.

Jack righted his hat. "Good man, de Groot."

"So you've said." Once again, a stab in Walt's chest. He sure missed Frank, someone to call buddy.

"Your friends send greetings," Jack said. "Betty Anello grows 'great with child.' Boy, is George proud."

"Yeah. Still can't believe he'll be a dad. So, how's Helen Carlisle? I'm worried about her."

"Didn't see her. Mom says she's practically taken over Riverview's Ladies' Circle, the Red Cross, and the Junior Red Cross. Guess it keeps her mind off Jim."

"At least we drove the Japanese off Guadalcanal. That's some vindication." Walt crossed his ankle over his knee and changed the subject. "How's Ray? Still can't believe the Army trained him to be a B-17 flight instructor."

"It'll be good for him. A change of pace, a transfer from San Antonio to Fort Worth—just what he needs in tough times."

"Tough?"

Jack groped in the inner pocket of his flight jacket. "Here you go. Hand-delivered. Read that one first—from Ray." He tapped the top envelope, his face grim.

Walt opened it. What could be wrong with Ray? He had a stateside job and a lovely fiancée planning a September wedding.

Dear Walt,

What great news that you will be back on U.S. soil soon. I'll count down those missions with you.

I appreciate your excitement that you might be able to attend my wedding; however, I'm afraid there won't be a wedding. Two weeks ago, Dolores returned my ring. After four years together, she decided she doesn't love me.

Although my heart and pride feel mortally

wounded, my mind has now turned philosophical. I thank the Lord I found out her true character before we were married.

Walt looked at Jack. This was the second time a woman had broken an engagement to Ray. First his college sweetheart and now Dolores. "I can't believe it."

"Think about it. How many times did Ray propose before Dolores said yes? How long did she put off setting a date? And when I was in Texas, I caught her making eyes at other men." Jack's lips twisted.

"You're kidding. Why? Can't do better than Ray."

"I agree. Dolores didn't. I'm glad he didn't get stuck with her."

"Yeah." He stared at Ray's letter, sure it showed only a glimpse of his heartache. How could Dolores do this to him? How could she hurt him like that?

"Four years." Walt smoothed the letter flat. "What kind of woman breaks an engagement after four years together?"

★

March 20, 1943

Wasn't that what he wanted Allie to do? Walt glanced around the hangar at the men in dress uniform, the women in bright spring dresses, and the band on the stage. That's what he wanted Allie to do, wasn't it? To break her engagement? To fall in love with him? To treat Baxter as Dolores treated Ray?

Jack nudged his shoulder. "What are you thinking?"

Walt smiled. "English bands don't know how to swing."

"That's okay. English girls don't know how to jitterbug."

"Neither do I."

"Emily doesn't mind. That girl's mad about you."

Across the hangar, the ladies were returning from powdering their noses or whatever ladies did. Cracker's girlfriend, Margaret, wore a light yellow dress—made the blonde look even sunnier. Emily's dress screamed at Walt with gigantic bright pink flowers. She waved, and Walt raised a hand in acknowledgment.

"Is the feeling mutual?" Jack asked.

Walt shrugged and bit back the temptation to lie. "I don't know. She's a nice girl, but I haven't known her long."

"Not real bright."

Walt turned to his brother. "You mean because she likes me."

Jack laughed. "No, she just isn't bright. Sure, the accent makes all the Brits sound intelligent. Can't fool me. But then a lot of fellows like the dumb, doting type."

"Yeah." Walt had seen plenty of men flee at the first sign of intelligence.

"Now me, I like a girl with brains, someone I can match wits with."

Walt smiled at the memory of bantering with a green-eyed lady in a rowboat. "Yeah. Me too."

"Huh?"

Emily returned and relieved him from explaining the contradiction between his words and his actions. She took his hand and pulled him away from Jack. "Come along, Wally. I so dreadfully want to dance."

"Wally?" Jack mouthed. His face fought between laughter and disgust.

Walt rolled his eyes and allowed her to drag him away. "Call me Walt," he said. "Walt, Walter, Novak, Preach, anything but Wally."

Emily faced him with wide, hurt eyes. "You don't like it?"

"Sorry. Never have."

"Oh, but you don't mind it from me. It's a special name only I can call you." She slipped her hand over his shoulder and snuggled close to dance.

Walt scrunched his face up. Why did he want to run screaming into the hills?

Emily's hair tickled his nose, and her fingers worked into his hair in the back. Reminded him he needed a haircut. He scooted her a bit in his arms to dislodge her.

Why? He'd loved Allie's curls tickling his nose. He dreamed of Allie's fingers in his hair. That was it, wasn't it? He didn't want to hold Emily; he wanted to hold Allie. This was wrong, all wrong. Emily, dancing, dating—all wrong. The sadness drilled like acid into his heart. Why couldn't Allie dump Baxter and fall for him?

Walt groaned loud enough to make Emily look up. He forced a smile, and she settled her cheek back on his shoulder. He had it all backward. Dating Emily wasn't wrong; loving Allie was wrong. Wrong, wrong, wrong. He was in love with another man's fiancée, and in a few months she'd be his wife. *Dear Lord in heaven, I can't covet another man's wife!*

Emily let out a contented sigh. In his tension, Walt had tightened his grip around her waist.

He loosened his hold.

Jack caught his eye and winked, even though he had three starry-eyed Bedford women around him. If only he could ask Jack's advice. But then he'd have to tell the whole messy tale.

A great wave of grief crashed over him. He wouldn't have to tell the whole messy tale to Frank. Frank already knew it, and he loved to talk everything to death. Walt closed his eyes. He couldn't handle this. He missed Frank, he didn't want to talk to Jack, and he didn't know what to do. All he knew was how much he loved Allie. Every letter made him love her more.

Every letter. Walt gritted his teeth. *No, Lord. Not the letters. Don't make me give up the letters.* But he saw it. The letters fed his love and his fantasy.

He argued with God while the band played "Moonlight Becomes You," but it had to be done. He had one more step of obedience to take, one more friendship to lose and mourn over, one more sacrifice to make.

But how? If he just stopped writing, she'd worry something had happened to him. He had to tell her he was stopping. But why? Was he supposed to tell her the real reason?

That's too much to ask, Lord. Let me keep a little dignity.

There had to be some other reason to give Allie, some excuse. Walt looked down at the young woman, the excuse in his arms. He'd barely have to stretch the truth. Allie wouldn't pity him, and Walt would save face.

One last ball bearing lie.

36

Riverside

April 3, 1943

The new Easter hat would be perfect. Soft cream, with a sage green ribbon and a spray of miniature lilies, it complemented Allie's crepe dress with the lily appliqué. She'd also wear Walt's lily cross.

Allie glanced out the sewing room window to the Victory Garden below, where tomato, corn, and pea plants folded in the fading light. Would Walt come home to see spring flowers or the summer fruit he loved? He'd come home soon. The mission list tucked under the model of *Flossie's Fort* grew faster than the tomato seedlings.

She leaned over the cutting table and marked blue chalk lines across the sleeves of a white blouse. The elbows had worn thin, and she was converting it to a summer blouse.

With censorship, could Walt tell her the date of his homecoming? She couldn't ask Betty, since she'd promised not to tell her of their correspondence, but somehow she'd find out and be there, even though travel was discouraged for civilians.

Allie cut through the fabric with her best shears. She'd tell her parents how Betty needed help setting up the nursery and how lonely Louise Morgan was in San Francisco. Both statements were true, and they needn't know about Walt.

She pinned a tissue pattern piece to the cast-off fabric to create cuffs for short, gathered sleeves. She'd meet Walt at the train station where he'd kissed her cheek and told her she was lovely and special. All his family and friends would be there, and she'd stand to the back of the crowd. The hat would keep her inconspicuous. She'd peek around the brim, watch him, and love him.

Allie cut around the pattern piece. When she stood before him, she'd study his reaction. He'd be pleased to see her, but how pleased? Their friendship had deepened as the letters increased in frequency, length, and intimacy, but could he return her love?

She sat at the sewing machine and threaded it with light pink thread to distinguish the gathering threads from the white stitching threads. Today she'd allow herself to dream.

When she tilted up her hat at the train station, perhaps Walt's confusion would burst into joy, and he'd hug her so tight she'd melt, and she'd burrow a kiss in the warm, rough stubble on his cheek. He'd remember she was engaged, release her, look around in embarrassment, and politely ask where Baxter was.

Allie smiled. "I broke my engagement. I don't love Baxter. I love you."

She gasped when she heard those words out loud. Oh, she could never tell him—not like that.

She ran pink basting stitches around the hem of a sleeve. Better to tell him only that she'd broken her engagement. Walt would understand. He'd be happy for her, proud of her as Cressie and Daisy were.

They wouldn't have time to talk at the depot, but they'd

be swept apart by family and friends, swept away to the Novak home. Throughout the evening he'd gaze at her over the crowd, and she'd try to go to him but be waylaid by well-meaning friends. Eventually he'd find her and lead her outside to walk under the stars.

They would discuss how meaningful their friendship had become. She'd reach into a tree for an orange and tell him all the things she loved about him, and maybe she'd let too much slip, and he'd be delighted, and all their emotions would tumble out, and he'd gather her into his arms and kiss her, really kiss her, like in the movies, like people in love.

"You said you were coming up here to sew."

Allie jumped and turned to see Father lean against the doorjamb. "I—I was—I am." She groped for the fabric on the sewing machine. How long had she been daydreaming and staring into space?

He flipped on the light. "In the dark?"

"I—I have enough light by the window." She knew her cheeks were a brilliant shade of pink.

"Every evening you come upstairs after dinner or go out. How long are you going to hide from your family?"

Allie turned in her chair to face him. "Until everyone accepts my decision."

"That won't happen."

"Then I'd rather be alone."

Father stepped into the room, his lips a narrow line. "What kind of gratitude is this? I always gave you everything you wanted, even sent you to college over your mother's objections. Maybe I let you have your way too often. I know I shouldn't have let you go to that wedding last summer. That's when this began. You were always such a sensible, loyal daughter, but now this. This is how you thank me?"

She gripped the white fabric, and her throat swelled.

Mother's love was limited by her disappointment in Allie's looks, but Father always stood up for her, took pride in her, and gave her a love to rest on. "I'm sorry, but I can't marry Baxter."

"You will. The wedding is three months from today, and you will be there."

"I—I won't." She couldn't suppress the quiver in her voice. "I love you, and I hate to disappoint you, I really do, but I can't marry a man I don't love."

Father's eyes darkened to a terrible indigo. "Whom do you love?"

"Excuse me?" The blood flushed from her face.

He picked up a pincushion from the cutting table and studied it. "Things aren't going well over there."

"Over where?" she asked, but she knew the answer.

"They lose almost 10 percent of their planes on each mission. Who could survive twenty-five missions?"

The coldness slapped Allie in the face and made her father's image waver in her eyes. "What an awful thing to say, and I don't like what you're insinuating. Nothing is going on."

"I'm not blind. I wasn't fooled when he asked Baxter's permission to write you. I should have spoken up, but I mistakenly trusted you. I see what's happening. I see how you light up when his letters come, how they get thicker and more frequent."

"It—it's not what you think. We're friends, but nothing more." She could dream of his love, but it was nothing but a dream.

"I won't let you hand over my company to that man—or anyone but Baxter."

That was the problem. She would inherit the company, and if she married . . .

"Baxter Hicks is the only man I trust to run my company.

He's earned the right to own it through his hard work, skill, and loyalty."

"I understand. I do. I agree he should run the company, but I refuse to marry him."

"You don't understand. I will not give my company to anyone but Baxter." Father slammed the pincushion onto the table.

In shock, Allie watched him storm from the room. She'd never seen her father, her defender, so angry. Would he deprive her of the company? Could he?

She rubbed her forehead and closed up the Singer for the night. Her father's point was clear. She couldn't have both Walt and Miller Ball Bearings. What a strange choice—a man whose love she could only fantasize about, a man in constant mortal danger thousands of miles away—or the company she had always expected to own, never with anticipation, but with assurance of lifelong security and position.

For the first time, she saw the dark side of her daydreams. Her parents would never accept Walt, never love him as they loved Baxter. Beyond the fantasy, what could her future hold with Walt?

She sat at the table and rested her forehead in her hands. Never had she imagined a future much different from her present. Privilege and luxury meant nothing—she could learn to live a more modest life. But how could she bear a life without her parents' favor?

Allie shivered. She loved Walt, but did she love him that much?

37

Thurleigh

April 17, 1943

Walt sipped his coffee and grimaced at the gritty brew. He had to choke down a cup to stay awake for the briefing.

"How's the grub?" Cracker set his tray across from Walt, and the rest of the crew joined him at the table.

"Eggs are good. Coffee's bad."

J.P.'s upper lip curled enough to show he didn't trust Walt's word even about the food.

Walt sighed. As a boy, he'd spend hours constructing a tower of blocks, and then knock it down with a sweep of his hand. Trust, also, took a whole lot longer to build than to destroy.

"Say, Preach, I hear you've got a big date tonight," Abe said.

"Um, yeah." His stomach contracted around the scrambled eggs he'd swallowed. Why did tonight's date make him more nervous than today's mission?

Louis pulled a bottle of Tabasco sauce from his pocket and sprinkled some on his eggs. "Where are you taking her?"

"Movie in town, I guess."

"She'll like that," Cracker said. "Chance to show off her American officer."

Walt spooned some oatmeal in his mouth and grunted. He never thought a girl would want to show him off, and now it bugged him. People called her Walt's girl, she'd given him an unmistakable "kiss me" look when he took her home last Saturday, and it all bothered him. However, he only had three more missions to fly. The whole thing would fall apart when he went home. In the meantime he should enjoy the attention, but he couldn't get Allie off his mind.

Her letters were still coming. Not much longer. Surely she'd read his last, stupid lie by now. That thought was bitterer than the coffee.

★

Riverside

Allie savored the cool night air. It was time to go in, but she hadn't enjoyed an evening on the porch with her family in ages, and she didn't want it to end.

Baxter was home with a cold, and she had ventured outside, determined to flee at the first mention of weddings. She'd been spared. They discussed the meeting in Tunisia of U.S. troops from the west and British troops from the east. Before long, the Axis would be driven from North Africa. Mother and Allie talked about how the recent rationing of fresh meat, butter, cheese, and canned goods affected menu planning, and Father added his opinion of Roosevelt's freeze on wages and prices.

"I think I shall retire," Mother said as she always did around ten o'clock.

"Me too." Allie gave her parents an appreciative smile and led the way into the house. She had two letters from Walt, but she kept a casual demeanor when she picked up her mail, as she had ever since Father confronted her.

She'd decided her future needn't be bleak. When Walt came home, he could be stationed anywhere in the country, so their relationship would be based primarily on letters for the duration. Perhaps Walt could come to love her, and perhaps her parents could come to accept him. If God performed one miracle, why couldn't he perform two?

Once upstairs, Allie changed into her nightgown and nestled into her bed with a pile of down pillows behind her back.

The letters were rather old, one from March 19, the other from March 21. She propped the letters on her knees and smiled. They wrote every other day now. Would they make the leap to daily letters?

He would have received a few letters written after she'd broken up with Baxter in February. Would he notice a change in tone? Would he notice she no longer mentioned Baxter or wedding plans?

Allie opened the first letter:

> Dear Allie,
>
> What a great day. Why not start with the letter I got from you? Whatever step of obedience you took, it must have been good, because you sound happier than you have for some time. I'm glad you chose to obey God.
>
> We flew an outstanding mission today. Best bombing we've ever done. Believe everything you read in the papers.
>
> Now for some news—my brother Jack is here. His group is coming to our part of the world, and

his squadron will train at our base. It's great to see him. I received plenty of news from home and letters so fresh you could smell the ink.

We stayed up late talking, and it's almost tomorrow. I'm writing by flashlight, or <u>torch</u> as they call it here.

I had a flash of insight tonight. Jack has a way about him that draws people, and he's never had to work at it. Late tonight I watched him talk with Cracker. I realized I envied Cracker's charisma as I envied Jack's, and I was just as much to blame as Cracker for the friction between us.

Wow, I shouldn't write so late at night. Another crazy look into the head of Walter Novak. My flashlight battery is dying. Earl Butterfield just threw something at me—you don't want to know what—and said my pen scratches make his head throb. More likely it's the whiskey.

We don't fly tomorrow, so I can get some sleep. You can too. Sleep well, Miss Miller.

"I will." Allie laid a kiss on his signature. How wonderful that Jack was in England. What a comfort his brother must be.

★

Jack set a hand on Walt's shoulder. "Now, when you push the wheel forward, the plane goes down. Pull it back, you go up. Forward—down, backward—up. Got it?"

Walt glared at his brother, seated next to him to observe the briefing, but Jack's grin made him laugh. He would never live down his first flying lesson with Grandpa. On takeoff, ten-year-old Walt had pushed the stick forward. Why didn't the plane go forward? Ray and Jack had rolled in the pasture grass, howling with laughter.

"I'll try to remember," Walt said.

"Good. I like having my kid brother around." Jack sat back and crossed his arms.

For once, Walt didn't mind being the kid brother. Jack had come with Walt's crew on a week's liberty to London early in the month when *Flossie* was in for an engine overhaul, and it was great getting to know his brother again as a grown man and fellow soldier.

Everything was looking up. Even though the 306th lost four planes over Antwerp on April 5, the worst was behind them. Four new bomb groups gearing up for battle, adequate replacement aircraft and crews, nose-mounted .50s in the B-17s, and three fighter groups with P-47s—Hitler didn't stand a chance.

★

Allie opened the second letter, and it was far too short. She hoped Walt wouldn't be so busy with Jack that he wouldn't have time for her. A selfish thought, but she cherished his letters as she cherished him. What a joy to love him, to admit it and savor it.

Every day her excitement grew. Walt would be home soon, and then . . .

Allie's heart went into a brief palpitation. It was one thing to make fantasy plans and another to put them into action. Events tended to turn out different than expected.

★

Walt struggled with the controls. The new formation would have been difficult anyway, but too many rookies made it downright tough.

Bomber Command kept tweaking the combat box to minimize losses. The lead squadron usually flew the low position, with the other squadrons in a diagonal line echeloned up and toward the sun. The lead bore the brunt of the Luftwaffe attack, earning the nickname "Purple Heart Corner."

Today they flew a "vertical wedge," like an arrowhead tilted to a forty-five degree angle. The 91st Group flew the tip of the arrow, the 306th behind at the lower corner, and the upper corner contained planes from both groups. The 303rd and 305th flew a similar wedge behind them. Any Germans foolish enough to attack the leaders would be demolished by the guns of the lower group on the way out. *Flossie's Fort* flew in the middle of the low group with rookies on either side.

"Tourists at three o'clock level," Pete called from the right waist.

Walt let out a low whistle. They were over the Frisian Islands in the North Sea, still an hour from the target at the Focke-Wulf factory in Bremen.

Behind Walt, J.P. swiveled his top turret around. "They're early, as if they knew we were coming."

"Thirty, forty Fw 190s," Pete said. "Just watching us."

"Yeah, but we've got 115 Forts," Mario said from the tail. "That's eleven hundred guns, Jerry. Eleven hundred. And I've got two of them."

Cracker turned to Walt. Above the oxygen mask, his cheeks lifted. "Tagger's going to add a few more swastikas to *Flossie's* nose today."

"I'll beat him," Al said from down in the ball turret, "if the cowards come closer and let me take a shot."

Walt let *Flossie* drift a bit north to avoid the rookie to his right, who was trying to hide from the schoolyard bully. Unlike his gunners, Walt was in no hurry for a fight. Let the Fw 190s track them for a while, burn off fuel, and lose nerve at the sight of the largest force ever dispatched by the Eighth Air Force.

The attack was inevitable. No need to rush it.

★

Dear Allie,

I have mixed feelings about writing this letter, and you may have mixed feelings about receiving it.

First the good news. Remember those talks we had about how hopeless I was with women? You'll be glad to know those days are over. I didn't mention Emily earlier, because I didn't want to get your hopes up—or mine. Emily's a local Red Cross girl who serves coffee and doughnuts after missions. Her best friend, Margaret, is Cracker's girlfriend, and Cracker said Emily had a crush on me. After I got over my shock, I asked her out. She's a real nice girl, and—hard as it is to believe—she's crazy about me.

Now the bad news. I'm afraid Emily's a bit jealous of my friendship with you. She appreciates how you listen to me, but she feels that should be her role now, and I agree. I can't tell you how much I'll miss our correspondence, or how much your friendship has meant to me.

But soon you'll be busy with your husband
and your new home, and you won't have time to
write scruffy pilots anyway.

I'll always remember what a special woman
you are, and how your letters, packages, and
most of all your prayers encouraged me. I'll
still pray for you, especially for God to bless
your marriage.

Your friend always, Walter Novak

Good news? Allie clapped her hand over her mouth. No, it was all bad news. Her stomach churned, and she pressed her hand more firmly over her mouth so she wouldn't become sick.

Walt had a girlfriend. No romantic meeting at the train station, no sweet kiss by the orange tree, no . . . no . . .

His handwriting blurred, danced, taunted her with what would never be. Some pretty English girl enjoyed his smile, his embrace, and his kiss. Allie never would.

Tears slithered down her cheeks. She curled up on her bed, one hand clutching her stomach, the other her mouth. No more letters, no more of Walt's humor and openness and understanding. Far worse than the loss of a silly and unfounded fantasy was the loss of a real and precious friendship.

A yawning chasm opened before her—life without Walt.

★

A trickle ran down the side of Walt's oxygen mask. He dragged the back of his hand across his forehead, but the leather glove only smeared the sweat.

"One o'clock level," J.P. called. "Heading for the rookie in front of us."

Walt blinked instinctively when he flew through a black cloud from a spent shell. Flak was "so thick you could walk on it," as the men said. The Germans had masses of antiaircraft guns in Bremen to protect the port and the aircraft plant.

Usually the fighters avoided their own flak, but this bunch pressed through it. Stupid, but strategic. On the bomb run, the B-17s spread out in a long trail and lost the clustering of machine guns they had in formation.

Was Allie praying for him? Did he even deserve her prayers after the tale he told her? She didn't know he'd lied, but God knew.

The Fw 190 rolled past the rookie, and *Flossie* vibrated from her own guns. Smoke poured out of the rookie's number two engine, then orange flames.

"Come on, put it out, put it out," Walt said.

The rookie lost altitude, slipped back, and as Walt coasted past, flames engulfed the left wing. "They're bailing out," Harry said from the left waist. "I count three chutes. Four, five."

"There goes another Fort," Mario said in a flat voice. "Direct flak hit, took off the tail. Too far off, can't see chutes."

Walt shook his head. That made four B-17s the 306th had lost so far, and they hadn't even reached the target.

"Watch it, Bayou Boy," Abe said. Down in the nose, Abe would be hunkered over the Norden bombsight, while Louis operated the nose gun just to the right over his head—something he'd never done before.

The interphone picked up Louis's swearing. "Unless you want those surgeon's hands filled with Nazi lead, I'd—"

"Come on, boys," Walt said. "Interphone discipline."

A Flying Fortress from the 91st spun far below, with three fighters all over her, and Walt forced himself to take a deep breath. He'd never seen such a savage attack.

"Bombs away," Abe called.

Flossie rose as five 1,000-pound general purpose bombs dropped to German soil 25,000 feet below.

"Let's go home, folks." Walt turned off the autopilot and pulled *Flossie* back into formation at the Rally Point. The low squadron of the 91st looked almost obliterated, and the 306th had an awful lot of holes.

Flak burst closer, closer. *Flossie* shuddered harder with each burst. Walt patted the wheel. "Come on, girl, don't be scared."

Another burst. Black as Satan's heart, red flames straight from the pit he lived in. The blast slammed Walt back in his seat. Shrapnel rained on the cockpit window. Cracker screamed. J.P. screamed. Walt heard himself scream too.

38

Allie rolled over in bed, and her hand landed on the damp spot on her sheet where she'd cried herself to sleep. She blinked in the darkness. No sliver of light peeked around the blackout curtains.

The prompting was familiar and unmistakable. The Lord wanted her to pray.

Did Emily pray for Walt? Did God prompt her to pray for him? Could she possibly love him as much as Allie did?

She groaned. Now was not the time for grief or jealousy or resentment. Now was the time to obey the Lord's call. She tucked her hand under her pillow and prayed.

Even if Walt didn't want her friendship, he still needed her prayers.

☆

Walt gasped. The cockpit windows were cracked and scratched, but intact. He glanced down the nose in front of him. Shards of Plexiglas. All that was left.

"Abe! Louis!" He spun around. "J.P.—"

"I'm going." J.P. stepped off the turret platform, grabbed a portable oxygen bottle, and dropped into the crawlway between the pilots' seats that led to the nose. Frigid wind blustered through the nose and up the crawlway.

Louis hated to wear his parachute. What if—no, Walt wouldn't even let himself think it.

Flossie lost airspeed. Walt pushed the throttles forward to stay in formation. The controls and engines were undamaged, but the shattered nose caused drag.

"They're here." J.P.'s voice crackled on the interphone. "Alive, but wounded. Must have gotten blown back by the explosion, blacked out."

"Thank you, Lord," Walt said.

"We've got to get them out of this wind," J.P. said.

"Hear that, Pete?" Walt asked. Pete was large, strong, and a medic to boot.

"On my way."

Walt and Cracker exchanged a look—relief that their friends were alive, worry that they wouldn't be alive when they reached Thurleigh, and fear that they'd never get back.

"Fighters forming up. Four o'clock high, coming round for a pass," Harry said from the waist, where he now had two guns to manage.

They had no forward protection at all. Not only had they lost their nose gun, but their top turret gunner was occupied.

"J.P., get up here," Walt said.

J.P. scrambled up the passageway, reconnected to the oxygen system, and entered his turret. "Here they come. Three bogies. Twelve o'clock high."

Walt stood his ground. Bomber Command frowned on evasive maneuvers, which broke up the formation and subjected everyone to danger.

One, two Fw 190s let loose on *Flossie*. Bullets pierced the right wing between engines three and four. J.P., Harry, and Al returned fire.

Harry whooped. "Got him!"

Walt jiggled the controls—still responsive. Fuel gauges holding steady. Good thing those bullets hadn't hit the control cables or fuel tanks.

The third fighter dived in, its single propeller a shimmering disc. Tracer bullets flashed in an arc toward *Flossie*.

"Get him." Walt eyed the enemy as if his hands were on a gun instead of the control wheel.

Black puff. The fighter exploded in a flurry of noise and metal and flame, nabbed by his own flak. Walt cheered.

Then a chunk of wing soared toward *Flossie*, clipped the number three engine. The prop ripped off, cartwheeled, and struck the right cockpit window. Walt whipped his head away, flung up his hand, felt sharp bites in his right cheek above his oxygen mask.

Cracker cried out. Walt snapped back to see Cracker clawing his face, his eyes.

"Cracker! Cracker, you okay?"

"Can't see! Can't see!"

"Pete, we need you up here." Walt huffed in frustration. Cracker needed help, and he couldn't do anything, couldn't leave the controls.

Pete came up from the nose with a yellow oxygen bottle slung across his back. "Cracker, calm down. You'll make it worse. Let me look." He straddled the crawlway and grabbed Cracker's hands in his fists.

Cracker screamed.

"J.P., hold him down. Let me get the glass out, get him some morphine."

Walt had to shut down engine three. On the center console he turned off the mixture control for number three, flipped off the ignition switch, shut the cowl flaps, and closed the throttle. All the while he braced himself against Cracker's cries, Pete bumping into him, and the tinkle of bloody glass flung to the floor.

"You're gonna live, Cracker," Pete said. "You're gonna live, okay?"

"I can't see! How can I fly if I can't see?"

Pete glanced down at Walt and shook his head.

Walt looked around. Forts falling, fighters swarming, flak exploding. One engine down and a gaping hole in the nose. With three officers out of action, Walt was on his own.

★

Allie gazed down—down through a blue sky. A patchwork spread below her with tiny toy buildings, so much like the ride in the biplane. However, this time she didn't feel peace and exhilaration, only dread gripping her heart.

Little clouds floated about her, black clouds, and birds, a flock of birds, diving at her, spinning, spitting birds with cruel faces.

★

Flossie lagged behind the group. Couldn't be helped. Couldn't keep up.

The Luftwaffe had left to harass another squadron, but they'd be back when they saw stragglers. Walt glanced at the fuel and oil gauges. Once J.P. was done with first aid duties, he could transfer fuel out of engine three. If everything held, they'd make it back.

Pete had taken Cracker back to the waist section, and J.P. had joined Bill in the nose. Grunts and shuffles rose from the passageway. Bill emerged with his arms hooked under Abe's shoulders.

"Abe's the worse off," Bill said. The bombardier lay

unconscious against Bill's chest with cuts to his forehead and bloody shredded flight gear.

"Get him to the waist. Afraid you'll be crowded back there."

Bill plunged backward with Abe's limp body. J.P. came out next and grabbed Abe's feet. Bill and J.P. huffed their way through the narrow door. In a few minutes, they returned for the injured navigator. Louis had fewer wounds. He groaned as Bill bumped him over the metal floor.

That groan was the best sound Walt had heard in hours. "Hey, Fontaine, no sleeping on the job. Wake up and help me out here."

J.P. climbed out of the passageway and looked Walt in the eye for the first time in months. "Even if he comes to, he can't help. Two broken arms, Pete said."

Flossie was a big plane to land with all this damage. Walt locked his gaze on his flight engineer. He'd let the kid down, but this was no time for resentment. "It's you and me if we want to get out of this alive."

J.P.'s face twitched, but he nodded, and then he and Bill lugged Louis back to the waist section, now an infirmary.

"We've got a visitor," Mario said. "Seven o'clock high, coming forward."

The Fw 190 circled at a distance. He'd come in high and head-on where *Flossie* had no manned guns. Walt could make evasive maneuvers since he was alone, but while *Flossie* was sleek, she wasn't built for a dogfight.

"J.P.? Could use you up here."

"He's coming, Preach," Bill said.

The German climbed for the attack. Walt felt like a sheriff in a Western who meets the villain in a showdown, reaches for his gun, and finds his holster empty.

"Father in heaven, help me." The fighter swooped down, and Walt put the B-17 into a climbing roll to the left.

Bullets sprayed toward *Flossie*, clattered around in the nose compartment, blasted into the cockpit, shrieked past Walt, pounded into the bulkhead. Walt's right arm snapped back—searing pain.

"Take that," Mario said. "Got his rudder. He'll leave us alone now."

"Good," Walt whispered, breath shallow, eyes fixed on three holes in the window in front of him. Missed him by inches. He turned, his motions slowed as if in a vat of syrup. Three holes punctured the bulkhead, right behind J.P.'s position.

J.P. came through the door.

"Good thing," Walt said, his voice thin and foggy. "Good thing you weren't here. You'd be dead."

J.P. didn't look for proof. He stared at the floor.

A red pool spread and froze on the olive drab floor. Walt laughed, a strange sound, from another room, another person. "Hydraulic fluid. Remember Al on our first mission? Not blood, hydraulic fluid."

"Novak. Your arm."

Walt looked to his right arm, to dripping red smears on his hand, his forearm, his elbow.

J.P. pulled on his headset, his brown eyes wide. "Pete! Novak's hit!"

Walt clutched his arm. Pain wrenched through his arm, his body. A long, low moan convulsed its way out.

39

Allie woke with a start. What a terrifying dream. How could she have fallen asleep when she was supposed to be praying? Faint light illuminated the edges of the blackout curtains.

Never before had her dreams been so vivid, so frightful. She folded back the covers and dropped to her knees on the rug beside her bed. "Oh Lord, he's half a world away. He belongs to another woman, but you want me to pray for him, and I'll do so."

Allie burrowed her forehead into the mattress and prayed harder than ever. She could feel her prayers swirl about her, mingle with the Holy Spirit, and waft across a continent and an ocean to the man she loved.

⋆

"Come on, Preach, hold still. Gotta get the tourniquet on."

Walt screamed, and his body contorted, but he raised his arm to let Pete work. This was nothing, nothing like any pain he'd felt before, like hitting his funny bone, but it wouldn't go away.

Pete cut through the sleeve of Walt's heavy B-3 flight jacket and eased it off his arm. The wool shirtsleeve, no longer olive drab, came off next. Pete wrapped a tourniquet above the elbow and bore down hard.

Walt cried out.

"Yeah, I know. We'll get you a new jacket."

He tried to smile. "You'd better."

"The cold will do you good, help close up the wounds."

Somehow in his pain-wracked head he remembered hearing about a B-24 gunner in the 93rd Group whose backside had been filled with flak over Vegesack. The crew saved his life by sticking the injured part outside through a hole in the fuselage.

Pete sprinkled sulphonamide powder on the wounds. "I'm ready for the morphine, J.P. Got it thawed?"

J.P. sat in the copilot's seat, his hands on the wheel. He reached inside his shirt and pulled out a syringe. "Yeah. Looks good."

"No morphine," Walt said. "Gotta fly this plane."

Pete leveled clear blue eyes at Walt. "You can't fly if you can't sit still."

He groaned and nodded. "All right, but not too much."

"Yes, sir," Pete said, but he sank the entire contents of the syringe into Walt's upper arm.

Walt sighed. Now he'd have to fight drowsiness as well as pain and blood loss. He was the only one left who could fly the ship. J.P. knew the mechanics of the bomber, but he'd never been behind the controls. Walt was the crew's only hope.

While Pete wrapped bandages around his elbow, forearm, and hand, Walt tried to engage his brain. It was 1430, an hour and a half past the target, and at least two hours from Thurleigh.

"Well, Pete, *Flossie* should make it to England, although it'll be tight. What about me? You think I can last two hours?"

Pete's pause didn't assure him. "Sure. I just—just need to stop the blood loss."

Walt screwed his eyes shut. "We've got about half an hour to decide. That's when we reach the Channel." They were over the North Sea with the continent in sight to the south, and they could drift over land to bail out. It'd be a tough jump with four wounded men, two unconscious. Most would survive, although as prisoners of war.

On the other hand, ditching a B-17 in the Channel was tough—not as bad as a B-24, which disintegrated when it hit the water—but still tough. Even if they got out of the plane in time, they had only a 28 percent chance of rescue, and the injured men wouldn't last in the icy water.

Before long, the morphine kicked in, and the pain lessened to a throbbing ache. The sensation of moving in syrup intensified. When he tried to look from the altimeter to the tachometers, his eyeballs took a second to respond.

"Good news, Preach," Pete said from back in the waist section. "Fontaine woke up. He wants to know what's for breakfast."

Walt looked at J.P., who grinned back under his mask. "Tell him he has a choice between German rations or American."

"American." Louis's voice came through weakly. "Y'all know the Jerries won't have Tabasco sauce."

"Okay, but we're alone up here. I need your help to plot a course. Can you do that?"

"Sure. Can't write with these broken arms, but Bill can help."

"Anyone want to bail now?" Walt said. "Our chances aren't great, and Abe would do better on land than in the water."

"Are you crazy?" Louis said. "He's Jewish. Once he said he'd go down with the plane rather than face the Nazis."

"All right," Walt said with a sigh. "Pray hard, everyone.

'The Lord is my rock, and my fortress, and my deliverer; my God, my strength, in whom I will trust.'" Psalm 18:2, inscribed on the nose of the B-17 and in Walt's mind and heart.

The continental coast faded behind him. He studied the fuel and oil gauges and made his fogged mind do the calculations. J.P. had transferred fuel from damaged engine number three to number one, but they needed every drop of fuel, every bit of airspeed.

Walt took *Flossie* down to five hundred feet. "Okay, men, let's lighten our load. Dump everything we don't need anymore—oxygen equipment, masks. Bill, get rid of whatever radio equipment you can. We're below German radar, so ditch the guns, the ammo. Al, go down into the nose, make sure that's clear."

"Okay," Al said. "But you ain't gonna get me to dump my fifty cases of whiskey."

For a moment, laughter took Walt's mind off his pain and his dilemma.

While the crew heaved equipment out the hatches, Walt talked J.P. through landing. J.P. shook his head at the mass of instruments on the panel. "You have to stay awake. I can't do this alone."

"I'm trying." Walt blinked hard against the fatigue. "But if I don't, you're in charge."

J.P. frowned. "We can't bail out over England. We're too low for a jump. But I can't land this plane."

"Don't say that. I know you can."

J.P. shot him a skeptical look.

Walt winced and shifted position on his seat-pack parachute. His arm lay numb, heavy, and icy in his lap. "Yes, I lied to you, and you have no idea how much I regret it, but I never lied about your ability. You're one of the smartest, most capable men I've ever met, and I'd rather have you up here than half the commissioned pilots I know."

J.P. snorted and glanced out the window.

This was why Walt would never lie again. "Listen, you have to admit I've never been a flatterer."

J.P. turned dark eyes to Walt and nodded.

"So do it. Land this bird."

"I'd rather have you around to do it." One side of his mouth hiked up, and Walt smiled at the glimmer of friendliness.

"All clear down here," Al called on the interphone from the nose.

"Thanks. How's the back, Bill?"

"Stripped to the bones. The only dead weight remaining is Worley."

"Preach, tell Bill I heard that, and I'm coming to get him."

Walt laughed, a mistake, used up too much energy. His lips tingled, and his vision darkened. He dropped his head to the control wheel until the sensation passed.

J.P. leaned over and tightened the tourniquet. "How are you doing?"

"Okay." He raised his head and looked to the gauges. They'd gained some airspeed. Good.

"Two B-17s approaching," Mario said from the tail. "Squadron letters *VK*—yeah, 303rd Group. Oh. And an escort."

"Spits? Thunderbolts?" They could guide *Flossie* to an airfield, or at least notify Air-Sea Rescue if she went down.

"Um, no. Fw 190. Oh no. He changed course. Coming our way."

★

Allie's alarm clock on the bedside table read seven-thirty. She needed to get dressed, take a long bus ride, and get to March Field by nine o'clock.

Her legs were cramped from kneeling so long. She got up, winced at the pins and needles, took a step, and slipped on papers underfoot—Walt's last letters. She retrieved them and crossed the cool hardwood floor to her desk.

Walt's portrait gazed at her, professionally stoic but good-natured. No wonder Emily fell for him. Allie added the letters to the thick stack in the top left drawer—for the last time. Something broke inside her.

She picked up the tiny grand piano and her face crumpled—"Für Allie. W.J.N. '42." Although he didn't love her, he'd been the dearest of friends.

Allie stroked *Flossie*'s wooden cockpit. Her prayers hung unresolved, like six notes in a musical scale.

What about the hospital?

Allie sat at the desk and opened her Bible to Psalm 91. As a volunteer, she could be admonished but she couldn't be fired.

★

"No guns," Walt whispered.

"We're dead," J.P. said.

Walt hated pessimism, but in this case it was warranted.

"Six o'clock level," Mario called.

Attacking a Fort from the rear was suicidal, and the German was too far off to know they had ditched their guns. Either he was confident or stupid.

"He's closing," Mario said.

Walt rolled to the right, but he was too low to dive. The left wing shook, and the fighter climbed up and away. Walt righted the plane. Oil pressure fell in number two, and the engine slowed, sputtered, and stopped. The prop windmilled, as useless as a child's pinwheel.

He had to get that prop feathered, couldn't afford the drag.

He ran through the feathering procedure but he didn't know why he bothered. The Fw 190 cut a loop in front of him, then a graceful saddle-shaped chandelle. Showing off. The German circled *Flossie* clockwise and pulled alongside the cockpit on Walt's side.

What was he doing? Inspecting the damage? Fine. Maybe if he saw the shattered nose, the two dead engines, and the lack of guns, he'd let them die of their own accord. No need to finish them off.

The pilot flipped up his goggles, squinted at *Flossie's* nose, and pulled off his oxygen mask. The man had a square chin and wide-set eyes, and his lips moved as if reading something out loud. Strange that the enemy was human.

Walt scanned the Fw 190's yellow nose, the black cross on the fuselage, and twenty hash marks on the rudder. Swell, an ace.

"Hey, Preach," Mario called. "I'm up in the waist. Cracker's pistol! I've got Cracker's pistol. I can get a shot in."

"Wait, no! Hold your fire." Walt whipped his gaze back to the Luftwaffe pilot, still moving his lips. He was reading the verse on Walt's plane. "Dear Lord, help him translate."

"Preach, have you lost your mind? You know I'm a good shot. I can get him."

"Tagger, no. That's an order." He met the eyes of the enemy. With his left hand he brought his shattered right arm up in a salute, biting back a scream from the pain that shot through him.

The German nodded and raised a traditional military salute, not a stiff-armed "Heil Hitler" salute. Then the fighter wheeled away.

"He's gone! He's really gone," Harry said from the waist. "What happened?"

"We're not worth the ammo." Cracker's voice was feeble.

"No," J.P. said, eyes on Walt. "It was the Bible verse—Novak's Bible verse. He read it and he left."

Louis cheered. "I told you it was good luck."

"No such thing," Walt said. "It was God's mercy. Pray for more mercy. We're in worse shape than before and a long way from home."

★

"Allie, I thought you were volunteering today."

She looked up from her desk to see Mother in the doorway. "I am but—"

"Goodness, you're not even dressed. You'd better hurry. What'll they say?"

"It doesn't matter." She squeezed her eyes shut, exhausted from hours of prayer.

"It always matters what people say."

Allie turned back to the desk. "I'll be down shortly." She frowned at her own rudeness, but the urgency and sweetness of her prayer time lured her back into the Lord's presence.

★

A sting on his face.

"Come on, Preach, don't you dare leave us."

Walt struggled to open his eyes.

"Come on." Pete shook Walt's shoulders. "You see the coast? We're gonna make it, but you've got to stay awake."

"Can't." His eyelids dropped like window shades.

"You have to." J.P. kicked him in the leg. "Louis found an RAF airfield, Bill's contacted them, but you need to land this plane."

"Yeah," Pete said. "What'll they tell Emily if you don't make it?"

★ 323 ★

"Allie." Walt forced his eyes open. If he died, Betty would tell Allie. She took Frank and Jim's deaths hard, and she barely knew them. How would she take Walt's death? And what about Mom and Dad? And Jack would be the first to know, would have to break the news.

He shook his head hard enough to make his cheeks flap. "What's our heading?"

"Can you see it?" J.P. said. "There's the control tower."

That tower perked him up better than a cup of coffee. Engine number four gave off smoke. "Come on, girl. Not much farther."

The fuel gauges stood on empty. No time to circle the field. No time to wait for clearance. Bill Perkins fired two red flares out the radio room roof hatch to indicate wounded men on board.

Down came the landing gear. White sparkles appeared before Walt's eyes. His approach was too fast, too low, and *Flossie* bounced hard.

The runway was short, built for fighters, trees at the end—and darkening. He groped for the brakes, but his foot wouldn't move. Darker and darker.

Lord God, help us.

40

Riverside

Allie's eyelids flickered along with the newsreel images until a warm drop trailed down her cheek.

She rose and fled the theater. In the ladies' room she splashed water on her face in a vain attempt to stanch the tears. She was too drained from the previous night's ordeal and a long day at March Field to control her emotions.

Daisy swung the door open. "Allie? Goodness. Figured something was wrong if you left in the middle of a newsreel. What's the matter?"

She pulled herself together. "Nothing, really. Walt told me he has a girlfriend. I shouldn't be upset. I should be pleased for him."

"No! Allie, no." Daisy clasped her in a tight hug. "What are you going to do?"

Daisy's despair startled Allie into composure. She drew back and offered a smile. "I'll be fine in time. I'm not the first woman with a broken heart."

Daisy harrumphed and crossed her arms. "Isn't that just like a man?"

Allie sighed. She didn't want to make Walt out to be a villain. "I'll be fine. But now I—I'm worried about him." She hesitated. She'd never mentioned her dreams to anyone but Walt. "I—well, I have dreams when he flies missions, and yesterday's was a nightmare."

Daisy raised half a smile. "Honey, you watch too many newsreels. Don't worry about that man ever again."

Allie coaxed out a smile. "Let's go watch the movie."

How could she help but worry? How would she ever know if Walt was all right? He wasn't writing anymore, and she couldn't ask Betty without breaking her promise to Walt.

She led the way back into the theater. *Lord, please let me know how he is. Please keep him safe in your arms.*

★

The man's voice was familiar. Deep and low. Dad? No, not Dad.

Walt tried to open his eyes. Nothing happened.

"Walt?" The man squeezed Walt's left hand. "Nurse, I think he's waking up. Walt? Come on, rise and shine. You've been in bed too long, lazybones."

Lazybones? That's what Mom called the boys in the morning. The voice—Ray? Jack? Yeah, Jack.

He tried every one of his facial muscles until he found the ones that operated his eyelids. Light stabbed his eyeballs. He cringed, then opened his eyes again. A face came into focus with black hair and a big grin under a mustache.

"Lazybones?" Walt croaked out. "You're the one too lazy to shave."

Jack's laugh tumbled out. "You're okay. Thank God, you're okay."

He was okay? Why wouldn't he be okay? His eyelids flopped shut, and he forced them up again. Why was he so tired? So numb?

"You had me worried. Sweating out the mission at the

control tower, counting the planes as they came in. No *Flossie*. Sure was relieved when we got the call that you landed at that RAF field. When I got down there and saw your plane—wow. That was some fine flying you did. I don't know how you got that Fort back."

Oh yeah, the mission to Bremen. The nose, Louis, Abe, Cracker, the engines, the wounds, the guns, the German, J.P. "I didn't do it. God did."

"That's the truth." Jack's voice choked.

Walt looked around. His eyes took moments to adjust to each sight. White walls. A blonde in a white uniform at the foot of his bed. "Where am I?"

"The hospital in Oxford. You've been out for two days. It's Monday the nineteenth."

"Oxford?"

"They—they brought you here for surgery."

Surgery. Oh yeah, his arm. They'd have to get the bullets out. No, they'd gone through. His gaze drifted to his right arm.

Jack's hand clapped on Walt's cheek and turned his face. "Walt, look at me. I want you to look at me."

He blinked at the intensity in Jack's gray blue eyes.

"You're alive. That's the important thing. You're alive."

He became aware of dull pain the whole length of his arm. "Yeah. Alive."

Jack's face twisted, and he gripped Walt's jaw. "You lost a lot of blood. A lot. They told me you might not make it. But you did. That's what matters."

"That's what I prayed for." And for the others to make it. He frowned. "The others?"

"It was—it was a bad mission. Worst yet by far. Sixteen Forts went down."

"Sixteen?"

Jack let his hand drop. "Yeah, and well—you've got to know the 306th took the worst of it. Ten—you folks lost ten B-17s."

"No. Ten? Can't be. That means—no—only sixteen made it back?" Walt slammed his eyes shut, slammed his mind shut. Ten Forts, a hundred men from Thurleigh.

"Afraid so. I'm sorry. And a lot were hit as hard as *Flossie*. You should have gone down too. You know that, don't you?"

Walt's head swam with the losses. "My crew?"

"They'll be okay, thanks to the Lord's grace and your piloting. Abe's got a big bump on his head and the doctors' embroidery all over his torso. Louis? He'll get lots of girls to sign his casts. They'll be back to duty before you know it, but ground jobs. They've done their share."

"Cracker?"

Jack's cheek twitched. "They shipped him home today for more surgery. The doctors say he may never see again."

"Oh no."

"The good news is he's going home. So are you."

"Me? Why? Broken bones, stitches. I can fly."

Jack's hand clamped on Walt's cheek again, and his gaze bore down. "You're alive, remember? That's what matters."

Walt strained against his brother's hand. He was alive, but . . .

"There was a lot of damage. A lot. Bones missing from your hand. Your elbow was shattered. Too much time without blood flow. The tourniquet saved your life but . . ."

"But what, Jack?" he said through clenched teeth. "Tell me or let me look."

"Walt, they had to take your arm."

"My arm? Take it where?"

Jack sighed and lowered his hand. "They had to amputate above the elbow."

"Amputate?" No. Impossible. His elbow hurt, his forearm, his hand. He could feel his fingers. His stomach churned, and he looked to his arm. Where was it? "No. Dear God, no."

"You're alive. That's what matters."

His entire insides recoiled. His arm lay on top of the blanket, but it ended. Stopped. Masses of white bandages formed a knob where his elbow should have been. No, he could feel it, feel his elbow.

"I'm so sorry, Walt, but you're alive."

A stump. He had a stump. Like a tree, chopped down, sawed in half. A stump. Like the Great War vets, like the old-timers from the Spanish-American War, like crotchety Old Man Horton, who lived alone in a run-down shed outside town. Children feared him, teenagers harassed him, women pitied him, and men ignored him.

Vile sickness wrenched his stomach.

"Nurse?" Jack said.

A hand on his shoulder rolled him to his side just in time for him to retch into an enameled pan. A stump. A stump.

"I'm like—" He spat out the last of the bile. "I'm like— like Old Man Horton."

"Don't say that. You won't be. You know what Grandpa always said. Horton was an angry, unhappy man before he went to Cuba. Yeah, his injury made him bitter, but he was halfway there beforehand."

The nurse wiped Walt's face. A stump. His right hand— gone.

He closed his eyes and pressed his head back on the pillow. This had to be a dream, a nightmare, and when he woke up he'd be whole again.

"I don't know what to say, Walt. I wish this hadn't happened. I wish I could take your place. I sure wish Dad or Ray were here instead of me. I'm the one who almost flunked out of seminary. They'd know what to say."

"Would they?" He opened his eyes to see Jack's face warped with concern. The nurse pressed a pill between his lips and handed him a glass. The water scorched its way down his throat. "What could they say? I—I lost my arm. My arm, Jack. My right arm. It's gone. My *right* arm. I can't—I can't write. Oh no, I can't fly. I can't fly, can't push the throttles."

His chest heaved. No—no, he wasn't going to cry like a stupid baby.

"You're an engineer. Thank the Lord for that. You can still use a slide rule, can't you? You'll be fine. Really, you'll be fine." Jack brushed the back of his hand across his eyes. No, he wasn't crying too, was he?

"Yeah? Who'll hire a cripple?" He screwed his eyes shut, hating the dampness, hating the huskiness in his voice. Twice in one year he'd cried. War was supposed to make him a man, not a blubbering baby.

"You're not a cripple. You're a war hero. You wouldn't believe the reporters beating down the doors, waiting for you to wake up. And your crew too. You saved their lives."

"I'm no hero." Walt lifted his hand to wipe his eyes. No—no hand. He had to use his left hand, felt clumsy.

"Sure, you are. I bet you'll have twenty job offers before you get home and at least that many marriage proposals."

Marriage. Walt stared at the clump of bandages. Any self-respecting woman would be repulsed. Allie would be. Good thing she had a whole man to marry.

41

Riverside

May 6, 1943

Allie checked the list in her hand: florist, photographer, bakery, printer, Mission Inn, St. Timothy's. Only the dress shop remained. It had been a long day, and her feet and head ached.

She caught a glimpse of herself in a shop window. At least she still looked fresh in her peach linen suit. To make the old outfit more fashionable, she had added four box pleats to the skirt and epaulettes to the shoulders.

She paused outside the door, took a deep breath, and plunged into the shop.

Miss Montclair knelt in front of a dress form in the back of the store. She wore a slim dress with broad, vertical black and white stripes. Few women could wear such a bold dress, much less dominate it as Agatha Montclair did.

"Excuse me?" Allie said.

Miss Montclair's eyes widened. She rose and set aside the tape measure. "Dearest Allie, I must say I'm astonished to see you."

"Oh? Mother made an appointment for me."

"Yes, but you haven't kept an appointment for months."

"I'm sorry. I truly am. But—well, I'm here today."

"Yes, I see." Miss Montclair's gaze grew steelier with each step. "Your mother will be quite pleased."

"No." She tried not to make an unladylike face. "She'll be most displeased."

"Is that right?" A smile cut a rocky canyon in Miss Montclair's face. "Come along. Let me show you what I've done."

Oh no. Mother's wedding gown.

Miss Montclair disappeared in a black and white blur behind a maroon curtain. She returned with a garment bag, which she hooked over a dressing room door. She glanced at Allie and chuckled. "Oh, if you could see your face."

Allie set down her pocketbook and joined Miss Montclair, who lifted the bag and removed a white gown with a deep, pointed lace collar, a blousy bodice, and narrow, elbow-length sleeves.

"Mother's gown! You put it back together."

"I thought you'd like that."

"I love it. You have no idea how thrilled I am." Allie fingered the delicate fabric, searched for signs of damage, and found none. "You did a beautiful job. Oh, I'm so pleased. The thought of Mother's dress ruined for—" She looked up to Miss Montclair's satisfied face. "How did you know I broke my engagement?"

"I had my suspicions. After our last conversation, I halted work. Then you stopped coming to your appointments, and Mary started avoiding me at church. She's rather upset, isn't she?"

Allie lifted the lacy sleeve and sighed. "Upset? To be upset would mean some degree of acceptance. No, she keeps making wedding plans, convinced I have cold feet. But today I cancelled all the arrangements. Now she'll have to accept it."

"Good for you." Miss Montclair scrutinized Allie's face. "Are you happy, dear?"

Her smile rose from a peaceful place in her heart, untouched by the chaos at home. "I am. I'll be much happier when my parents take me seriously, but I made the right decision. I can't describe how wonderful it feels."

"You've forgotten, dear. I already know." She returned the gown to the bag. "Is there another man waiting in the wings?"

Wings—what an unfortunate choice of words. Allie managed to smile. "No. This is between Baxter and the Lord and me."

On the bus ride home, her feelings for Walt disrupted her peace—unremitting love, loneliness for his friendship, and nagging worry about his fate.

Her dreams had stopped. Had God released her from her responsibility? Had *Flossie* been damaged? Did Walt have a break from missions? Had he been transferred to a ground position? Or had something horrible happened to him? Betty hadn't mentioned him in her letters, but then she never did.

Allie could still see the headline: "Forts flatten Nazi factory." Then the subhead: "Sixteen B-17s lost."

Sixteen! She'd never read of losses so high. Why, Walt's chances . . .

No, she wouldn't allow herself to worry. Besides, many of the men survived as prisoners of war. Some even managed to avoid capture and work their way to England via the underground. If anyone could make it back, Walt could.

However, the thought of Walt in a prison camp or hiding from Nazi soldiers in a French cellar made her shudder.

Allie stepped off the bus and walked up the long drive-way under rustling citrus leaves. "Oh Lord, wherever he is, whatever has happened to him, please keep him safe. Please comfort him and strengthen him."

Over dinner, Allie steered conversation away from wedding plans and toward the resolution of the coal strike that had infuriated Father.

After a peaceful meal, Mother brought in fresh strawberries from the Victory Garden for dessert. "So, Allie, you had several appointments today. Did you keep them?" Her voice was stiffened by too many broken appointments.

Allie nodded, her mouth full of a strawberry she should have sliced.

Mother's smile electrified. "See, Baxter, I told you she'd come around."

Oh dear. She misunderstood. Allie chewed vigorously to clear her mouth.

"I told you she'd come to her senses, didn't I?" Father said with a smile Allie had missed the last few months. "I didn't have to change the will after all. Baxter, you still have that ring?"

"Of course."

Allie swallowed too large a bite, and the acid ate into her throat. "The will?"

Mother poured cream over her berries. "You didn't leave us much of a choice, dear. We were going to tell you next week when it's finalized, to give you an incentive to do what's proper."

"What—what did you do?"

Mother's smile fluttered. "Well, Baxter is now the sole heir of our estate. You told your father it was only right. But it's nothing to worry about anymore."

"The—the estate?" Her voice strangled in her throat. "You mean the company—just the company."

"The whole estate." Father lowered his spoon and the corners of his mouth.

It couldn't be. He didn't want to leave his company to another man, even though there was no other man. But the whole estate? It couldn't be. "You disinherited me?"

"No, no, no," Mother said. "When you marry Baxter, you'll inherit as before."

Allie's breath bounced off the top of her lungs as on a too firm mattress. "You chose Baxter over your only daughter? You—you disinherited me?"

Father's gaze hardened. "Not if you marry Baxter as you promised."

Baxter twirled his spoon in his bowl. "I thought you'd come to your senses."

"No. I mean, yes. Yes, I did—back in February. I won't marry you and I won't change my mind."

"Why not? You changed it once before."

"I won't—I won't marry you." How could they? How could they do this to her?

"But, Allie." Mother gripped her bowl in both hands, her eyes enormous. "You said you kept your appointments."

"I did, but not as you think. I cancelled everything—the flowers, the invitations, the reservations—everything."

"No! How could you?" Mother's voice shook.

"I had to." Allie's voice echoed her mother's. "You wouldn't take me seriously. You need to accept this."

"No, you need to accept *this*." Father stood and planted his palms on the table. "Baxter is my sole heir. If you don't marry him, you'll receive nothing. I trust you'll make the right choice."

Her jaw set as firmly as her mind. "I already have." She dashed from the dining room past the elegant furniture of the home she'd never inherit.

"Allie! Allie, wait." Baxter's voice and footsteps followed her.

"What?" She whirled around under the crystal chandelier in the entry. "What more could you possibly want?"

He thumped to a stop and smoothed back an errant strand of hair. "I want you to know I'm willing to give you a second chance. Over the past three months you've embarrassed me in front of your parents, and now in front of half of Riverside. Nevertheless, I'm willing to forgive you and take you back."

"Why?" She flung out her hands. "Why on earth would you want to marry me? J. Baxter Hicks has already accomplished his goals. J. Baxter Hicks has taken everything he wanted from the boss's daughter. You took the company, my inheritance, my home—why, you even took my parents' love and approval. You're done. What more could you want from me?"

His face softened, and he reached for her hand. "I want you for my wife. I want to raise a family with you."

Allie stepped back, away. "No. Don't you understand? You've taken it all, but I won't, I won't let you take my soul." She turned, and her feet pounded up the stairs.

"They're right to disinherit you," he yelled after her. "You fickle, ungrateful, disobedient—"

"Disobedient?" She spun around at the top of the stairs. "You can call me anything you want but disobedient. My obedience got me into this mess." She ran down the hall, fumbled with her doorknob, and entered her bedroom, bathed golden in the sunset.

She walked in circles past her bed, her bureau, the window, her desk, her armoire, the door, around and around, aching in her loss and her parents' betrayal. The light turned to orange, to red, to purple gray.

"What now, Lord? What can I do?"

Allie paused in front of her desk, in front of Walt's portrait. She longed for his insight, his humor, his comfort, his advice. Her face puckered up.

"Oh, Walt," she whispered. "You may not need my friendship, but I certainly need yours."

42

2nd General Hospital, Oxford

May 9, 1943

Walt labored over each stroke of his pen. Sloppy. A six-year-old could do better.

He crumpled the paper, which wasn't easy with his left hand, and lobbed it at the trash can. Missed. He huffed and raked the curl off his forehead. Even that took two tries.

More to add to his list of things he couldn't do well—eat with a fork, brush his teeth, dress himself. Buttons and buckles and socks made him want to break something.

Never mind the list of things he'd never do again—fly a plane, play the piano, carve wood, drive a car, tie his shoes, cut meat.

Sure, the therapists said be patient, keep trying, chin up, smile, and everything would come together in time. Easy for them to say. They didn't have to live with one lousy, stinking, useless left hand.

Over Bremen he'd prayed to stay alive. He might have re-worded his prayer if he'd spent some time in this hospital beforehand. Maybe Frank didn't have it so bad.

Walt groaned at his line of thought. Frank wouldn't agree.

Eileen and the kids would rather have Frank alive in any condition, and so would he.

Walt sighed. The letter would have to wait until Jack came today after church. He could transcribe.

No, Walt needed to try. He had one lousy, stinking, useless left hand, and he had to learn to live with it. Dad and Mom would worry less if they read something cheerful in Walt's own handwriting—if they could read it. Too bad he couldn't write Allie and tell her his frustrations without having to sound cheerful. He pulled out a new sheet of paper.

Dear Dad and Mom,

I'm getting better, and I'm not in pain anymore. They let me walk the halls every day now. Everything's hard, but I'll learn. I should be going to a stateside hospital by the end of the month. They'll put me as close to Antioch as—

"Hiya, Wally. Brought a letter from your girlfriend."

Walt groaned at his brother's teasing. "Don't call me Wally, and she's not my—J.P.! What are you doing here?" He hadn't seen J.P. since Bremen.

Jack sat on the edge of the bed. "It's a long train ride. I wanted company, ordered him to join me. One of the advantages of being an officer, which J.P. can experience firsthand now."

For the first time, Walt noticed J.P. wore the darker olive drab trousers of an officer and gold second lieutenant's bars on his flight jacket. "It went through?"

J.P. settled into the chair beside the bed. "You're talking to Thurleigh's newest gunnery officer. You should warn a man when you recommend him for a commission."

"How could he?" Jack said. "You weren't speaking to him."

J.P. made a face. "Listen, Novak, I'm sorry—"

"Don't. It's all right."

"No, it's not. I—well, you earned my respect back over Bremen, and then some. Now I find out you recommended my commission while I was giving you the cold shoulder."

Walt shrugged. "You deserve the commission, and I deserved the cold shoulder."

"Still can't believe you told that load of baloney. Liar, liar, pants on fire." Jack reached over and ruffled Walt's hair.

"Yeah, you taught me how to lie so *you* wouldn't get in trouble." He laughed and batted away Jack's hand. Nope, wrong arm again.

Jack's smile flickered, and he lowered his hand. He motioned to the bedside table. "Say, who sent candy?"

Walt glanced at J.P., who was trying not to stare at his empty pajama sleeve. His stomach twisted up. Every day for the rest of his life, people would try not to stare, and then when they thought he wasn't looking, they would stare. Even the prostheses the doctors showed him wouldn't help. If anything they were worse—shiny, pinching metal hooks with cables and buckles and straps. As an engineer, he admired the machinery, but he didn't want it on his body.

"Who's the candy from?" Jack repeated.

"Emily. Want some? I don't like it." As sickly sweet as Emily's tearful visit. Good thing she only came once. He didn't want to know how much of her family's sugar ration she wasted on him.

"Brought a letter from her and the rest of your mail." Jack popped a red hard candy in his mouth and pulled envelopes from his jacket.

"Thanks." Walt set the pile in his lap and flipped through. Emily, George Anello, Grandpa Novak—Allie. Hadn't she received that letter yet?

"What'd she say?" Jack asked, the candy jutting his cheek out. "Haven't seen her."

How could he see Allie? Oh—Emily. "Um, I don't know." He opened her letter.

Dear Wally,

I hear you'll be going home soon. I do so wish I could follow you, but my father says I mustn't be daft. I've had a simply smashing time with you, and I'll miss you dreadfully. Perhaps later you can send for me. California sounds like a smashing place. I'd love to meet some movie stars.

Walt ran his hand down over his face. "Wow, that girl scares me."

"Why? What'd she say?"

"She thinks I'm her ticket to Hollywood."

Jack laughed. "Antioch's a good four hundred miles from Hollywood."

"I doubt she can count that high."

Next, he opened the letter from George, written in early April, before Bremen, which told of wildflowers blooming on green hills, nursery preparations in the bungalow, and high school kids pulling pranks on history teachers. Hard to believe normal life continued in small towns in America, while insanity reigned over Europe.

He set down the letter. "What's new at Thurleigh?"

"Reeling from Bremen," J.P. said. "Recovering from St. Nazaire on the first."

"Read about that in the *Stars and Stripes*." Felt disconnected to hear about missions secondhand.

"I flew with another crew," J.P. said. "Bad visibility. After bombing, the group turned too early for England, headed right over Brest, straight into flak and fighters. Lost three planes. Another two were Category E back in England."

"Good day for medals, though." Jack took a green candy and grimaced at the taste.

"Did you read about Snuffy Smith from our group?" J.P. asked. "First mission, flying ball turret with Johnson's crew."

"Yeah, it was in the paper." A rip-roaring fire in the radio room drove the radio operator and two gunners to bail out. Smith fought the fires, tossed burning equipment out through holes in the fuselage, manned the waist guns, and gave first aid to the tail gunner. "Sounds as if they want to give him the Congressional Medal of Honor."

"If he gets it, you should too," J.P. said.

"Nah." At least Snuffy Smith's story distracted the reporters from Walt. He opened the letter from Grandpa dated April 21.

> Dear Walt,
>
> Jack's telegram arrived yesterday. Your mother and grandmother are upset but relieved you're alive. They're strong women, and their faith will see them through.
>
> I'm not worried about you at all. You're a clever boy with a full share of Novak stubbornness. You'll figure out any task you put your mind to. I looked over old _Jenny_. I bet we can rig an extension to the throttle so you can fly her. Same thing on the gearshift of the

car. The car will have to wait until after the war.

The last tire blew out the other day.

Walt looked up with more hope than he'd felt in weeks. "Grandpa's figuring out how to modify *Jenny* so I can fly."

Jack laughed. "Good old Grandpa. The two of you will design all sorts of contraptions."

"Just might." He fingered Allie's envelope, postmarked April 15.

"Aren't you going to read it?"

"Later." Might be his last letter from her. He wanted to take his time, and he sure didn't want his brother to watch him read it.

J.P. leaned his elbows on his knees. "From Allie?"

"Yeah." Walt set his face in a neutral expression.

"Your pretend girlfriend?" Unlike *Flossie*'s crew, Jack was amused by the story.

"That's the one." He put the envelope on the table. "Her wedding is sometime in July." At least her last few letters spared him the details.

J.P.'s eyes narrowed to slits. "You really do love her, don't you?"

Walt's jaw flopped open, a lie ready to spill out, especially in front of Jack. He groaned. No more dishonesty. "Yeah, I do."

"What?" Jack said.

"So it was only half a lie," J.P. said.

"No such thing."

Jack backhanded Walt's knee. "What's going on here?"

"Nothing, nothing." Walt scrunched up his face. "Your brother's a fool."

"I know that, but what's going on?"

He shot Jack a glare. "All right. Might as well tell the

whole messy tale. I met her at George and Betty's wedding, fell for her hard, found out she had a boyfriend, decided to write her anyway. That was a mistake, because I fell in love with her. No, I take that back. It wasn't a mistake. She's been a real good friend."

"Bet her fiancé's steamed that you love her."

"Are you kidding? He doesn't know. Neither does she."

"You haven't told her?"

Walt raised an eyebrow. "Didn't you hear? She's getting married."

"You're just going to let it happen?"

"Of course. It's the honorable thing to do."

Jack rolled his eyes, got up, and poked around in the candy box. "Come on. Fight for her. Tell her you love her. At least give her a chance to reject you."

"Try the orange ones. They're not so nasty."

"Fight for her."

"Jack's got a point," J.P. said. "What's the worst that can happen? She marries the other guy, which she'll do anyway if you don't act. The best . . . ?"

"You beat your brothers to the altar." Jack put a pink candy in his mouth. "Boy, is that awful."

"That's what Allie would say too."

Jack spat the candy into the trash, sat on the bed, and bounced a few times. "Come on, Wally. Emily thinks you're smashing. Maybe Allie will too."

"Uh-uh. Allie's smart." He kicked his brother's backside as hard as he could with the blanket over his legs. "She's filthy rich, she's got a filthy rich fiancé and a mansion to move in to, she doesn't know I'm a cripple, she doesn't know about my lies, and I'm not about to tell her."

"Tell her," Jack said. "What have you got to lose?"

"You sound like the nurse I had back in the winter when I had pneumonia. She told me the same thing."

"Smart woman." Jack scanned the ward. "Is she pretty too?"

"Yes." Walt balled up an empty envelope and hit Jack smack in the ear. Not bad for a southpaw. "She's not here. She was at Diddington. Too bad. It'd be fun to watch you strike out with a woman for once."

"A challenge, huh?" Jack tossed the wad of paper up and down. "Nothing I love more than a challenge, especially a challenging woman. Which brings me back to you. Novaks never turn away from a challenge. Fight for the woman you love."

"I agree," J.P. said. "She feels something for you. The lady writes two, three letters a week, and thick ones. Tell her."

Tell her he loved her? Tell her he lied to his crew about her? Tell her he directly disobeyed the Lord and told one last rankling, festering lie?

No. There was a thin line between honesty and stupidity, and he wasn't about to cross it.

43

March Army Air Base

Saturday, June 26, 1943

"We'll sure miss you here," Regina Romero said.

Allie signed her name on the volunteer check-in list for the last time. "Thank you, but I'll miss this place more." She looked forward to her job in the business office of the Citrus Machinery Company, which now manufactured the Water Buffalo amphibious tank, but she'd miss her Red Cross work.

She walked down the hall and said good-bye to doctors, nurses, and patients. After the brutal shock of the loss of her inheritance, she'd forged ahead. Her parents were young and healthy, but someday they'd be gone, and Allie would be homeless and penniless. Women had opportunities now, but who knew how things would change after the war? Allie's business education told her it was prudent to get a job now, save as much as possible, and establish herself in a career.

"Hi, Miss Miller."

"Miss Miller, right over here."

Allie smiled around the ward. How she'd miss these men. A heavy young nurse with her cap askew approached

Allie. "Could you talk to the new fellow first? Whiny, I tell you. Keeps clamoring about how he has to write his girl." She pointed to a man propped up in bed, a tuft of dark blond hair rising from the bandages around his head. "Lieutenant Hunter. Yeah, that'd help me out, make the ward more peaceful. You know how short staffed we are on Saturdays."

"I'd be glad to." Allie patted her arm and pulled up a chair beside Lieutenant Hunter's bed. "Good morning, Lieutenant. My name is Miss Miller, and I'm with the Red Cross. Would you like me to take a letter for you?"

"Yeah, could you?" He had a straight nose and a square jaw below his bandages. "Dear Maggie—"

She chuckled. "Just a minute. Let me get situated." She put a piece of airmail stationery on her clipboard. "Now I'm ready. Dear Maggie?"

"Yeah. Maggie, I miss you so much. No letters from you since I left. None from anyone over there. I know mail is slow, and I've been transported from hospital to hospital, but two months is a long time without word.

"Had another surgery last week. The doctors sound optimistic, but even with these bandages, I can see what's happening. The surgeries aren't working. I'm blind, and they can't do anything about it." His mouth clamped into a hard, grim line.

Allie's heart ached at the masculine determination not to show emotion. "I'm so sorry."

He jutted his chin out. "That's why I'm writing, Maggie. We talked about how I'd send for my English rose so she could bloom on American soil. That can't happen now. I refuse to burden you."

"Please don't think that way," Allie said as she penned the dismal words. "There's so much—"

He held up one hand. "I don't want Red Cross perkiness. I want a letter transcribed."

"Yes, sir."

"Do me one favor, Maggie. Stay off the air base. If you have to date a Yank, stay away from the combat crews. You don't deserve this heartache. I love you, Maggie, and I hate to send this letter, but it's for the best."

Allie couldn't leave it like this. "Just a minute, sir."

She wrote on the bottom of the page, "An unsolicited post-script: It's clear how much he loves you. Even if he never sees again, his future needn't be bleak. You both will be in my prayers."

"All caught up?" he asked in an impatient tone.

"Yes, sir. Please continue."

"Maggie, it's not right to ask more of you, but could you send news on my crew? I don't even know if they're alive or dead. Fontaine's probably okay, but Ruben was unconscious when we landed and a mess from what Wisniewski said."

"Wisniewski?" she whispered. Fontaine? Ruben? Two months, he'd said. That was the middle of April, when she had her last dream. No, it couldn't be.

"Yeah. W-I-S-N-I-E-W-S-K-I."

She already knew how to spell it, and knew the man wasn't Lieutenant Hunter but Lieutenant Huntington. Somehow she forced her pen over the paper.

"Got it?" he asked. Cracker—it was Cracker. If he only knew how much she knew of him, both good and bad.

"Yes," she choked out.

"Preach is the man I'm really worried about."

Terror trampled the hope she'd built up. "Preach?" she said.

"It's a nickname. The letter?"

"Yes, yes. I—I'm writing." *Oh, please, Lord. Please let Walt be all right.*

"Preach was in bad shape. Real bad. I don't know how he landed the plane with only one good arm, but that tells you the kind of man he is. He blacked out after we landed. Wisniewski says it's a miracle he lived as long as he did, that he got us all home. I just hope he made it."

Allie's hand formed the words that confirmed her worst fears—Walt had been gravely injured, maybe even—oh, please, not killed.

"You need her address," Cracker said. "Sooner this gets out, sooner she can get on with her life."

Allie wrote it down. Bedford—Walt was in Bedford. Where was he now? Was he even alive? She knew of only one way to find out, but it required breaking a promise. However, this was necessary for Cracker's peace of mind and hers.

"I—I can obtain information for you. Walter Novak is— was—is a good friend of mine."

Cracker's jaw went slack. "You know Preach?"

"Mm-hmm." She hated how her voice squeaked. "We— we have a mutual friend. I'll contact her. She'll know about Walt—maybe Abe and Louis too."

"Wow. You do know him. I can't believe it. Listen, I'm sorry you had to find out like this, Miss—Miss . . ."

Tears beaded on her eyelashes. "Miller. Allie Miller."

"Allie?" Cracker's jaw hung even lower. "Not the Allie he was always writing to? Not—oh boy, have I heard a lot about you."

"I need to go now." The tears threatened to brim over, but she needed to maintain a cheerful façade for the patients. She stood and stumbled around the chair and the beds. Once out the door, she leaned her forehead against the corridor wall. *Please, Lord, let Walt be all right. I don't care if he loves another woman. I just want him to live.*

"Allie?"

She lifted her head to see Cressie in her gray uniform.

"The last day is hard, isn't it?"

"It's not—it's—" Her throat swelled shut.

"Let's go talk in Regina's office." Cressie put her arm around Allie's waist and guided her down the corridor. "Was it one of the patients?"

Allie shook her head, afraid to open her mouth and release a torrent of sobs.

Cressie led her into the empty office and shut the door. "Heavens alive. I don't know how Regina does such a good job in this pigsty." She hefted piles of papers from two chairs to the floor and motioned for Allie to sit. "Tell me what happened, love."

The privacy of the office, the warmth of Cressie's hands around hers, and the concern in her little blue eyes loosed something. "The—the new patient—he was on Walt's crew—my friend Walt. He—Walt was wounded, and I don't know if he's alive or dead, or where he is, and I never told him I broke my engagement, and I never told him I love him, and he should know, even though he loves someone else, he should know. I have to tell him, and now I may never—may never have the chance."

"Hush. Hush. Oh dear, what a pickle." Cressie squeezed Allie's hands. "Now, first we've got to find out Walt's condition."

"Betty would know."

"All right, love, all right. You're going home right this minute to call her. Don't you fuss. I'll tell Regina. You can't work like this. Now, don't you wait for the mail. Call Betty. Then if Walt's alive—and I know he is—you'll write him a letter and tell him everything you want him to know."

"But—"

"Didn't you hear yourself? First you fretted about his welfare, then you fretted because you never told him you love him. So tell him, love. Tell him. One thing this war should teach you is life is short, and you've got to seize each day."

"*Carpe diem*," Allie whispered. She had never adopted that motto, but perhaps she should.

★

A warm wind shut the door behind Allie. She tossed her pocketbook on the mail table, dashed for the phone in the hallway, and gave the operator Betty's number.

"Allie? My, you're home early."

She turned as the phone jingled. Mother stood in the archway to the sitting room in a pale pink dress. "Hello, Mother."

"I'm glad you're home. Your father and I have something to discuss with you."

"Not now. I—I have to call Betty. It's urgent." She turned away. How could she get Mother to leave? She didn't want to ask about Walt in front of her.

"Anello residence," George's deep voice declared.

"George? Hello, it's Allie Miller."

"Allie! It's good to hear your voice. Betty will be sorry she missed you. Say, you must have gotten the announcement."

"Announcement?"

"Wouldn't you know my daughter showed up two weeks early? Impatient like her father."

"Oh, congratulations." She swerved from concern for Walt to joy for George and Betty. "What's her name? How's Betty?"

"Judith Anne, and she's the cutest little thing you've ever seen. Betty's just as happy as can be."

"That's wonderful." Allie bit her lower lip. While thrilled about the baby, she was desperate for news of Walt, and

★ 351 ★

long-distance phone calls were restricted to five minutes. How could she politely change subjects? "So—so when was she born?"

"June 14. I'm on my way to fetch Betty from the hospital right now. Wait, I thought you got the announcement."

"No, not yet. I was calling—"

"Uh-oh. If you didn't get the announcement, you didn't get the reply to your wedding invitation. I mailed them the same day. Betty will be fit to be tied."

Allie stared at her own drained face in the mirror over the telephone. "Wedding invitation?"

"Last month you tell her you broke your engagement, and now this," he said with a laugh. "Wow, that's some fancy engraving. Betty's got it on her bedside table at the hospital. Sure sorry we can't come. Say, that's a week from today, isn't it?"

Allie had cancelled the printing order. She looked to her mother in the archway. "George, I'll talk to you later." She settled the receiver back on the hook.

"Mother?" She held a lid over her simmering emotions. "George Anello says he received my invitation. How can that be? I cancelled the order."

"I know. I had a terrible time setting everything back up again and locating all your friends' addresses. I'm afraid the invitations were a trifle late."

The lid came off to release a roiling boil. Allie marched up to her mother. "How dare you send invitations when I called off the wedding?"

Mother stepped back from her steam. "Don't raise your voice at me."

"Don't plan my life for me. Did you honestly think I'd marry Baxter just because you planned a wedding?"

"Well, yes. We have over a hundred people coming. That's what your father and I wanted to discuss with you today. We raised you to value propriety, and it would be most improper not to show up for your own wedding."

Allie strode across the marble entry. "This is absolutely unbelievable. First you thought I'd marry Baxter just to make everyone happy. You were wrong. Then you thought I'd cave in when you stripped me of my inheritance. I didn't. What makes you think I'd give in to this scheme? Did you think I'd disobey God for the sake of propriety? I don't care about gossip or scandal or propriety. I don't!"

"Allie Miller!" Father stormed down the hallway from his study and to Mother's side. "Don't you dare raise your voice at your mother. You owe her an apology."

"No, I don't," she said, satisfied by her own indignation. "I am twenty-three years old and perfectly capable of making my own decisions. You can't force me into an arranged marriage. This is 1943!"

Mother's face reddened. "That's no excuse for treating us with disrespect."

"I've never shown you anything but respect, but you refuse to respond likewise. I am an adult, and it's time you treated me like one."

Father's face set into shattering steel. "You want to be treated like an adult? Fine. As of July 3, we are no longer responsible for your support or housing. Marry Baxter, or you're on your own. I doubt you'll care for that aspect of adulthood."

Sad, calm determination settled in Allie's soul. On her own? It was for the best. How could she live with people who didn't truly love or respect her? She turned for the stairs. A week was too long to remain. Perhaps she could sleep on Cressie's couch while she made plans.

"July 3," Father said. "Show up at St. Timothy's, or you will no longer be our daughter."

"We'll only welcome you in this house as Mrs. Baxter Hicks," Mother said.

Allie placed her hand on the graceful banister she never dared slide down as a child. She gazed down at her mother's beauty, marred by angry tears, and at her father, no longer her defender.

"I shall miss you both very much."

✦

"Have some more tea, love," Cressie said.

"No, thank you." The saucer rattled when Allie set the teacup down. Everything shook inside her from the day's turbulence—the news from Cracker, the worry over Walt, the confrontation with her parents, the hurried packing of her belongings into Herb Galloway's cab, and her conversation with Betty on Cressie's phone.

Walt was alive. Praise the Lord, he was alive. Betty had told her of his grueling mission, his wounds, the amputation of his right arm, and his transport to the Army hospital at the Presidio in San Francisco.

Allie's tears of joyous relief mixed with selfish grief for his right hand. The hand that smashed hers on the piano keys. The hand that circled her waist when they danced and cupped her chin when he kissed her cheek. The hand that carved the cow, the plane, and the tiny piano. The hand that penned the letters she cherished.

He would adjust. Walter Novak, with his ingenuity, faith, and good humor would adjust, but she couldn't imagine what he must be going through.

Cressie settled among the red and orange upholstery roosters, and rested her elbow on a purple doily. "Well, love, you need to make plans. I'm sure someone needs a boarder. We'll put out the word tomorrow at church."

Allie folded her hands in the skirt of her Red Cross uniform. She hadn't taken the time to change. "I can't stay in Riverside."

Cressie frowned. "Why ever not?"

"I need to start over, away from reminders of my home and family. I'll miss Groveside and all my friends, especially you and Daisy, but I need to go away."

"Hmm. Hmm. A bit hasty, but maybe you're right. Where will you go?"

"Antioch. I can't stay long because of Walt, but I'll visit Betty a few days while I look for a job in San Francisco. My friend Louise said one of her boarders moved out."

"You stay here as long as you need."

Allie shook her head. "I'll leave Tuesday. Tomorrow I'll say good-bye at church and resign my pianist position. On Monday I'll quit my new job and go to March to tell Cracker about Walt."

"A right good plan. I'm flabbergasted, plumb flabbergasted. I'd have thought you'd be completely discombobulated."

"Oh, I am." Allie lifted a trembling hand and smile. "Discombobulated and terrified, but I know the Lord will see me through."

"That he will, love. That he will."

⭐

Union Station

Tuesday, June 29, 1943

"No tickets, miss. Trains are full. Civilians aren't supposed to travel." The ticket agent scowled over his glasses at Allie and pointed to a Southern Pacific poster on the wall, which read, "Don't take the train unless your trip is essential."

"It—it is essential."

He grunted and waved her off. "Come back tomorrow and earlier in the day."

Allie stepped away from the window. How could she come back tomorrow? She couldn't afford a round-trip to Riverside or a hotel in LA. She had emptied her savings account of the earnings from her pianist job, but she needed every penny for her trip north, job-hunting trips into San Francisco, and a deposit for an apartment if Louise couldn't take her in.

What could she do tonight? She glanced around the cavernous station, filled with the echoes of hundreds of conversations. A sailor bumped into Allie and apologized without meeting her eye.

She was alone, utterly alone. What was she doing? She should go home, marry Baxter, and make everyone happy.

She groaned and headed across the lobby. She should disobey God, be miserable for the rest of her life, and forget everything she learned the past year? Impossible.

A year ago to the day, she'd been in the same station, Walt's kiss still tingling on her left cheek, Baxter leaning to kiss the same cheek, Allie offering her right cheek instead.

She wore the same brick-red traveling suit, but everything else had changed. A year ago she never would have considered spending the night in Union Station, but tonight that was exactly what she would do. Her luggage resided with the porter, and she had a new book, *The Robe*, to read and stationery so she could write Walt. She would tell him in person, but a letter would help her compose her thoughts.

Allie stepped outside, walked a bit, and turned onto Olvera Street, the heart of Mexican Los Angeles. She passed a stall with souvenir sombreros for men on furlough and another with tooled leatherwork.

Her letter, her speech, would have to be as well crafted. First she'd give words of appreciation for his sacrifice and encouragement for his future. Then she'd tell him she'd broken her engagement and why she'd done so. Next she'd confess why she hadn't told him before—she loved him and wanted to tell him in person.

Allie proceeded to a stall with shelves of painted clay pots. That would be hard to write, near impossible to say to his face.

She'd preface the statement of her love: "I feel led to relate things that may make you uncomfortable. Cressie told me life is fleeting, so seize the day. I'd rather say this and humiliate myself than keep it secret and regret it forever."

Allie traced a red bloom on a round pot. She felt a tug on the hem of her skirt. A tiny girl wrapped pudgy arms around her knee. She wore a dress with a profusion of red and green ruffles, much against War Production Board standards. Perhaps the dress had been in the family for years, a part of her heritage.

Allie set her hand on the girl's silky black hair. "Hello, there. Shall we find your mother?"

The girl raised startled black eyes, let go, and stepped back. "Mama?"

"Rosita? *Aquí*," a woman called from across the way.

Rosita scampered over, and her mother kissed her and swung her up on her hip.

Allie smiled at the pair, but an empty pit developed inside her. Never again would she savor her parents' love. Never again would she experience her heritage—her home, her groves, her city. The loss stung her fresh. She'd never even visited San Francisco, and she knew none of its ways.

"No friends," she whispered. "No work, no church, not even a family." She had to start over with nothing. She took a deep breath, sick and tired of crying.

Would Walt worry about her, feel sorry for her? The last

thing she wanted was to increase his burden. She had to assure him she would be fine, which she would.

She followed the scent of savory pork to a vendor and bought a taco for an inexpensive lunch. She sat on a low wall to eat her taco and compose her farewell:

"Walt, you deserve much love and joy in your life, and I truly am glad you found it with Emily. Please don't worry about me. I am content and have no regrets. You'll always be in my heart and prayers as a beloved friend."

44

Letterman General Hospital, San Francisco

Thursday, July 1, 1943

Walt slammed his Bible shut. He had to stop reading Proverbs.

He'd stopped lying, confessed to his crew, and taken the consequences. He'd changed, but it wasn't enough. That last lie to Allie, that stupid, prideful lie. Didn't want her to pity him, which was nothing but pride. He was supposed to tell her the truth but no, he disobeyed, and now it ate away at him.

Walt leaned forward in his chair and looked out the window of his hospital ward. A BT-13 Valiant trainer flew overhead. Now he had to write Allie and confess his lie as well as his love. Her wedding was next month—no, this month. Swell. Wouldn't that make a classy wedding gift?

Proverbs 27:5 only deepened his guilt: "Open rebuke is better than secret love." What kind of man was he? Cowering from rebuke and a wounded ego? Some war hero.

"There's our war hero."

Walt groaned and looked over his shoulder to see Mom, Dad, and Ray, who was home on furlough. Walt had been glad to arrive in California two weeks before, but now he was sick of watching other pilots fly, sick of doctors and nurses, and sick of false cheer from his family.

"We have quite a collection here." Dad sat on the edge of the bed and opened the scrapbook he was compiling for Walt. He had a similar one for Jack's combat exploits. "Nice article last week in the Oakland paper, and one in the *San Francisco Chronicle*—no picture, though. The *Antioch Ledger* ran a follow-up yesterday." He turned the scrapbook around.

Walt peered at the headline: "Local hero convalescing." Reporters—he was absolutely sick of reporters.

"Isn't that nice?" Mom said with the wide smile she'd worn since he came home. This situation was beyond her soothing mothering, beyond Dad's buck-up-and-make-the-most-of-it fathering, beyond Ray's eager pastoring. Ironically, Jack, who didn't know what to say, made him feel better than the rest of the family combined. Walt didn't blame them. They'd braced themselves for death, not for maiming.

"Any word from Jack?" On the 94th Bomb Group's first mission, Jack's left thigh and backside had been filled with flak.

Ray straddled a wooden chair. "I got a letter yesterday. He's doing well, wants to get out of the hospital. And you know Jack—he's set his sights on one of the nurses." He said this without smiling.

"Sounds like Jack."

"He says she knows you, took care of you when you had pneumonia."

"Lieutenant Doherty? The redhead? Boy, does he have his work cut out for him."

"Yeah, he said you warned him, as if a warning ever stopped him." Something sad flickered in Ray's gray eyes. "He should listen to warnings. Wish I had."

Walt frowned. How could he expect Ray to make him feel better when he was reeling from a broken heart?

"Before I forget," Mom said, "I brought more of Grandma's strawberries."

"Thanks," he said, unable to muster a smile. He'd lost an arm, Jack lay in a hospital bed, Ray had been dumped by the woman he loved, and fruit was supposed to help? Nothing tasted good anymore, not even strawberries.

"How are you, dear?" Mom's forehead wrinkled with pity.

"No change. Arm didn't grow back."

Mom's mouth twitched.

Walt sighed. She didn't deserve his cynicism. "Sorry."

"We—we ran into your doctor on the way in. He said you're ready for a short trip home."

"Yeah." He looked out the window. As much as he hated the hospital, he didn't want to go home and face a town full of pity. "Maybe later."

"Your mother's ready for you to come home," Dad said.

"Well, I'm not, okay?"

"Walter Jacob Novak!"

He squeezed his eyes shut. How could he explain without hurting Mom's feelings more? "I—well—"

"If your mother wants—"

"Dad, leave him alone," Ray said.

Walt opened his eyes in surprise.

Ray ran a hand through his straight black hair. "You know, ever since—well, I have some days when I want to be with family and other days when I just want everyone to leave me alone. I think Walt's having one of those days."

"Yeah. Yeah, that's it exactly." He gave his oldest brother a grateful look. "I know you're here because you want to help but . . ."

"I know." Ray stood and extended his hand—his left hand—for Walt to shake. "Sometimes doing nothing is the best kind of help."

★

The Key System train clattered over the lower level of the Bay Bridge. Allie tried to concentrate on the visions of the San Francisco Bay flashing between the steel girders, but she had other matters on her mind. Within the hour she'd face the man she loved. No fantasy or letter could prepare her. Her body weighed heavy from Tuesday's poor sleep in Union Station's lobby, yesterday's crowded train ride, and a late night talk with Betty.

Allie rested her temple against the cool window glass and watched the wooded mound of Treasure Island pass by. She refused to dwell on one thing Betty said, that Walt hadn't mentioned Emily. Betty also said he was depressed. Allie understood. He'd lost his arm, he wasn't able to do what he did best, and he was ripped from the woman he loved. He didn't mention Emily because he didn't want to talk about her.

In the past Walt might have told Allie in a long letter. Not anymore.

She swallowed hard. She was tired of crying. She would not cry today, especially before she saw Walt.

She folded her hands on top of her handbag with the letter inside. She hesitated to bring it, afraid she'd use it as a crutch to avoid speaking the words. At the last moment she stashed it inside. What if the ward was crowded? What if he had visitors? Whether oral or written, she had a message to deliver and a day to seize.

★

Walt flopped one shoelace across the shoe, then crossed

the other lace on top and tucked it under. He anchored one lace with his stump and tugged the other. At least the stump no longer hurt and the stitches were out. He kept the sleeve pinned up so he wouldn't have to see. Grotesque, useless.

He formed a loop and braced it with his stump while he looped the other lace. His shoes looked ridiculous with the striped pajamas and blue bathrobe, but he had to get out. He had to get away from the stench of cigarette smoke and disinfectant. He had to get out into the sunshine before the fog rolled in and reminded him of England, where men were flying and dying, and Walt couldn't do a thing to help.

The first loop slipped loose. A low growl rumbled in his throat. He started again. Last thing he wanted was to ask for help from one of the Red Cross ladies in their gray uniforms like Allie Miller wore. Some time this month she'd be Allie Hicks.

The loop popped free. For the first time in his life, Walt wished he were a swearing man. How could he hold down a job when it took fifteen minutes to tie his stupid shoes?

Walt glanced outside, where fog crept over the treetops. Too late. He yanked off a shoe and hurled it across the room.

★

Butterflies flitted in Allie's stomach as she walked the unfamiliar corridor. No, not butterflies, but a swarm of locusts, chewing, jumping, gnawing.

Allie paused at the door to the ward. She shouldn't be there. She should leave.

Outside the door she closed her eyes and leaned back against the wall. No, she had to see him. She had to tell him she loved him. She promised herself, she promised Cressie, and she promised the Lord.

"May I help you, miss?"

Allie opened her eyes to see a brunette in a white nurse's uniform. "I'm here to see Capt. Walter Novak."

The nurse tilted her head to the door. "Right in here, but let me warn you. He's in a foul temper."

Allie gave her a stiff smile. How inappropriate. Regina would never allow such talk about patients. Nevertheless, the comment stirred the locusts into a frenzy.

"Are you waiting for me to announce you?" the nurse asked.

Allie blinked at her sarcasm. "No, of course not."

She ducked in the door and stopped. Twelve beds lined the walls. Men lounged in bed or stood chatting and smoking. Which one was Walt?

At Betty's wedding, Allie said she'd recognize him in fifty years, but now? Why, it had only been one year. How could she love a man she didn't even recognize?

"Hiya, doll." A man with bushy brown hair passed Allie and winked.

She gave him the thinnest of smiles. Then she saw Walt.

By the last bed on the left, he sat in a chair at a window with his back to her. The right sleeve of his bathrobe was pinned up over the stump of his arm. Fresh sorrow coursed through her. How little she knew of his suffering.

Allie forced her feet down the room, surprised she hadn't bent the frame of her handbag in her grasp. A shaft of sunlight pierced the fog and illuminated tiny, adorable curls at the nape of his neck. He wore only one shoe, with laces lying limp on the floor.

She drew a deep breath. "Walter Novak?" she said in a tinny voice.

He didn't turn from the window, but he let out an interminable sigh. "Listen, lady, I'm not doing any more interviews. I know you're a fine writer, and you'd do my story justice, and your editor sent you all the way here, but I'm sick of interviews. No more. Besides, taking a few bullets through my arm doesn't make me a hero."

Despite the cold tone, the sound of his voice was a warm tune to her ear. "Perhaps not, but landing a heavy bomber when you're close to death makes you a hero in my eyes."

He whipped sideways in his chair to face her, fire in his eyes. "Listen, I'm not doing any—" The fire extinguished. "Allie?"

She raised a soft smile. "Hello, Walt."

✯

He stared. He blinked. She was still there in that green dress with the big white flower, the lily. Was she—yeah, she wore the cross he sent her. She looked prettier than he remembered, prettier than her pictures. Something new glowed in her smile. That's right. She was about to be a bride.

"What are you doing here?"

Allie's eyebrows lifted. "I—I'm visiting Betty. I arrived yesterday, but I'll only stay a week or so."

He thought he'd never see her again, and there she was, right in front of him. "But why are you *here*?"

She tucked a curl behind her ear. "Well . . ."

Walt's stomach soured, and he turned to his window. "Oh yeah, the pity visit."

"No. No, I—I have something to tell you, and yes, of course I wanted to see you, to make sure you were all right. Why, when I heard what happened . . ."

Outside the window, fog shackled the trees. "Betty told you."

"Actually, I found out from Cracker."

He snapped his gaze back to Allie. "Cracker?"

"I was as surprised as you. He's a patient at March Field.

I transcribed a letter for him the other day. That—that's how I found out you'd been injured."

"Cracker? You saw Cracker? How is he?"

"He still—he still can't see, and he's pessimistic about ever seeing again. He was also worried sick about you and Abe and Louis. He—he didn't know if you were dead or alive." Her voice broke. "I—well, I had to call Betty."

Walt scrunched his eyes shut. He was such an idiot. If he hadn't lied, he could have told her what happened so she wouldn't worry. Some friend he was.

"I know I promised I wouldn't tell Betty of our correspondence, but I had to know how you were, and so did Cracker."

Walt formed his hand into a fist and rapped his knee. Yet another lie. He made her miserable for no reason.

"I'm sorry, but I had no choice."

He swung his head heavily from side to side, unable to meet her eye. "That's not the problem."

"Oh."

Silence separated them, a chasm carved by his lying lips. Now he could tell her the truth and throw off the last weight of his sin. Sure, the chasm would deepen, but he'd already destroyed the friendship. Might as well do it right—with the truth.

He pressed his hand hard over his eyes. If only he had more time to think this through.

"If that's not the problem, what is?"

He let his hand fall, looked up at Allie, and loved her more than ever. The glow was gone, but strength showed in the set of her chin and the directness of her gaze. She was going to be another man's wife, and he had to tell her how much he loved her.

"This isn't proper," he whispered.

"That's right. Your girlfriend." Her eyelashes blurred brown over green. "If it isn't proper for us to write, it certainly isn't proper for me to be here."

Walt chewed over words in his mouth. None of them worked. None came out.

"Oh dear. I have to. I have to do this." Allie clamped her lips together, popped open her purse, and pulled out an envelope. "This—this is for you."

"Huh?" He was the one with things to say. Why was she giving him a letter? He reached for it. For an instant, his hand was only an inch from hers. He set the envelope in his lap and worked a clumsy finger under the seal.

"No, wait."

Walt looked up.

Her eyes got big and pleading. "Please wait until after I leave. You—you'll still be in my prayers." Allegra spun away so fast, she lived up to her name.

"Allie, no. Wait." He stood, tripped on his untied shoelace, and caught himself on the edge of the bed. He got up in time to see the woman he loved dash out the door. How could he catch her with one shoe off, one shoe on? How could he catch her when it took fifteen minutes to tie his stinking shoelaces?

He plopped on the bed, wrenched off his shoe—

"Novak, if you throw another shoe at me, I swear I'll beat you to a pulp."

Walt glared at the officer across the way and slammed his shoe to the floor. Everything had gone wrong. He hadn't told a lie, but he hadn't told the truth, and now she was gone.

Allie's letter lay on the floor, the nice, thick kind he loved to receive from her. He opened the envelope and pulled out several pages covered with her pretty handwriting.

Dear Walt,

I have so many things to tell you. Some may encourage you, many will surprise you, and some may bother you. Please bear with me.

First, please accept my condolences on your injuries.

Walt groaned and dropped the letter in his lap. Why was he reading this?

She meant well. Of course, she did. But what could she offer him? He'd heard all the platitudes. Maybe she'd quote some uplifting Bible verses, but he'd heard them all. Then she'd say she wished him the best, more about praying for him, maybe something nauseating about how she and Baxter would name a child after him.

Walt strode down the aisle and dropped the letter in the trash can.

"I don't want to hear it."

45

San Francisco

Friday, July 2, 1943

"You have a lovely flat, Louise." Allie settled on the couch and gazed out the bay window to the tall, lush trees of Golden Gate Park across the street.

"It's awfully small, much smaller than you're used to in Riverside." Louise Morgan sat beside her and nodded to the miniature kitchen.

"So much larger than we had in Grace Scripps Clark Hall."

Louise laughed. "We had so much fun there, didn't we? I don't have a mosaic courtyard where we can lounge in the sun and pretend to study, or a piano to sing around, but we could still have fun. Please tell me you'll stay."

"Please tell me you'll have me—and soon."

Louise's brown eyes magnified to unnatural proportions behind her glasses. "Tomorrow?"

"Tomorrow would be perfect." Betty was more than hospitable, but everything in Antioch reminded Allie of Walt.

Louise sprang to her feet and pulled Allie to standing. "If you're moving in tomorrow, you need to pack. We can chat later. I can't wait to hear the whole story about Baxter. I'm glad you broke up. Such a cold fish."

Allie smiled. Louise had always been quiet, but with her husband in North Africa, she seemed hungry for company.

Louise opened the front door. "Tomorrow you'll wear a coat."

"I can't believe I need a coat in July." Allie shivered when she stepped out into the damp air. Fog swirled above the tops of the trees in the park. "It must be thirty degrees cooler here than in the rest of California."

"It's like this all summer." Louise gave her a hug. "Run along, now. I'll see you tomorrow."

Allie trotted down the steps to Lincoln Avenue. She had a steep climb to the blue and gold Muni train, which would take her downtown. Then she'd take an orange, black, and gray Key System train to Oakland, where she'd catch a bus to Antioch.

The day had revived her. She'd submitted job applications at a dozen companies eager to hire her, she had an apartment, and Louise had invited her to church.

Allie pulled her peach linen jacket tight about her. A new setting was exactly what she needed to recover from the loss of her home and parents.

Getting over Walt would take far less time, thanks to the previous day's visit. Although she understood his depression, he had no right to be gruff. Why, he was positively rude, and that was before he received the letter.

She turned the corner and climbed uphill to the Muni line.

Allie thought she'd regret telling Walt she loved him because she'd embarrass them both. Now she regretted it only because in very short time it would no longer be true.

★

Letterman General Hospital

Mr. and Mrs. Stanley Miller
request the honor of your presence
at the marriage of their daughter
Allegra Marie
to
Mr. Joseph Baxter Hicks

Cruel. After Walt made such a mess of Allie's visit, he didn't need a reminder that she was marrying another man, and a fop at that.

What was a woman who preferred down-to-earth *Allie* to frilly *Allegra* doing with a man who preferred stuffy *Baxter* to good old *Joe*? Was Baxter even a Christian? Not once had she mentioned his faith, and she attended Groveside alone. Maybe she valued money more than God after all.

Yep, she did. The wedding was at St. Timothy's. Might be fun to show up for the fancy society wedding, see how pretentious she really was.

Nope. Couldn't go. The wedding was July 3—tomorrow. He didn't even have time to RSVP. Bet they'd get their high-falutin noses out of joint about that.

Walt glanced out the window at the same tired scenery. Tomorrow she'd be married. He could put her behind him and get on with his life. He'd work harder at his therapy so he could get his medical discharge, go to Seattle, and take the engineering position with Boeing his CO had arranged. Then he could contribute to the war effort again.

He stood and lifted his arms for a stretch. Tomorrow would be a new start for him.

He swung his arms behind him, grasped what remained of his right arm, and stretched his chest. A new start for Allie too. He needed to stop grumbling about her marriage and pray for God to bless it.

"Wait a second." Walt frowned and checked the invitation. Yes, it said July 3. What was Allie doing in northern California two days before her wedding? That was cutting it close, considering how hard it was for civilians to travel. And wouldn't she have all those fussy last minute arrangements?

He stared at the spot where she'd stood only the day before.

"I arrived yesterday, but I'll only stay a week or so."

He shook his head hard. Must have heard wrong. No, her voice came through clearly in his head. He stared at the invitation—"Saturday, the third of July." He'd read right and he'd heard right. But that meant . . .

No, he couldn't allow himself to think that.

But what if it were true?

Walt glanced around the room, the double line of beds, the tan walls, the men he never bothered to talk to. The only explanation was that the wedding was postponed or cancelled. But she would have said something.

He groaned. How could she have said anything when his grumpiness and thoughtless words drove her away?

"The letter!" He whipped toward the door, the trash can. *"So many things to tell you? Many will surprise you?"*

Walt ran down the ward. Why on earth hadn't he read that letter? He slid to his knees, dumped the trash, and spread it in front of him. "Please, Lord, let it be here."

"Told you Novak was a nut case," someone said.

"Flak-happy, I tell you."

Walt ignored them and flipped through the trash. Nothing. He sat back on his heels and heaved a sigh. What did he expect? They emptied the trash every night.

He gathered up the garbage. What had Allie written? He passed the sidelong glances and whispers, and sat on his bed to study the envelope for the invitation. It was addressed in feminine handwriting, probably Mrs. Miller's, because it wasn't Allie's. Forwarding marks covered the surface, but he could still read the postmark from June 1. Would Allie postpone the wedding less than a month in advance, after the invitations were mailed? Not Allie. Too messy, too scatterbrained, too improper.

Come to think of it, she hadn't mentioned wedding plans in her last letter. Or had it been longer? He got up, opened his duffel, and pulled out the stationery box where he stored Allie's letters.

For the rest of the afternoon, he read her letters. He could see her changes over the year, could see her strengthening determination to follow God's will, her increasing independence, and her growth in friendship and service.

Walt set down the last letter and rubbed his eyes. Swell. Just what he needed, to fall deeper in love with her.

Something else clarified. She went through three distinct phases over the year. At first her letters were cheerful—scared to defy her parents but excited about the changes in her life. Then right after Christmas something changed. That was when she got engaged. That was when her letters got flat. That was when she rambled about obedience and sacrifice.

Didn't make sense. She was engaged. Wasn't she supposed to be happy? Why hadn't he picked up on it before? Maybe because it didn't last long.

There. Walt jabbed a letter with his finger. Yeah, he remembered this. February 20. She'd gone a week between letters, and then suddenly her mood improved, happier and more assured than ever.

What was going on with the wedding? He skimmed through the last two months of letters—twice, because he couldn't believe it. Not one word about Baxter. Not one word about the wedding.

Walt's heart thumped harder than an unbalanced propeller. No Baxter, no wedding. It was cancelled in February by Allie, not by Baxter. Otherwise she would have been depressed when they broke up.

Why hadn't she said anything in February? That didn't make sense. What about the invitation sent in June? Why would they send invitations to a cancelled wedding? That made absolutely no sense.

He had to find out. Walt stood, tightened the belt on his bathrobe, and jammed his feet into his slippers. He had to find Dr. Sutherland and get out of this place—now.

Allie was staying in Antioch for a week. The doc would give him a few days to go home, but he wouldn't let him take a longer trip to Riverside.

Walt caught a whiff of chipped beef on toast and looked down to the tray on his bedside table. When had that been delivered? He touched the plate and checked his watch. Six o'clock.

His heart went as cold as his dinner. Dr. Sutherland went home at five. He'd be gone for the weekend, leaving only interns who couldn't discharge him. The doc wouldn't let him go home during the week when therapy took place.

Walt stormed down the ward and kicked the trash can. "No! I've gotta get out of here."

46

Antioch

"Tomorrow!" Betty clamped a hand over her mouth when the baby squirmed under her chin. "Tomorrow?" she whispered. "You'll stay longer, won't you?"

Allie sent an apologetic smile to Betty over in the rocking chair. "I'm sorry. Tomorrow is best."

Betty's lip pushed out in a pout. "I want you to stay longer, but I suppose it's hard for you to be here."

"I want a new start."

"I don't blame you. I can't believe Walt acted like such a louse. I have a good mind never to speak to him again."

"Please don't say that. He needs his friends now more than ever."

Betty tapped her fingers on little Judith's rump. "You're too good for him."

Sadness plunged fresh into Allie's soul. "You have that backward."

"Ooh, you are in love."

"Not for long." Allie headed down the hallway to the nursery. Since the baby still slept in a cradle in her parents' room, Allie had been sleeping on a cot in the nursery. "Where's George?"

"Over at Helen's. Leaky faucet." Betty turned into her room and laid the baby in her cradle.

Allie opened the trunk and pulled her bridesmaid's dress out of the closet, a silly, sentimental item to bring. Betty joined her, folded another dress, and set it in the trunk.

"What's this?" Betty lifted the B-17 model from the trunk. "Oh my goodness. Did Walt make this?"

"Yes. Please don't tell him. It's humiliating enough that he's read my letter and knows I love him. I'd rather he didn't know I kept every letter, every gift."

"Don't worry, darling, I won't say a thing." Betty spun a tiny propeller. "Isn't this something?"

"He does beautiful work, doesn't he? He made models for all his family and . . ." She stopped with her hand on the next hanger, and turned back.

Betty raised an eyebrow. "Friends? I don't think so. Not George, not Art. I haven't seen one at his parents' either."

Allie's hand shook as she slipped the lily dress off the hanger. He must have been too busy to make more, but why would she have been first?

"What else did he give you?" Betty peered into the trunk.

"Well, this necklace." She fingered the cross around her neck. Regardless of how Walt felt, the cross was a sign of her faith, and she refused to hide it in a drawer. "He also made this music box." She laid the dress in the trunk and pulled the piano from the sweater in which it was wrapped.

Betty gasped. "It's beautiful." She turned it over, read the inscription, and looked at Allie with wide blue eyes. "No wonder you fell in love. This is—I can't believe I'm saying this about Walt—this is romantic."

"No, it's not." Allie gave her a firm look, took back the gifts, and stashed them in the trunk. "Friendly, not romantic."

Betty flourished two tall stacks of envelopes tied with ribbons. "This is some friendship."

"Was." Allie sighed and took back the letters. "Yes, it was a wonderful friendship. Now would you stop undoing my packing?"

The front door banged open, and laughing voices entered the house.

Betty poked her head into the hallway. "George Anello, you'll wake the baby."

"Sorry." George trotted down the hall, shut the bedroom door, and stepped into the nursery. "Hi, darling. Hi, Allie. You've got to hear the news."

Allie didn't feel like a social gathering, but George grabbed her hand and Betty's and dragged them to the little living room. Art Wayne and Dorothy Carlisle stood by the fireplace.

Helen Carlisle rummaged in the desk in the corner, while Jay-Jay, her one-year-old son, clung to her leg. "Betty, you are the most disorganized person. Where is your paper?"

Dorothy waved a hand at her sister-in-law. "Not yet. Let me tell the news."

"If I let you start, I'll never get a word in." Art looked down at Dorothy with all the usual adoration but none of the usual fear.

Then Allie noticed Art and Dorothy held hands.

"Oh my goodness." Betty lowered her plump form into a wingback chair. "Don't tell me—"

Art grinned. "I got my draft notice this morning."

"Oh no," Betty gasped.

"No, I want to go. You know I do. Especially after what happened to Jim and now Walt."

Allie's gaze flew to Helen, who intensified her search of the desk. Poor thing. Jim had only been gone eight months or so.

"Besides, it spurred me to action." Art's smile lifted his brown mustache even higher. "Went into Della's Dress Shop today at lunch."

"Not even a hello, mind you," Dorothy said. "Just immediately—"

"Hush. My story." Art pressed a finger to her lips. "I said what I should have said years ago: 'Dorothy, I love you, I've always loved you, and I'll never love anyone but you. I can't go to war without knowing whether you love me too.'"

"Arthur Wayne!" Betty said. "All these years—"

Dorothy set her free hand on her hip. "Don't you want to hear what I said?"

Betty laughed. "We already know."

Allie nodded, her eyes damp from the sweet knowledge that their story had a happy ending, and the bitterness that hers didn't.

"You don't know," Dorothy said. "Sure, he pulled the rug from under me, but I recovered. I said, 'You've never given me any reason to love you whatsoever.' So he . . ." Her cheeks flushed in pretty contrast with her dark hair.

Art slipped his arm around her waist and pulled her close to his side. "I grabbed her and kissed her and gave her a reason to love me."

Dorothy's face glowed scarlet. "Yes. Yes, he did."

"Arthur Wayne!" Betty said. "You're actually a romantic. I can't believe it. You and—" She shot an alarmed look at Allie. "Well, I can't believe it."

Allie gripped the pole of a brass lamp. Betty had almost said, "You and Walt."

"Wait till you hear this." George sat on the arm of Betty's chair until she swatted his backside.

"We're getting married," Art said. "Tomorrow."

Betty squealed and ran over to hug Dorothy, then Art. "But how? It takes time."

"Helps to know people." Art pried himself from Betty's embrace. "Your dad did the blood tests, Judge Llewellyn pulled strings at City Hall, and Pastor Novak said he'd do the ceremony. I have two weeks before I'm inducted, and I want to spend them as a married man."

"We have work to do." Helen concentrated on the paper before her on the desk. "Mom will do the cake. I loaned Dorothy my—my dress."

The waver in her voice shook Allie to the core. Allie understood a fraction of Helen's pain from her own broken heart and the loss of her family and security. And Allie's flight to San Francisco promised similar comfort as Helen's frenzied activity.

"George is best man. Ray Novak said he'd fill in. Art's cousin too." Helen wrote at a fast clip. "I have my dress from Betty's wedding. Betty, Mrs. Carlisle will loan you a dress in the shop that'll fit. Allie, do you have something to wear?"

"Me?" She stared at the back of Helen's blonde head.

"Oh, please," Dorothy said. "The timing of your visit is perfect."

"You have your dress from my wedding," Betty said.

An image of the wedding portrait flashed through Allie's mind—a portrait Walt would see. Would he see her pining over him, trying to insert herself into his group? She managed a smile. "I'm sorry, but I told Louise I'd move in tomorrow." She immediately saw the hole in her excuse.

"You have to stay anyway to attend the wedding," Dorothy said.

Betty beckoned, and Allie stooped so Betty could whisper in her ear. "He refuses to leave the hospital. You're safe."

Allie smiled at her friend, grateful for her discretion. She went to Dorothy and gave her a hug. "How could I turn down such an honor?"

47

Antioch

Saturday, July 3, 1943

Not exactly the homecoming Walt dreamed about.

Dr. Sutherland had been delayed by an emergency surgery the night before, but by the time Walt tracked him down, convinced him he wasn't crazy, and persuaded him to write the order, it was too late to call his parents. When he called that morning, no one answered, and now the house was deserted.

Walt dropped his duffel on his bed and glanced around the room he hadn't seen in a year. Model planes dangled from the ceiling, including a Sopwith Camel and a Fokker Triplane. How often had he imagined their glamorous duel? Now he'd been in real air battles. Nothing glamorous about terror and death.

Silence hummed in his ears. Just as well. He needed to find Allie, and his family would slow him down.

He headed downstairs and straightened his service cap. Full dress uniform felt strange after two and a half months in pajamas. Felt heavier too, with the rows of ribbons on his chest—the European Theater ribbon, the air medal with three oak leaf clusters for more than twenty missions, and the Distinguished Flying Cross he received after Romilly. After Bremen he added the Purple Heart and the most prestigious, the Silver Star.

What good would medals do when Allie heard what he'd done? He swung open the front door and crossed the street toward George and Betty's house in the next block. No matter what, he had to put that last lie behind him forever.

And what was her story? All he knew was something had happened with Baxter, and Allie cared enough for Walt to visit him in the hospital. Beyond that, the possibilities were endless.

What if she was available? What if she could forgive him? What if she could fall in love with him? Walt grumbled and rang George's doorbell. What if he *was* flak-happy?

He waited. His blood pulsed in his neck. No answer. Where on earth was Allie?

Walt scanned the houses behind giant sycamores and oaks and maples, a familiar scene, yet details popped out at him—a bird twittering in the plum tree, the Anellos' red mailbox by the curb, the new roof on the Jamisons' house.

Where would George and Betty go on a Saturday afternoon? He jogged across the street, but the Jamisons weren't home. Across the street, no Carlisles. Down a few houses—no sign of George's parents. Kitty-corner and no Waynes.

"Where is everybody?" Walt clenched his fist. "Okay, Lord, how can I talk to Allie if I can't find her?"

★

When Allie met Ray Novak the night before, she wouldn't have known he was Walt's brother except for the gentleness of his smile, but now as she stood at the front of the church and observed him from the corner of her eye, she saw a resemblance in Ray's solid build in the Army Air Force uniform and the way he stood and moved, and a longing like homesickness swirled in her heart. It was best if she never saw Walt again, yet she yearned for his smile and laugh. At the hospital, he did neither.

Allie sighed and turned her attention to Walt's father, who had the same curly black hair, although less of it and peppered with gray, the same unusual nose, and the same vocal tones. Monday—on Monday she could get away from Antioch and the Novaks.

A year ago she'd stood in a wedding in the same building in the same dress. That time Walt couldn't take his eyes off her, but now he couldn't even be polite.

Next to her, Betty turned toward a creak in the back of the sanctuary. "Allie . . ."

She lifted a finger to her lips. Betty couldn't ever be silent, in class, during Sunday services, even during the wedding of two dear friends.

Betty faced front. "Allie," she hissed. "Slowly, very slowly, look toward the door. Oh no."

Dread flowed cold in Allie's veins. No. He was in the hospital.

In the light of the open church doors, a man stood silhouetted, a man with one hand. The light flashed to a slit and vanished. Walt stood, mouth agape, eyes on Allie.

"Oh no." She whipped her head forward and hoped her hair concealed her face. "What's he doing here?" she whispered.

"The wedding. Oh my goodness. His parents—his parents must have called him. Oh, Allie, I'm so sorry. If I'd known—"

"Betty, the letter. He read my letter." Her stomach coiled in dismay. "He knows."

"Oh no." She didn't turn, but Allie read the concern in the set of her cheeks. "All right, darling, I'll see you through."

Allie's grip tightened on her bouquet. Only the Lord could see her through this mess.

* * *

Walt lowered his body into the back pew. Art and Dorothy getting married? When had that happened? That mystery should have occupied him, but his eyes and mind filled with Allie.

She was a bridesmaid today, not a bride. She was available. She knew him, understood him, and cared for him. If he'd been honest, if he still had both hands, he might have had a chance with her, but not now. At least he could talk to her—if she ever looked his way. How could he blame her after how he acted on Thursday?

The organ blasted out the recessional and startled him. Art and Dorothy faced the guests and swept down the aisle. Art's face lit up even more when he saw Walt. He nudged Dorothy, who looked glad to see Walt for once. A grin from George, a strange scowl from Betty, then Allie glided past him, chin high, face bright pink.

He wanted to chase after her and get it over with, but the ushers dismissed from the front of the church, and after Ray came by with Helen on his arm, the aisle packed full. Forget etiquette—Walt tried to ease into the crowd.

"Look who's here." Mrs. Anello stepped in front of him, blocking his way, and called into the aisle. "Edie, you didn't tell me Walter was home."

"I didn't know." Mom worked her way over and embraced him. "Oh, honey, I'm so glad you're home."

"Me too." He pulled out of her hug to see half of Antioch descend on him.

"That's my grandson," Grandpa Novak said. "Back from bombing the Huns. Silver Star, no less."

The older men shook his hand and thanked him for what he'd done for America and freedom. No one seemed to mind that he offered his left hand. The women hugged him, grateful he was safely home. The children looked up to him, some with a million questions, some too awed to speak.

He'd left home just another Antioch kid, the least promising of the Novak boys, but now? Well, the attention was the kind of thing he thought he wanted until he got it. Dozens of people surrounded him with questions and requests for stories. He gave a quick, sanitized version of the Bremen mission, but he didn't tell it well. All he wanted was to find Allie.

"Shouldn't we get to the reception?" he asked. "Where is it anyway?"

"At the Carlisles' house, and they're probably wondering where we are," Mom said. "Come along, everyone. We'll have plenty of time for Walt's stories at the reception."

How could he get away? How could he get Allie alone?

Mom strolled down the street, one arm hooked around Walt's elbow, the other around Dad's. Walt tried to pick up the pace, but they lagged behind and told the whole story of Art and Dorothy, which he wanted to hear, but not so slowly.

At the Carlisles' he stepped into a crowd of people eager to waylay him, but he had a job to do. He smiled at his parents. "Excuse me. I need to find someone."

He edged through the crowd, offered smiles and handshakes, but kept moving and searching, intent on his objective. Where was she? He heard Betty's giggle near the kitchen door. She'd know Allie's story. He made his way over and dodged snoopy Mrs. Llewellyn.

He laid a hand on Betty's shoulder. "Betty, hi."

She looked up and raised an eyebrow. "Surprised to see *you* here."

Walt ignored her icy tone and nodded to George's youngest sister, whom Betty was talking to. "Hi, Mary Jane."

"Hi, Walt." She patted Betty's arm. "I'll go see if Mrs. Carlisle needs help."

Walt dug his hand into his trouser pocket and surveyed the room for any sign of brown curls or green eyes. "Wow. This is amazing. Art and Dorothy—about time."

"Mm-hmm." Betty glared at him.

Allie must have told her how he acted when she visited the hospital, but he kept his expression casual. "Yeah, amazing. Also amazing to see Allie Miller here."

"Why would that surprise you? She's my friend. She's allowed to visit me."

"No, I mean—well, isn't she supposed to marry that Baxter fellow today?"

Betty's eyes grew wider and wider until Walt thought they'd fall out of her head. "Didn't she tell you she broke her engagement? Didn't she give you a letter?"

He screwed up his face. "I threw it away."

"You *what*? Why'd you do that?" She whacked him in the stomach with the back of her hand.

"Hey! I had my reasons. I thought—well, I thought it was Get Well Card stuff—every cloud has a silver lining and all that. I didn't want to hear it."

"You're a jerk, Walter Novak."

"Believe me, I know." Inside his pocket, he drummed his knuckles against his leg. "So she—she broke her engagement? The wedding is cancelled, not postponed? And Baxter . . . ?"

"Baxter's out of the picture."

"Oh, wow." Walt renewed his search for Allie. She really

was available. "Wow. But—but why? Her dad picked him out for her, right?"

"That was the problem. Allie said they never loved each other."

"Really?" Hope did funny, bubbly stuff inside him. So he was right a year ago when he thought Allie had never been loved, had never been in love. Maybe he wasn't so dumb about women after all.

Betty's gaze flicked around Walt's face. "Yes, really. But the main reason Allie broke up with him was because Baxter insisted she give up her volunteer work and her church, but she refused to disobey God."

"Oh, wow. Wow." Hadn't he told her to obey God whatever the consequences? Apparently he counseled her to break up with Baxter. Walt realized his face was twitching, and he strained to calm down. "She broke up with him. I can't believe it. That took guts. Wow, her parents must be furious."

"You have no idea."

Walt nodded, too much nodding. "That's why she's here, isn't it? Let them cool down until it's safe to go home."

Furrows crossed Betty's forehead. "She can't go home again."

"What?" He felt as if someone tied a tourniquet around his waist.

"She called off the wedding months ago, but her parents kept on as if nothing changed—sent invitations and everything. Isn't that medieval? Arranged marriages went out ages ago. Oh, and are the Millers steamed. They rewrote their will and gave everything to Baxter. Allie can't inherit a penny unless she marries him."

Numbness from the tourniquet spread down Walt's legs. Allie wasn't a society snob. She gave up her inheritance to obey God.

"Then last week they told her if she didn't marry Baxter today, they'd disown her."

Walt's jaw went slack. "They—don't tell me they kicked her out."

"That's why she's here, until Monday at least. She's moving in with our friend Louise in San Francisco."

"Wow. San Francisco?" He ran his hand over his mouth. "How can she leave Riverside? She loves her parents, that city, her church, her friends."

Betty tilted her head, and her gaze dissected Walt. "She's not as weak as you think. She'll be fine. She wants a fresh start."

"I didn't say she was weak. I mean, wow, she turned her world upside-down. That's one strong woman. A fresh start? Wow."

"It's what she needs."

"Yeah. Wow." He rubbed the back of his neck and scanned the room again. Where was she? "All this—I can't believe all this was happening and I didn't know. When did she call off the wedding?"

"Valentine's Day. Don't you love the irony?"

February, as he figured from her letters. He frowned. "She never said anything."

"She didn't tell me either for a couple months because—" Betty clamped her lips shut.

"Why not?" He narrowed his eyes at her. "Why didn't she tell us?"

Her lips curved up slightly. "Ask her yourself."

Walt huffed and whipped his gaze over the heads of the guests. "I would if I could find her. Where on earth is she?"

"I haven't seen her since we left the church. Oh, I bet she's hiding from you in the kitchen. Can't believe how rude you were." Betty reached for her sister's arm as she passed with an empty tray. "Helen, is Allie in the kitchen?"

"Allie? I wish. She promised to help, but no, she hasn't lifted one manicured hand—" Helen sighed and rebalanced the tray. "I'm sorry. I'm just so frazzled."

"Helen, darling, sit down and enjoy the party."

"I know, I know. I'm Martha and you're Mary, but the work has to be done."

"I'll be in to help in a minute."

"Thank you, Betts." She turned for the kitchen.

"Wait, have you seen Allie?" Walt asked.

Helen faced him and nudged back a blonde lock with her shoulder. "We walked back from the church together. She stopped at Betty's, said she needed to do something."

Betty's house. Swell. Back to the chase. "Thanks. See you later."

"Wait." Betty grasped his arm and waited until Helen disappeared into the kitchen. Then she looked up at Walt, her eyebrows fused together. "You're rather concerned about Allie."

He shifted his weight from one foot to the other. "Well, yeah. She's a real good friend."

"Won't your girlfriend be jealous?"

He winced. "Oh boy. I don't—I don't have a girlfriend. It's—wow, it's a long and ugly story."

"Are you going to tell Allie?"

"I'm trying to. That's why I came today. That's why I'm looking for her."

"Just how much do you care for her?"

Walt froze. Betty's gaze was so intent, so intense, her grip on his arm so firm. She knew. She knew he loved Allie. This was no time to add another lie to his list. He raised half a smile. "Don't you think I should tell her first?"

Her smile lifted the corners of her eyes. "I suppose so. Now go."

"Wait. What do you think she'll say? Does she—"

"Uh-uh. You can't make me talk. Go. Now." She grasped his shoulders and spun him toward the door.

He nearly bowled over Mrs. Llewellyn, which served the old busybody right for eavesdropping. He shouldered his way outside and loped down the street. Each step pounded hope into his heart. Betty seemed eager for Walt to find Allie. She seemed pleased that Walt loved Allie. What did she know?

Walt threw open the Anellos' front door. "Allie!"

Forget the speech. First he'd pull her into his embrace, and kiss her and kiss her, and tell her he loved her, and make her say she loved him or cared for him or maybe thought she could learn to care for him, and kiss her over and over. Then the speech.

"Allie!" He ran down the hall, swung around the doorjamb and into the bedroom. No Allie. The nursery? The closet stood open and empty, hangers askew. He thumped his fist on the doorjamb. "No! She left."

Back down the hall and into the kitchen. A note sat on the table:

> I've left for Louise's. I'm sorry to leave in such
> haste, but I know you understand why, Betty.
> Thank you so much for your hospitality.

The note crackled in Walt's fist. "Swell. Just swell."

Santa Fe or Southern Pacific? Santa Fe was closer, but Southern Pacific had a later train to San Francisco. Swell. Southern Pacific was a good mile south.

Out the door, down the street. Now each step pounded the hope out of his heart. He was the reason she was running away, and she didn't even have the whole story yet.

She had already broken her engagement in March, when

he lied about Emily, when he was supposed to tell Allie he loved her. It wouldn't have been improper at all. God knew that. Why did he think he knew better than the Creator of the universe?

Walt rounded the corner onto A Street, caught sight of himself in the window of Wayne's Hardware, and stopped in his tracks. One arm. He had one arm, and worse, he was a liar.

Who was he kidding? Grab her and kiss her? Might as well slap her in the face. No, he had to tell her the whole ugly truth before he told her he loved her.

"Is that Walter Novak?"

He looked across A Street to see little white-haired Mr. Burton, his high school math teacher. Nice fellow, and he was heading for Walt.

"Hi, Mr. Burton. Sorry, I'm in a hurry." He sent a wave and strode on.

He had no time to lose.

48

"Just in time, miss. The last train for San Francisco arrives in ten minutes."

"Good." Allie counted out the fare. Once again she almost mistook a steel penny for a dime. She had so little money left. Would it cover bus fare and groceries until she received a paycheck?

"Going somewhere fancy?"

"Oh. I came from a wedding." She felt color rise in her cheeks. She should have changed out of her formal gown, but if she had, she would have missed the train.

Allie stowed the precious ticket in her handbag and checked in her baggage. The platform stretched empty around her, and so did the next five minutes.

Tonight she'd indulge in a good cry, but not now. She wouldn't dwell on the shame of standing naked in her love before Walt's pitying eyes.

Tomorrow she'd wake up in a new city, go to a new church, and make new friends.

"Allie?"

Her heart lurched at the beloved voice, and she turned. Walt stood not five feet away, breathing hard, his face flushed.

War had matured him, slimmed his face, and made him even more handsome. Her chest contracted so hard it hurt.

"I know you don't want to see me," he said. "But I've got to talk to you."

She lifted her chin, determined not to show her rampaging emotions. He wanted to discuss her letter? Why couldn't he respect her enough to leave her alone? Didn't he understand the humiliation of unrequited love? "This isn't necessary."

"Yes, it is." He frowned and wiped his forehead. "There's a bunch of stuff I should have told you the other day, in May, in March, in January even."

What could he have to tell her? Allie glanced down the track to the east, willing her train to come.

"I'll try to make it fast, but I've got to do this. Got to."

She turned back. The late afternoon sun illuminated the insistence in his hazel eyes, and she nodded in spite of the knowledge that she was about to receive a heaping portion of pity.

"First, I'm real sorry about what happened with your parents. I can't believe they did that."

"I'll be fine."

"I know you will." He looked her in the eye with warmth that threatened to melt her knees. "Breaking up with Baxter—that was the step of obedience, wasn't it?"

All the intimacy of their friendship returned in those words. Allie nodded, unable to speak.

"I'm glad you obeyed. Real glad. But wow, I had no idea the consequences would be that bad. Do you think your parents—they'll forgive you, won't they?"

Allie shook her head. Walt's disappointment and understanding made her want to bury her face in his chest and tell him every hurt and worry and care, but he belonged to another woman.

She pulled herself tall. "I think you should return to the reception. If our letters weren't proper and my visit wasn't proper, then this is most unseemly."

★

Walt grimaced, punched in the chest with his own lie, but he had to take it like a man, and he had to say what he'd come to say, every ugly word. "Listen, Allie, I lied to you and I lied about you."

"Oh." She didn't sound as surprised as he'd expected.

"The orange, that was the first lie. You know that." He walked past Allie to the edge of the platform. "Remember when we picked strawberries? I said I hadn't seen the juice on your cheek. Not true. Thought it was cute and didn't want you to clean up."

He turned on his heel and strode past her again, toward the station building. "Next, the wedding. I said George wanted us to dance for Art and Dorothy's sake. That was a whopper so I could back out on our deal and dance with you."

He whipped around, back across the platform, and looked up the tracks—no sign of the train. "When I visited your house, you want to know what really happened? I threw away your address. Threw it away. I—well, I was attracted to you. Boy, was I mad when I learned about Baxter, but I changed my mind and wanted to write you, so Frank and I drove all over—"

"I know."

Walt turned. "How did you know?"

Allie wiped a finger under one eye. Swell, she was already crying, and he'd just gotten started. "My friend Daisy—her father was your cab driver."

All this time she'd known. He'd worked so hard to conceal it and for what? "Why didn't you say anything?"

"I—I didn't want to embarrass you—or—or myself." She wiped her cheek, made a face, and opened her purse.

He wanted to go to her and hold her and kiss away those tears, but he had so much more to say. "Embarrassment. Pride. That's where lies start. I'm sick of it. I even made you promise not to tell Betty we were writing. What did I say? Betty didn't think it was proper? Nowhere near the truth. I just didn't want her to know what I did to get your address."

"I—I figured as much."

"You figured that one out too? Well, here's one you don't know." He marched right up to her, right into her tear-stained face. "Every man at Thurleigh thought you were my girlfriend. Bet you didn't know that."

"What?" Her pretty lips barely moved.

He hadn't been that close to her for a year, close enough to smell her sweetness. "Yeah, I told them you were my girl-friend."

"But—but why?"

She was too close. He had to get away, had to keep moving. Back toward the building. "So I'd be one of the guys, so they wouldn't bug me, so they'd respect me. It worked. And you helped—the letters, the applesauce, the cookies—wow, they thought you were crazy about me."

"Is—is that what this was about? I was just a decoy, a trophy—"

"No." Walt wheeled around. "No, never. You have no idea. Would I have written everything I did—I mean, when Frank—" He set his hand on his hip and looked at the ground until the thickness in his throat went away. Then he locked his gaze on her. "I wrote stuff to you I didn't tell anyone else. You have no idea how much your friendship's meant to me."

Allie's mouth twisted. "Or yours to me."

This was when he was supposed to embrace her and kiss her and tell her he loved her, if he didn't have one last big lie around his neck ready to hang him.

She pulled a handkerchief from her purse. "You said you confessed a lie to your crew. Was—was that it?"

"Yep. Cracker, of all people, he's the one who got them to forgive me. They didn't have to. I don't deserve it. I don't deserve your forgiveness either."

"Walt, I—"

"No, wait." He held up his hand. Nope, no hand on that side anymore. He lifted his left hand. "I'm not done yet."

Allie flipped open her handkerchief and pressed it to her cheek. "But you said you stopped lying after that."

"Well, there was an exception. I thought it would fix everything, but it just made everything worse. Lies do. Remember when I told you white lies were like ball bearings in the machinery of society? Wrong. Lies are like incendiary bombs, burning and melting and mangling everything—trust, hopes, everyone you love."

She dabbed at her eyes. "I—I think I understand."

"Good. Not that it'll make a difference. You see, my last letter to you was a lie."

"Excuse me?"

"Yeah, a lie." He paced to the edge of the platform. He had to finish before the train came. "Emily. Yeah, I went out with her a few times. She was actually crazy about me, but I wasn't crazy about her. She was never my girlfriend."

Back around to the station. The motion of his feet pumped out the words. "I couldn't talk to her like I could talk to you—I mean, Flossie the cow has more brains. And Emily never told me I couldn't write to you."

"What?" Her voice cracked. "Why did you say she said that?"

"I needed an excuse to stop writing you or else I would have had to tell you the truth."

"And what truth is that?" She stood tall, and a breeze ruffled her long green dress.

Walt groaned and strode toward the tracks. "That I cared for your correspondence too much."

"I—I don't understand."

"Of course not. How could you? I'm messing this up." He kicked a chunk of gravel down to the tracks. "How come it's easier to tell a lie, even when the truth is the same as one of your lies?"

"I really don't understand."

He faced her and planted his feet in the at-ease position, except he couldn't clasp his hands behind his back. "I knew I had to stop writing when I prayed, 'Lord, why can't she dump Baxter and fall for me?'"

Her eyes widened, bigger and greener than ever.

"It was wrong. You were engaged. Well, I guess you weren't anymore, but I thought you were. If you married him, I'd be in love with another man's wife, and that's against one of the Ten Commandments. Well, so is lying but . . ."

Allie's mouth opened, closed, opened. "You don't mean . . ."

"I love you." At last, the blessed, painful truth.

"You—you—"

"I love you. I thought dating Emily would help. It didn't. The more time I spent with her, the more I missed you, the more I loved you. I had to stop writing. Doesn't make it right, but that's why I lied."

"Why didn't you just tell me the truth?" Her face crumpled, and she clapped her hand over her mouth.

Her distress socked him in the gut. "I'm sorry. I should have. I knew you couldn't feel the same way about me, and I didn't want to make a fool of myself. Stupid pride. And pride is why I didn't confess earlier. Once you said silence was a truthful solution to a dilemma. Not in my case. I allowed you to believe a lie. Silence isn't truthful when it perpetuates a lie."

Allie mumbled something, then moved her trembling hand from her mouth. "Didn't you think how your letter would make me feel? I cried myself to sleep that night."

"You did?" His insides felt as if they were stuck in Mom's wringer. He didn't think she'd miss his friendship that much.

"That was the night—" She glanced to his stump and back to his face. "I had a horrible dream. You didn't want my friendship, but you needed me to pray, and I did."

A kick to his wrung-out soul. "Good thing one of us obeyed. Listen, Allie, I'm sorry about this. I'm sorry I lied. I'm sorry I hurt you. And what a lousy way this is for a man to tell a woman he loves her."

Allie hugged her stomach and looked around the train station, her face wet and agitated. "I daydreamed about this moment. I'd be here at this depot, and I'd wear my Easter hat, and you'd step off the train, and all your friends and family would be there, and I'd hug you and tell you about my broken engagement, and if you seemed pleased, I might whisper in your ear how much I loved you, but only if I felt bold, because I didn't—I didn't know you loved me too."

Walt stared, his mouth wide open, his eyes wide open, but his ears had to be blocked. He couldn't have heard what he thought he heard.

Tears streamed down her face, but she didn't stop them. "It would have been wonderful, so sweet and romantic. If you'd been truthful, that's what would have happened, instead of this—this—crying and pacing and apologizing and—"

"Wait. You didn't say—did I hear right? Did you say you loved me?"

She met his eyes and blinked. "You read my letter, didn't you?"

"That was in the letter?" The air rushed out of his chest.

Allie groaned and covered her eyes. "Oh no. I thought you knew. Oh no. I thought—but you knew everything else— Baxter, the wedding, my parents."

"Betty told me. The letter—I threw it away." He stepped closer, he had to be closer. "I thought you wrote a bunch of mush like, 'God makes us stronger in our sufferings,' and I didn't want to hear it. You—you love me?"

She nodded, and she squished up her face with her hand.

With a surge of joy, he reached for her but stopped himself. "You still love me? Even after you saw my—my arm?"

Her hand fell away to reveal all her hurt and anger. "Your arm? How shallow do you think I am? You say you love me, but how well do you know me if you can ask such a thing?"

Oh boy. How much worse could he make this?

"I don't care about your arm. I care about you being truthful with me."

Walt stared down at her. So much to love—the vulnerability in her eyes, the strength in her chin, the truth in her words. She loved him, but it didn't matter.

"Well?" she said.

"What can I say? I could say I lied because I love you, which is true, but it doesn't make it right. I could point out evidence that I've changed—I did tell you the whole ugly truth after all. But I can't make excuses. I can only take the consequences and pray you'll forgive me."

Allie's mouth softened and quivered.

"I can't love a man I can't trust."

His chest crushed under the weight of her statement. "I once told my crew, 'Dishonesty always has a price.' Boy, a steep price."

49

The blast of a train whistle tore Allie's gaze from Walt's resigned anguish. At last, her escape. Walt's eyes darkened as the train pulled in. "Ironic, isn't it? I love you and you love me, but what stands between us is bigger than Baxter and Emily combined—trust. I'm so sorry."

"Don't be." She fumbled inside her pocketbook for her ticket. "I'm glad I found out now before I wasted any more time pining over you."

A twitch in his cheek told her she'd struck a nerve. Good. He deserved it for lying to her, lying about her, and stomping on her heart twice now. She stepped around him toward the sanctuary of the train.

"Good-bye, Allie."

The sadness in his voice wrenched her, but she didn't turn around. "Good-bye," she said in her coolest tone.

The conductor punched her ticket and eyed her dress. While elegant at a wedding, the gown looked clownish on a train. Allie held her head high and made her way down the crowded aisle. At least there was room, and since she was the only passenger boarding, they would depart soon.

"Here, miss." A corporal stood and offered his seat.

"Thank you, sir."

"Say, you're all dressed for dancing. How 'bout you and me—"

"No, thank you." She settled in the seat and ventured a glance out the window. Walt stood alone on the platform.

He sat on a bench, set his cap beside him, and lowered his head. His eyes closed and his lips moved. Was this another deception designed to elicit her forgiveness?

It wouldn't succeed. He said it himself—he was a liar, and she couldn't trust him.

In a few hours she'd be in San Francisco, away from this selfish man who cared more for his own pride than the feelings of the woman he claimed to love.

"He loves me." A low moan rose in her throat. She'd dreamed of hearing those words on his lips, but her dreams always ended with an embrace and a kiss, not with her departure.

Allie looked away to the sailor's cap of the man in front of her. Walt didn't deserve embraces or kisses. He lied to her. Why, he even lied about her to his friends. Oh dear, that was why Cracker said he'd heard a lot about her.

She glanced out the window to Walt's slumped shoulders and bowed head. He didn't have to tell her that. She never would have known. He chose to tell her, to obey.

"No." She slammed back in the seat. He lied about Emily for selfish reasons. He allowed Allie to live in despair for two months when she could have lived in hope—hope that would have been fulfilled if he hadn't lied.

A burst of steam, a growl of engines, and Allie looked out the window. Walt sat up straight on the bench, his face distraught, and he shoved the curl off his forehead. Why did he have to do that? Did he know how endearing she found that gesture?

"But I could never trust what he says." She'd never deceive

him like that. She hugged her stomach over the delicate chiffon dress she'd worn when she danced with Walt and she . . .

Allie gathered the fabric in her grip. She chose not to tell him about Baxter.

What did Walt just say? Silence wasn't truthful when it perpetuated a lie? She allowed him to believe she didn't have a boyfriend—a lie, and what a hurtful lie.

"Oh no," she whispered. Her bare left hand rubbed against the inside of her right arm. When she didn't tell Walt she broke her engagement, she allowed him to believe she was still engaged—also a lie.

"Oh, dear Lord, I'm as guilty as he is." All this spring he must have lived in despair, dreading her marriage, when he could have lived in hope—hope that would have been fulfilled if she hadn't deceived him.

The train lurched to a start. Walt stood, put on his cap, raised a heart-wrenching, left-handed salute, and walked away.

"No!" Allie sprang to her feet. "Stop the train!"

"Something the matter, miss?" the conductor called behind her.

"I have to get off this train."

"Sorry. Can't do that. You can get off at Pittsburg."

"No, I have to get off now." She headed down the aisle.

The corporal grasped her arm and turned to the conductor. "Talking to herself, you know what I mean?"

Allie leveled a gaze at him. "I assure you, sir, I am perfectly sane. Now please let go." She tugged her arm free and plunged down the aisle.

"Hey, lady! Where do you think you're going?"

The train lumbered along. Surely she could get off. She excused her way past curious passengers to the end of the car, where the door stood open for a breeze. She grabbed the handrail. Walt was opening the station door.

"Walt!" she screamed. "Walter Novak!"

Then she looked down. The wind whipped her hair about her face, and the platform blurred before her eyes. What was she thinking? She couldn't jump off a moving train! The prudent course of action was to continue to San Francisco and return the next day. After all, her luggage was on board.

"Lady! Hey, lady, are you crazy?"

Allie looked over her shoulder. The conductor was almost upon her. Back to the station, where Walt stood, hand on the door, gaping at her. The train gained speed. The end of the platform neared.

"Oh, dear Lord, help me."

The conductor's hand brushed her sleeve.

"Walter!" she cried and she jumped and she screamed. The ground rushed up. Her right ankle crumpled. Down she tumbled, over and over, a blur of wood and sky and pain around her.

"Allie! Allie!"

Her cheek rested on the rough wood platform. She moaned. Every limb ached.

"Allie! What on earth?" Walt pounded to a stop and dropped to his knees.

She rolled to her side and pushed up partway. "I lied to—"

"Are you okay? Allie, what on earth?" He scanned up and down her body, placed his arm behind her back, and eased her up so she sat on her hip. "Where are you hurt?"

"Walt, I lied to you."

He met her eyes and frowned. "Must have hit your head." He nudged her forward and ducked around to examine the back of her head.

She ignored the throbbing pain in her ankle and the soreness in her hip. "Walt, please listen. I lied to you."

"What are you talking about? I'm the one who lied. Now, where's it hurt?"

"I did. I lied to you." She reached up and gripped his shoulder. "Remember when we met last year? I didn't tell you about Baxter."

Walt sighed. "Just an oversight."

"At first it was. I thought you knew. But when we danced, I realized you were attracted to me and you didn't know about Baxter, and I chose silence. You're right. Silence isn't truthful when it perpetuates a lie."

"It's not the same."

She clutched the thick shoulder she'd admired that evening. "Yes, it is. You know why I didn't say anything? Pride—I didn't want to make a scene. And selfishness—I wanted to stay in the arms of the most wonderful man I'd ever met, stay where I felt lovely and special for the first time in my life."

Walt's face fell still for a long moment. "Allie, don't do this."

"I let you speak. Now it's my turn." She lifted her hand to his cheek, exhilarated by the proximity of the man she loved, by the intensity of her own gaze, by honesty itself. "I also lied when I didn't tell you I broke my engagement."

"That's not—"

"Yes, it is. I allowed you to believe something that wasn't true and I didn't consider your feelings."

"You didn't know I loved—"

"It doesn't matter. If I had told the truth, you never would have lied to me about Emily."

His gaze bore down on her. "That's no excuse."

"No, but if I'd told the truth, you wouldn't have lied. Please forgive me."

"Allie . . ." His voice grew thick and husky.

"Please." She ran her hand back into his hair. Although short in the back, it felt even more luxurious than she imagined. "Please forgive me."

Walt wrapped his arm around her shoulder and pressed her tight. "Of course, I forgive you but—"

"And I forgive you." She nestled her face in the hollow at the base of his neck and inhaled soap and aftershave and wool, forgiveness and love and joy.

"You shouldn't. You shouldn't do this." He held her even tighter. "You're not thinking straight. I'm a cripple—a cripple, Allie. And I can't provide for you as you're used to."

"Please don't say that. Oh, darling, no." She caught her breath. She'd called him darling, but it was true. "As for providing for me, I walked away from my inheritance. I don't need money. I only need the Lord. Well, it would be nice to have you too." She pressed her lips to his neck, just below his ear, where his skin was smooth and warm. A rumble in his throat told her she'd struck a nerve again, but a pleasant one this time.

"I love you so much, but you're used to grand pianos and crystal chandeliers."

Allie drew back and traced the rainbow of ribbons on Walt's chest. "A man who can earn these medals will never be impoverished, but even if you were, I—I'd rather have your love in poverty than—than a hundred grand pianos."

"But I'm a—"

"Please, I never want to hear you say you're a cripple again. You're intelligent and inventive. You can do anything you put your mind to doing." She trailed her hand down his right arm.

He flinched.

Allie glanced up. "I'm sorry. Does it still hurt?"

"No." His forehead creased. "But you don't want to touch it."

She folded her hand around the end of his arm, as if she could infuse her love and mend his brokenness. "Maybe this is why God led me to March Field. I used to be jarred by such things, but no longer. Besides, this represents one of the things I love in you—your willingness to sacrifice."

Walt's struggle to control his face jarred her far more than his arm. After he gained control, he hiked up one eyebrow and bent one corner of his mouth. "I thought obedience was better than sacrifice."

Thank goodness, both his smile and his sense of humor survived after all. "Yes, and I love even more how you've done what God asked. What more could I want? Would you rather I didn't forgive you, so we both could be miserable?"

Walt squeezed her shoulder and gave her another twitch of a smile. "I'd resigned myself to misery as the price of obedience."

"Goodness. Don't you think it's time obedience was rewarded?" She worked her hand up into his curls and knocked off his cap. "Oops. Sorry, darling." His smile creaked into place as if on rusty hinges.

She smiled then glowered at him. "However, there is one lie I'll never forgive. The strawberry juice. How could you let me walk around in such an undignified state?"

He chuckled, a welcome sound. "That's why it was cute. You're always so ladylike, and there you were with this red streak." He nuzzled his nose into her cheek and settled a kiss on the crest of her cheekbone. "Right here."

"Oh," she sighed. She'd never truly recovered from the first time he kissed her cheek, but now—oh, now she would never recover and she didn't want to, not when his lips drifted down her cheek.

Her eyes fluttered shut. They were going to kiss—a real kiss, like in the movies, like people in love, and she turned her head to seek his lips.

Walt pulled back. "Say, you're not the woman I fell in love with."

He didn't kiss her? She blinked, her eyes out of focus. "Hmm?"

"You're not." His scowl couldn't hide the twinkle in his hazel eyes. "The woman I fell in love with would never be seen in public like this. Would you look at yourself? One shoe off, one shoe on, dress all torn up."

Allie glanced at the gashes in the chiffon over her knees, her hip, and on her sleeves. Oh dear, she did like that dress.

"The woman I love is too proper to throw herself off a train."

She slipped both arms around his neck and smiled. "You're teasing me, Walter Novak."

"She definitely wouldn't embrace a scruffy flyboy in public." He rubbed his delightfully scruffy cheek against hers.

Music soared, tumbling over itself, a lyrical fountain of melody. "And she'd never dream of kissing that flyboy in public."

Walt stilled. "We haven't—oh boy. You know, we should go someplace—"

"No one's around, and I'm not that woman anymore, remember?" She kissed him in front of his ear.

"Oh yeah. Yeah, I remember."

He met her halfway and pressed his lips to hers. Were there a thousand kisses, or only one in a symphony with a thousand movements? Some gentle, some insistent, some longing, some tender, all a culmination of friendship and dreams and prayers.

She never wanted the kiss to end, but she had so much to say to him. "Walt?" she mumbled against his lips.

"Hmm?" He let his mouth linger on hers for a moment, then drew back.

Her lips felt gelatinous from his kisses. "I—I lost count," she said, and realized she didn't make sense. "Oh, you wouldn't remember."

Walt smiled slowly, as if he had the same lip problem she did. "'Course I remember. Tried to forget and couldn't. Never figured out why he—why he didn't—was that true? Is this your first—"

Allie nodded, her throat tight. "He didn't love me and I didn't love him. But you—oh, darling, I love you so much."

Walt leaned his forehead against hers, and his eyes melted into a lovely blur. "And boy, do I love you." He paused and swallowed. "Sweetheart."

A sudden pain clenched her heart. Father used to call her sweetheart. But now Walt would, and the pain mellowed to warmth. She tipped up her face for another kiss, and Walt obliged.

Footsteps thumped. Wooden boards creaked. Allie snapped out of Walt's embrace to see the ticket agent run toward them.

"Just got a telegraph. Some crazy lady jumped off the train." He stopped and cocked his head at Allie seated on the ground. "You're not the crazy lady, are you?"

Flaming heat rose up Allie's cheeks. "I—I'm afraid so."

Walt chuckled. "She's my crazy lady, Mr. Putnam."

He frowned. "You're one of the Novak boys, aren't you? I'd recognize Jacob Novak's nose anywhere. So, what's going on? You all right, miss?"

"I've never felt better." She gave Walt a warm smile, which

collapsed into an apologetic one. "But I think I twisted my ankle."

"You what?" Walt scooted down to her feet. "Why didn't you say something?"

She winced as she stretched her sore legs before her. "I had more important matters to tend to."

He shot her half a smile, then frowned at her foot. "Look how swollen it is. Hope you didn't break it."

"Oh dear." Her right ankle throbbed, visibly larger than the other.

Mr. Putnam leaned forward and rested his hands on knobby knees. "Want me to call Doc Jamison?"

"Yeah, could you? Oh, wait. He's not home."

Allie laughed. "The wedding reception."

Walt grinned. "Forgot about that. Say, Mr. Putnam, could you call us a cab?"

"Can do." The men helped her to standing. Mr. Putnam retrieved her shoe and handbag and Walt's cap. "Say, miss, what about your luggage?"

Allie held on to Walt's shoulder. "Oh dear. It's halfway to San Francisco."

"Could you wire them, have them send it back?" Walt settled a sturdy arm around Allie's waist and smiled down at her. "Let's get you to the doctor."

"Oh my. We have some explaining to do."

"Not *we*. You. I'm not the one who jumped off a train."

Allie rested her head on Walt's shoulder and laughed.

When they reached the Carlisles', Walt helped her out of the cab. She leaned on him to hobble up the walk, and she swung open the front door.

"Hiya, Walt. Thought you'd forgotten us."

"Allie! Oh my goodness. What happened?"

People swarmed about her, fussed over her dress and her

injuries, pulled her from Walt's side, seated her in an arm-chair, and elevated her foot on an ottoman.

Dr. Jamison probed her ankle. "Looks like a sprain. I'll have to do X-rays to rule out a fracture. How did this happen?"

"Oh, I—Walter?" she called out. Where was he? These were his relatives, his friends. She'd rather he told the story. There he was, talking to a tall, gray-haired man. "Walt, would you come over here, please?"

"Yeah?" He worked into the circle.

"Dr. Jamison wants to know what happened."

"Tell him. Tell everyone," he said with a grin. "I've got an errand to run, but in the meantime, tell them everything."

"You're not leaving now, are you?"

"I'll be back." He cupped her chin in his hand and glanced at his family and friends. Then he kissed her gently. "Tell them everything, okay? I love you."

"Okay." Her voice was drowned out by gasps and Betty's squeal.

Walt straightened up with a flushed face, waved to the crowd, beckoned to the gray-haired man, and ran out the door.

Surprised, delighted, confused eyes turned to Allie.

She looked around and smiled. "Where on earth do I begin?"

50

Walt reined himself back to a walk. He wanted to get back to Allie, but he didn't want to arrive winded and sweaty.

This had to be right, but why wouldn't it be? She loved him. She forgave him. She actually jumped off a train for him. And wow, she kissed great.

He caught himself running again and slowed down. "Lord, help us make the right decisions." He took it as a sign that Mr. Lindstrom was at the reception and was willing to help, even though Walt had plowed a go-cart through his vegetable garden in sixth grade.

Walt took the Carlisles' porch steps two at a time. The parlor had thinned out to close family and friends, seated on chairs around the room. There was Allie, talking, laughing, all red in the face, her foot propped and bandaged.

He kept his eyes on the target, ignored the friendly flak around him, knelt beside Allie, and took her hand.

She beamed at him. "Hello, darling."

"Hi." No small talk. He had a big old bomb to drop. "Will you marry me?"

The room went dead silent, and Allie's lips parted. "Wh-what?"

"Yeah, you heard right. Will you marry me?"

"Walter, I—oh my goodness. I mean, just an hour ago—and now?"

"I know. Same for me." He squeezed her hand. "I know it's fast, but hear me out. You have three marital options and three geographical options. Choose your objective."

George's laugh rang from across the room. "Novak, you're the only man I know who could make a marriage proposal sound like a military campaign."

"Stay out of this, Anello. I'm proposing to Allie, not to you."

A smile dimpled the corner of her mouth. "Marital options?"

"Yeah. First option—you accept the proposal, and we get married right away, like Art and Dorothy. Second option—you accept but we wait a year, whatever. Third option—you turn me down but I'll keep asking."

Her smile glowed even more, but she didn't say anything.

If his heart were a B-17 engine, he'd have to feather it, because it was out of control. "Well, which one?"

"I'd like to hear my geographical options first." She stroked the back of his hand with her thumb.

Walt sat back on his heels to get farther away. If she played with his hair again, he wouldn't be able to concentrate on the mission.

"Okay, I've got a job lined up at Boeing in Seattle after I'm discharged. Your first option—go to San Francisco as planned. Of course, now you don't have to run away from me. Second option—stay in Antioch. You can find a room and get a job if you want. When I come home on vacation, I won't have to split my time between Antioch and San Francisco. Third option—Seattle. My radio operator, Bill Perkins, he's from Seattle, and he's stateside now. He can help you find a nice place to stay. Maybe Boeing could use a business major."

Uh-oh. He saw tears. "You—you don't have to decide today."

"I've already decided," she said, her voice as moist as her eyes.

Too late for feathering—his heart went into a stall. "Yeah?"

"The second option and the third."

Now the stall spread to his brain. "Huh?"

Allie laughed, shaky and cute. "I've heard Seattle is lovely."

He grinned, and rose back up onto his knees. "That's what Bill says. Islands and ferries and lots of trees. You want to come?"

"Oh yes. I want to be near you. We fell in love on paper. I want to get to know you even better in person."

"Yeah, exactly. Seattle was my first choice." He lifted her hand and kissed it. "What about—what about the marital option? Will you? Will you marry me?"

Allie's green eyes gleamed brighter, quicker, more allegro than ever.

"Please, sweetheart. I want to look into those eyes for the rest of my life."

She smiled, slow and quiet and adagio. "Yes, Walt. I would be honored to be your wife."

"You would?" A laugh erupted. He put his arm around her shoulder and pulled her close so her curls could tickle his nose. "You really would?"

She wrapped her arms around him and chuckled in his ear. "You are adorable."

"Mr. Putnam was right. You are crazy." He planted a kiss on her cheek. "So when? Now? Later? Any time's fine with me."

"A little later." She settled back in the chair, leaving her hand on his shoulder. "Would you mind horribly? As I said, I'd like to get to know you better in person."

He smiled and wound his finger around one of her curls. "That was my first choice too."

"Wise woman you found, son," Dad said from over at the bridge table. "I don't approve of these rushed wartime weddings."

Everyone laughed. Art sat on the sofa with his arm around his wartime bride's shoulder. "You just officiated at one," he said.

"That's different," Dad said. "You've known each other since you were babies."

Betty came to Walt, leaned over, and whispered in his ear. "A ring. You should have waited until you had a ring. Promise her you'll get one Monday."

"How hopeless do you think I am? Boy, I tell you." Walt grumbled and dug in the pocket of his uniform jacket. "Where do you think I went with Mr. Lindstrom?"

"You bought a ring?" Allie asked in a small voice.

"Um, yeah." He frowned. How stupid to propose to her on the day she was supposed to marry Baxter.

"Show her," Betty said.

He might as well. Too late to undo that mistake. He struggled to open the lid with one hand, and then handed the box to her. The diamond looked smaller than it did in the store. "I'm sure it's not what—well, not what you're used to."

Tears puddled in her eyes. "It's much more beautiful and much, much more welcome."

He studied her face. She meant it. She'd rather have a simple ring from him than whatever she had before. He pulled the ring from the box and slipped it on her finger. The stone swung around to the underside of her hand, and they laughed together.

"We'll get it sized," he said.

"Well, let's see," Betty said.

Walt stood to let the women swoop down on Allie. He had his own set of congratulations to endure. The men gave him hearty handshakes, but Ray's congratulations seemed subdued by his own bad history with engagements. Then the women fell on him with joyful hugs, although Helen didn't exactly look joyful. Had to be a hard day for her—first Jim's sister married his best friend, and now another friend proposed.

Walt glanced over to Allie's chair.

Mom held Allie's cheeks between her hands and kissed her on the forehead. "I couldn't be more pleased. I can't imagine a better wife for Walt, or a sweeter daughter-in-law."

Allie's smile looked forced and sad. Everyone was there, and everyone was happy, except her parents. Walt had a hunch the Millers wouldn't be so pleased with their future son-in-law.

He rushed to Allie's side and took her hand. "Hi, there."

"Hi." Her voice shook. "I wish—"

"I know." He gave her a little kiss. "They're probably at dreary old St. Lucifer's right this minute, waiting for you to come down that aisle, and here you are with a sprained ankle, a tattered dress, and a tiny diamond, being seen in public kissing a one-armed flyboy."

Allie's mouth quivered. "Oh, how I love my flyboy."

"I sure am glad. That ring isn't returnable."

She reached up and caressed his cheek. "Return it? An entire bovine army couldn't get it away from me."

"Good, because loving you is better than—well, I was about to say it's better than flying but . . ."

Allie's eyebrows lifted, then relaxed. She knew he was teasing.

Walt grinned and kissed her. "Yeah, it's even better than flying."

Discussion Questions

1. In the 306th Bombardment Group, 315 men went to England in September 1942 in the 35 original 9-man combat crews. Of these, 106 were killed, 88 became POWs, 10 left combat due to wounds, and 9 were evadees. How do you think the men coped with such distressing statistics? What coping techniques did you see among the characters? How do you think modern Americans would tolerate such circumstances?

2. Allie experiences rationing and shortages on the home front. Do you have any personal or family experiences of World War II home front life? How would you have dealt with these difficulties?

3. Walt and Allie's love is built by letters. In this day of email and instant messages, it's hard to imagine a letter taking two to six weeks to go overseas, and waiting twice that long for a response. How does this delay affect Walt and Allie's communication and decisions?

4. Our world harshly judges those born less than attractive. How much of Allie's self-image problem stems from having a gorgeous mother who values beauty? How does Agatha Montclair's story shape Mary Miller's perception of her daughter? What problems arise from Allie's view of herself as plain?

5. Allie says, "Self-pity is nothing but pride in disguise." Agree or disagree? Why?

6. Describe Walt's relationship with his brothers. How have comparisons to Jack and Ray affected Walt? Have you noticed similar issues in your family?

7. At the beginning of the story, Walt says white lies are like "ball bearings in the machinery of society," but by the end he says they're like "incendiary bombs, burning and melting and mangling." How is this revealed in Walt's life? In your experience, which statement is closer to the truth?

8. To Allie, "silence is a truthful solution to a dilemma." Can silence be dishonest? Was it for Allie? For Walt?

9. Walt realizes his lies stem from pride. How is this manifested in his story? In general, what part does pride play in sin?

10. When Walt confesses his lie to his crew, many of the men are angry. How do you feel about their response? Does the ongoing nature of his dishonesty make it worse in their eyes? Does his faith make them come down on him harder?

11. Describe Allie's spiritual home life. How did she change when she met Betty? How does she grow throughout the book? What part does Walt play? How about Cressie?

12. What contributes to Allie's decision to marry Baxter (personality, family, background)? Why do you think Baxter wants to marry her—just the money?

13. Allie struggles with whether she should marry a man who doesn't share her faith. How do you feel about this matter?

14. Throughout the story, Allie is torn between honoring her parents and obeying God. Why do you think it takes Allie so long to stand up to her parents? Have you ever felt torn between two "good" things?

15. What sacrifices does Walt make? How do they affect the people around him?

16. Cressie says, "Sometimes we choose our sacrifices," and Daisy says some sacrifices "make you feel holy without making you holy." How do you see this in Allie's life? In Walt's? Have you ever noticed it in your life?

17. 1 Samuel 15:22 states, "Hath the Lord as great delight in burnt-offerings and sacrifices, as in obeying the voice of the Lord? Behold, to obey is better than sacrifice." Why is this true? How is this seen in Walt and Allie's lives?

18. What do you think of Walt's reaction to his injury?

How about Allie's reaction? How would you feel if you or someone you loved faced a similar situation?

19. The second book in the series focuses on Walt's brother Jack and his nurse, Lt. Ruth Doherty. From what you've seen of these characters, what might you expect?

Acknowledgments

For years I've dreamed of writing this page for this is a group project.

Above all, thanks to my Lord, the giver of dreams, who fulfills his purpose in his way and in his time.

My family deserves my undying gratitude. My poor husband, Dave, married a pharmacist and ended up with a writer. And my sweet children, Stephen, Anna, and Matthew, have suffered several late pickups at school. I love you all more than I can say.

Few writers come from homes without books. My parents, Ronald and Nancy Stewart, infused my sister and me with a love of reading. Dad, Mom, and Martha (Groeber), thanks for your support—and fine-toothed editing.

Thanks also to those who taught me, critiqued me, encouraged me, and prayed for me, especially the faculty at the Mount Hermon Christian Writers Conference, the members of American Christian Fiction Writers, and most of all Diablo Valley Christian Writers Group—Jessica Brophy, Alice Ann Cantelow, Kathleen Casey, Ron Clelland, Carol Green, Cynthia Herrmann, Susan Lawson, Marilynn Lindahl, Debbie Maselli, Sue Massie, Paula Nunley, Evelyn Sanders, Marcy Weydemuller, and Linda Wright.

As for prayer, I've been slathered in it! My church, my small group, and my book club have held me up. And thanks to those who read my manuscript—Marilyn and Kristina Baham, Andrea Balderrama, Jill Combs, Cindi Grovhoug, Jeanne Horgan, Rosanna Hunter, Laura Juranek, Sue Matt, Joy Benson, Twilla Bordley, MaryAnn Buchanan, Tami Fanucchi, Angelique Foster, Laquetta Franz, Sonja Grovhoug, Michelle Lippincott, Don and Nancy McDaniels, Janice Moore, Lisa Prevost, Laurie Ratterree, Denise Sterud, Susan Stuteville, Donna Ubeda, and Sandy Wall. And thanks to Suzanne Russo for printing a portable version.

I also thank the staff at the Antioch Public Library and Charles Vercelli of the Western Railway Museum for help with obscure research questions. And my story would have been flat without the opportunity to walk through the restored B-17s of the Collings Foundation and the Experimental Aircraft Association.

Last but definitely not least, I thank my editor, Vicki Crumpton at Revell, and my agent, Rachel Zurakowski at Books & Such Literary Agency, for taking a chance on an unknown writer. Thanks for showing me much mercy and grace.

Thanks to you, dear reader, for taking a chance on a new author as well. I hope you enjoyed getting to know Walt and Allie as much as I did. Please visit my website at www. sarahsundin.com to see a diagram of a B-17, or to drop me an email. I'd love to hear from you.

Sarah Sundin is an on-call hospital pharmacist and lives in northern California with her husband and three children. Her great-uncle flew with the U.S. Eighth Air Force in England. Sarah holds a BS in chemistry from UCLA and a doctorate in pharmacy from UC San Francisco. This is her first novel.